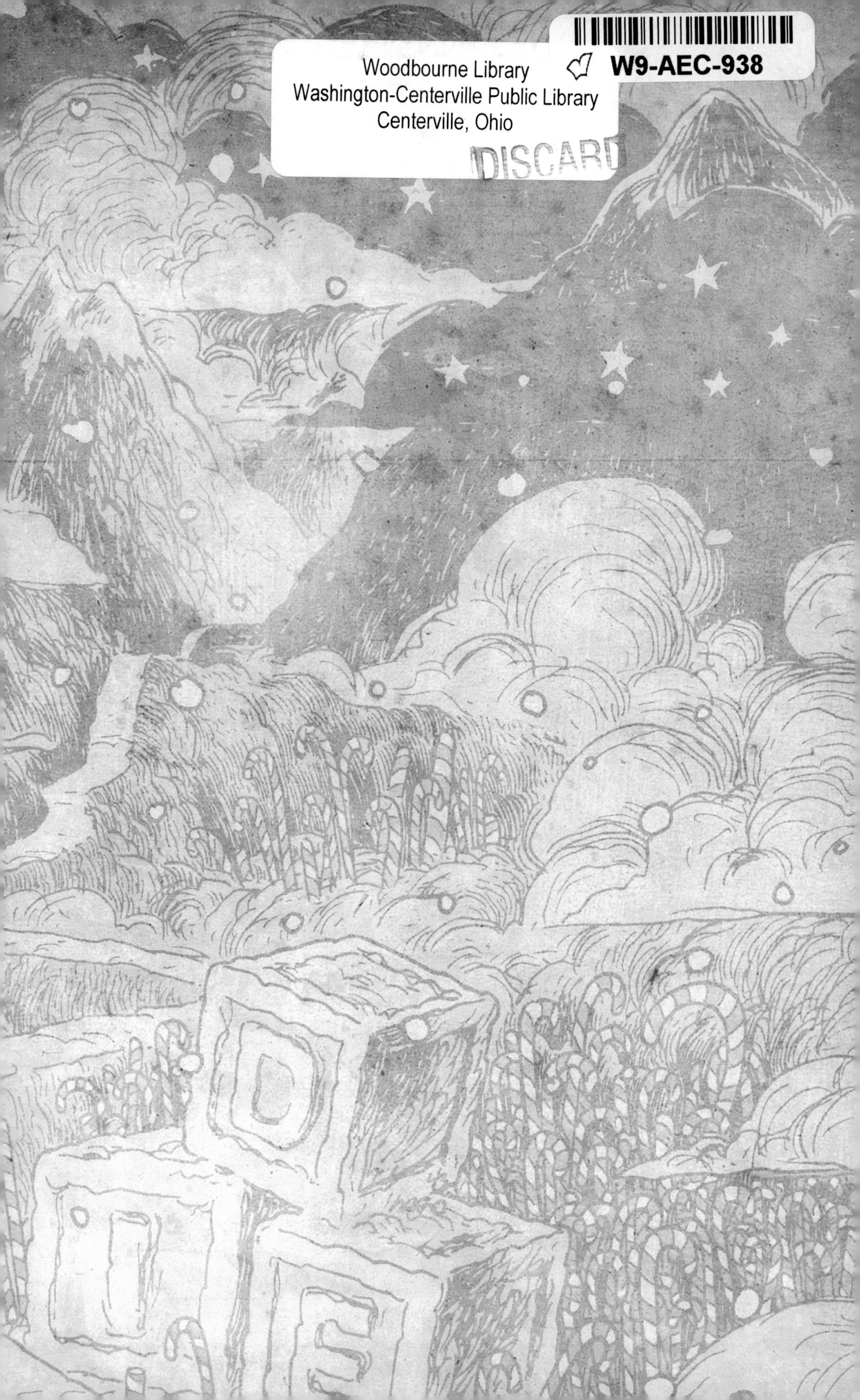

WRAITH

"After many years I became old and white; I heard a great deal, many lies and falsehoods, but the longer I lived, the more I understood that there were really no lies. Whatever doesn't really happen is dreamed at night. It happens to one if it doesn't happen to another, tomorrow if not today, or a century hence if not next year. What difference can it make? Often I heard tales of which I said, 'Now this is a thing that cannot happen.' But before a year had elapsed I heard that it actually had come to pass somewhere."

—Isaac Bashevis Singer, "Gimpel the Fool"
(translated by Saul Bellow)

LETTERS BY
Robbie Robbins
SERIES EDITS BY
Chris Ryall
COVER ART BY
Gabriel Rodriguez
COVER COLORS BY
Nelson Daniel
COLLECTION EDITS BY
Justin Eisinger & Alonzo Simon
COLLECTION DESIGN BY
Robbie Robbins

Special thanks to Mickey Choate.

ISBN: 978-1-61377-898-2

17 16 15 14   1 2 3 4

Ted Adams, CEO & Publisher
Greg Goldstein, President & COO
Robbie Robbins, EVP/Sr. Graphic Artist
Chris Ryall, Chief Creative Officer/Editor-in-Chief
Matthew Ruzicka, CPA, Chief Financial Officer
Alan Payne, VP of Sales
Dirk Wood, VP of Marketing
Lorelei Bunjes, VP of Digital Services
Jeff Webber, VP of Digital Publishing & Business Development

www.IDWPUBLISHING.com
IDW founded by Ted Adams, Alex Garner, Kris Oprisko, and Robbie Robbins

Facebook: **facebook.com/idwpublishing**
Twitter: **@idwpublishing**
YouTube: **youtube.com/idwpublishing**
Instagram: **instagram.com/idwpublishing**
deviantART: **idwpublishing.deviantart.com**
Pinterest: **pinterest.com/idwpublishing/idw-staff-faves**

WRAITH. JULY 2014. FIRST PRINTING. © 2014 Joe Hill. Art © 2014 Idea and Design Works, LLC. All Rights Reserved. IDW Publishing, a division of Idea and Design Works, LLC. Editorial offices: 5080 Santa Fe Street, San Diego, CA 92109. The IDW logo is registered in the U.S. Patent and Trademark Office. Any similarities to persons living or dead are purely coincidental. With the exception of artwork used for review purposes, none of the contents of this publication may be reprinted without the permission of Idea and Design Works, LLC. Printed in Korea.

"Gimpel the Fool" by Isaac Bashevis Singer, translated by Saul Bellow, copyright 1953 by Partisan Review. Copyright renewed (c) 1981 by Isaac Bashevis Singer, from A TREASURY OF YIDDISH STORIES, REVISED AND UPDATED EDITION, edited by Irving Howe & Eliezer Greenberg. Used by permission of Viking Penguin, a division of Penguin Group (USA) LLC.

IDW Publishing does not read or accept unsolicited submissions of ideas, stories, or artwork.
Originally published as WRAITH issues #1–7.

WRAITH

CREATED & WRITTEN BY
Joe Hill

ART BY
Charles Paul Wilson III

COLORS BY
Jay Fotos

To Jim, Stephanie, Jon, and Justin Leonard.
—Joe Hill

To Stephanie. Thanks for putting up with me while I drew this.
—Charles Paul Wilson III

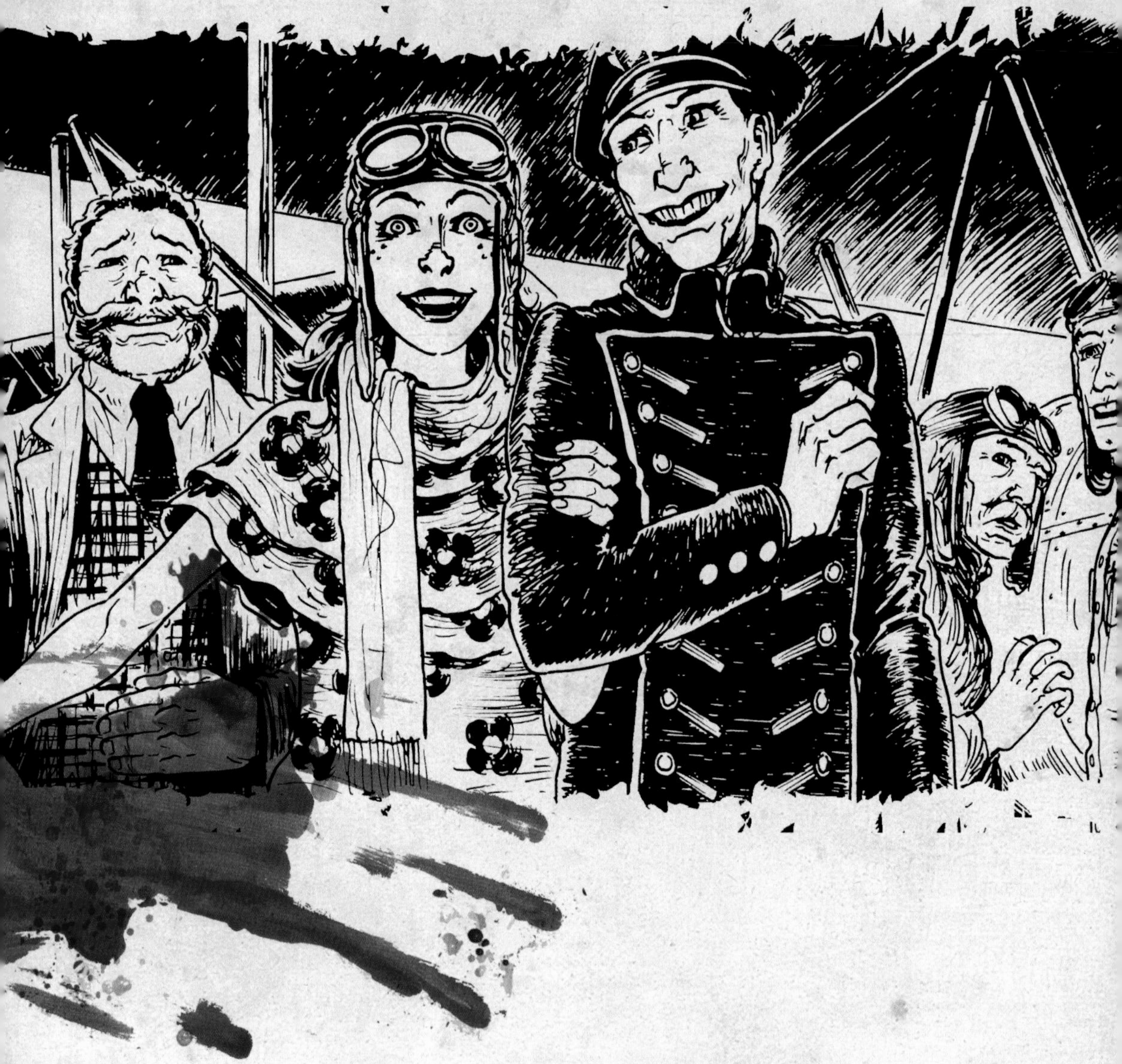

prologue

FANTOMS

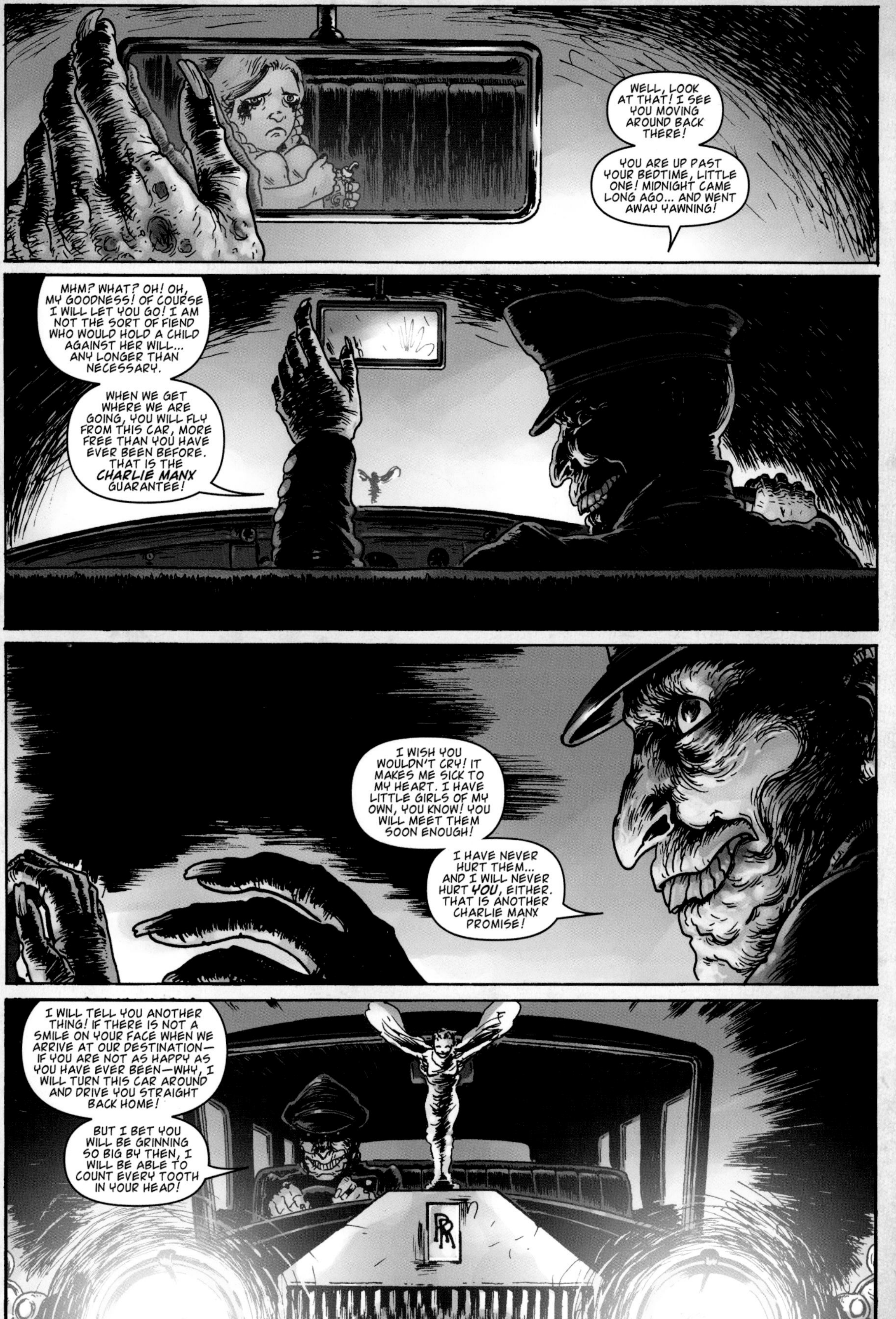
WELL, LOOK AT THAT! I SEE YOU MOVING AROUND BACK THERE!
YOU ARE UP PAST YOUR BEDTIME, LITTLE ONE! MIDNIGHT CAME LONG AGO... AND WENT AWAY YAWNING!
MHM? WHAT? OH! OH, MY GOODNESS! OF COURSE I WILL LET YOU GO! I AM NOT THE SORT OF FIEND WHO WOULD HOLD A CHILD AGAINST HER WILL... ANY LONGER THAN NECESSARY.
WHEN WE GET WHERE WE ARE GOING, YOU WILL FLY FROM THIS CAR, MORE FREE THAN YOU HAVE EVER BEEN BEFORE. THAT IS THE CHARLIE MANX GUARANTEE!
I WISH YOU WOULDN'T CRY! IT MAKES ME SICK TO MY HEART. I HAVE LITTLE GIRLS OF MY OWN, YOU KNOW! YOU WILL MEET THEM SOON ENOUGH!
I HAVE NEVER HURT THEM... AND I WILL NEVER HURT YOU, EITHER. THAT IS ANOTHER CHARLIE MANX PROMISE!
I WILL TELL YOU ANOTHER THING! IF THERE IS NOT A SMILE ON YOUR FACE WHEN WE ARRIVE AT OUR DESTINATION—IF YOU ARE NOT AS HAPPY AS YOU HAVE EVER BEEN—WHY, I WILL TURN THIS CAR AROUND AND DRIVE YOU STRAIGHT BACK HOME!
BUT I BET YOU WILL BE GRINNING SO BIG BY THEN, I WILL BE ABLE TO COUNT EVERY TOOTH IN YOUR HEAD!

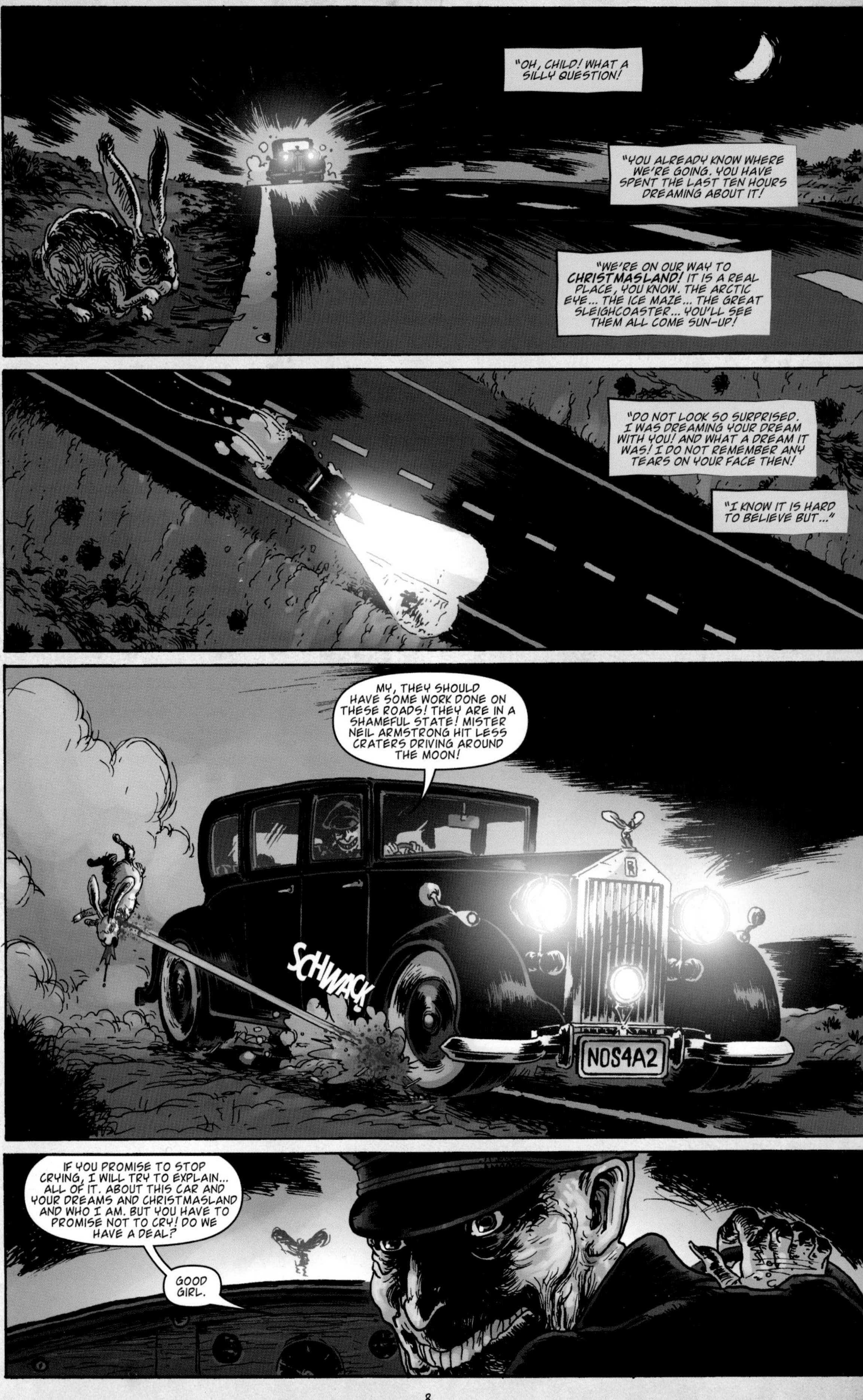
"OH, CHILD! WHAT A SILLY QUESTION!
"YOU ALREADY KNOW WHERE WE'RE GOING. YOU HAVE SPENT THE LAST TEN HOURS DREAMING ABOUT IT!
"WE'RE ON OUR WAY TO CHRISTMASLAND! IT IS A REAL PLACE, YOU KNOW. THE ARCTIC EYE... THE ICE MAZE... THE GREAT SLEIGHCOASTER... YOU'LL SEE THEM ALL COME SUN-UP!
"DO NOT LOOK SO SURPRISED. I WAS DREAMING YOUR DREAM WITH YOU! AND WHAT A DREAM IT WAS! I DO NOT REMEMBER ANY TEARS ON YOUR FACE THEN!
"I KNOW IT IS HARD TO BELIEVE BUT..."
MY, THEY SHOULD HAVE SOME WORK DONE ON THESE ROADS! THEY ARE IN A SHAMEFUL STATE! MISTER NEIL ARMSTRONG HIT LESS CRATERS DRIVING AROUND THE MOON!
SCHWACK!
NOS4A2
IF YOU PROMISE TO STOP CRYING, I WILL TRY TO EXPLAIN... ALL OF IT. ABOUT THIS CAR AND YOUR DREAMS AND CHRISTMASLAND AND WHO I AM. BUT YOU HAVE TO PROMISE NOT TO CRY! DO WE HAVE A DEAL?
GOOD GIRL.

"KNOW NOW THAT THERE ARE TWO KINDS OF ROADS, CHILD.

"THERE ARE ROADS LIKE THESE, ALL BLACKTOP AND POTHOLES AND NOISY TRUCKS AND TOLLS AND TRAFFIC AND STINK.

"AND THEN THERE ARE THE PRIVATE ROADS OF THOUGHT, WHERE EMOTIONS ARE WEATHER, BLOWING ACROSS THE LANDSCAPES OF YOUR IMAGINATION. I HAVE HEARD SUCH TERRITORIES CALLED INSCAPES. THE NAME WILL SERVE.

DESOLATION CANYON
Colorado 20 mi

"WITH THE RIGHT KIND OF RIDE AND THE RIGHT KIND OF DRIVER, YOU CAN START OUT ON THE FIRST SORT OF ROAD, AND WIND UP... EVENTUALLY... ON THE OTHER SORT.

"WELL, LET ME TELL YOU, THIS 1938 ROLLS-ROYCE WRAITH IS THE RIGHT KIND OF RIDE! AND I AM THE RIGHT KIND OF DRIVER! CHARLES TALENT MANX THE THIRD, BORN IN CRIPPLE CREEK, COLORADO! YOU WOULD NOT BELIEVE HOW LONG AGO, EITHER!

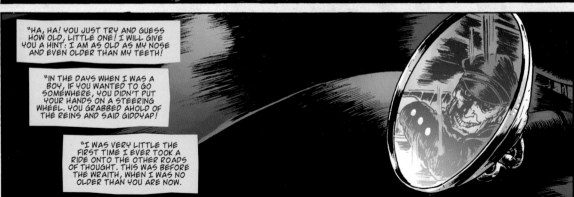

"HA, HA! YOU JUST TRY AND GUESS HOW OLD, LITTLE ONE! I WILL GIVE YOU A HINT: I AM AS OLD AS MY NOSE AND EVEN OLDER THAN MY TEETH!

"IN THE DAYS WHEN I WAS A BOY, IF YOU WANTED TO GO SOMEWHERE, YOU DIDN'T PUT YOUR HANDS ON A STEERING WHEEL. YOU GRABBED AHOLD OF THE REINS AND SAID GIDDYAP!

"I WAS VERY LITTLE THE FIRST TIME I EVER TOOK A RIDE ONTO THE OTHER ROADS OF THOUGHT. THIS WAS BEFORE THE WRAITH, WHEN I WAS NO OLDER THAN YOU ARE NOW.

"I HAD A DIFFERENT RIDE THEN. I SMILE TO THINK OF IT.

"IT WAS MY CHRISTMAS PRESENT. IT WAS MY SPECIAL CHRISTMAS PRESENT.

"IT WAS MY FANTOM."

"MY FATHER WAS A LOW RASCAL WHO LEFT ME NOTHING BUT MY NAME AND WAS SHOT OVER A WOMAN WHO I REGRET TO SAY WAS NOT MY MOTHER.
PORTIS & McMURTRY'S INN AND MORTUARY
"HE DIED IN THE ARMS OF A FAT LADY NAMED SALLY GRAPEFRUITS AND SHE WAS CALLING HIM A FOOL AS HIS LIFE TRICKLED AWAY BETWEEN HIS FINGERS!
"SUCH IS THE FATE OF THE FAITHLESS MAN! TO DIE IN THE GRIP OF AN ABUSIVE FAT WOMAN AND WAKE IN THE EMBRACE OF SATAN!
SCRIBBLED BY JOE HILL
DRAWN BY CHARLES "TALENT" WILSON THE III
SPELT JUST RIGHT BY SHAWN LEE & ROBBIE ROBBINS
PAINTED PRETTY BY JAY FOTOS
THREATS AND DEMANDS ISSUED BY CHRIS RYALL
WRAITH NUMERO UNO
PROLOG: FANTOMS
"SOME WOMEN ARE BORN TO BE MOTHERS, BUT I AM AFRAID FANNY MANX WAS NOT THE MATERNAL SORT! OH, SHE DID WHAT SHE COULD TO EARN FOR US, WORKING AS A HOUSEMAID IN PORTIS AND MCMURTRY'S INN AND MORTUARY.
"I WILL SAY OUR MOUTHS NEVER WENT EMPTY!
"IT WAS NO EASY LIFE IN A ONE-WHORE TOWN—AHEM, ONE-HORSE, I MEAN TO SAY—LIKE CRIPPLE CREEK, AND MY MOTHER WAS BITTER ABOUT OUR LOT. WHEN FANNY WAS IN HER CUPS, SHE WOULD BLAME ME FOR ALL MISFORTUNES AND COULD BE QUITE CRUEL.
"SHE WOULD CALL ME THE BAT-FACED BOY AND TELL ME BABIES ARE VAMPIRES, AND WHEN THEY SUCK AT THE BREAST, THEY ARE REALLY DRAINING A WOMAN'S YOUTH. SHE SAID IT SERVED ME RIGHT I SLEPT IN A COFFIN—IT WAS WHERE I BELONGED!
MERRY CHRISTMAS TO ALL
A VISIT FROM SAINT NIC
"MR. PORTIS AND MR. McMURTRY HAD AN INGENIOUS BUSINESS MODEL, YOU SEE. IN THE FRONT ROOM, THE MINERS AND ROUSTABOUTS COULD DRINK THEMSELVES TO DEATH.
"IN THE BACK ROOM, THEIR NEXT OF KIN COULD SELECT A COFFIN AND ONE OF SEVERAL AFFORDABLE FUNERAL SERVICES!
"SO IT'S TRUE, I HAD A COFFIN OF MY OWN AND SLEPT IN IT EVERY NIGHT. IT SOUNDS MACABRE, BUT BELIEVE ME, I HAD THE QUIETEST ROOM IN THE WHOLE INN AND THE ONLY BED THAT WAS NOT FULL OF LICE!
"I MADE A LITTLE COIN BY DRIVING MR. McMURTRY'S HORSE-DRAWN HEARSE IN THE PROCESSIONS TO THE CEMETERY. IT WAS MY FIRST JOB. I HAVE ALWAYS BEEN A DRIVER.
"MY MOTHER KEPT THE MONEY I EARNED FOR HERSELF, BUT ON CHRISTMAS, AT LEAST, SHE WOULD LET ME SPEND A LITTLE ON SOMETHING I WANTED."

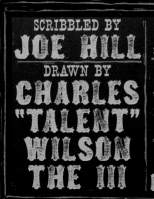

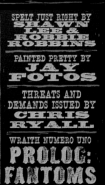

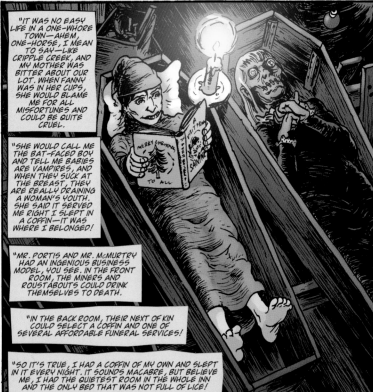

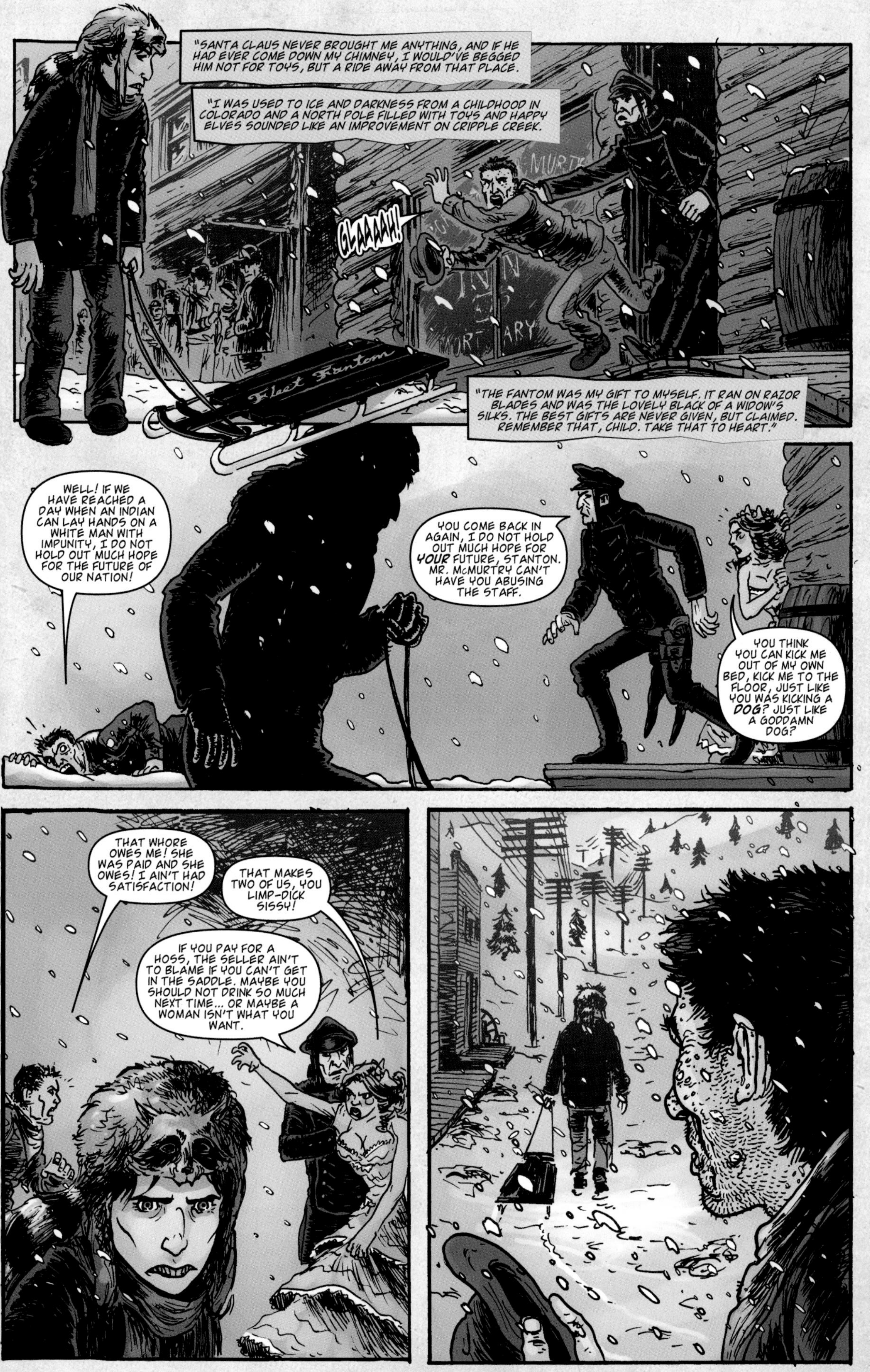
"SANTA CLAUS NEVER BROUGHT ME ANYTHING, AND IF HE HAD EVER COME DOWN MY CHIMNEY, I WOULD'VE BEGGED HIM NOT FOR TOYS, BUT A RIDE AWAY FROM THAT PLACE.
"I WAS USED TO ICE AND DARKNESS FROM A CHILDHOOD IN COLORADO AND A NORTH POLE FILLED WITH TOYS AND HAPPY ELVES SOUNDED LIKE AN IMPROVEMENT ON CRIPPLE CREEK.
GLAAAAH!
"THE FANTOM WAS MY GIFT TO MYSELF. IT RAN ON RAZOR BLADES AND WAS THE LOVELY BLACK OF A WIDOW'S SILKS. THE BEST GIFTS ARE NEVER GIVEN, BUT CLAIMED. REMEMBER THAT, CHILD. TAKE THAT TO HEART."
Fleet Fantom
WELL! IF WE HAVE REACHED A DAY WHEN AN INDIAN CAN LAY HANDS ON A WHITE MAN WITH IMPUNITY, I DO NOT HOLD OUT MUCH HOPE FOR THE FUTURE OF OUR NATION!
YOU COME BACK IN AGAIN, I DO NOT HOLD OUT MUCH HOPE FOR YOUR FUTURE, STANTON. MR. McMURTRY CAN'T HAVE YOU ABUSING THE STAFF.
YOU THINK YOU CAN KICK ME OUT OF MY OWN BED, KICK ME TO THE FLOOR, JUST LIKE YOU WAS KICKING A DOG? JUST LIKE A GODDAMN DOG?
THAT WHORE OWES ME! SHE WAS PAID AND SHE OWES! I AIN'T HAD SATISFACTION!
THAT MAKES TWO OF US, YOU LIMP-DICK SISSY!
IF YOU PAY FOR A HOSS, THE SELLER AIN'T TO BLAME IF YOU CAN'T GET IN THE SADDLE. MAYBE YOU SHOULD NOT DRINK SO MUCH NEXT TIME... OR MAYBE A WOMAN ISN'T WHAT YOU WANT.

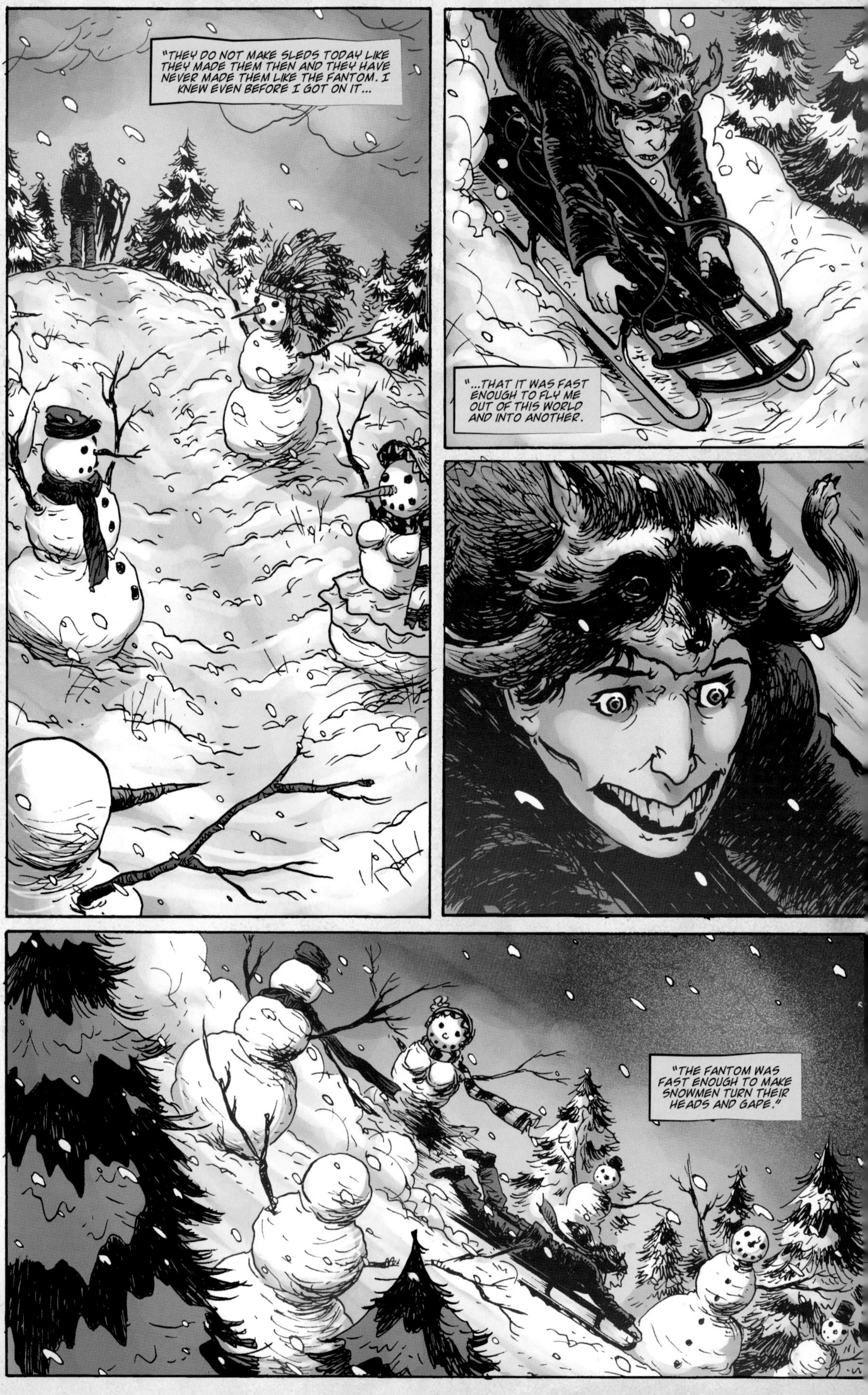
"THEY DO NOT MAKE SLEDS TODAY LIKE THEY MADE THEM THEN AND THEY HAVE NEVER MADE THEM LIKE THE FANTOM. I KNEW EVEN BEFORE I GOT ON IT...
"...THAT IT WAS FAST ENOUGH TO FLY ME OUT OF THIS WORLD AND INTO ANOTHER.
"THE FANTOM WAS FAST ENOUGH TO MAKE SNOWMEN TURN THEIR HEADS AND GAPE."

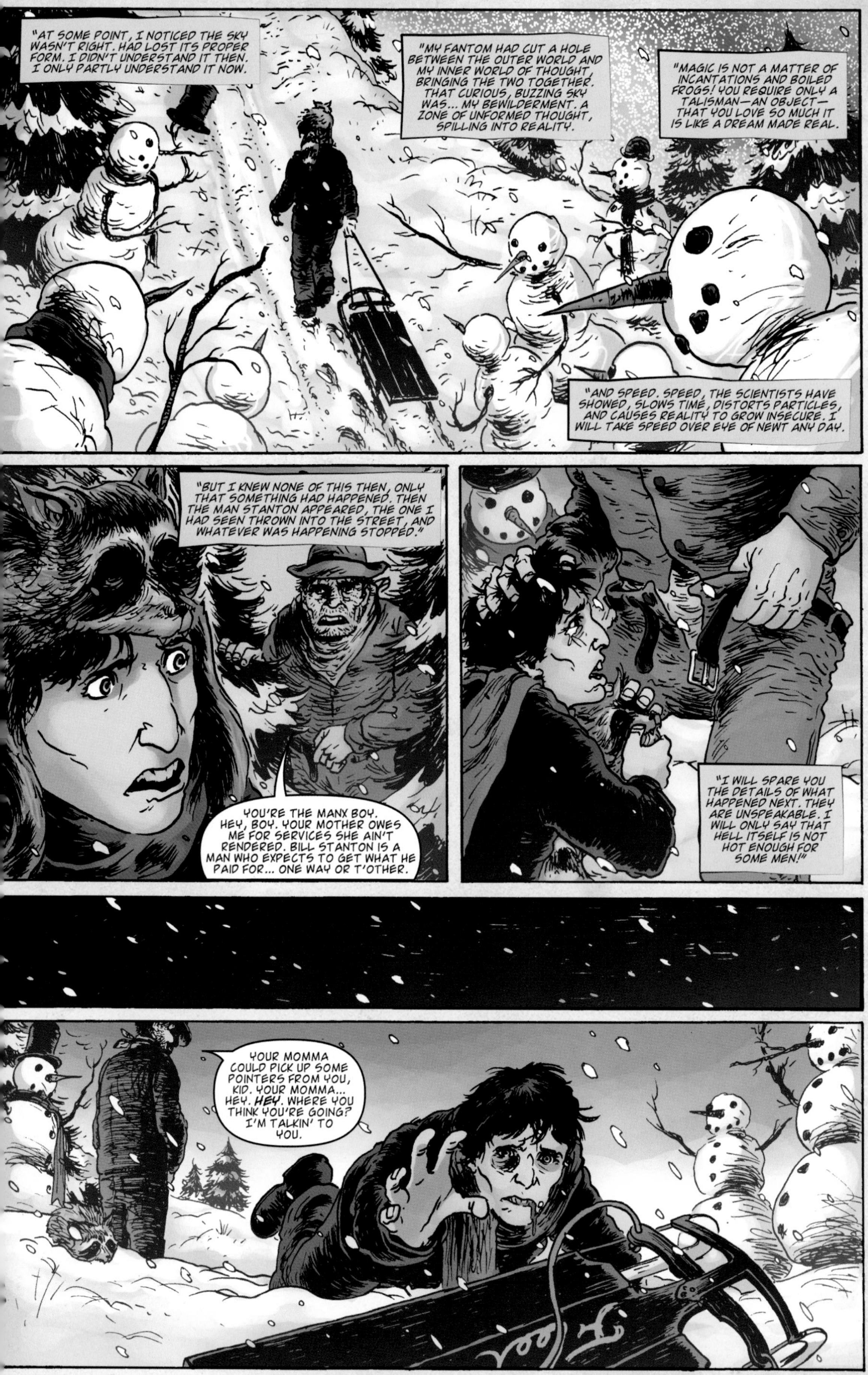
"AT SOME POINT, I NOTICED THE SKY WASN'T RIGHT. HAD LOST ITS PROPER FORM. I DIDN'T UNDERSTAND IT THEN. I ONLY PARTLY UNDERSTAND IT NOW.
"MY FANTOM HAD CUT A HOLE BETWEEN THE OUTER WORLD AND MY INNER WORLD OF THOUGHT, BRINGING THE TWO TOGETHER. THAT CURIOUS, BUZZING SKY WAS... MY BEWILDERMENT. A ZONE OF UNFORMED THOUGHT, SPILLING INTO REALITY.
"MAGIC IS NOT A MATTER OF INCANTATIONS AND BOILED FROGS! YOU REQUIRE ONLY A TALISMAN—AN OBJECT—THAT YOU LOVE SO MUCH IT IS LIKE A DREAM MADE REAL.
"AND SPEED. SPEED, THE SCIENTISTS HAVE SHOWED, SLOWS TIME, DISTORTS PARTICLES, AND CAUSES REALITY TO GROW INSECURE. I WILL TAKE SPEED OVER EYE OF NEWT ANY DAY.
"BUT I KNEW NONE OF THIS THEN, ONLY THAT SOMETHING HAD HAPPENED. THEN THE MAN STANTON APPEARED, THE ONE I HAD SEEN THROWN INTO THE STREET, AND WHATEVER WAS HAPPENING STOPPED."
YOU'RE THE MANX BOY. HEY, BOY. YOUR MOTHER OWES ME FOR SERVICES SHE AIN'T RENDERED. BILL STANTON IS A MAN WHO EXPECTS TO GET WHAT HE PAID FOR... ONE WAY OR T'OTHER.
"I WILL SPARE YOU THE DETAILS OF WHAT HAPPENED NEXT. THEY ARE UNSPEAKABLE. I WILL ONLY SAY THAT HELL ITSELF IS NOT HOT ENOUGH FOR SOME MEN!"
YOUR MOMMA COULD PICK UP SOME POINTERS FROM YOU, KID. YOUR MOMMA... HEY. **HEY**. WHERE YOU THINK YOU'RE GOING? I'M TALKIN' TO YOU.

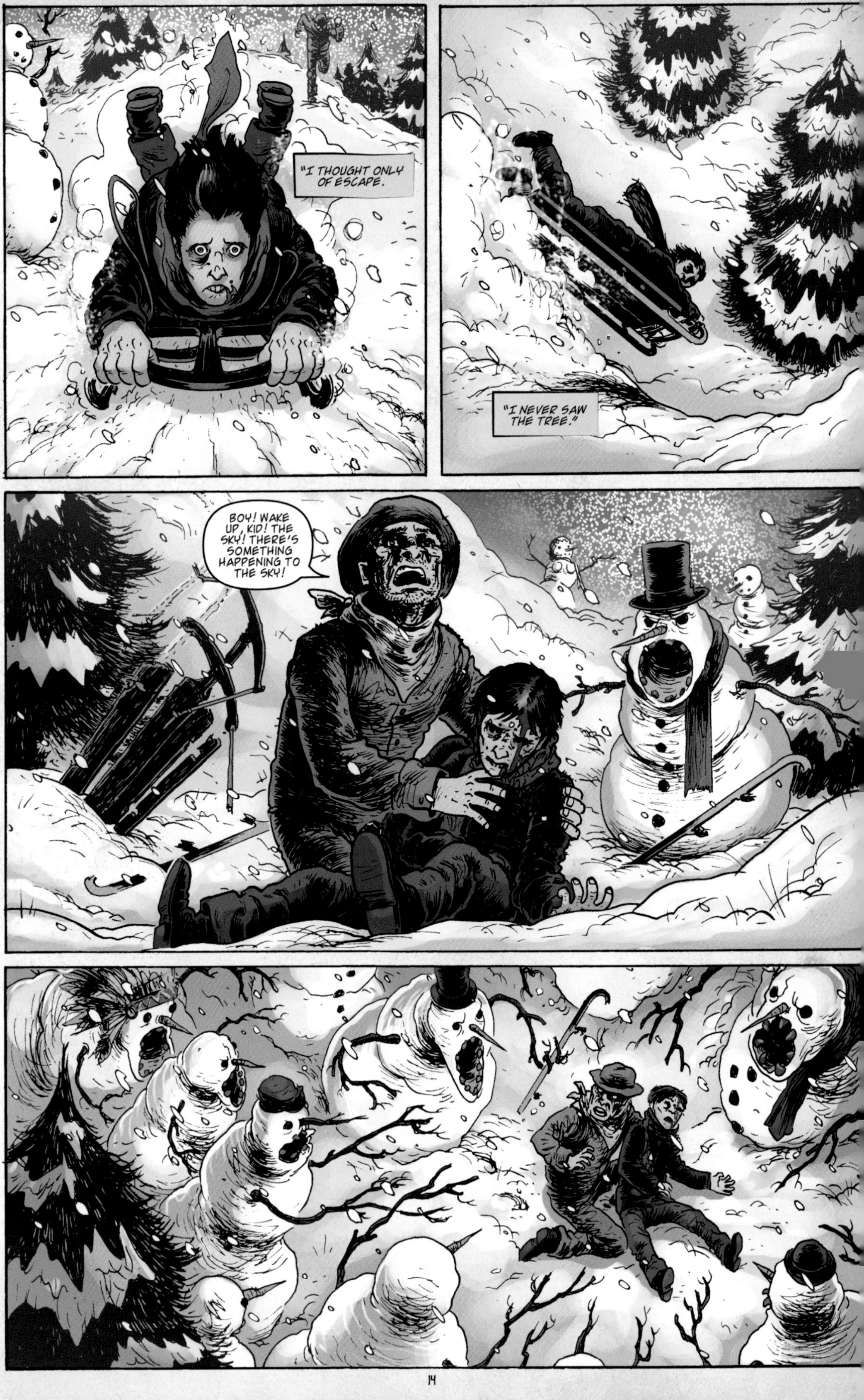
"I THOUGHT ONLY OF ESCAPE.
"I NEVER SAW THE TREE."
BOY! WAKE UP, KID! THE SKY! THERE'S SOMETHING HAPPENING TO THE SKY!

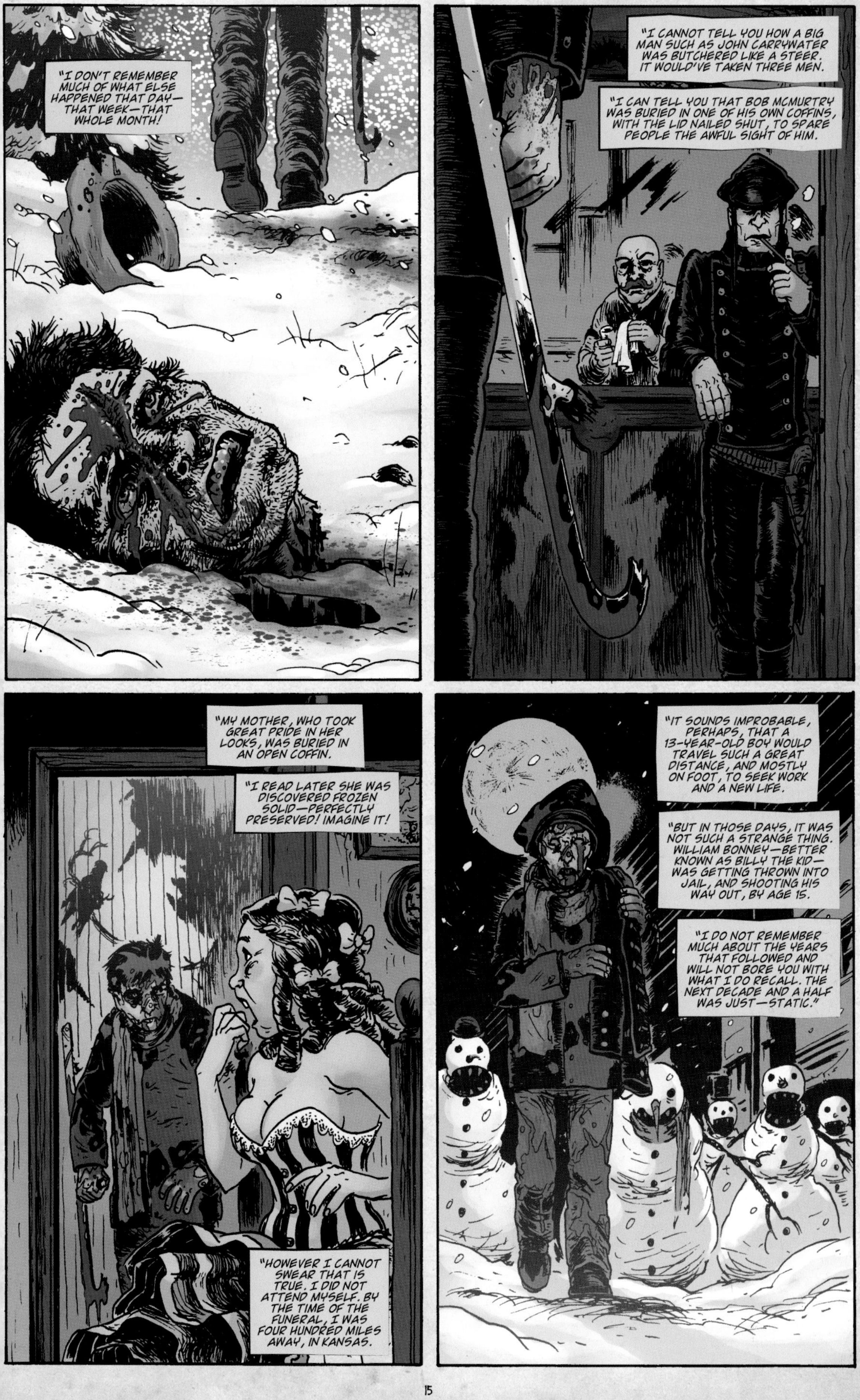
"I DON'T REMEMBER MUCH OF WHAT ELSE HAPPENED THAT DAY—THAT WEEK—THAT WHOLE MONTH!
"I CANNOT TELL YOU HOW A BIG MAN SUCH AS JOHN CARRYWATER WAS BUTCHERED LIKE A STEER. IT WOULD'VE TAKEN THREE MEN.
"I CAN TELL YOU THAT BOB MCMURTRY WAS BURIED IN ONE OF HIS OWN COFFINS, WITH THE LID NAILED SHUT, TO SPARE PEOPLE THE AWFUL SIGHT OF HIM.
"MY MOTHER, WHO TOOK GREAT PRIDE IN HER LOOKS, WAS BURIED IN AN OPEN COFFIN.
"I READ LATER SHE WAS DISCOVERED FROZEN SOLID—PERFECTLY PRESERVED! IMAGINE IT!
"HOWEVER I CANNOT SWEAR THAT IS TRUE. I DID NOT ATTEND MYSELF. BY THE TIME OF THE FUNERAL, I WAS FOUR HUNDRED MILES AWAY, IN KANSAS.
"IT SOUNDS IMPROBABLE, PERHAPS, THAT A 13-YEAR-OLD BOY WOULD TRAVEL SUCH A GREAT DISTANCE, AND MOSTLY ON FOOT, TO SEEK WORK AND A NEW LIFE.
"BUT IN THOSE DAYS, IT WAS NOT SUCH A STRANGE THING. WILLIAM BONNEY—BETTER KNOWN AS BILLY THE KID—WAS GETTING THROWN INTO JAIL, AND SHOOTING HIS WAY OUT, BY AGE 15.
"I DO NOT REMEMBER MUCH ABOUT THE YEARS THAT FOLLOWED AND WILL NOT BORE YOU WITH WHAT I DO RECALL. THE NEXT DECADE AND A HALF WAS JUST—STATIC."

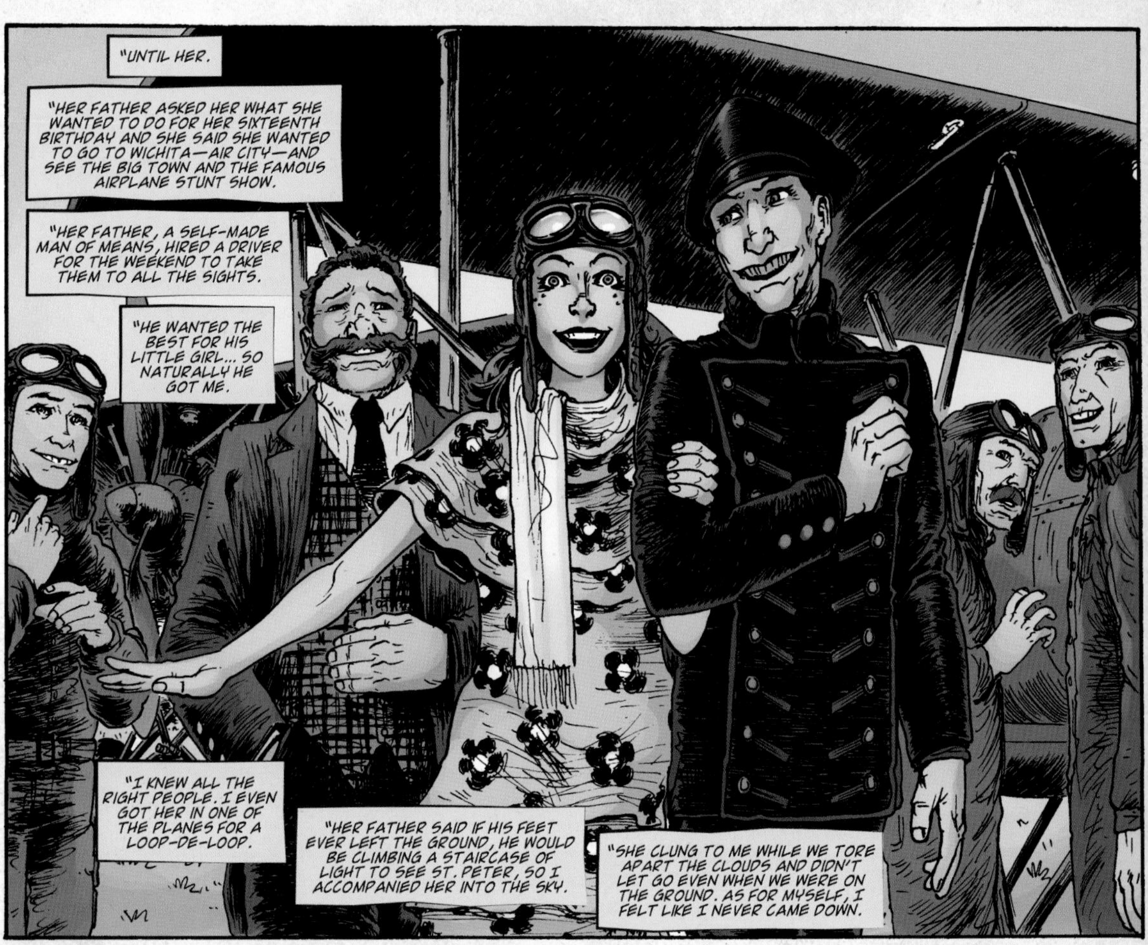
"UNTIL HER.
"HER FATHER ASKED HER WHAT SHE WANTED TO DO FOR HER SIXTEENTH BIRTHDAY AND SHE SAID SHE WANTED TO GO TO WICHITA—AIR CITY—AND SEE THE BIG TOWN AND THE FAMOUS AIRPLANE STUNT SHOW.
"HER FATHER, A SELF-MADE MAN OF MEANS, HIRED A DRIVER FOR THE WEEKEND TO TAKE THEM TO ALL THE SIGHTS.
"HE WANTED THE BEST FOR HIS LITTLE GIRL... SO NATURALLY HE GOT ME.
"I KNEW ALL THE RIGHT PEOPLE. I EVEN GOT HER IN ONE OF THE PLANES FOR A LOOP-DE-LOOP.
"HER FATHER SAID IF HIS FEET EVER LEFT THE GROUND, HE WOULD BE CLIMBING A STAIRCASE OF LIGHT TO SEE ST. PETER, SO I ACCOMPANIED HER INTO THE SKY.
"SHE CLUNG TO ME WHILE WE TORE APART THE CLOUDS AND DIDN'T LET GO EVEN WHEN WE WERE ON THE GROUND. AS FOR MYSELF, I FELT LIKE I NEVER CAME DOWN.

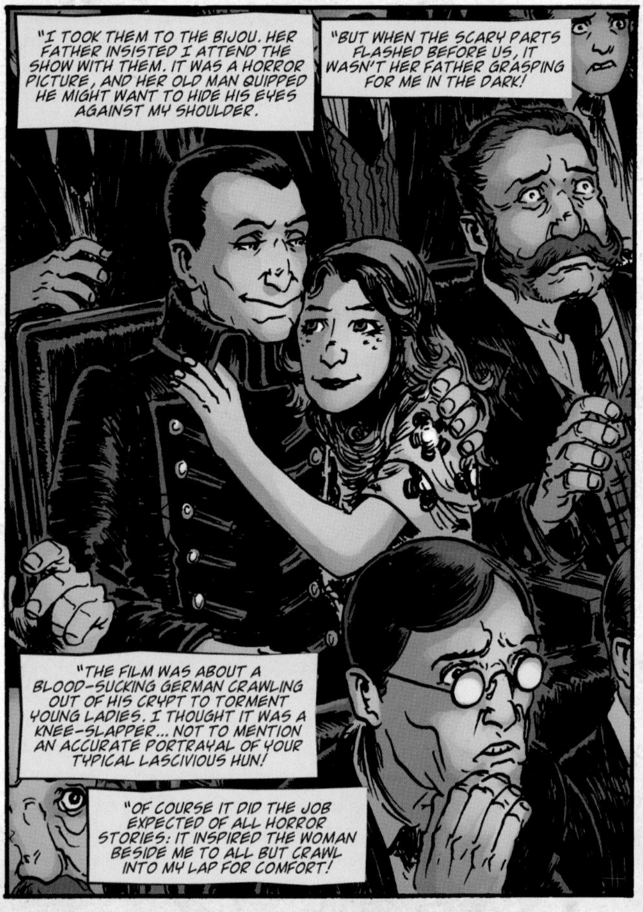
"I TOOK THEM TO THE BIJOU. HER FATHER INSISTED I ATTEND THE SHOW WITH THEM. IT WAS A HORROR PICTURE, AND HER OLD MAN QUIPPED HE MIGHT WANT TO HIDE HIS EYES AGAINST MY SHOULDER.
"BUT WHEN THE SCARY PARTS FLASHED BEFORE US, IT WASN'T HER FATHER GRASPING FOR ME IN THE DARK!
"THE FILM WAS ABOUT A BLOOD-SUCKING GERMAN CRAWLING OUT OF HIS CRYPT TO TORMENT YOUNG LADIES. I THOUGHT IT WAS A KNEE-SLAPPER... NOT TO MENTION AN ACCURATE PORTRAYAL OF YOUR TYPICAL LASCIVIOUS HUN!
"OF COURSE IT DID THE JOB EXPECTED OF ALL HORROR STORIES: IT INSPIRED THE WOMAN BESIDE ME TO ALL BUT CRAWL INTO MY LAP FOR COMFORT!

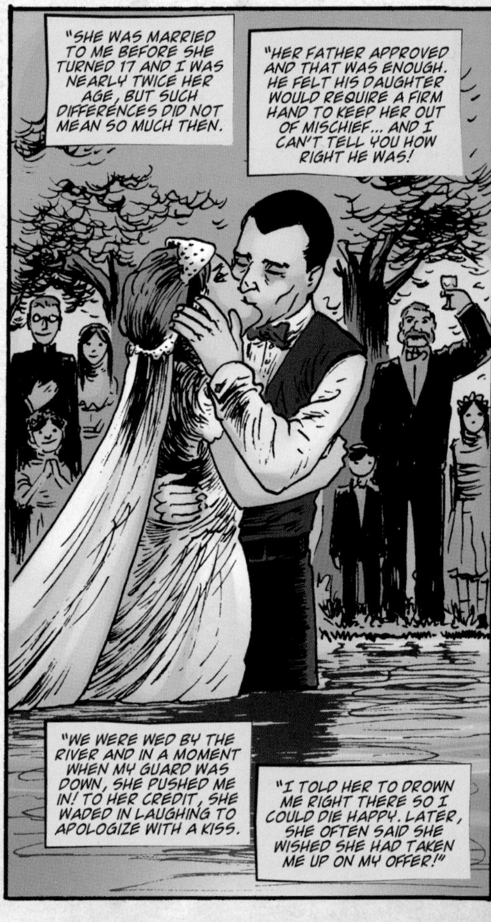
"SHE WAS MARRIED TO ME BEFORE SHE TURNED 17 AND I WAS NEARLY TWICE HER AGE, BUT SUCH DIFFERENCES DID NOT MEAN SO MUCH THEN.
"HER FATHER APPROVED AND THAT WAS ENOUGH. HE FELT HIS DAUGHTER WOULD REQUIRE A FIRM HAND TO KEEP HER OUT OF MISCHIEF... AND I CAN'T TELL YOU HOW RIGHT HE WAS!
"WE WERE WED BY THE RIVER AND IN A MOMENT WHEN MY GUARD WAS DOWN, SHE PUSHED ME IN! TO HER CREDIT, SHE WADED IN LAUGHING TO APOLOGIZE WITH A KISS.
"I TOLD HER TO DROWN ME RIGHT THERE SO I COULD DIE HAPPY. LATER, SHE OFTEN SAID SHE WISHED SHE HAD TAKEN ME UP ON MY OFFER!"

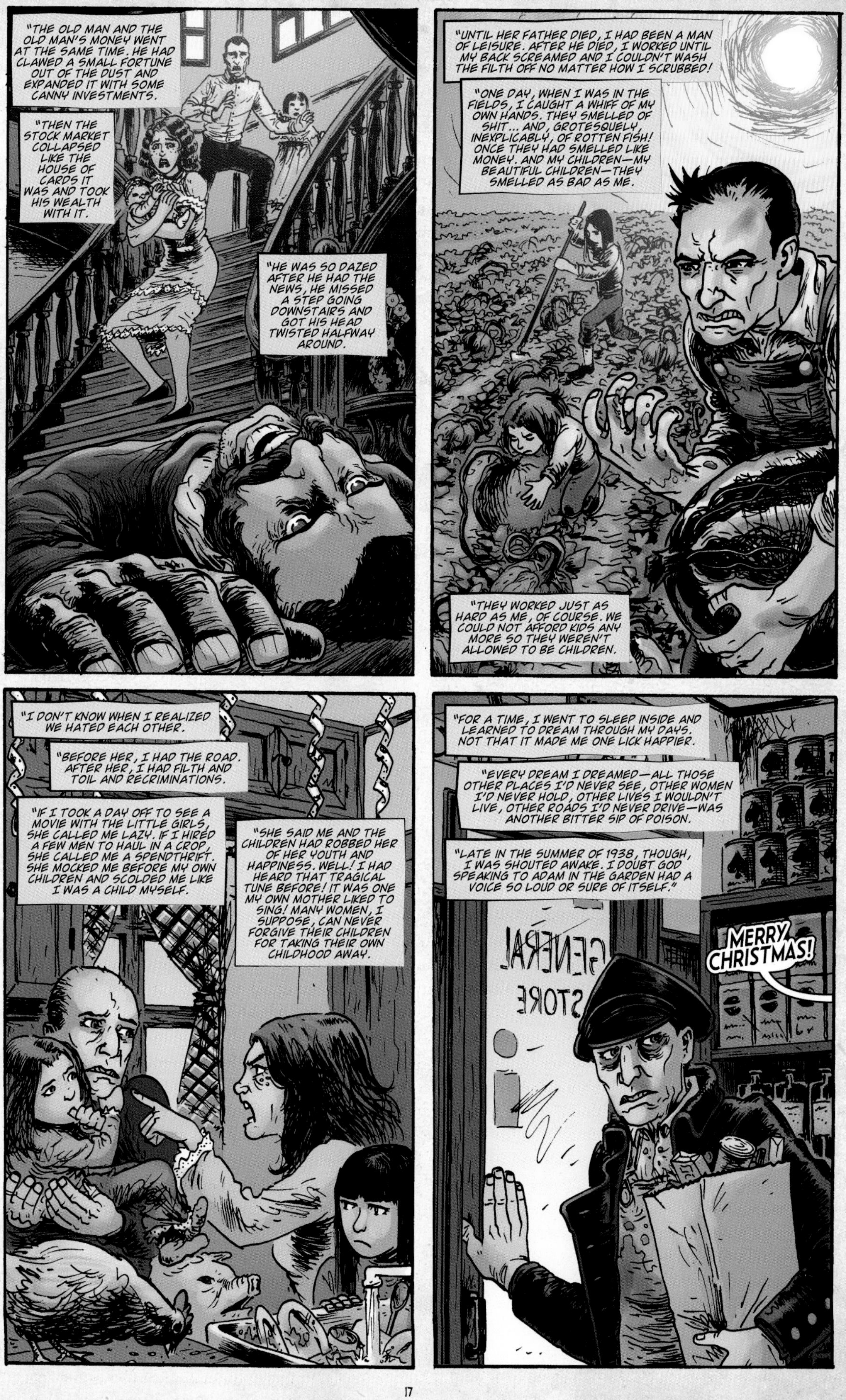
"THE OLD MAN AND THE OLD MAN'S MONEY WENT AT THE SAME TIME. HE HAD CLAWED A SMALL FORTUNE OUT OF THE DUST AND EXPANDED IT WITH SOME CANNY INVESTMENTS.
"THEN THE STOCK MARKET COLLAPSED LIKE THE HOUSE OF CARDS IT WAS AND TOOK HIS WEALTH WITH IT.
"HE WAS SO DAZED AFTER HE HAD THE NEWS, HE MISSED A STEP GOING DOWNSTAIRS AND GOT HIS HEAD TWISTED HALFWAY AROUND.
"UNTIL HER FATHER DIED, I HAD BEEN A MAN OF LEISURE. AFTER HE DIED, I WORKED UNTIL MY BACK SCREAMED AND I COULDN'T WASH THE FILTH OFF NO MATTER HOW I SCRUBBED!
"ONE DAY, WHEN I WAS IN THE FIELDS, I CAUGHT A WHIFF OF MY OWN HANDS. THEY SMELLED OF SHIT... AND, GROTESQUELY, INEXPLICABLY, OF ROTTEN FISH! ONCE THEY HAD SMELLED LIKE MONEY. AND MY CHILDREN—MY BEAUTIFUL CHILDREN—THEY SMELLED AS BAD AS ME.
"THEY WORKED JUST AS HARD AS ME, OF COURSE. WE COULD NOT AFFORD KIDS ANY MORE SO THEY WEREN'T ALLOWED TO BE CHILDREN.
"I DON'T KNOW WHEN I REALIZED WE HATED EACH OTHER.
"BEFORE HER, I HAD THE ROAD. AFTER HER, I HAD FILTH AND TOIL AND RECRIMINATIONS.
"IF I TOOK A DAY OFF TO SEE A MOVIE WITH THE LITTLE GIRLS, SHE CALLED ME LAZY. IF I HIRED A FEW MEN TO HAUL IN A CROP, SHE CALLED ME A SPENDTHRIFT. SHE MOCKED ME BEFORE MY OWN CHILDREN AND SCOLDED ME LIKE I WAS A CHILD MYSELF.
"SHE SAID ME AND THE CHILDREN HAD ROBBED HER OF HER YOUTH AND HAPPINESS. WELL! I HAD HEARD THAT TRAGICAL TUNE BEFORE! IT WAS ONE MY OWN MOTHER LIKED TO SING! MANY WOMEN, I SUPPOSE, CAN NEVER FORGIVE THEIR CHILDREN FOR TAKING THEIR OWN CHILDHOOD AWAY.
"FOR A TIME, I WENT TO SLEEP INSIDE AND LEARNED TO DREAM THROUGH MY DAYS. NOT THAT IT MADE ME ONE LICK HAPPIER.
"EVERY DREAM I DREAMED—ALL THOSE OTHER PLACES I'D NEVER SEE, OTHER WOMEN I'D NEVER HOLD, OTHER LIVES I WOULDN'T LIVE, OTHER ROADS I'D NEVER DRIVE—WAS ANOTHER BITTER SIP OF POISON.
"LATE IN THE SUMMER OF 1938, THOUGH, I WAS SHOUTED AWAKE. I DOUBT GOD SPEAKING TO ADAM IN THE GARDEN HAD A VOICE SO LOUD OR SURE OF ITSELF."
GENERAL STORE
MERRY CHRISTMAS!

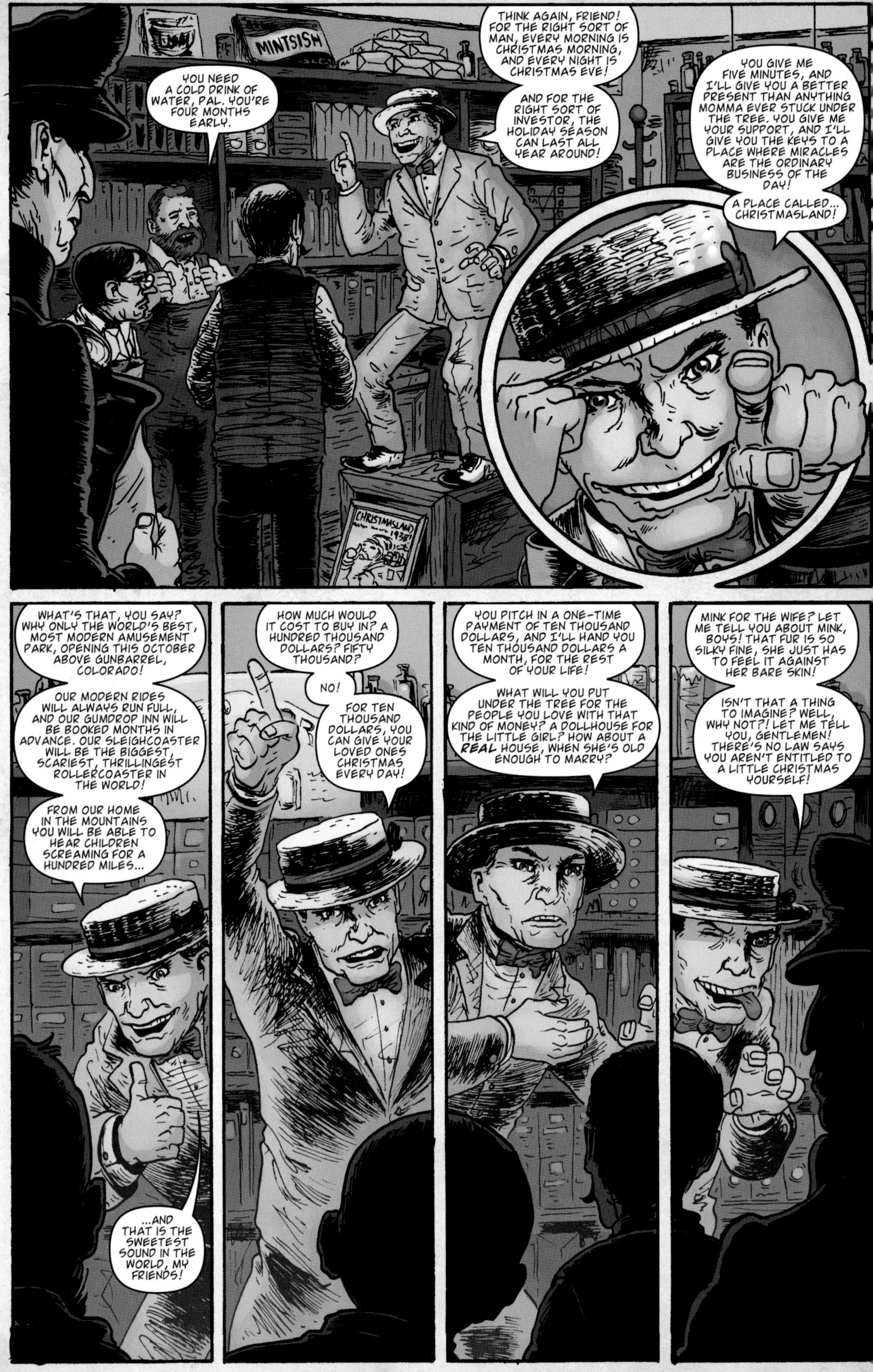
THINK AGAIN, FRIEND! FOR THE RIGHT SORT OF MAN, EVERY MORNING IS CHRISTMAS MORNING, AND EVERY NIGHT IS CHRISTMAS EVE!
YOU NEED A COLD DRINK OF WATER, PAL. YOU'RE FOUR MONTHS EARLY.
AND FOR THE RIGHT SORT OF INVESTOR, THE HOLIDAY SEASON CAN LAST ALL YEAR AROUND!
YOU GIVE ME FIVE MINUTES, AND I'LL GIVE YOU A BETTER PRESENT THAN ANYTHING MOMMA EVER STUCK UNDER THE TREE. YOU GIVE ME YOUR SUPPORT, AND I'LL GIVE YOU THE KEYS TO A PLACE WHERE MIRACLES ARE THE ORDINARY BUSINESS OF THE DAY!
A PLACE CALLED... CHRISTMASLAND!
MINTSISH
CHRISTMASLAND
WHAT'S THAT, YOU SAY? WHY ONLY THE WORLD'S BEST, MOST MODERN AMUSEMENT PARK, OPENING THIS OCTOBER ABOVE GUNBARREL, COLORADO!
OUR MODERN RIDES WILL ALWAYS RUN FULL, AND OUR GUMDROP INN WILL BE BOOKED MONTHS IN ADVANCE. OUR SLEIGHCOASTER WILL BE THE BIGGEST, SCARIEST, THRILLINGEST ROLLERCOASTER IN THE WORLD!
FROM OUR HOME IN THE MOUNTAINS YOU WILL BE ABLE TO HEAR CHILDREN SCREAMING FOR A HUNDRED MILES...
...AND THAT IS THE SWEETEST SOUND IN THE WORLD, MY FRIENDS!
HOW MUCH WOULD IT COST TO BUY IN? A HUNDRED THOUSAND DOLLARS? FIFTY THOUSAND?
NO!
FOR TEN THOUSAND DOLLARS, YOU CAN GIVE YOUR LOVED ONES CHRISTMAS EVERY DAY!
YOU PITCH IN A ONE-TIME PAYMENT OF TEN THOUSAND DOLLARS, AND I'LL HAND YOU TEN THOUSAND DOLLARS A MONTH, FOR THE REST OF YOUR LIFE!
WHAT WILL YOU PUT UNDER THE TREE FOR THE PEOPLE YOU LOVE WITH THAT KIND OF MONEY? A DOLLHOUSE FOR THE LITTLE GIRL? HOW ABOUT A REAL HOUSE, WHEN SHE'S OLD ENOUGH TO MARRY?
MINK FOR THE WIFE? LET ME TELL YOU ABOUT MINK, BOYS! THAT FUR IS SO SILKY FINE, SHE JUST HAS TO FEEL IT AGAINST HER BARE SKIN!
ISN'T THAT A THING TO IMAGINE? WELL, WHY NOT?! LET ME TELL YOU, GENTLEMEN! THERE'S NO LAW SAYS YOU AREN'T ENTITLED TO A LITTLE CHRISTMAS YOURSELF!

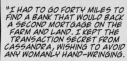

"I HAD TO GO FORTY MILES TO FIND A BANK THAT WOULD BACK A SECOND MORTGAGE ON THE FARM AND LAND. I KEPT THE TRANSACTION SECRET FROM CASSANDRA, WISHING TO AVOID ANY WOMANLY HAND-WRINGING.

"THE MAN FROM CHRISTMASLAND LIMITED SAID EVEN IF THE PARK ONLY RAN AT 10 PERCENT CAPACITY, I WOULD MAKE BACK MY INITIAL INVESTMENT IN SIX WEEKS.

"HIS NAME WAS NICHOLAS. HE ENCOURAGED ME TO CALL HIM ST. NICK, BUT I WAS TOO BASHFUL FOR SUCH FAMILIARITIES! WHEN I SPOKE TO HIM, I ALWAYS ADDRESSED HIM AS MR. LeMARC.

"THE THIRD DAY OF OCTOBER, MR. LeMARC MAILED PASSES FOR OPENING DAY... AND THE NEWS THAT MY INVESTMENT HAD ALREADY EARNED OUT ON ADVANCE SALES. HE WOULD WRITE ME A CHECK WHEN HE SAW ME. I ADMIT I SAT ON THE CURB AND WEPT WITH RELIEF.

Christmasland
Coming October 1938

"I COULDN'T BEAR TO DRIVE US THERE IN A 12-YEAR-OLD TRUCK WITH NO FLOORBOARDS, AND I KNEW WE HAD PLENTY OF MONEY WAITING IN COLORADO.

"WE WERE ON THE WAY TO EARNING MORE IN A FEW MONTHS THAN CASS'S FATHER HAD MADE IN HIS ENTIRE HARD-SCRABBLE LIFE.

"I WENT TO A DEALERSHIP IN TOWN. THE WRAITH WAS WAITING.

"IT HAD COME INTO THEIR HANDS LIGHTLY USED AND THEY WERE ALMOST GIVING IT AWAY.

"THE PREVIOUS OWNER HAD KILLED HIMSELF AND HIS CHILDREN IN IT. PIPED EXHAUST IN AND POISONED THEM, AND HIMSELF WITH THEM.

"IT WAS IN ALMOST NEW CONDITION, BUT GIVEN ITS... DISAGREEABLE PROVENANCE, IT WAS HARD TO FIND A BUYER. I GOT IT FOR NEXT TO NOTHING.

"THE CHILDREN COULD NOT HAVE BEEN MORE AMAZED IF I HAD COME HOME IN A SLEIGH DRAWN BY FLYING REINDEER!

"MY WIFE WAS AMAZED AS WELL, AND EXPRESSED HER SURPRISE IN NO UNCERTAIN TERMS. I SOMETIMES REGRET THAT I DID NOT TAKE A HAND TO HER AND REMIND HER WHO WORE THE BELT!

"WHO KNOWS! THINGS MIGHT'VE ENDED BETTER FOR HER IF I HAD!

"I SLEPT IN THE CAR FOR A WEEK. SHE TOLD ME SHE WOULD NOT ALLOW ME BACK IN OUR BED UNTIL I RETURNED THE WRAITH TO THE DEALER AND BEGGED FOR OUR MONEY BACK."

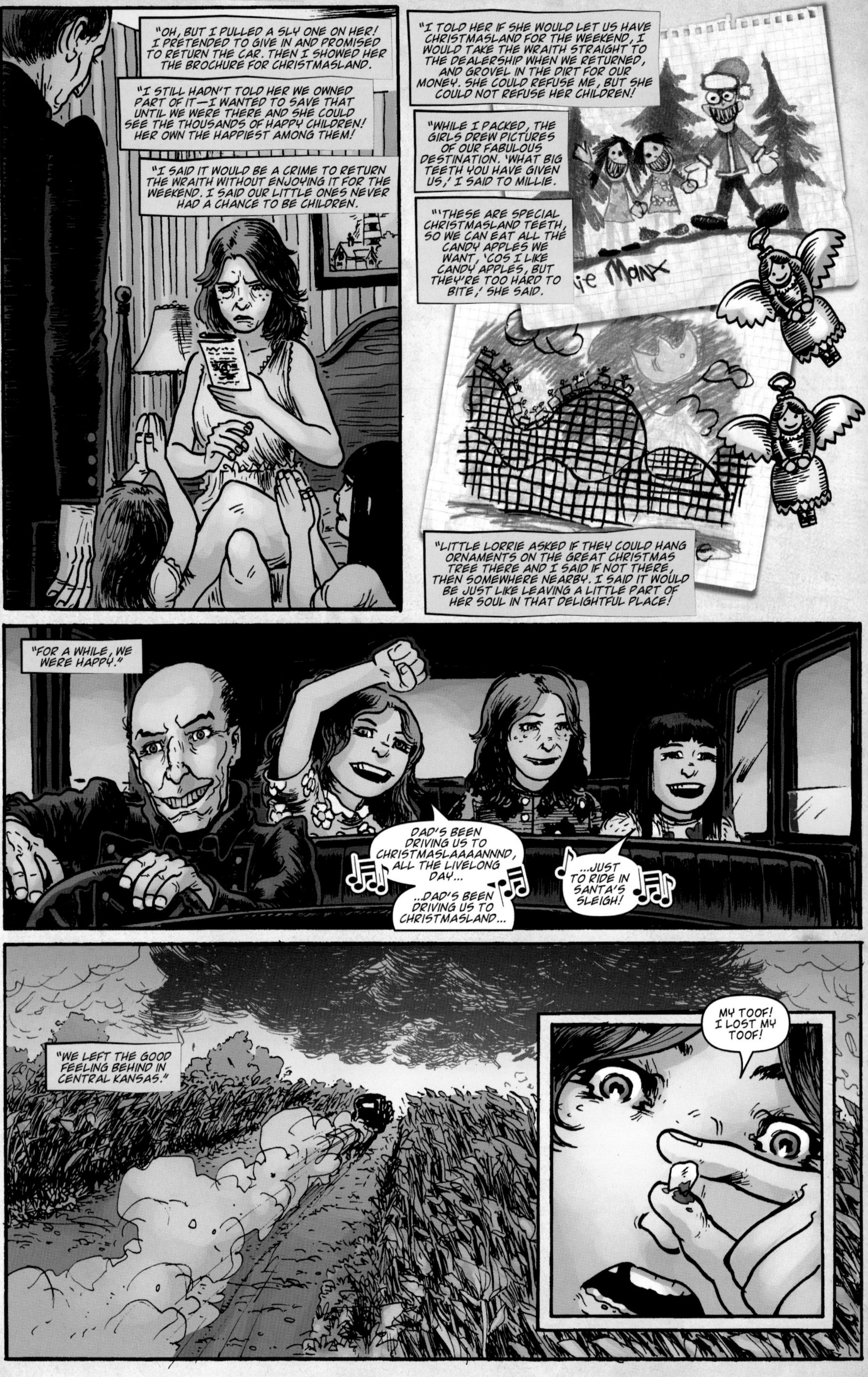
"OH, BUT I PULLED A SLY ONE ON HER! I PRETENDED TO GIVE IN AND PROMISED TO RETURN THE CAR. THEN I SHOWED HER THE BROCHURE FOR CHRISTMASLAND.
"I STILL HADN'T TOLD HER WE OWNED PART OF IT—I WANTED TO SAVE THAT UNTIL WE WERE THERE AND SHE COULD SEE THE THOUSANDS OF HAPPY CHILDREN! HER OWN THE HAPPIEST AMONG THEM!
"I SAID IT WOULD BE A CRIME TO RETURN THE WRAITH WITHOUT ENJOYING IT FOR THE WEEKEND. I SAID OUR LITTLE ONES NEVER HAD A CHANCE TO BE CHILDREN.
"I TOLD HER IF SHE WOULD LET US HAVE CHRISTMASLAND FOR THE WEEKEND, I WOULD TAKE THE WRAITH STRAIGHT TO THE DEALERSHIP WHEN WE RETURNED, AND GROVEL IN THE DIRT FOR OUR MONEY. SHE COULD REFUSE ME, BUT SHE COULD NOT REFUSE HER CHILDREN!
"WHILE I PACKED, THE GIRLS DREW PICTURES OF OUR FABULOUS DESTINATION. 'WHAT BIG TEETH YOU HAVE GIVEN US,' I SAID TO MILLIE.
"'THESE ARE SPECIAL CHRISTMASLAND TEETH, SO WE CAN EAT ALL THE CANDY APPLES WE WANT, 'COS I LIKE CANDY APPLES, BUT THEY'RE TOO HARD TO BITE,' SHE SAID.
"LITTLE LORRIE ASKED IF THEY COULD HANG ORNAMENTS ON THE GREAT CHRISTMAS TREE THERE AND I SAID IF NOT THERE, THEN SOMEWHERE NEARBY. I SAID IT WOULD BE JUST LIKE LEAVING A LITTLE PART OF HER SOUL IN THAT DELIGHTFUL PLACE!
"FOR A WHILE, WE WERE HAPPY."
DAD'S BEEN DRIVING US TO CHRISTMASLAAAANNND, ALL THE LIVELONG DAY...
...DAD'S BEEN DRIVING US TO CHRISTMASLAND...
...JUST TO RIDE IN SANTA'S SLEIGH!
"WE LEFT THE GOOD FEELING BEHIND IN CENTRAL KANSAS."
MY TOOF! I LOST MY TOOF!

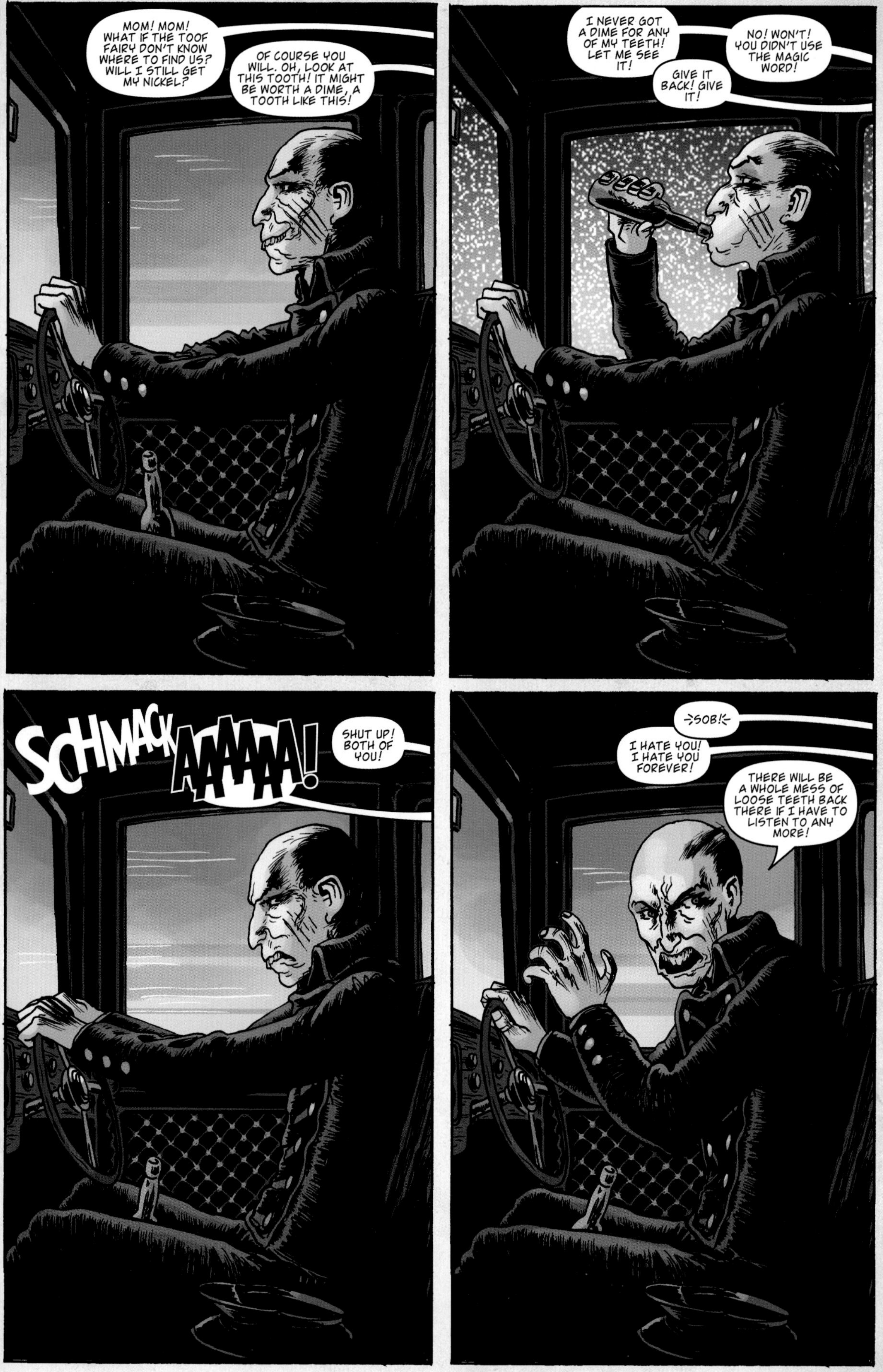
MOM! MOM! WHAT IF THE TOOF FAIRY DON'T KNOW WHERE TO FIND US? WILL I STILL GET MY NICKEL?
OF COURSE YOU WILL. OH, LOOK AT THIS TOOTH! IT MIGHT BE WORTH A DIME, A TOOTH LIKE THIS!
I NEVER GOT A DIME FOR ANY OF MY TEETH! LET ME SEE IT!
NO! WON'T! YOU DIDN'T USE THE MAGIC WORD!
GIVE IT BACK! GIVE IT!
SCHMACK
AAAAAA!
SHUT UP! BOTH OF YOU!
SOB!
I HATE YOU! I HATE YOU FOREVER!
THERE WILL BE A WHOLE MESS OF LOOSE TEETH BACK THERE IF I HAVE TO LISTEN TO ANY MORE!

I KNOW THIS SKY. HUH.

I THOUGHT YOU ONLY CAME AROUND WHEN I NEEDED TO MAKE A SECRET ESCAPE. DO I NEED TO ESCAPE AGAIN?

IT'S LIKE A GODDAMN THUNDERSTORM ARMAGEDDON HOLOCAUST OUT THERE. YOU CAN'T DRIVE IN THIS, CHARLIE. WE NEED TO FIND A PLACE TO BUNK FOR THE NIGHT.

THE GIRLS APPEAR TO HAVE BUNKED ALREADY. THEY ARE SLEEPING NICELY. WHY DON'T YOU SNOOZE YOURSELF?

THESE GIRLS ARE HALF-FROZE. I CAN SEE THEIR BREATH. THEY NEED WARM BEDS AND A REGULAR NIGHT OF REST. BESIDES... I DON'T LIKE THE WAY THEY LOOK. THEY'RE... PALE.

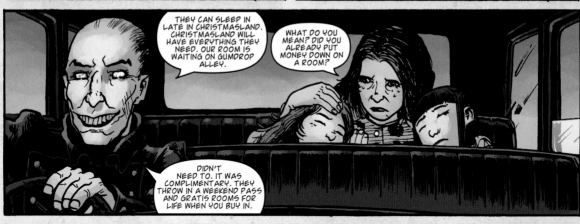

THEY CAN SLEEP IN LATE IN CHRISTMASLAND. CHRISTMASLAND WILL HAVE EVERYTHING THEY NEED. OUR ROOM IS WAITING ON GUMDROP ALLEY.

WHAT DO YOU MEAN? DID YOU ALREADY PUT MONEY DOWN ON A ROOM?

DIDN'T NEED TO. IT WAS COMPLIMENTARY. THEY THROW IN A WEEKEND PASS AND GRATIS ROOMS FOR LIFE WHEN YOU BUY IN.

WHAT DO YOU MEAN... BUY IN?

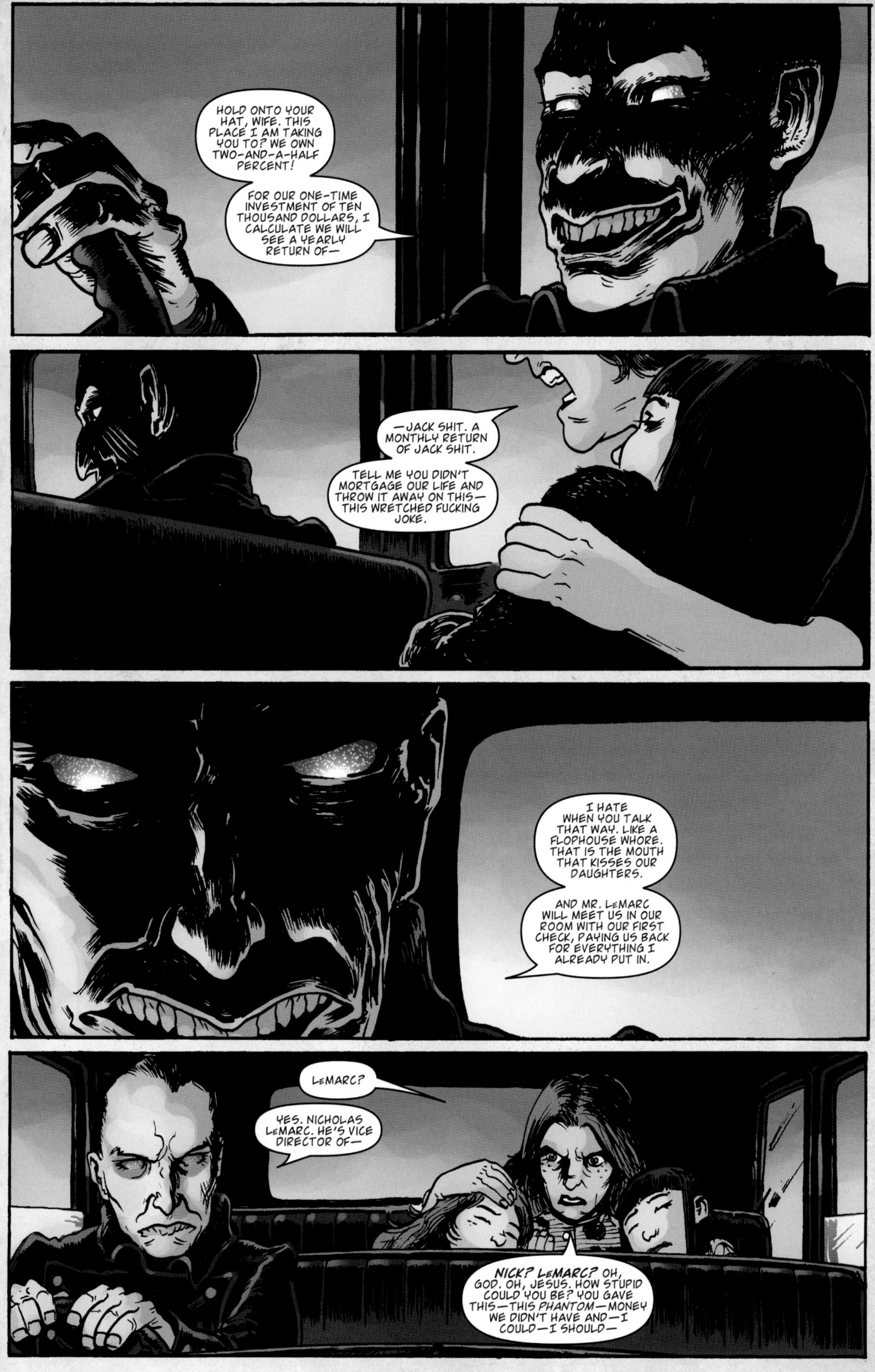
HOLD ONTO YOUR HAT, WIFE. THIS PLACE I AM TAKING YOU TO? WE OWN TWO-AND-A-HALF PERCENT!
FOR OUR ONE-TIME INVESTMENT OF TEN THOUSAND DOLLARS, I CALCULATE WE WILL SEE A YEARLY RETURN OF—
—JACK SHIT. A MONTHLY RETURN OF JACK SHIT.
TELL ME YOU DIDN'T MORTGAGE OUR LIFE AND THROW IT AWAY ON THIS— THIS WRETCHED FUCKING JOKE.
I HATE WHEN YOU TALK THAT WAY. LIKE A FLOPHOUSE WHORE. THAT IS THE MOUTH THAT KISSES OUR DAUGHTERS.
AND MR. LeMARC WILL MEET US IN OUR ROOM WITH OUR FIRST CHECK, PAYING US BACK FOR EVERYTHING I ALREADY PUT IN.
LeMARC?
YES. NICHOLAS LeMARC. HE'S VICE DIRECTOR OF—
NICK? LeMARC? OH, GOD. OH, JESUS. HOW STUPID COULD YOU BE? YOU GAVE THIS—THIS PHANTOM—MONEY WE DIDN'T HAVE AND—I COULD—I SHOULD—

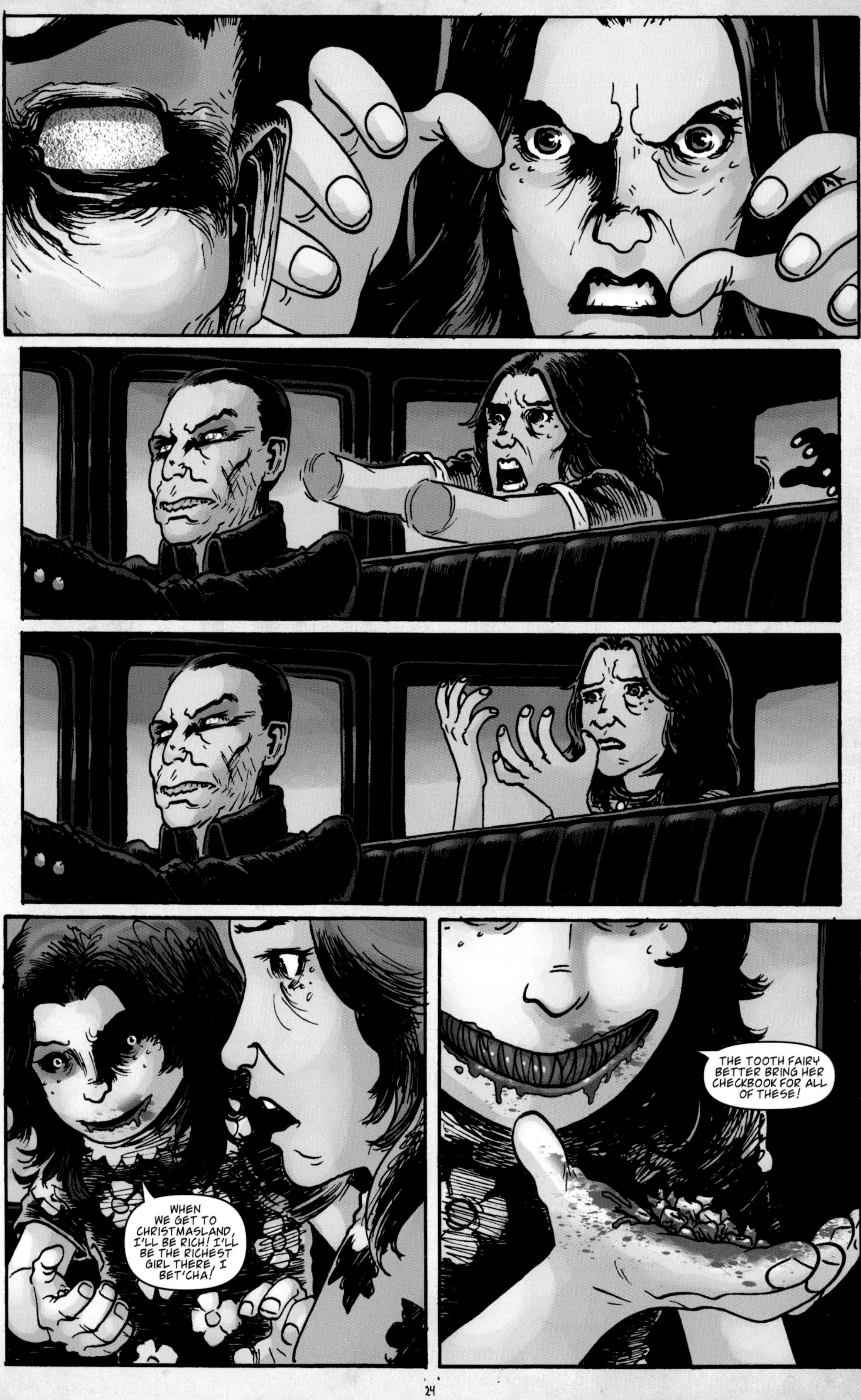
WHEN WE GET TO CHRISTMASLAND, I'LL BE RICH! I'LL BE THE RICHEST GIRL THERE, I BET'CHA!
THE TOOTH FAIRY BETTER BRING HER CHECKBOOK FOR ALL OF THESE!

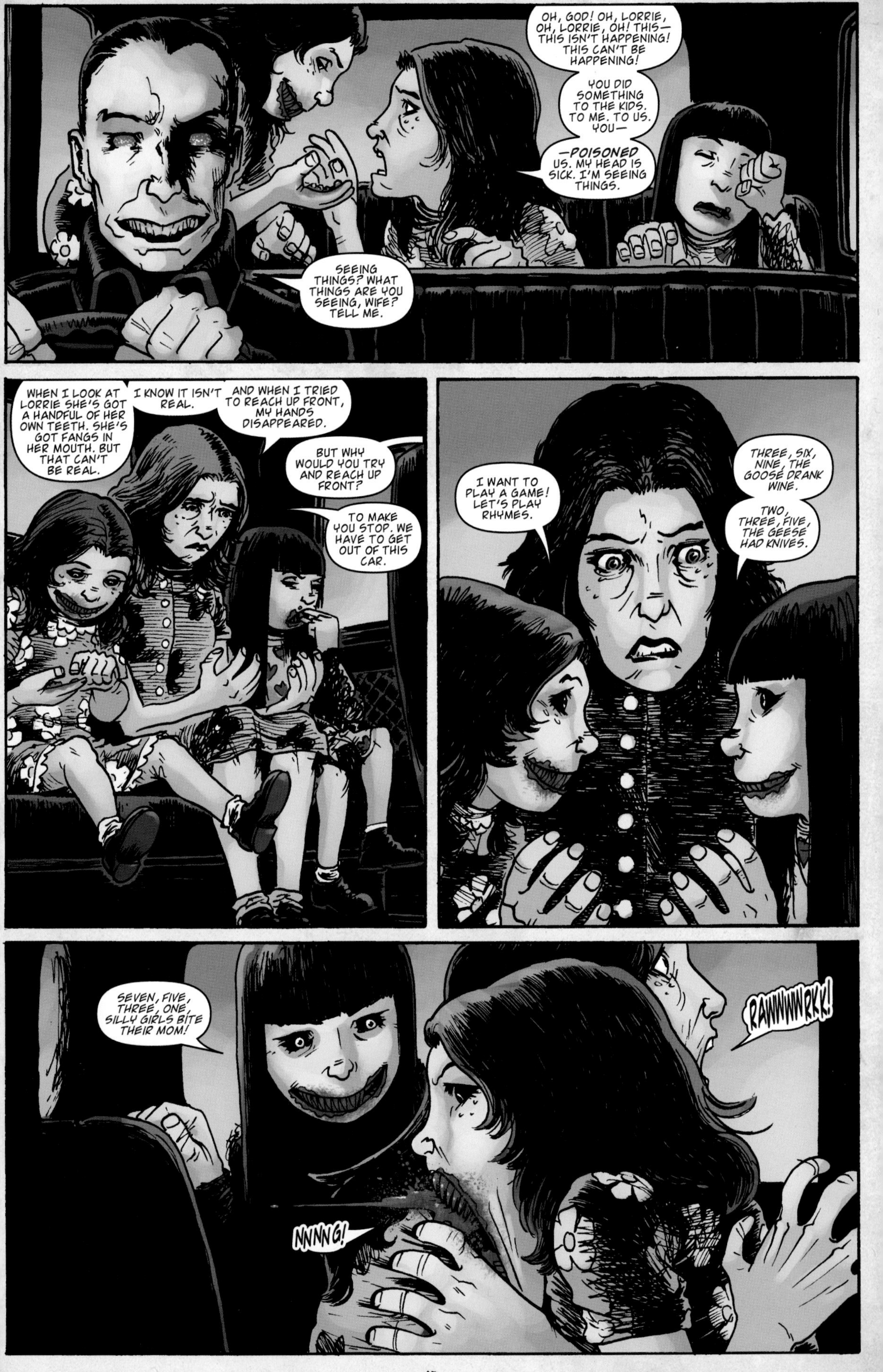
OH, GOD! OH, LORRIE, OH, LORRIE, OH! THIS— THIS ISN'T HAPPENING! THIS CAN'T BE HAPPENING!
YOU DID SOMETHING TO THE KIDS. TO ME. TO US. YOU—
—POISONED US. MY HEAD IS SICK. I'M SEEING THINGS.
SEEING THINGS? WHAT THINGS ARE YOU SEEING, WIFE? TELL ME.
WHEN I LOOK AT LORRIE SHE'S GOT A HANDFUL OF HER OWN TEETH. SHE'S GOT FANGS IN HER MOUTH. BUT THAT CAN'T BE REAL.
I KNOW IT ISN'T REAL.
AND WHEN I TRIED TO REACH UP FRONT, MY HANDS DISAPPEARED.
BUT WHY WOULD YOU TRY AND REACH UP FRONT?
TO MAKE YOU STOP. WE HAVE TO GET OUT OF THIS CAR.
I WANT TO PLAY A GAME! LET'S PLAY RHYMES.
THREE, SIX, NINE, THE GOOSE DRANK WINE.
TWO, THREE, FIVE, THE GEESE HAD KNIVES.
SEVEN, FIVE, THREE, ONE, SILLY GIRLS BITE THEIR MOM!
RAWWWWRKK!
NNNNG!

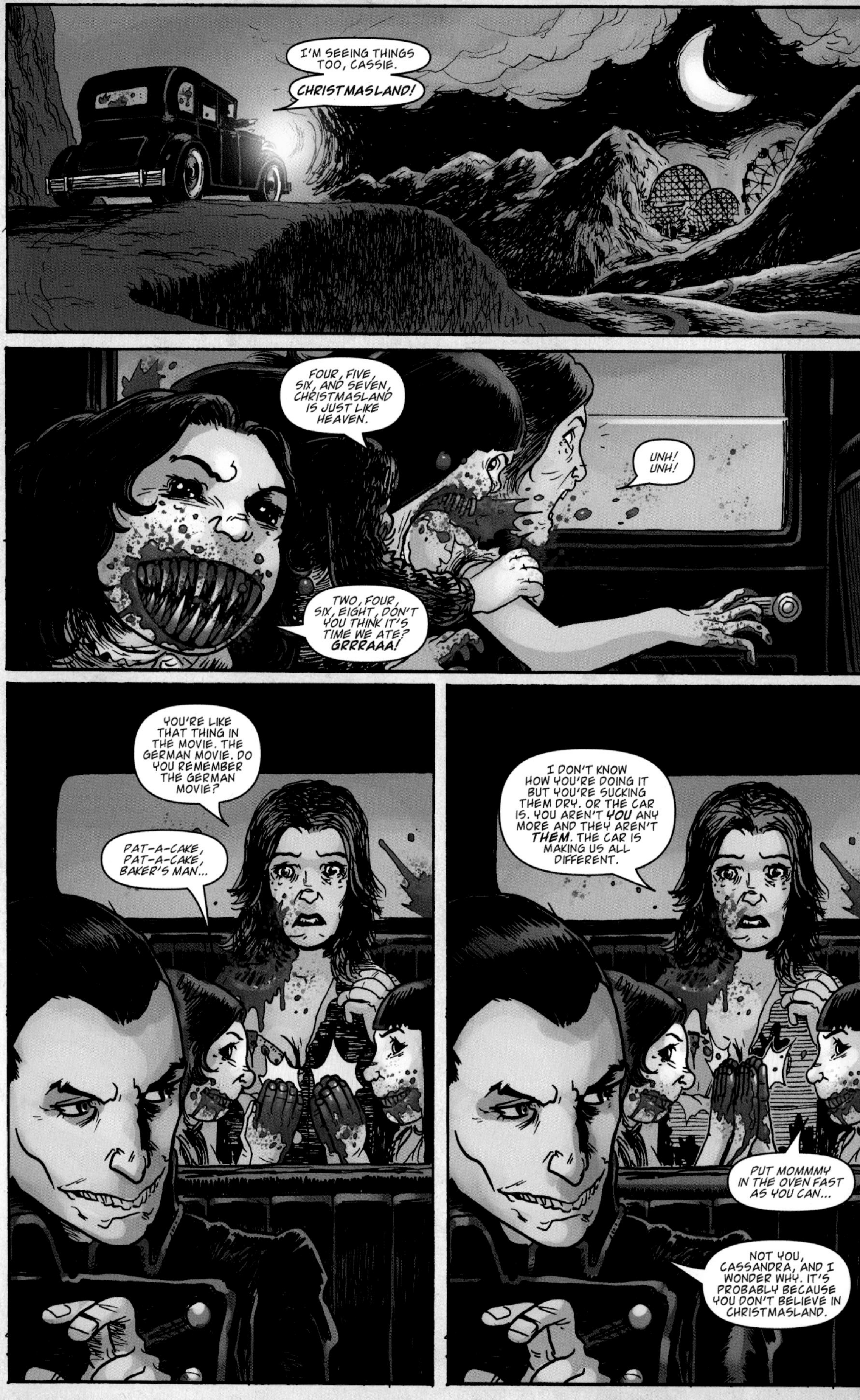

I'M SEEING THINGS TOO, CASSIE.
CHRISTMASLAND!
FOUR, FIVE, SIX, AND SEVEN, CHRISTMASLAND IS JUST LIKE HEAVEN.
UNH! UNH!
TWO, FOUR, SIX, EIGHT, DON'T YOU THINK IT'S TIME WE ATE? GRRRAAA!
YOU'RE LIKE THAT THING IN THE MOVIE. THE GERMAN MOVIE. DO YOU REMEMBER THE GERMAN MOVIE?
PAT-A-CAKE, PAT-A-CAKE, BAKER'S MAN...
I DON'T KNOW HOW YOU'RE DOING IT BUT YOU'RE SUCKING THEM DRY. OR THE CAR IS. YOU AREN'T YOU ANY MORE AND THEY AREN'T THEM. THE CAR IS MAKING US ALL DIFFERENT.
PUT MOMMMY IN THE OVEN FAST AS YOU CAN...
NOT YOU, CASSANDRA, AND I WONDER WHY. IT'S PROBABLY BECAUSE YOU DON'T BELIEVE IN CHRISTMASLAND.

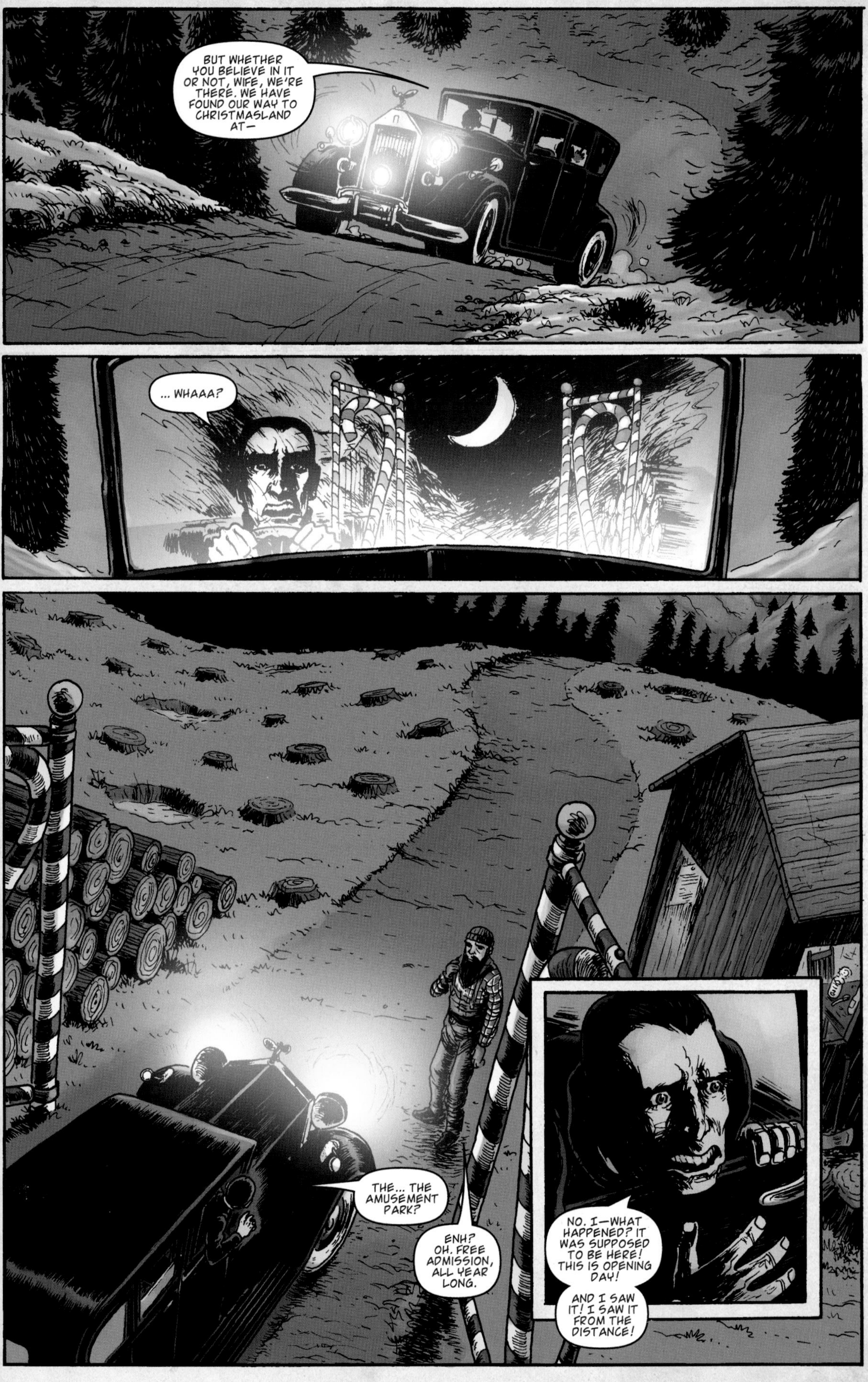
BUT WHETHER YOU BELIEVE IN IT OR NOT, WIFE, WE'RE THERE. WE HAVE FOUND OUR WAY TO CHRISTMASLAND AT—
... WHAAA?
THE... THE AMUSEMENT PARK?
ENH? OH. FREE ADMISSION, ALL YEAR LONG.
NO. I—WHAT HAPPENED? IT WAS SUPPOSED TO BE HERE! THIS IS OPENING DAY!
AND I SAW IT! I SAW IT FROM THE DISTANCE!

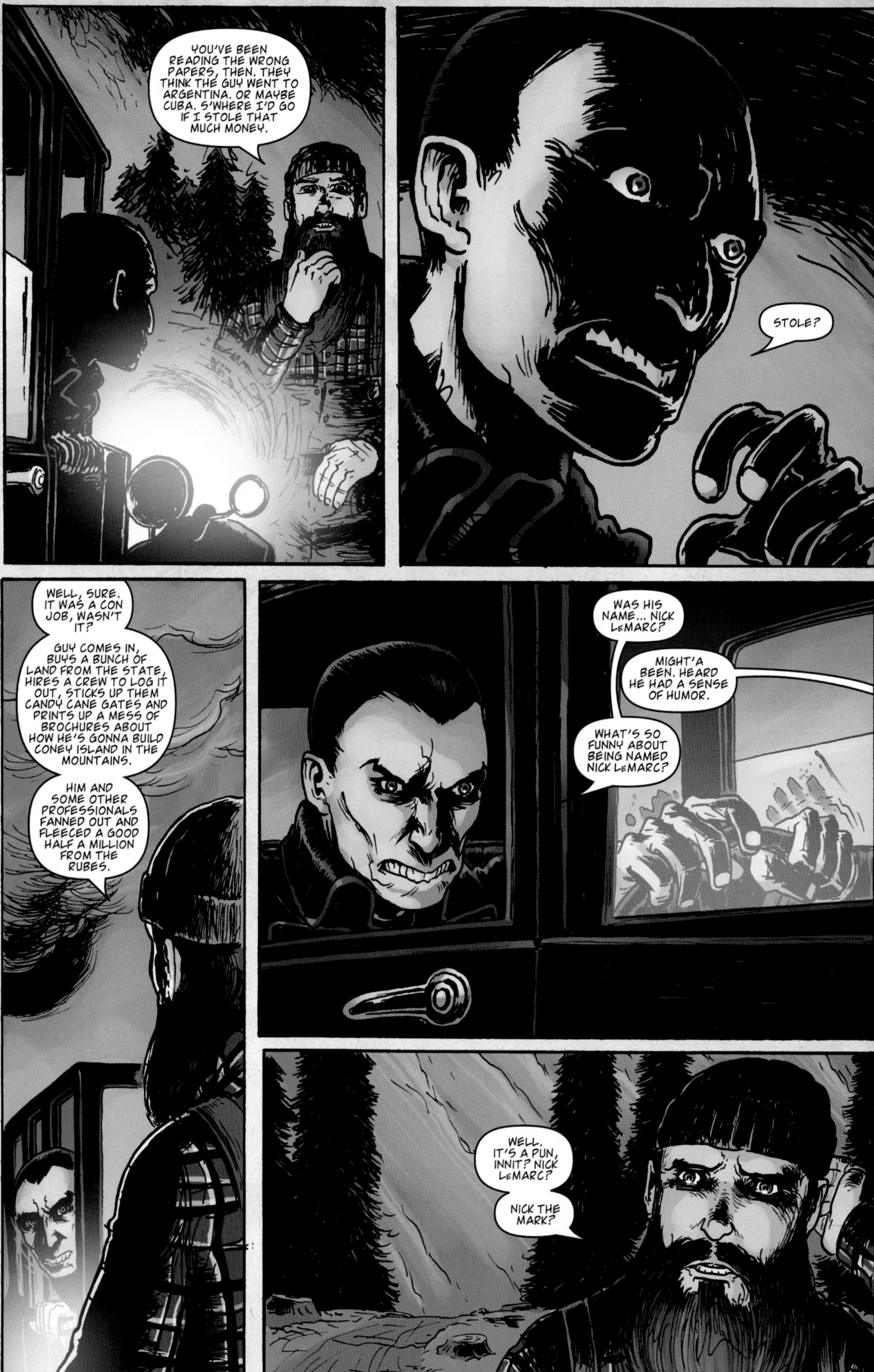

YOU'VE BEEN READING THE WRONG PAPERS, THEN. THEY THINK THE GUY WENT TO ARGENTINA. OR MAYBE CUBA. S'WHERE I'D GO IF I STOLE THAT MUCH MONEY.
STOLE?
WELL, SURE. IT WAS A CON JOB, WASN'T IT?
GUY COMES IN, BUYS A BUNCH OF LAND FROM THE STATE, HIRES A CREW TO LOG IT OUT, STICKS UP THEM CANDY CANE GATES AND PRINTS UP A MESS OF BROCHURES ABOUT HOW HE'S GONNA BUILD CONEY ISLAND IN THE MOUNTAINS.
HIM AND SOME OTHER PROFESSIONALS FANNED OUT AND FLEECED A GOOD HALF A MILLION FROM THE RUBES.
WAS HIS NAME... NICK LEMARC?
MIGHT'A BEEN. HEARD HE HAD A SENSE OF HUMOR.
WHAT'S SO FUNNY ABOUT BEING NAMED NICK LEMARC?
WELL. IT'S A PUN, INNIT? NICK LEMARC?
NICK THE MARK?

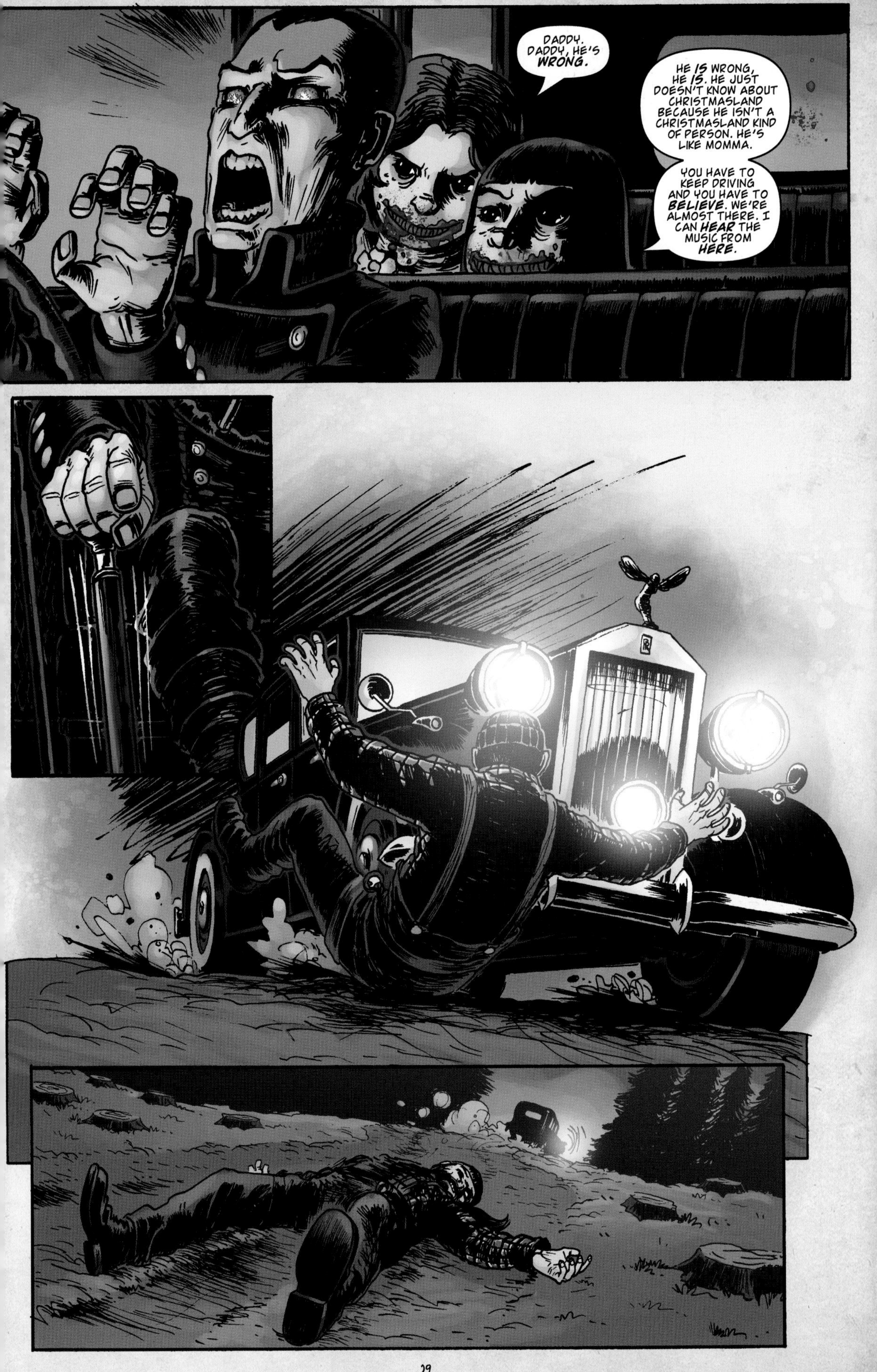
DADDY. DADDY, HE'S WRONG.
HE IS WRONG, HE IS. HE JUST DOESN'T KNOW ABOUT CHRISTMASLAND BECAUSE HE ISN'T A CHRISTMASLAND KIND OF PERSON. HE'S LIKE MOMMA.
YOU HAVE TO KEEP DRIVING AND YOU HAVE TO BELIEVE. WE'RE ALMOST THERE. I CAN HEAR THE MUSIC FROM HERE.

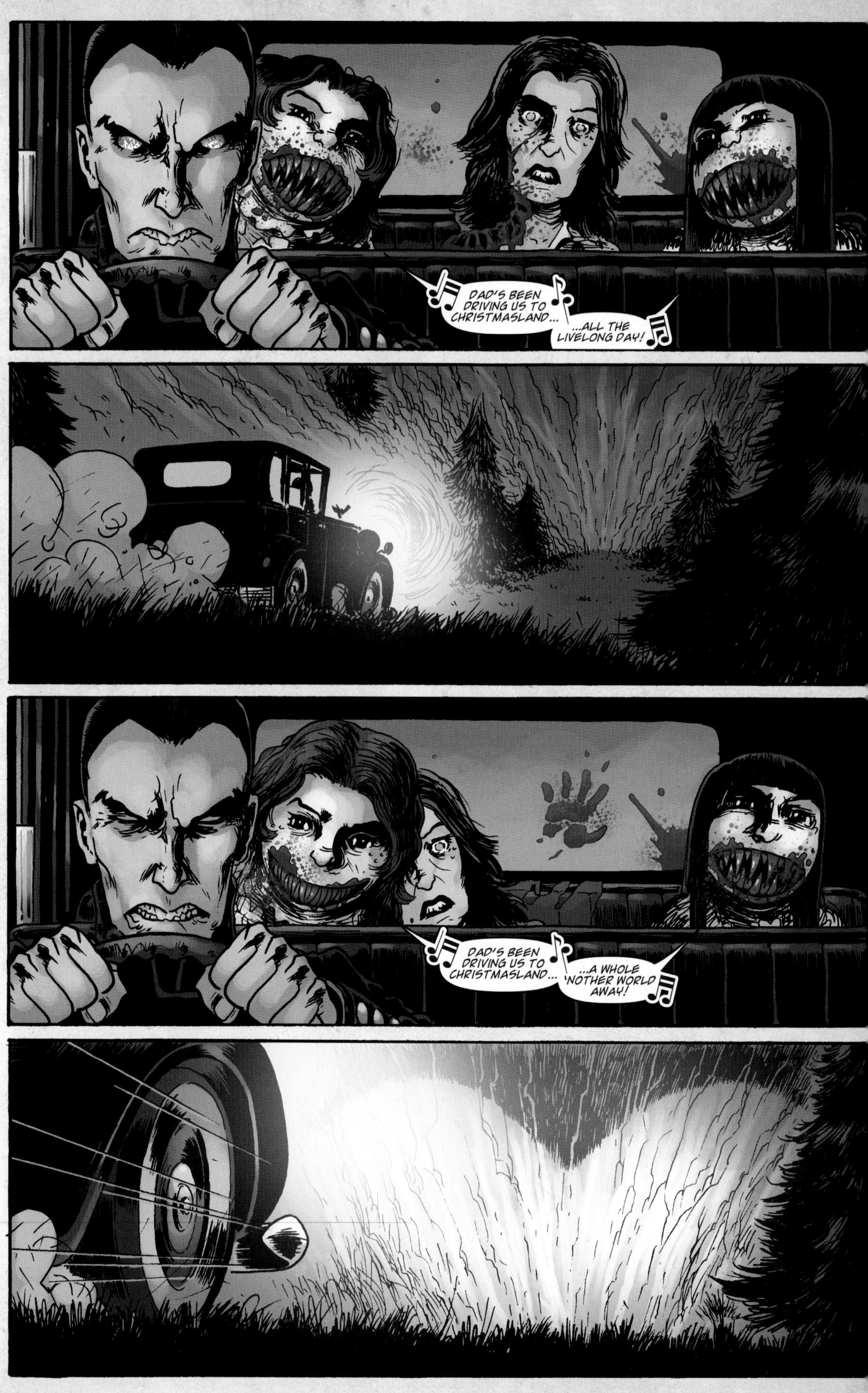
DAD'S BEEN DRIVING US TO CHRISTMASLAND...
...ALL THE LIVELONG DAY!
DAD'S BEEN DRIVING US TO CHRISTMASLAND...
...A WHOLE 'NOTHER WORLD AWAY!

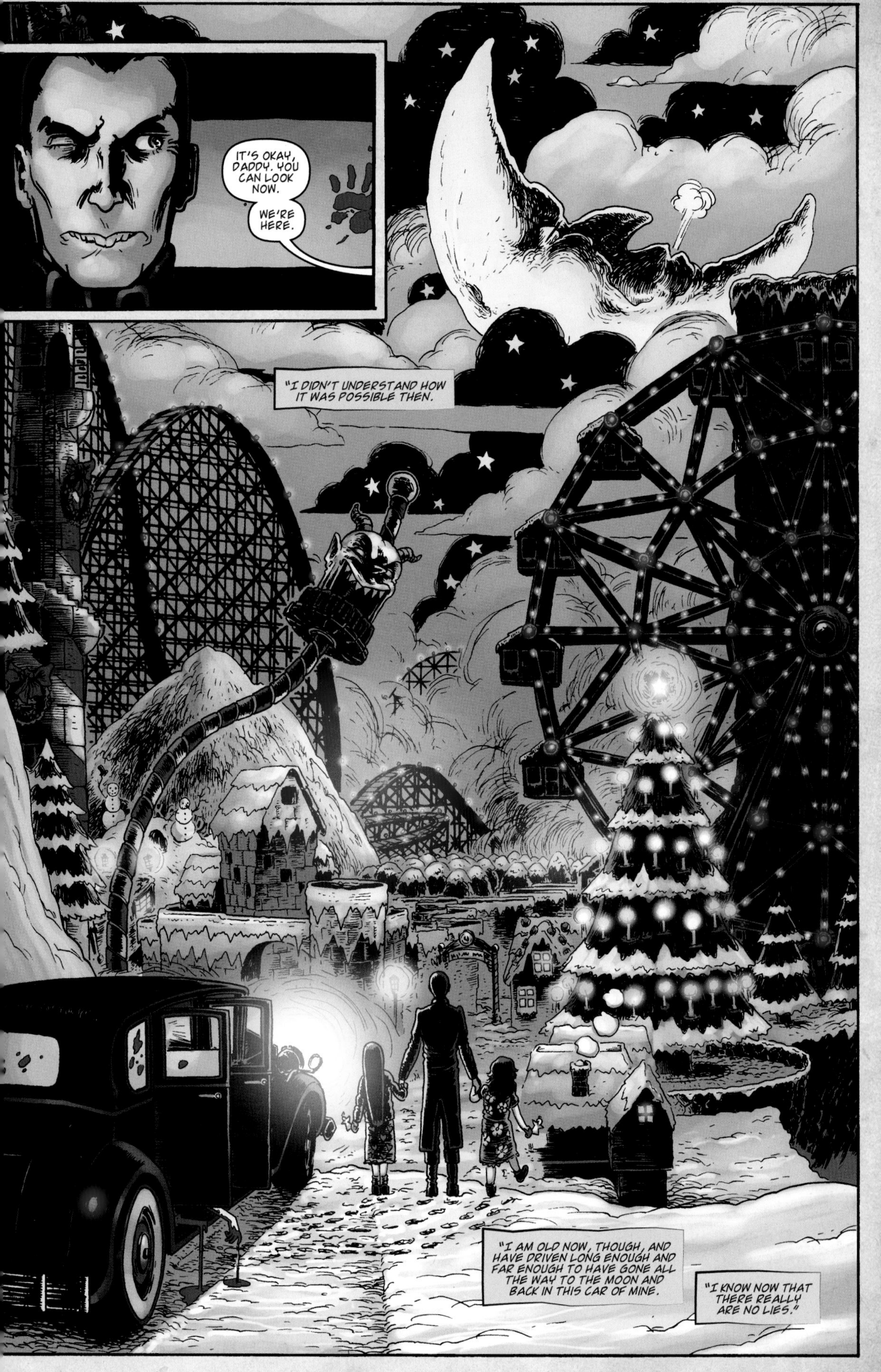

IT'S OKAY, DADDY. YOU CAN LOOK NOW.
WE'RE HERE.
"I DIDN'T UNDERSTAND HOW IT WAS POSSIBLE THEN.
"I AM OLD NOW, THOUGH, AND HAVE DRIVEN LONG ENOUGH AND FAR ENOUGH TO HAVE GONE ALL THE WAY TO THE MOON AND BACK IN THIS CAR OF MINE.
"I KNOW NOW THAT THERE REALLY ARE NO LIES."

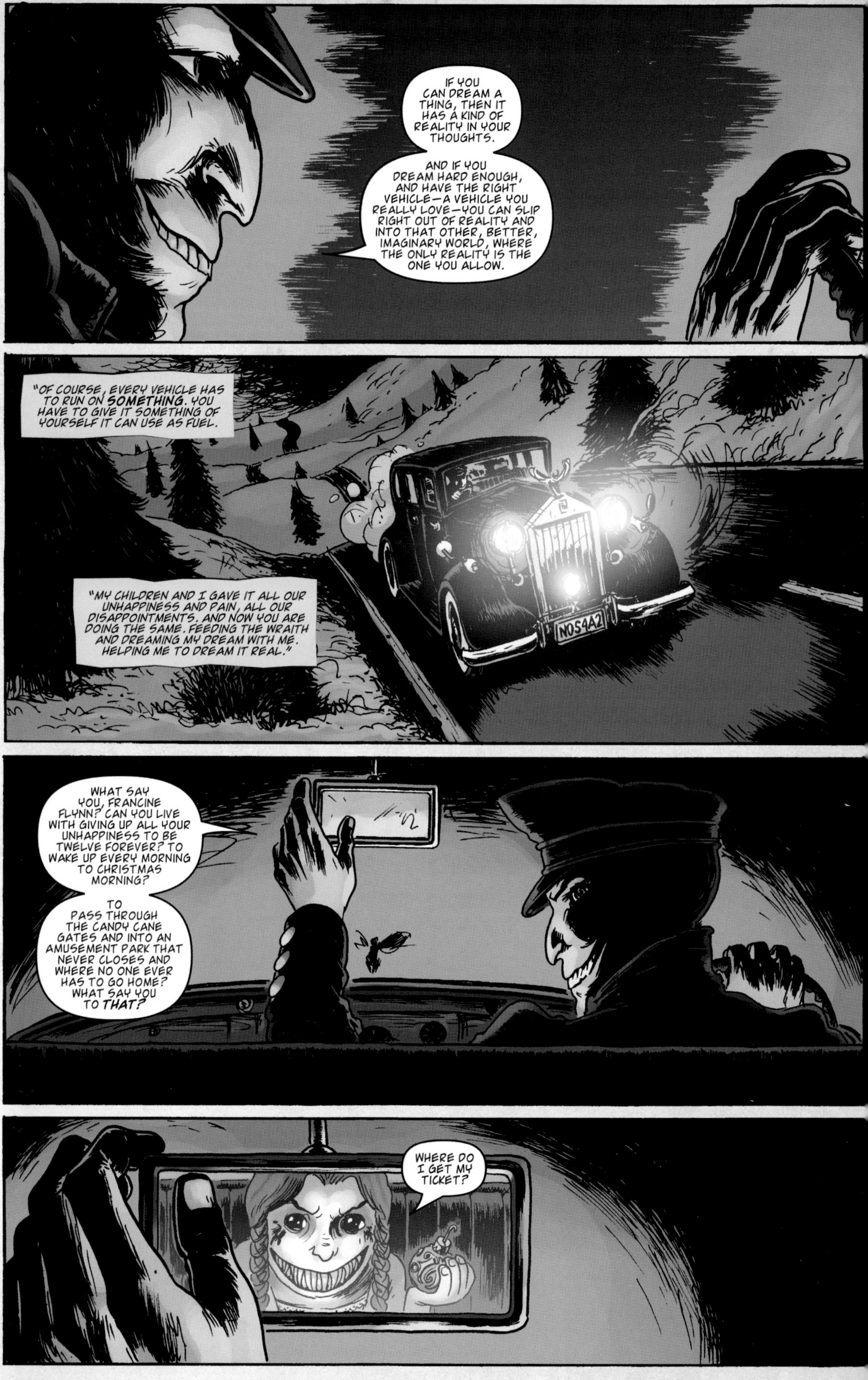
IF YOU CAN DREAM A THING, THEN IT HAS A KIND OF REALITY IN YOUR THOUGHTS.
AND IF YOU DREAM HARD ENOUGH, AND HAVE THE RIGHT VEHICLE—A VEHICLE YOU REALLY LOVE—YOU CAN SLIP RIGHT OUT OF REALITY AND INTO THAT OTHER, BETTER, IMAGINARY WORLD, WHERE THE ONLY REALITY IS THE ONE YOU ALLOW.
"OF COURSE, EVERY VEHICLE HAS TO RUN ON SOMETHING. YOU HAVE TO GIVE IT SOMETHING OF YOURSELF IT CAN USE AS FUEL.
NOS4A2
"MY CHILDREN AND I GAVE IT ALL OUR UNHAPPINESS AND PAIN, ALL OUR DISAPPOINTMENTS. AND NOW YOU ARE DOING THE SAME. FEEDING THE WRAITH AND DREAMING MY DREAM WITH ME. HELPING ME TO DREAM IT REAL."
WHAT SAY YOU, FRANCINE FLYNN? CAN YOU LIVE WITH GIVING UP ALL YOUR UNHAPPINESS TO BE TWELVE FOREVER? TO WAKE UP EVERY MORNING TO CHRISTMAS MORNING?
TO PASS THROUGH THE CANDY CANE GATES AND INTO AN AMUSEMENT PARK THAT NEVER CLOSES AND WHERE NO ONE EVER HAS TO GO HOME? WHAT SAY YOU TO THAT?
WHERE DO I GET MY TICKET?

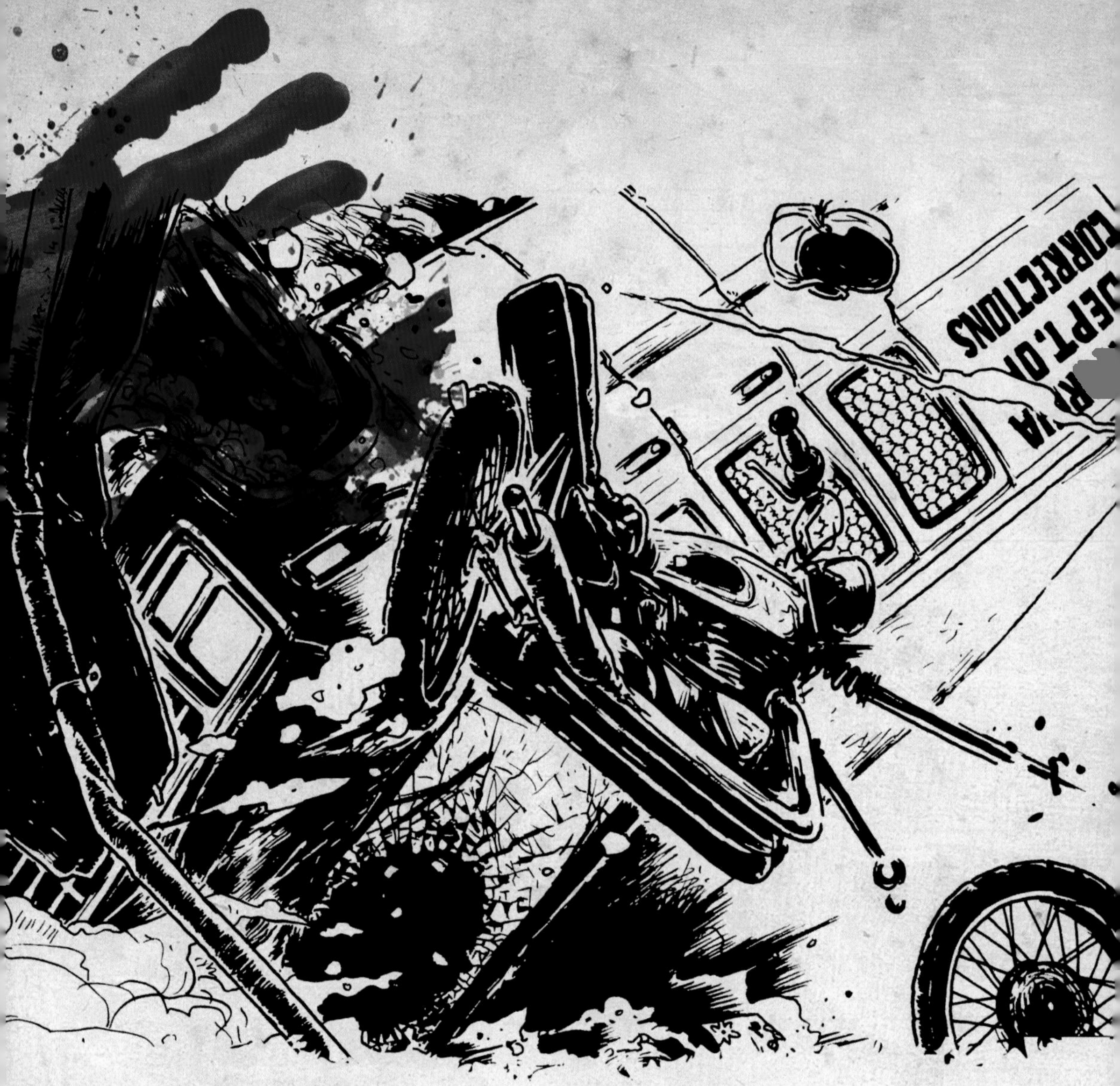
CORRECTIONS

WELCOME TO CHRISTMASLAND chapter one

THE GET-AWAY

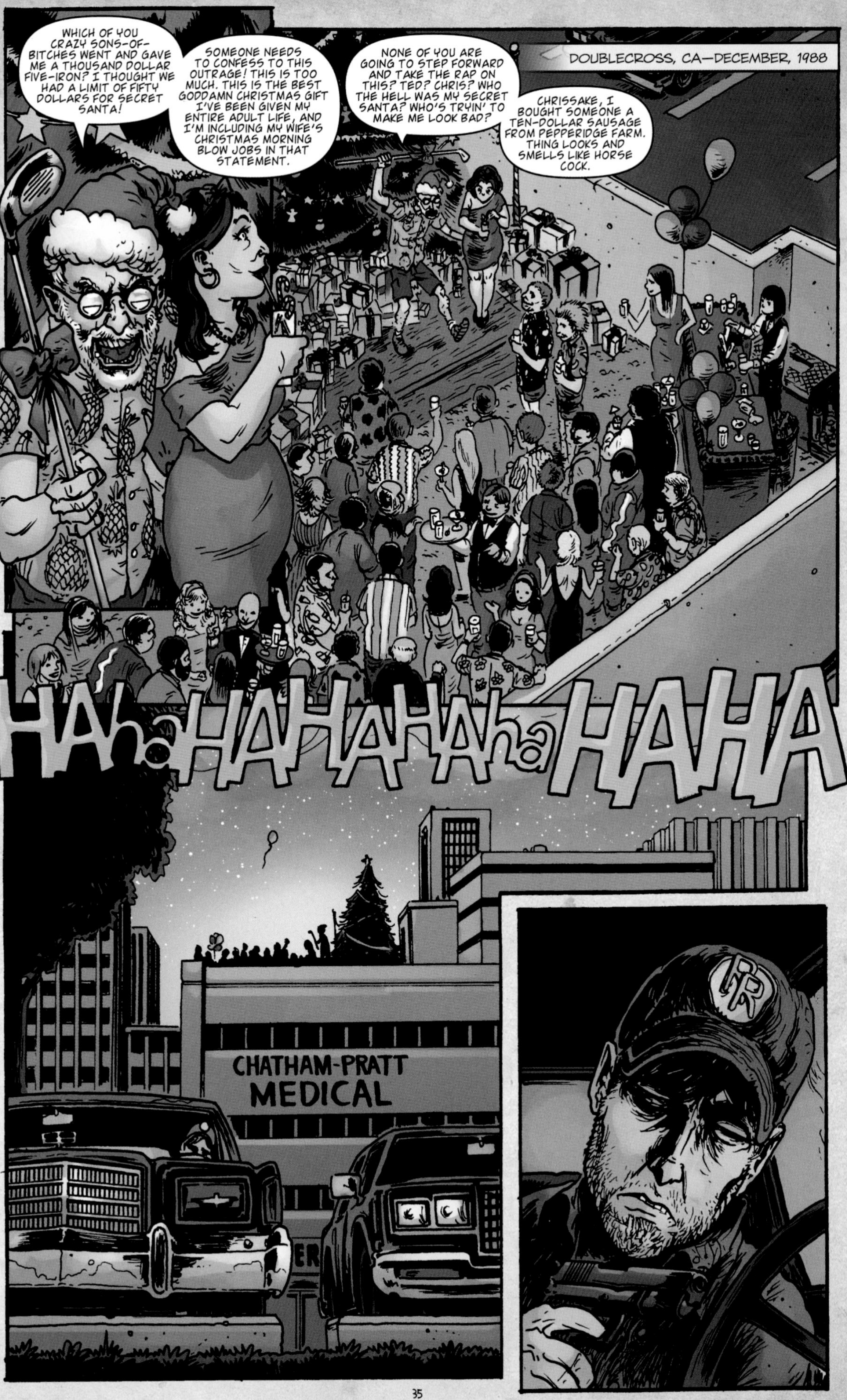
DOUBLECROSS, CA—DECEMBER, 1988
WHICH OF YOU CRAZY SONS-OF-BITCHES WENT AND GAVE ME A THOUSAND DOLLAR FIVE-IRON? I THOUGHT WE HAD A LIMIT OF FIFTY DOLLARS FOR SECRET SANTA!
SOMEONE NEEDS TO CONFESS TO THIS OUTRAGE! THIS IS TOO MUCH. THIS IS THE BEST GODDAMN CHRISTMAS GIFT I'VE BEEN GIVEN MY ENTIRE ADULT LIFE, AND I'M INCLUDING MY WIFE'S CHRISTMAS MORNING BLOW JOBS IN THAT STATEMENT.
NONE OF YOU ARE GOING TO STEP FORWARD AND TAKE THE RAP ON THIS? TED? CHRIS? WHO THE HELL WAS MY SECRET SANTA? WHO'S TRYIN' TO MAKE ME LOOK BAD?
CHRISSAKE, I BOUGHT SOMEONE A TEN-DOLLAR SAUSAGE FROM PEPPERIDGE FARM. THING LOOKS AND SMELLS LIKE HORSE COCK.
HAHAHAHAHAHAHAhaHAHA
CHATHAM-PRATT
MEDICAL

HEY. HEY, TEACH, YOU GONNA SLEEP THE WHOLE WAY? WE'RE HAVING A PHILOSOPHICAL CONVERSATION HERE.

WE COULD USE THE PERSPECTIVE OF AN EDUCATED MAN.

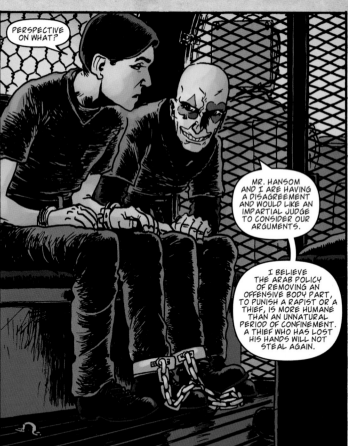

PERSPECTIVE ON WHAT?

MR. HANSOM AND I ARE HAVING A DISAGREEMENT AND WOULD LIKE AN IMPARTIAL JUDGE TO CONSIDER OUR ARGUMENTS.

I BELIEVE THE ARAB POLICY OF REMOVING AN OFFENSIVE BODY PART, TO PUNISH A RAPIST OR A THIEF, IS MORE HUMANE THAN AN UNNATURAL PERIOD OF CONFINEMENT. A THIEF WHO HAS LOST HIS HANDS WILL NOT STEAL AGAIN.

I NEED NOT DESCRIBE THE ANATOMICAL HORROR TO BE VISITED UPON THE RAPIST.

PERHAPS FOR THAT REASON, MR. HANSOM HERE IS OF THE MIND THAT INCARCERATION IS, SOMEHOW, KINDER.

OF COURSE IT IS. YOU WANT PEOPLE WHO HAVE MADE—WELL, MISTAKES—A CHANCE TO BECOME USEFUL MEMBERS OF THEIR COMMUNITIES AGAIN.

YOU GO AMPUTATING THINGS, OFFENDERS ARE JUST GOING TO BE MORE OF A DRAG ON SOCIETY.

YET I HAVE BEEN JAILED BEFORE AND I KNOW IT TO BE ANOTHER KIND OF AMPUTATION. IT IS AN AMPUTATION OF TIME, WHICH IS MORE VALUABLE TO A MAN THAN A HAND OR A FOOT OR A TONGUE. WHAT SAY YOU TO THAT, CHESS LLEWELLYN?

I DON'T KNOW. I'M KIND OF ATTACHED TO MY HANDS.

IN THE SCENARIO I ENVISION, THAT WOULD CHANGE.

36

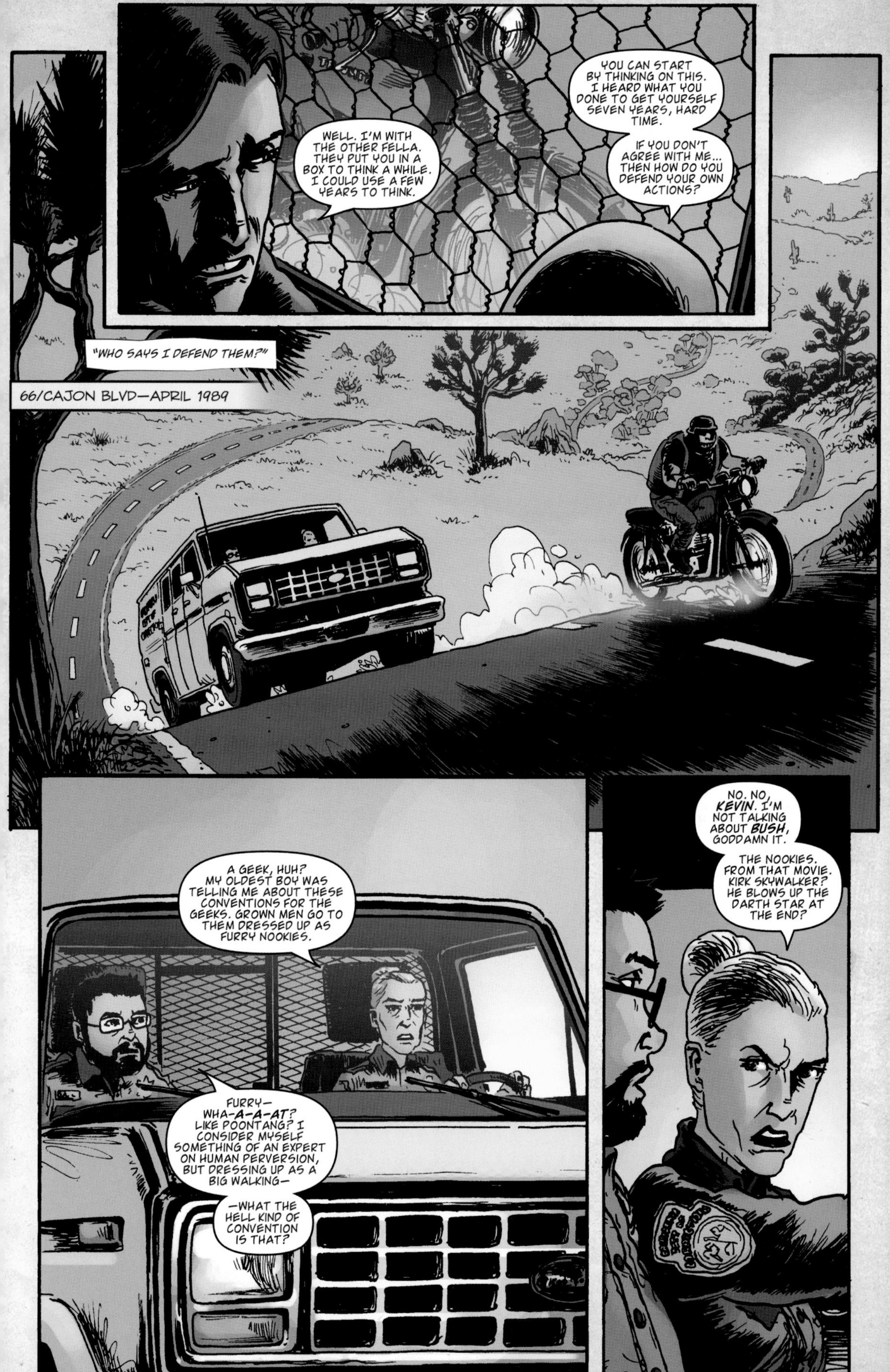
WELL. I'M WITH THE OTHER FELLA. THEY PUT YOU IN A BOX TO THINK A WHILE. I COULD USE A FEW YEARS TO THINK.
YOU CAN START BY THINKING ON THIS. I HEARD WHAT YOU DONE TO GET YOURSELF SEVEN YEARS, HARD TIME.
IF YOU DON'T AGREE WITH ME... THEN HOW DO YOU DEFEND YOUR OWN ACTIONS?
"WHO SAYS I DEFEND THEM?"
66/CAJON BLVD—APRIL 1989
A GEEK, HUH? MY OLDEST BOY WAS TELLING ME ABOUT THESE CONVENTIONS FOR THE GEEKS. GROWN MEN GO TO THEM DRESSED UP AS FURRY NOOKIES.
FURRY—WHA-A-A-AT? LIKE POONTANG? I CONSIDER MYSELF SOMETHING OF AN EXPERT ON HUMAN PERVERSION, BUT DRESSING UP AS A BIG WALKING—
—WHAT THE HELL KIND OF CONVENTION IS THAT?
NO. NO, KEVIN. I'M NOT TALKING ABOUT BUSH, GODDAMN IT.
THE NOOKIES. FROM THAT MOVIE. KIRK SKYWALKER? HE BLOWS UP THE DARTH STAR AT THE END?

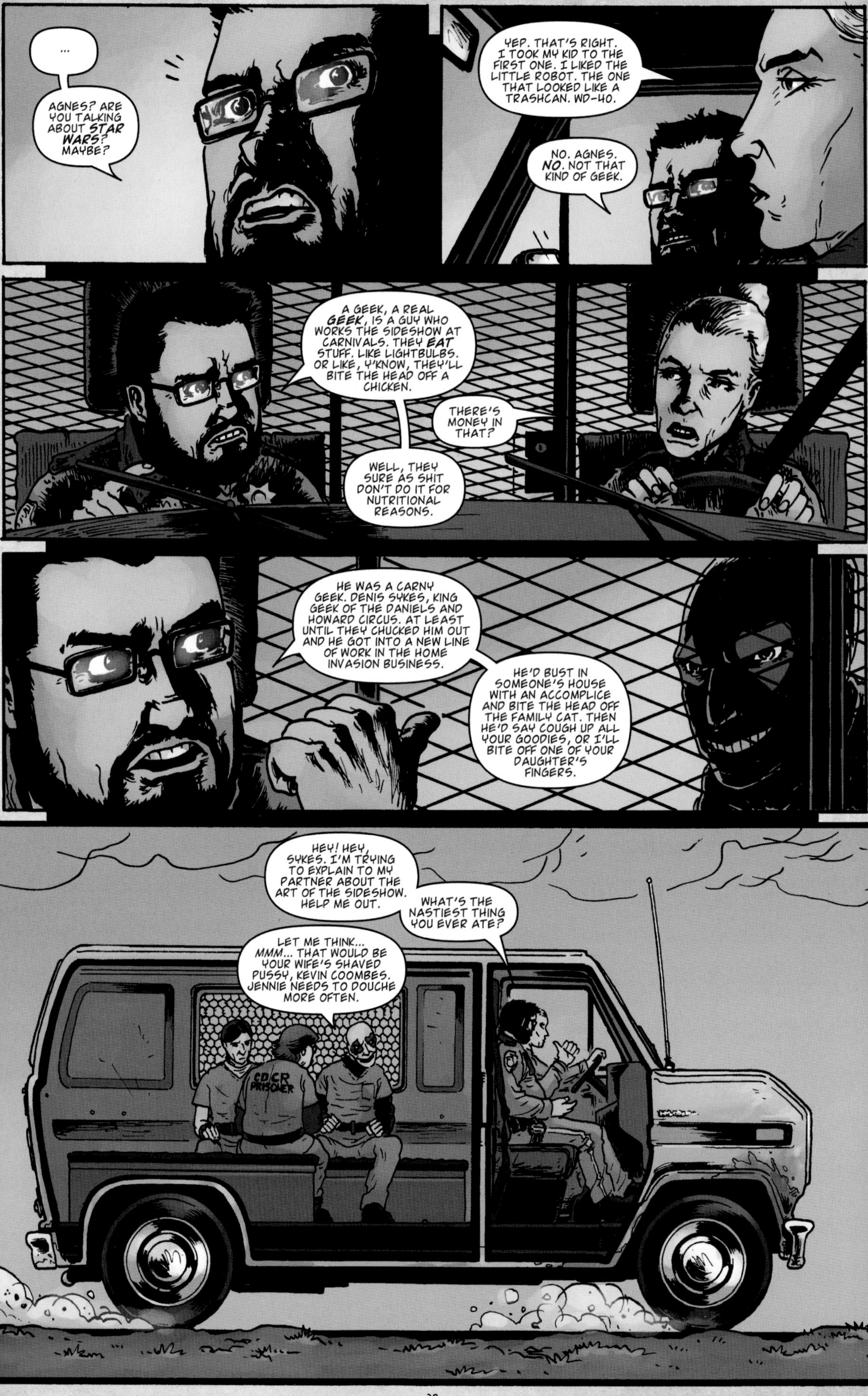
...
AGNES? ARE YOU TALKING ABOUT STAR WARS? MAYBE?
YEP. THAT'S RIGHT. I TOOK MY KID TO THE FIRST ONE. I LIKED THE LITTLE ROBOT. THE ONE THAT LOOKED LIKE A TRASHCAN. WD-40.
NO. AGNES. NO. NOT THAT KIND OF GEEK.
A GEEK, A REAL GEEK, IS A GUY WHO WORKS THE SIDESHOW AT CARNIVALS. THEY EAT STUFF. LIKE LIGHTBULBS. OR LIKE, Y'KNOW, THEY'LL BITE THE HEAD OFF A CHICKEN.
THERE'S MONEY IN THAT?
WELL, THEY SURE AS SHIT DON'T DO IT FOR NUTRITIONAL REASONS.
HE WAS A CARNY GEEK. DENIS SYKES, KING GEEK OF THE DANIELS AND HOWARD CIRCUS. AT LEAST UNTIL THEY CHUCKED HIM OUT AND HE GOT INTO A NEW LINE OF WORK IN THE HOME INVASION BUSINESS.
HE'D BUST IN SOMEONE'S HOUSE WITH AN ACCOMPLICE AND BITE THE HEAD OFF THE FAMILY CAT. THEN HE'D SAY COUGH UP ALL YOUR GOODIES, OR I'LL BITE OFF ONE OF YOUR DAUGHTER'S FINGERS.
HEY! HEY, SYKES. I'M TRYING TO EXPLAIN TO MY PARTNER ABOUT THE ART OF THE SIDESHOW. HELP ME OUT.
WHAT'S THE NASTIEST THING YOU EVER ATE?
LET ME THINK... MMM... THAT WOULD BE YOUR WIFE'S SHAVED PUSSY, KEVIN COOMBES. JENNIE NEEDS TO DOUCHE MORE OFTEN.
CDCR PRISONER

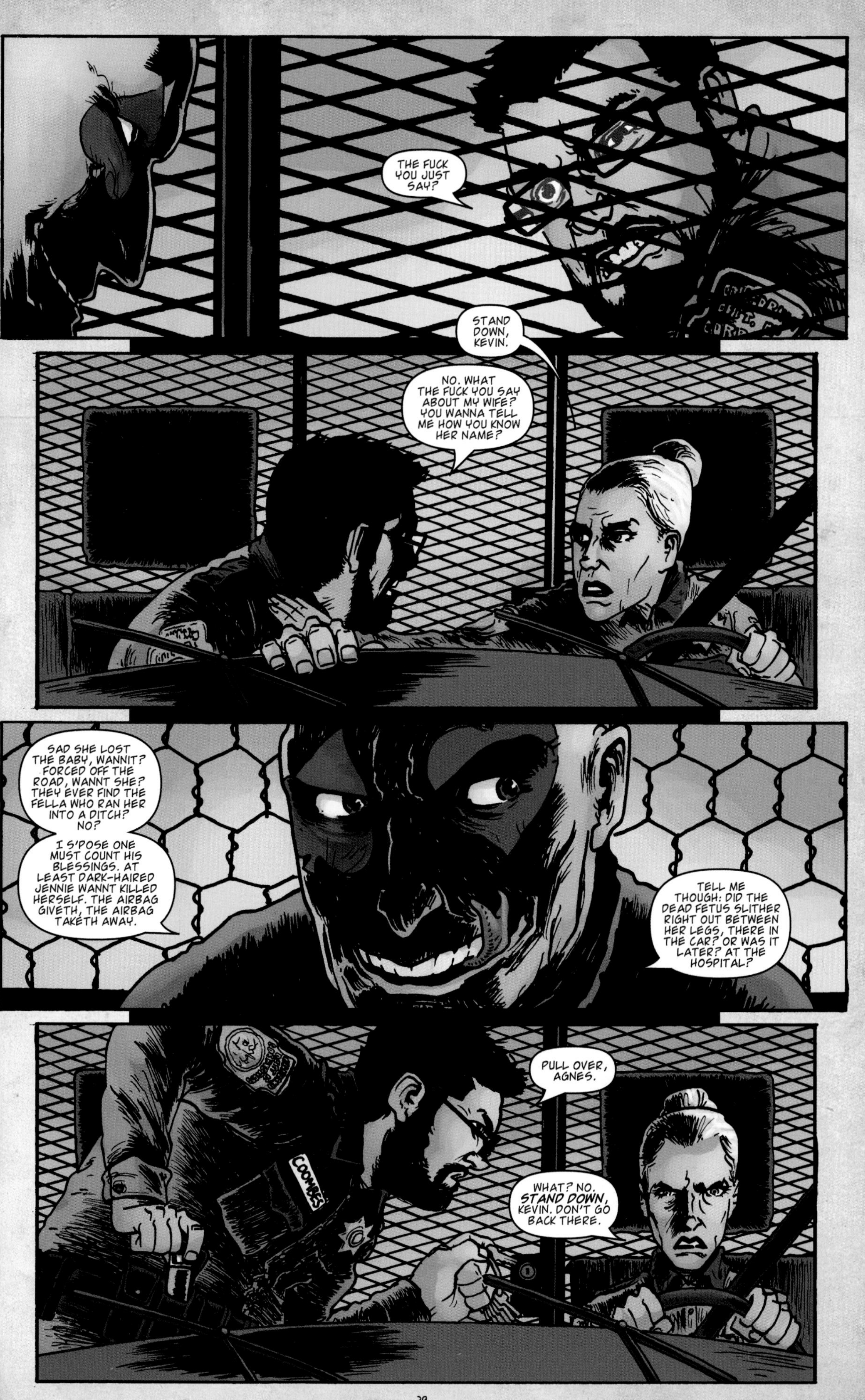
THE FUCK YOU JUST SAY?
STAND DOWN, KEVIN.
NO. WHAT THE FUCK YOU SAY ABOUT MY WIFE? YOU WANNA TELL ME HOW YOU KNOW HER NAME?
SAD SHE LOST THE BABY, WANNIT? FORCED OFF THE ROAD, WANNT SHE? THEY EVER FIND THE FELLA WHO RAN HER INTO A DITCH? NO?
I S'POSE ONE MUST COUNT HIS BLESSINGS. AT LEAST DARK-HAIRED JENNIE WANNT KILLED HERSELF. THE AIRBAG GIVETH, THE AIRBAG TAKETH AWAY.
TELL ME THOUGH: DID THE DEAD FETUS SLITHER RIGHT OUT BETWEEN HER LEGS, THERE IN THE CAR? OR WAS IT LATER? AT THE HOSPITAL?
PULL OVER, AGNES.
COOMBES
WHAT? NO. STAND DOWN, KEVIN. DON'T GO BACK THERE.

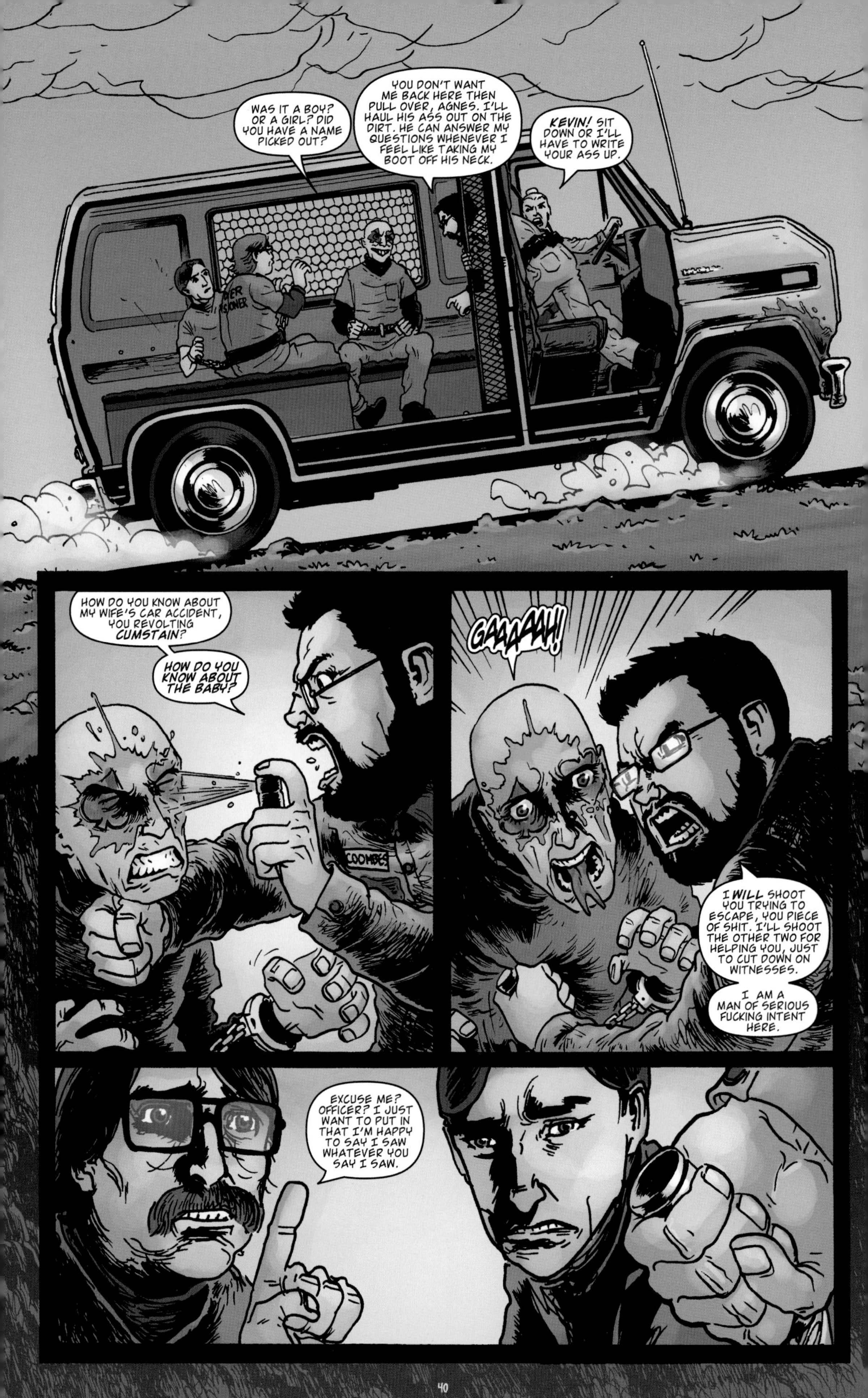
WAS IT A BOY? OR A GIRL? DID YOU HAVE A NAME PICKED OUT?
YOU DON'T WANT ME BACK HERE THEN PULL OVER, AGNES. I'LL HAUL HIS ASS OUT ON THE DIRT. HE CAN ANSWER MY QUESTIONS WHENEVER I FEEL LIKE TAKING MY BOOT OFF HIS NECK.
KEVIN! SIT DOWN OR I'LL HAVE TO WRITE YOUR ASS UP.
HOW DO YOU KNOW ABOUT MY WIFE'S CAR ACCIDENT, YOU REVOLTING CUMSTAIN?
HOW DO YOU KNOW ABOUT THE BABY?
COOMBES
GAAAAAH!
I WILL SHOOT YOU TRYING TO ESCAPE, YOU PIECE OF SHIT. I'LL SHOOT THE OTHER TWO FOR HELPING YOU, JUST TO CUT DOWN ON WITNESSES.
I AM A MAN OF SERIOUS FUCKING INTENT HERE.
EXCUSE ME? OFFICER? I JUST WANT TO PUT IN THAT I'M HAPPY TO SAY I SAW WHATEVER YOU SAY I SAW.

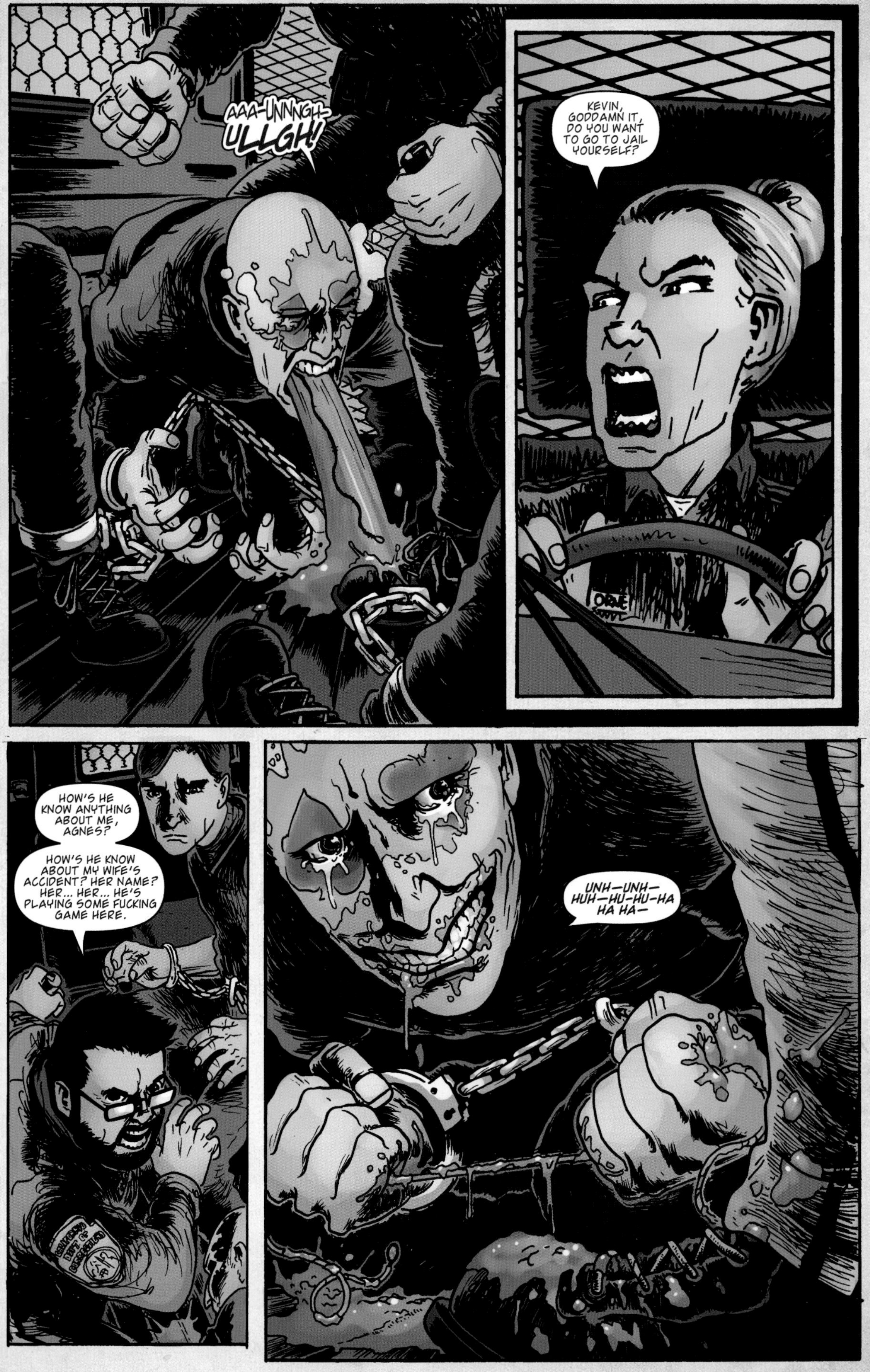
AAA-UNNNGH-
ULLGH!
KEVIN, GODDAMN IT, DO YOU WANT TO GO TO JAIL YOURSELF?
HOW'S HE KNOW ANYTHING ABOUT ME, AGNES?
HOW'S HE KNOW ABOUT MY WIFE'S ACCIDENT? HER NAME? HER... HER... HE'S PLAYING SOME FUCKING GAME HERE.
UNH—UNH—HUH—HU—HU—HA HA HA—

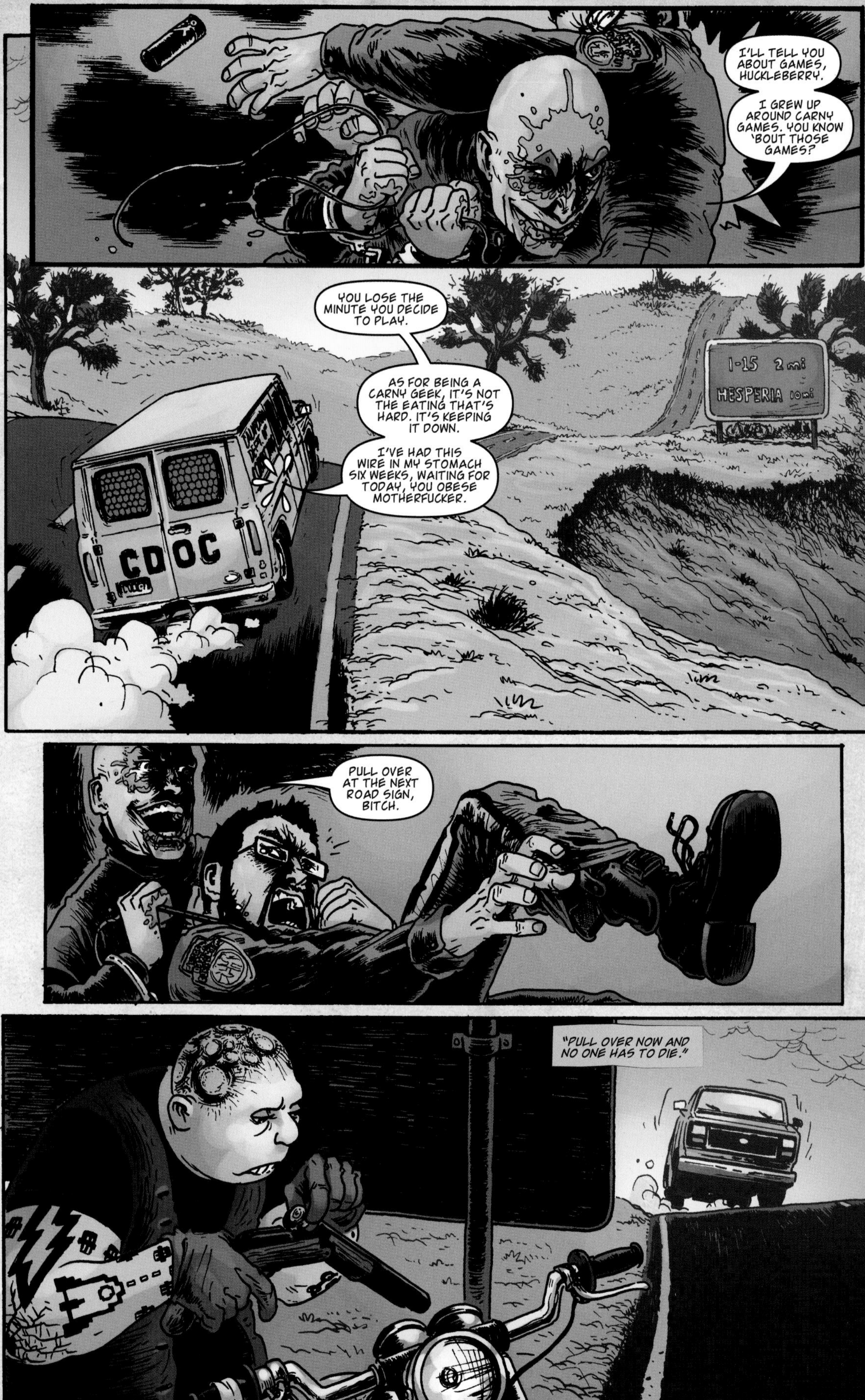

I'LL TELL YOU ABOUT GAMES, HUCKLEBERRY.
I GREW UP AROUND CARNY GAMES. YOU KNOW 'BOUT THOSE GAMES?
YOU LOSE THE MINUTE YOU DECIDE TO PLAY.
I-15 2 mi
HESPERIA 10 mi
AS FOR BEING A CARNY GEEK, IT'S NOT THE EATING THAT'S HARD. IT'S KEEPING IT DOWN.
I'VE HAD THIS WIRE IN MY STOMACH SIX WEEKS, WAITING FOR TODAY, YOU OBESE MOTHERFUCKER.
CDOC
PULL OVER AT THE NEXT ROAD SIGN, BITCH.
"PULL OVER NOW AND NO ONE HAS TO DIE."

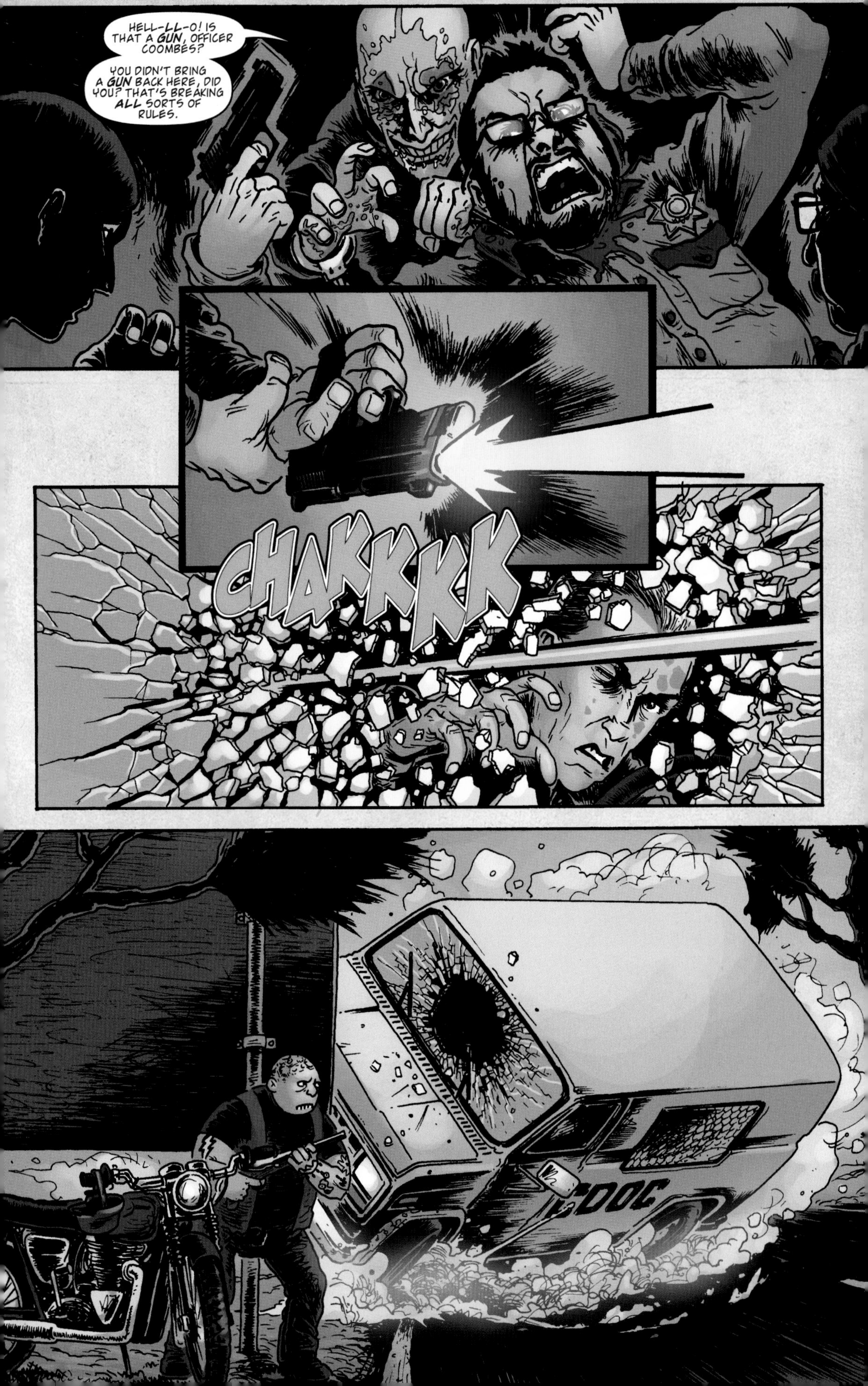
HELL-LL-O! IS THAT A GUN, OFFICER COOMBES?
YOU DIDN'T BRING A GUN BACK HERE, DID YOU? THAT'S BREAKING ALL SORTS OF RULES.
CHAKKKK
DOC

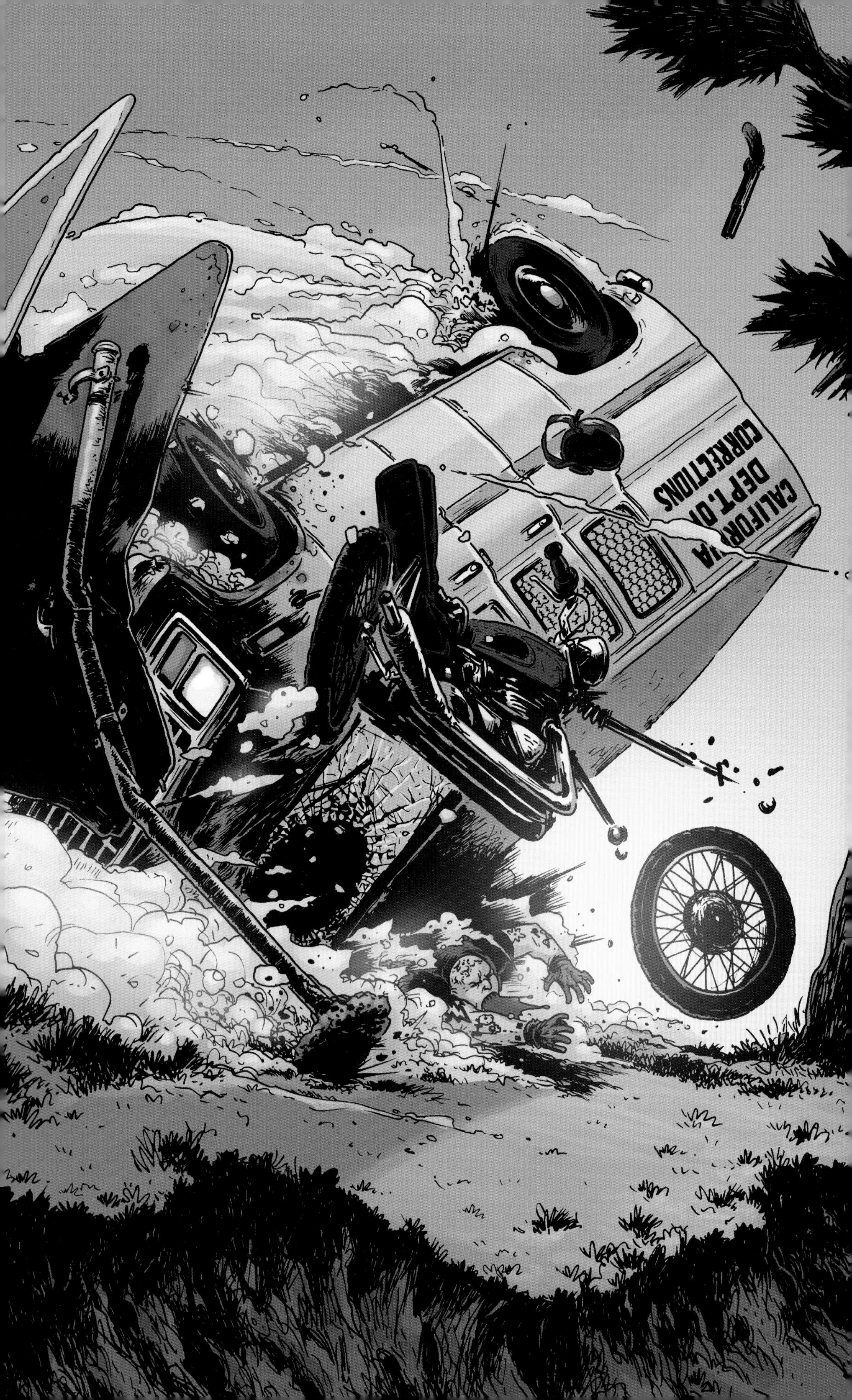
CORRECTIONS

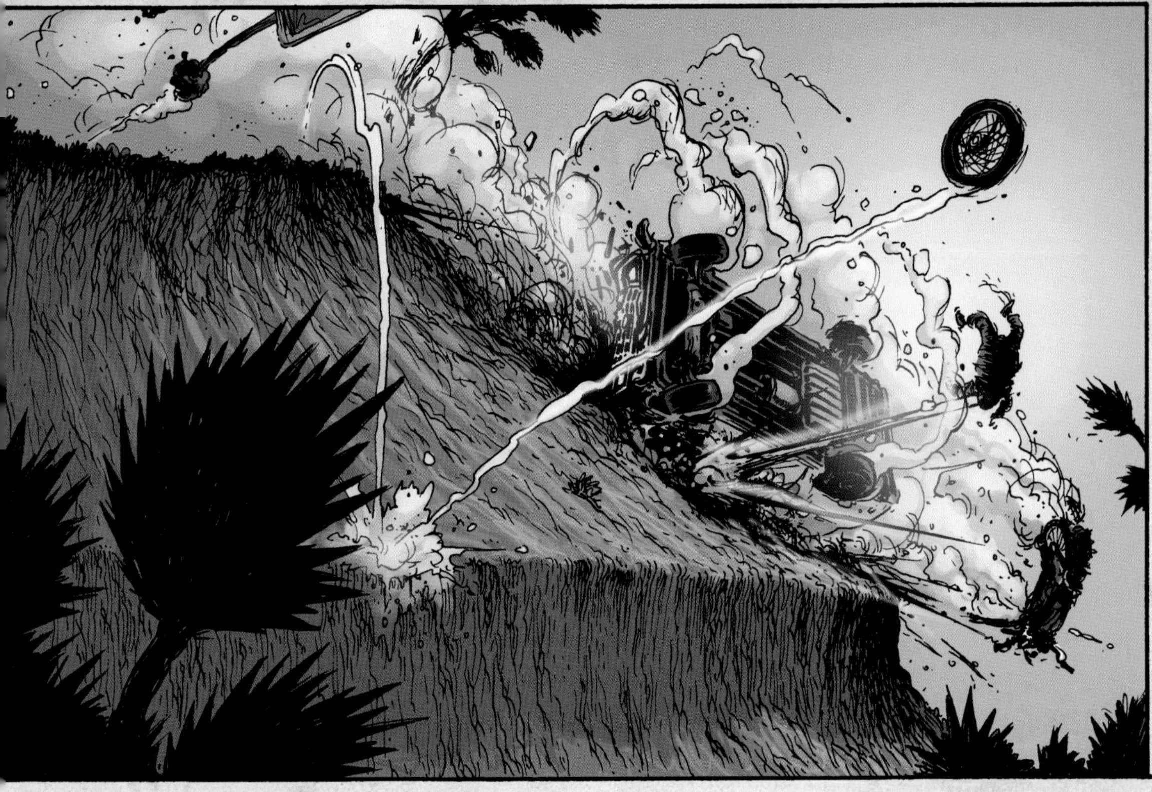

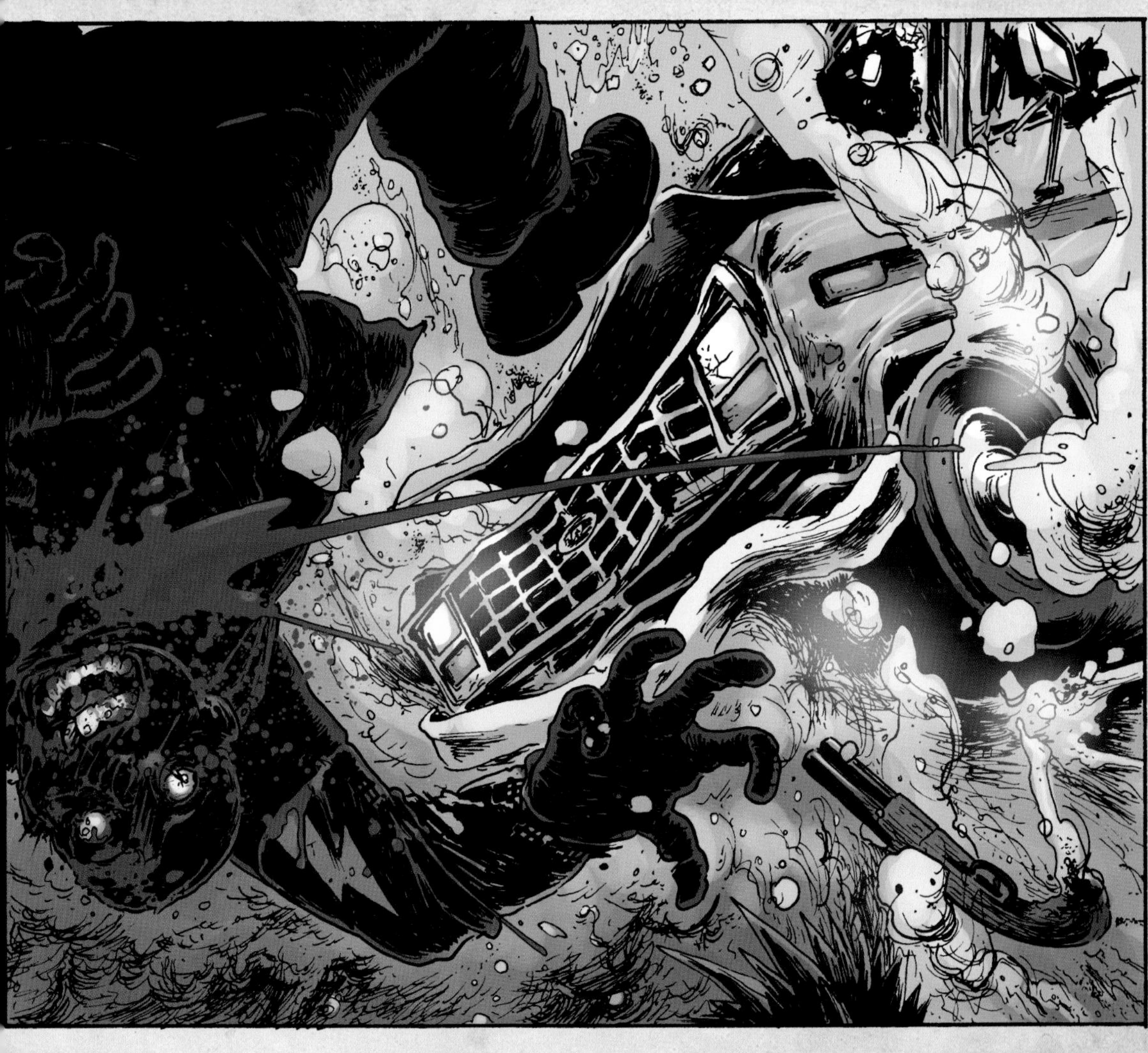

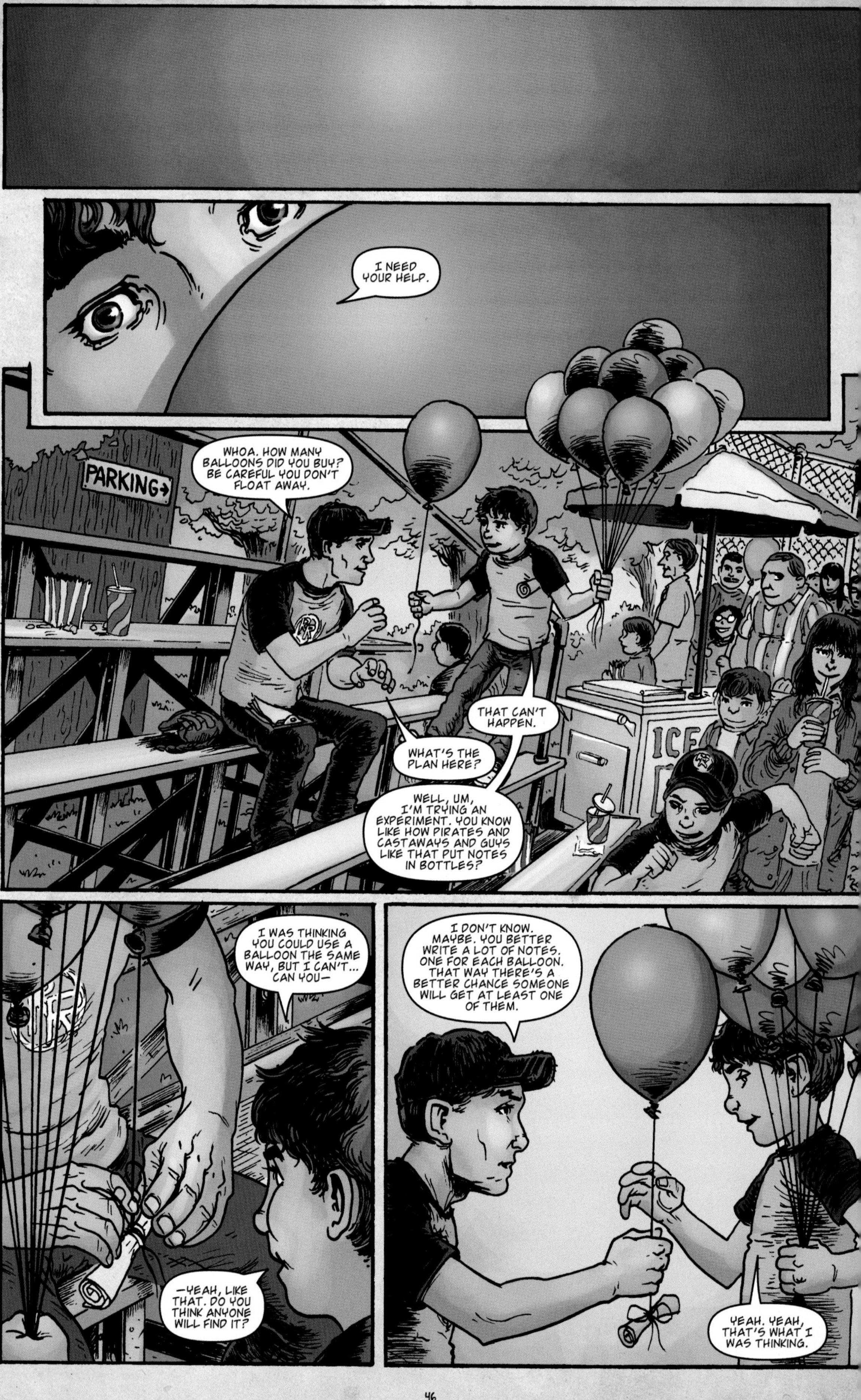
I NEED YOUR HELP.
WHOA. HOW MANY BALLOONS DID YOU BUY? BE CAREFUL YOU DON'T FLOAT AWAY.
PARKING
THAT CAN'T HAPPEN.
WHAT'S THE PLAN HERE?
WELL, UM, I'M TRYING AN EXPERIMENT. YOU KNOW LIKE HOW PIRATES AND CASTAWAYS AND GUYS LIKE THAT PUT NOTES IN BOTTLES?
I WAS THINKING YOU COULD USE A BALLOON THE SAME WAY, BUT I CAN'T... CAN YOU—
—YEAH, LIKE THAT. DO YOU THINK ANYONE WILL FIND IT?
I DON'T KNOW. MAYBE. YOU BETTER WRITE A LOT OF NOTES. ONE FOR EACH BALLOON. THAT WAY THERE'S A BETTER CHANCE SOMEONE WILL GET AT LEAST ONE OF THEM.
YEAH. YEAH, THAT'S WHAT I WAS THINKING.

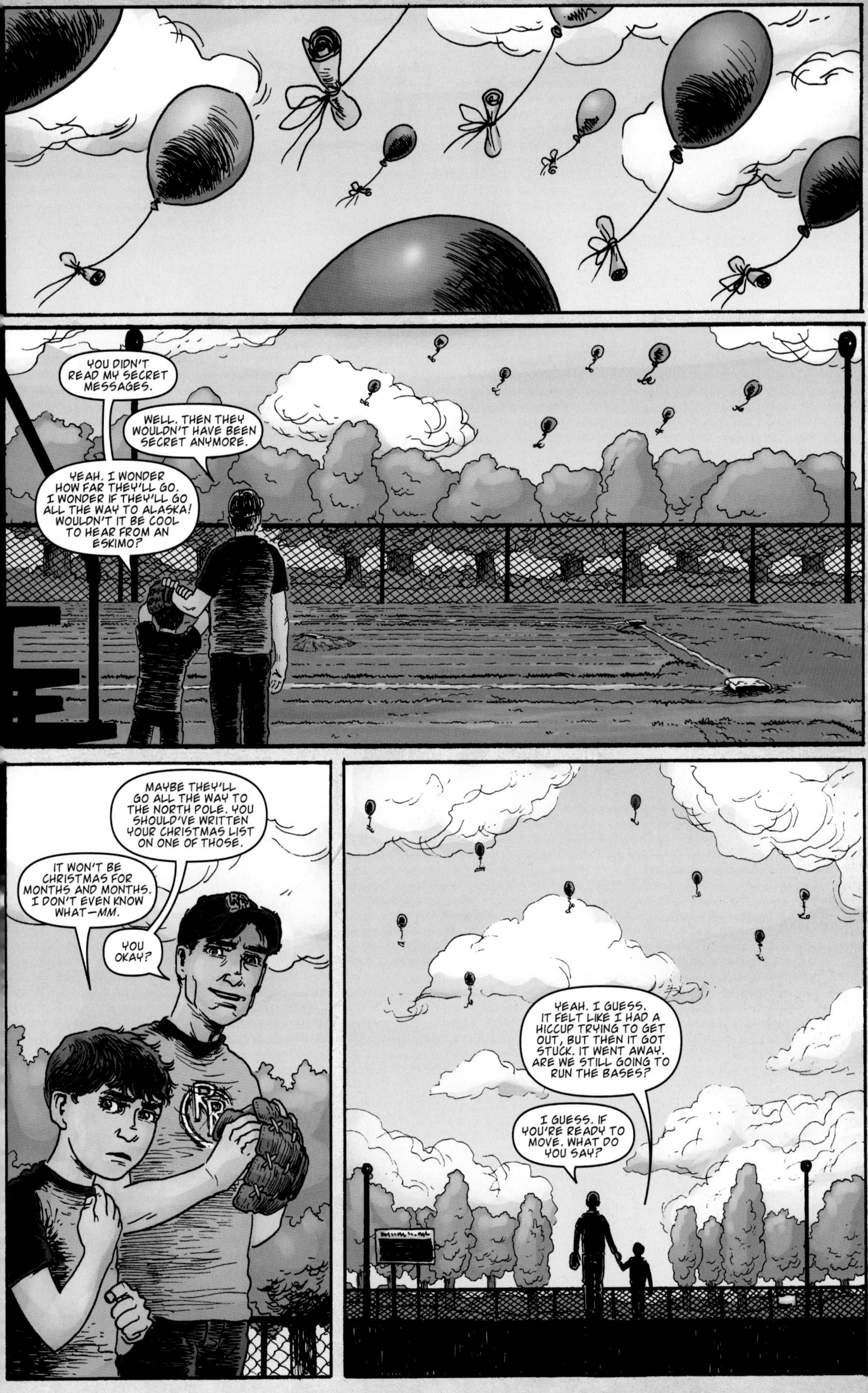
YOU DIDN'T READ MY SECRET MESSAGES.
WELL. THEN THEY WOULDN'T HAVE BEEN SECRET ANYMORE.
YEAH. I WONDER HOW FAR THEY'LL GO. I WONDER IF THEY'LL GO ALL THE WAY TO ALASKA! WOULDN'T IT BE COOL TO HEAR FROM AN ESKIMO?
MAYBE THEY'LL GO ALL THE WAY TO THE NORTH POLE. YOU SHOULD'VE WRITTEN YOUR CHRISTMAS LIST ON ONE OF THOSE.
IT WON'T BE CHRISTMAS FOR MONTHS AND MONTHS. I DON'T EVEN KNOW WHAT—MM.
YOU OKAY?
YEAH. I GUESS. IT FELT LIKE I HAD A HICCUP TRYING TO GET OUT, BUT THEN IT GOT STUCK. IT WENT AWAY. ARE WE STILL GOING TO RUN THE BASES?
I GUESS. IF YOU'RE READY TO MOVE. WHAT DO YOU SAY?

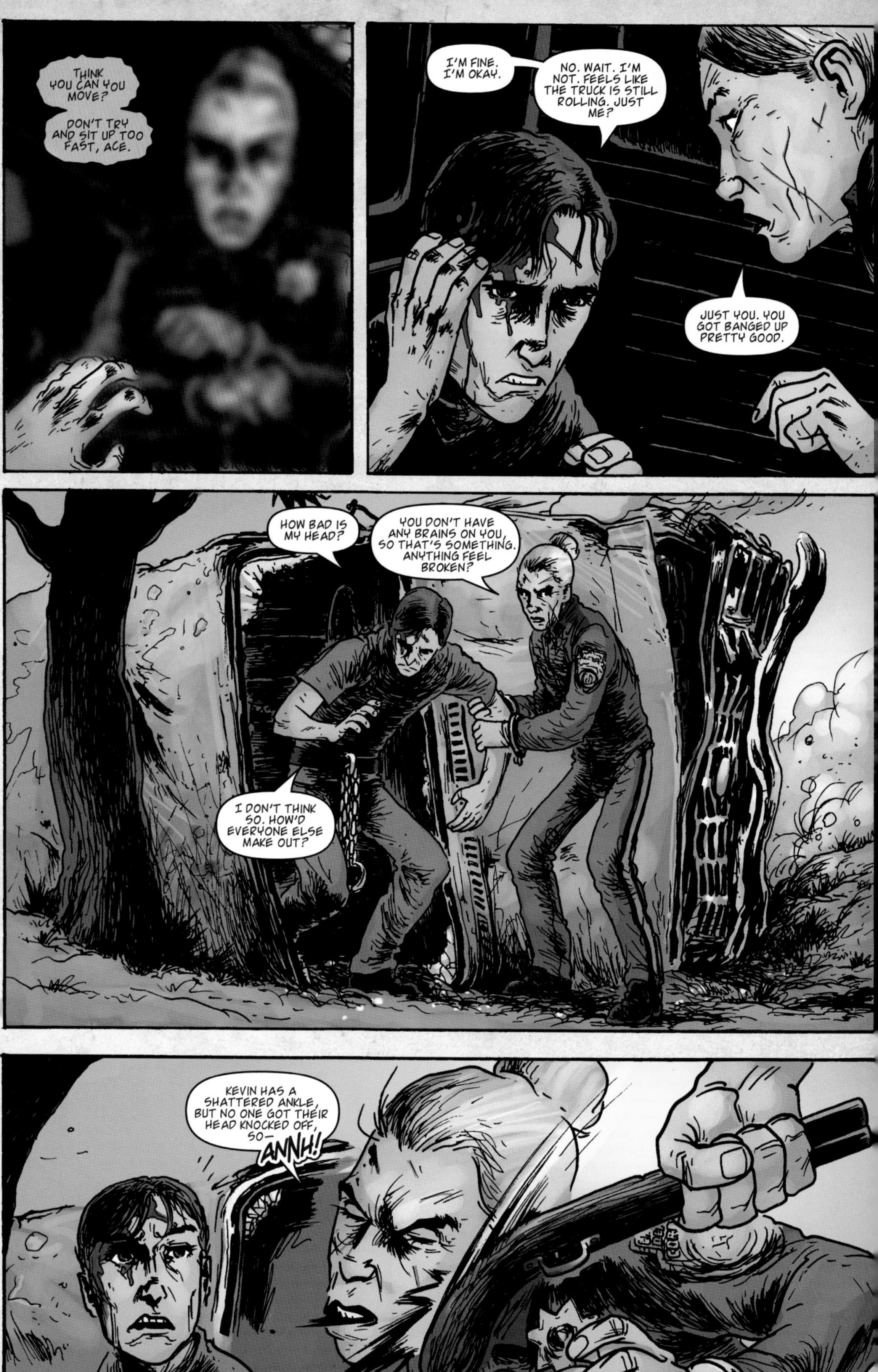
THINK YOU CAN YOU MOVE?
DON'T TRY AND SIT UP TOO FAST, ACE.
I'M FINE. I'M OKAY.
NO. WAIT. I'M NOT. FEELS LIKE THE TRUCK IS STILL ROLLING. JUST ME?
JUST YOU. YOU GOT BANGED UP PRETTY GOOD.
HOW BAD IS MY HEAD?
YOU DON'T HAVE ANY BRAINS ON YOU, SO THAT'S SOMETHING. ANYTHING FEEL BROKEN?
I DON'T THINK SO. HOW'D EVERYONE ELSE MAKE OUT?
KEVIN HAS A SHATTERED ANKLE, BUT NO ONE GOT THEIR HEAD KNOCKED OFF, SO—
ANNH!

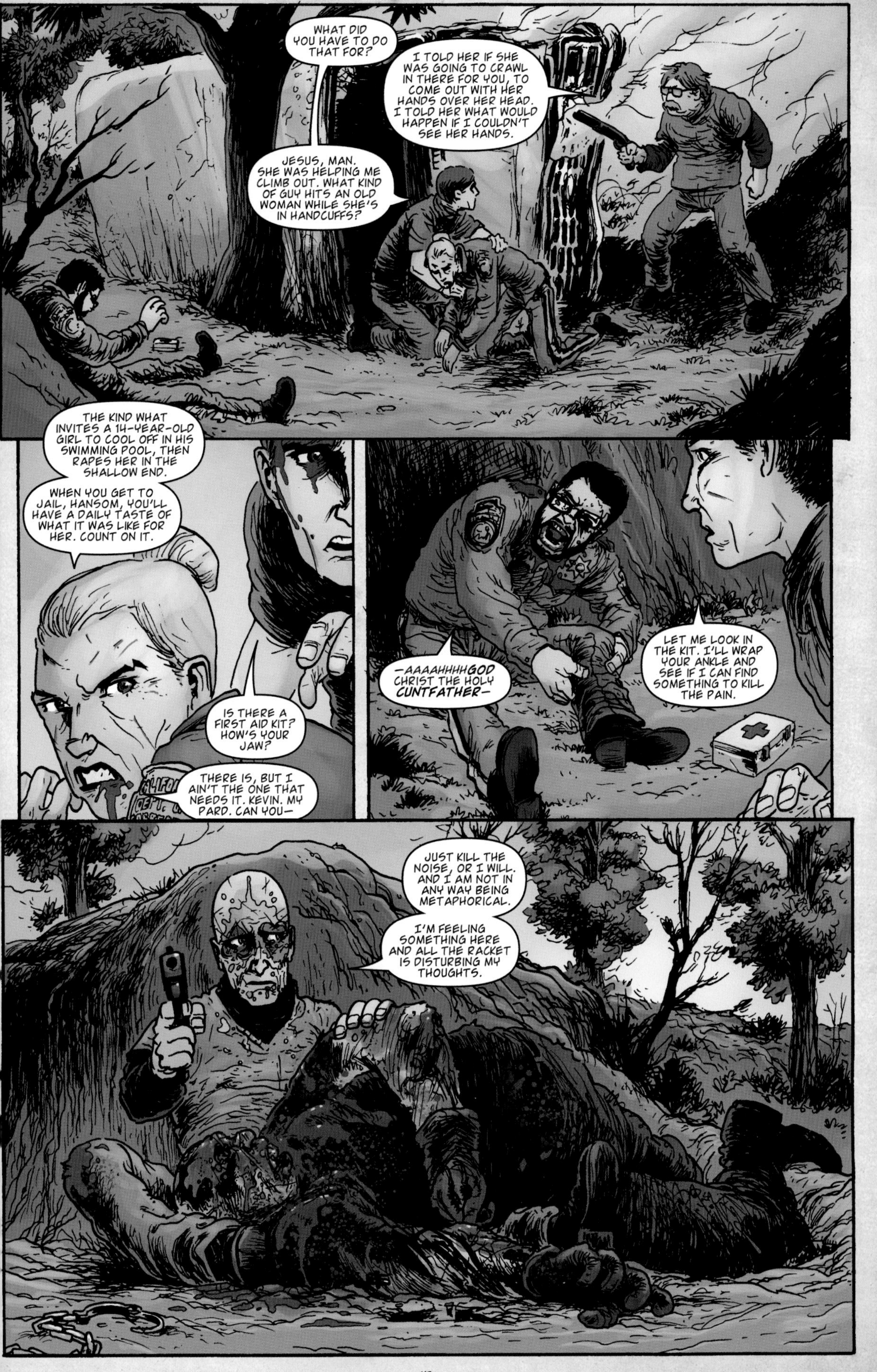
WHAT DID YOU HAVE TO DO THAT FOR?
I TOLD HER IF SHE WAS GOING TO CRAWL IN THERE FOR YOU, TO COME OUT WITH HER HANDS OVER HER HEAD. I TOLD HER WHAT WOULD HAPPEN IF I COULDN'T SEE HER HANDS.
JESUS, MAN. SHE WAS HELPING ME CLIMB OUT. WHAT KIND OF GUY HITS AN OLD WOMAN WHILE SHE'S IN HANDCUFFS?
THE KIND WHAT INVITES A 14-YEAR-OLD GIRL TO COOL OFF IN HIS SWIMMING POOL, THEN RAPES HER IN THE SHALLOW END.
WHEN YOU GET TO JAIL, HANSOM, YOU'LL HAVE A DAILY TASTE OF WHAT IT WAS LIKE FOR HER. COUNT ON IT.
IS THERE A FIRST AID KIT? HOW'S YOUR JAW?
THERE IS, BUT I AIN'T THE ONE THAT NEEDS IT. KEVIN. MY PARD. CAN YOU—
—AAAAHHHHGOD CHRIST THE HOLY CUNTFATHER—
LET ME LOOK IN THE KIT. I'LL WRAP YOUR ANKLE AND SEE IF I CAN FIND SOMETHING TO KILL THE PAIN.
JUST KILL THE NOISE, OR I WILL. AND I AM NOT IN ANY WAY BEING METAPHORICAL.
I'M FEELING SOMETHING HERE AND ALL THE RACKET IS DISTURBING MY THOUGHTS.

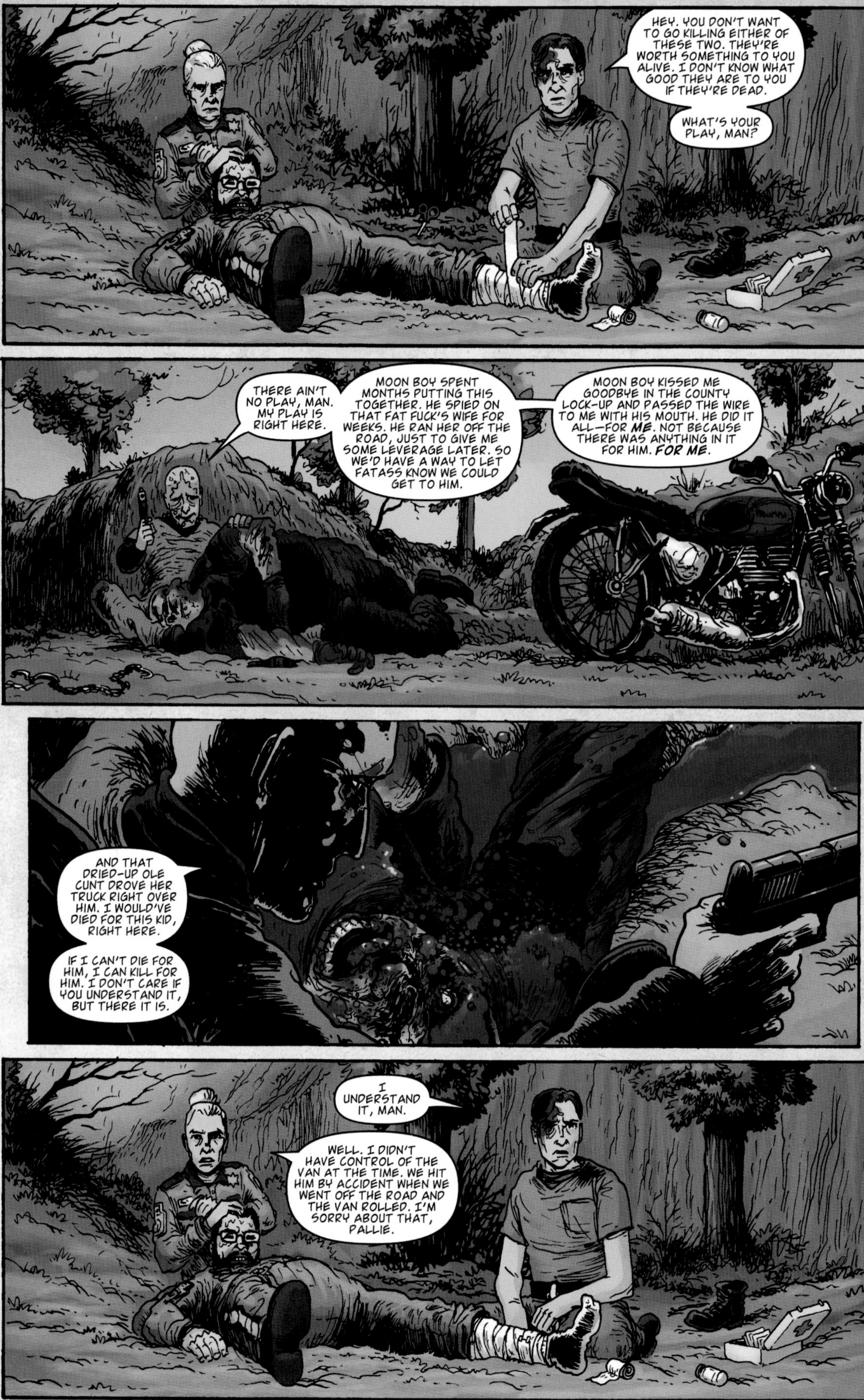

HEY. YOU DON'T WANT TO GO KILLING EITHER OF THESE TWO. THEY'RE WORTH SOMETHING TO YOU ALIVE. I DON'T KNOW WHAT GOOD THEY ARE TO YOU IF THEY'RE DEAD.
WHAT'S YOUR PLAY, MAN?
THERE AIN'T NO PLAY, MAN. MY PLAY IS RIGHT HERE.
MOON BOY SPENT MONTHS PUTTING THIS TOGETHER. HE SPIED ON THAT FAT FUCK'S WIFE FOR WEEKS. HE RAN HER OFF THE ROAD, JUST TO GIVE ME SOME LEVERAGE LATER. SO WE'D HAVE A WAY TO LET FATASS KNOW WE COULD GET TO HIM.
MOON BOY KISSED ME GOODBYE IN THE COUNTY LOCK-UP AND PASSED THE WIRE TO ME WITH HIS MOUTH. HE DID IT ALL—FOR ME. NOT BECAUSE THERE WAS ANYTHING IN IT FOR HIM. FOR ME.
AND THAT DRIED-UP OLE CUNT DROVE HER TRUCK RIGHT OVER HIM. I WOULD'VE DIED FOR THIS KID, RIGHT HERE.
IF I CAN'T DIE FOR HIM, I CAN KILL FOR HIM. I DON'T CARE IF YOU UNDERSTAND IT, BUT THERE IT IS.
I UNDERSTAND IT, MAN.
WELL. I DIDN'T HAVE CONTROL OF THE VAN AT THE TIME. WE HIT HIM BY ACCIDENT WHEN WE WENT OFF THE ROAD AND THE VAN ROLLED. I'M SORRY ABOUT THAT, PALLIE.

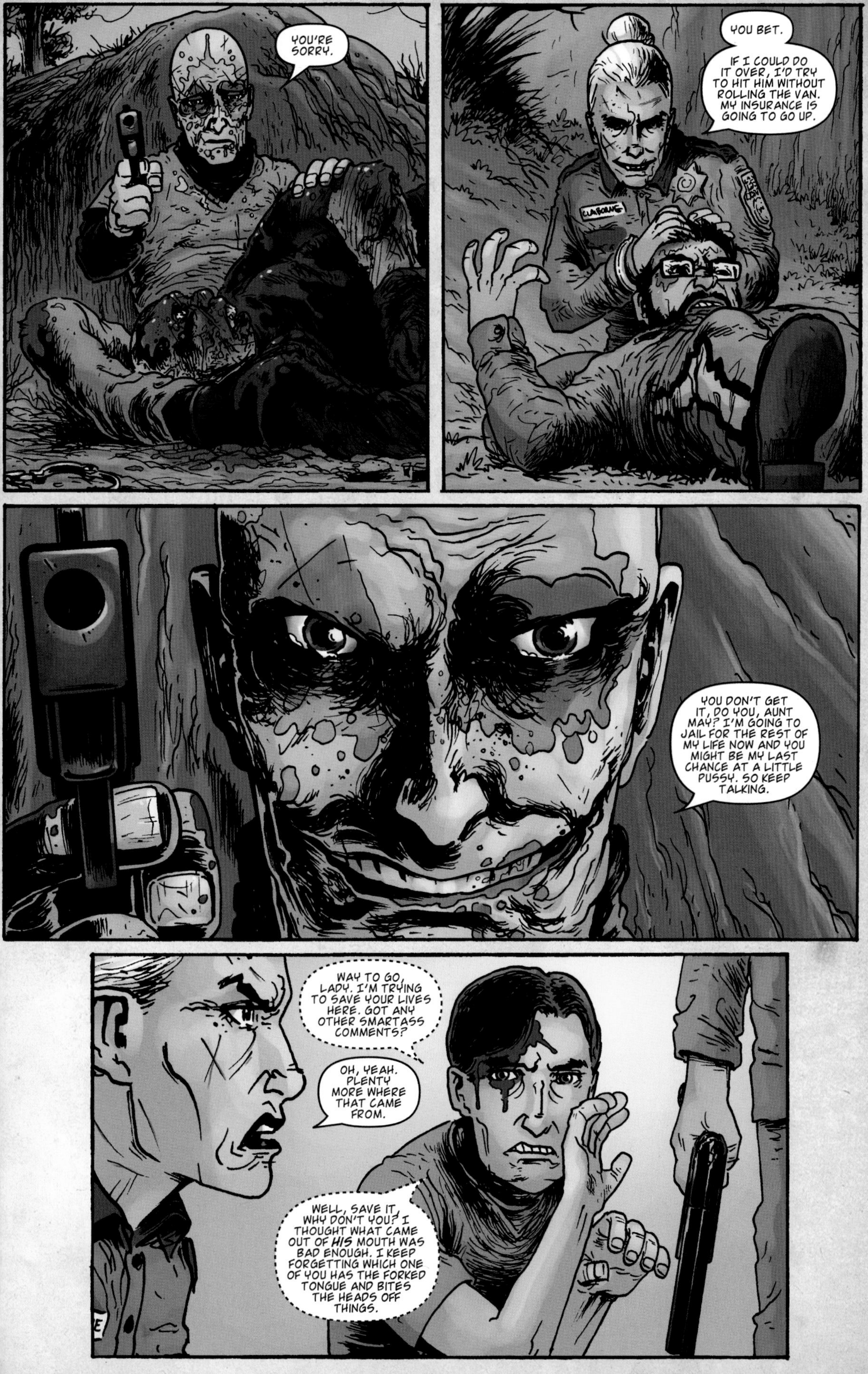
YOU'RE SORRY.
YOU BET.
IF I COULD DO IT OVER, I'D TRY TO HIT HIM WITHOUT ROLLING THE VAN. MY INSURANCE IS GOING TO GO UP.
YOU DON'T GET IT, DO YOU, AUNT MAY? I'M GOING TO JAIL FOR THE REST OF MY LIFE NOW AND YOU MIGHT BE MY LAST CHANCE AT A LITTLE PUSSY. SO KEEP TALKING.
WAY TO GO, LADY. I'M TRYING TO SAVE YOUR LIVES HERE. GOT ANY OTHER SMARTASS COMMENTS?
OH, YEAH. PLENTY MORE WHERE THAT CAME FROM.
WELL, SAVE IT, WHY DON'T YOU? I THOUGHT WHAT CAME OUT OF HIS MOUTH WAS BAD ENOUGH. I KEEP FORGETTING WHICH ONE OF YOU HAS THE FORKED TONGUE AND BITES THE HEADS OFF THINGS.

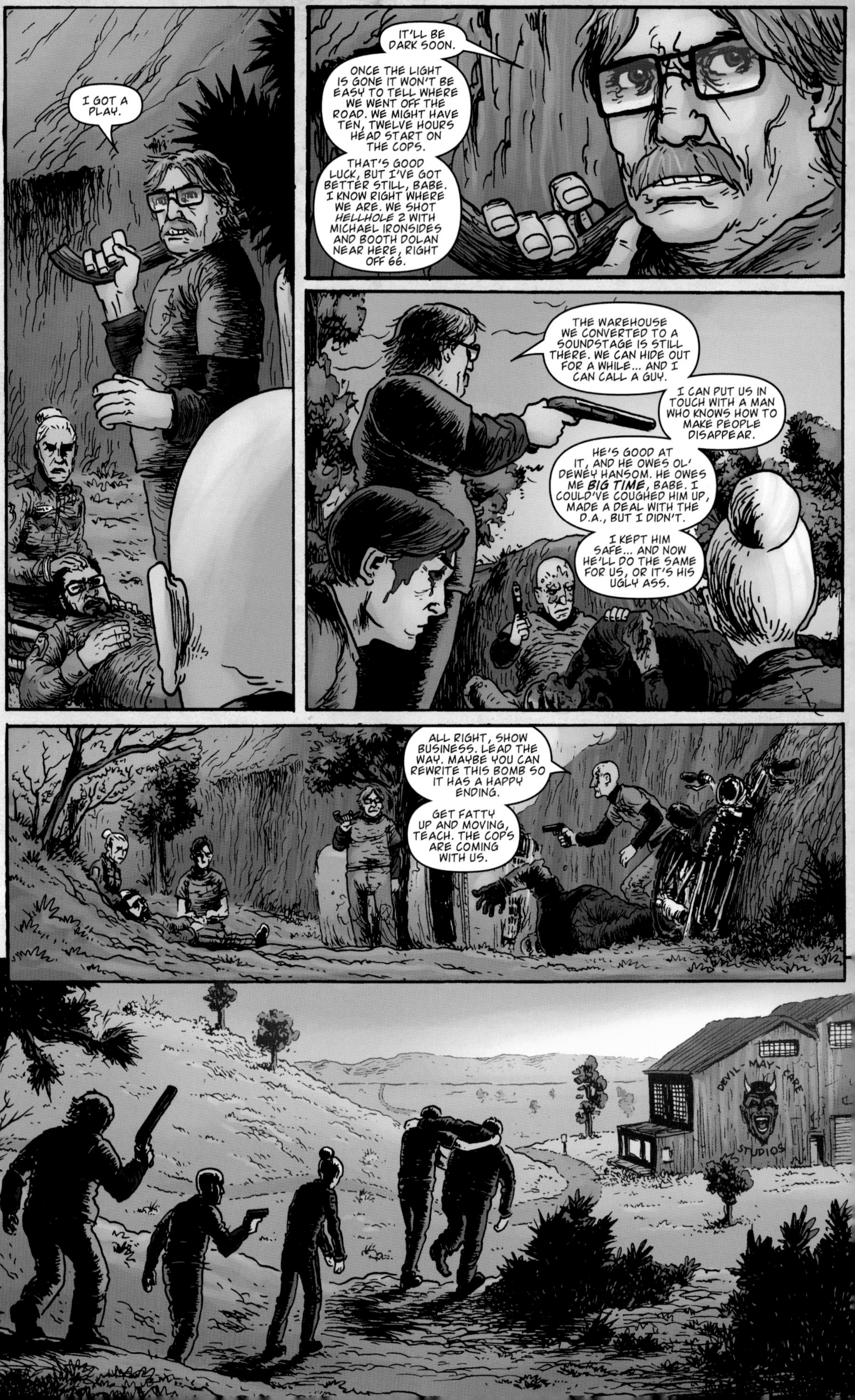
I GOT A PLAY.
IT'LL BE DARK SOON.
ONCE THE LIGHT IS GONE IT WON'T BE EASY TO TELL WHERE WE WENT OFF THE ROAD. WE MIGHT HAVE TEN, TWELVE HOURS HEAD START ON THE COPS.
THAT'S GOOD LUCK, BUT I'VE GOT BETTER STILL, BABE. I KNOW RIGHT WHERE WE ARE. WE SHOT *HELLHOLE 2* WITH MICHAEL IRONSIDES AND BOOTH DOLAN NEAR HERE, RIGHT OFF 66.
THE WAREHOUSE WE CONVERTED TO A SOUNDSTAGE IS STILL THERE. WE CAN HIDE OUT FOR A WHILE... AND I CAN CALL A GUY.
I CAN PUT US IN TOUCH WITH A MAN WHO KNOWS HOW TO MAKE PEOPLE DISAPPEAR.
HE'S GOOD AT IT, AND HE OWES OL' DEWEY HANSOM. HE OWES ME ***BIG TIME***, BABE. I COULD'VE COUGHED HIM UP, MADE A DEAL WITH THE D.A., BUT I DIDN'T.
I KEPT HIM SAFE... AND NOW HE'LL DO THE SAME FOR US, OR IT'S HIS UGLY ASS.
ALL RIGHT, SHOW BUSINESS. LEAD THE WAY. MAYBE YOU CAN REWRITE THIS BOMB SO IT HAS A HAPPY ENDING.
GET FATTY UP AND MOVING, TEACH. THE COPS ARE COMING WITH US.
DEVIL-MAY-CARE STUDIOS

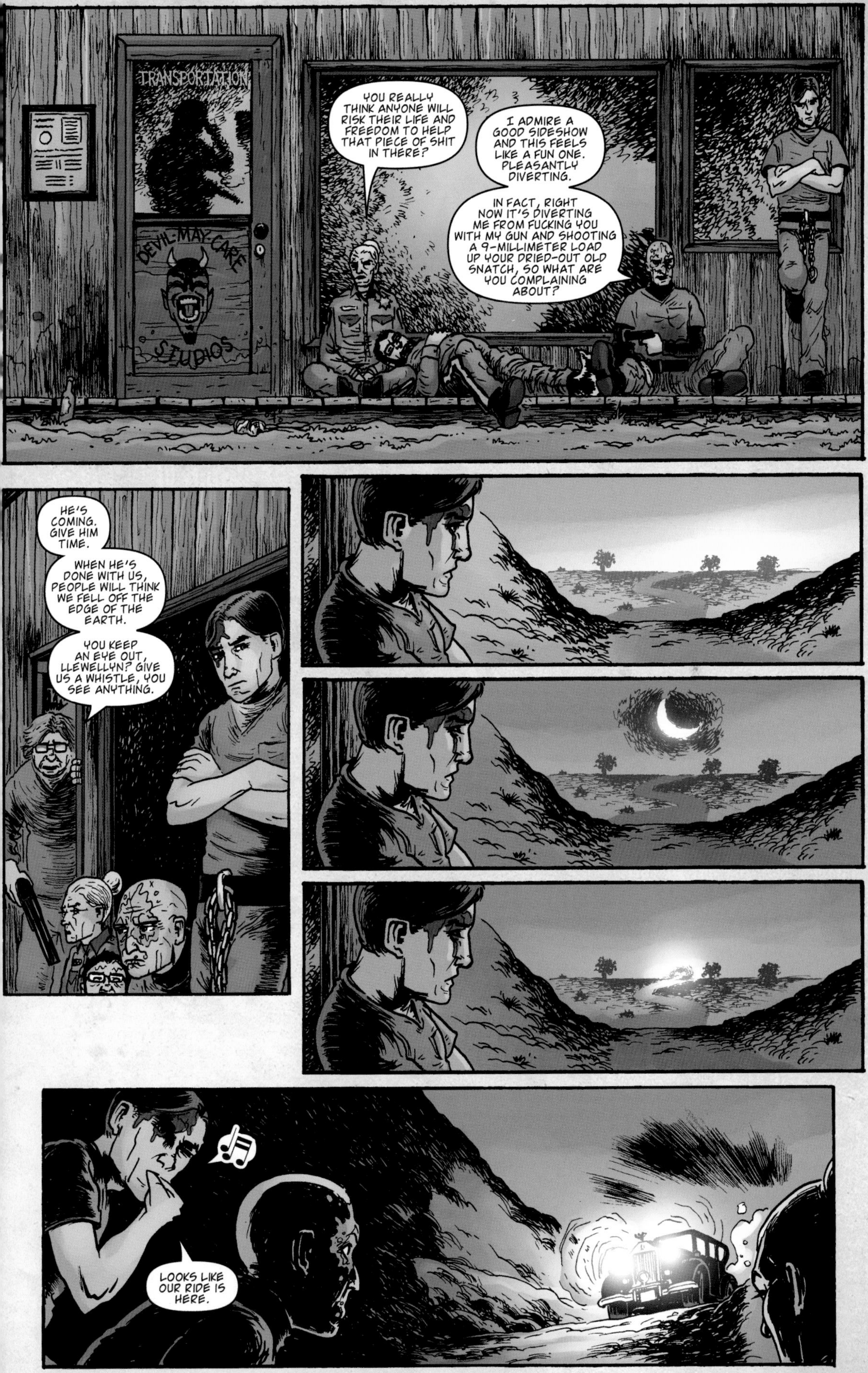
TRANSPORTATION
DEVIL-MAY-CARE
STUDIOS
YOU REALLY THINK ANYONE WILL RISK THEIR LIFE AND FREEDOM TO HELP THAT PIECE OF SHIT IN THERE?
I ADMIRE A GOOD SIDESHOW AND THIS FEELS LIKE A FUN ONE. PLEASANTLY DIVERTING.
IN FACT, RIGHT NOW IT'S DIVERTING ME FROM FUCKING YOU WITH MY GUN AND SHOOTING A 9-MILLIMETER LOAD UP YOUR DRIED-OUT OLD SNATCH, SO WHAT ARE YOU COMPLAINING ABOUT?
HE'S COMING. GIVE HIM TIME.
WHEN HE'S DONE WITH US, PEOPLE WILL THINK WE FELL OFF THE EDGE OF THE EARTH.
YOU KEEP AN EYE OUT, LLEWELLYN? GIVE US A WHISTLE, YOU SEE ANYTHING.
LOOKS LIKE OUR RIDE IS HERE.

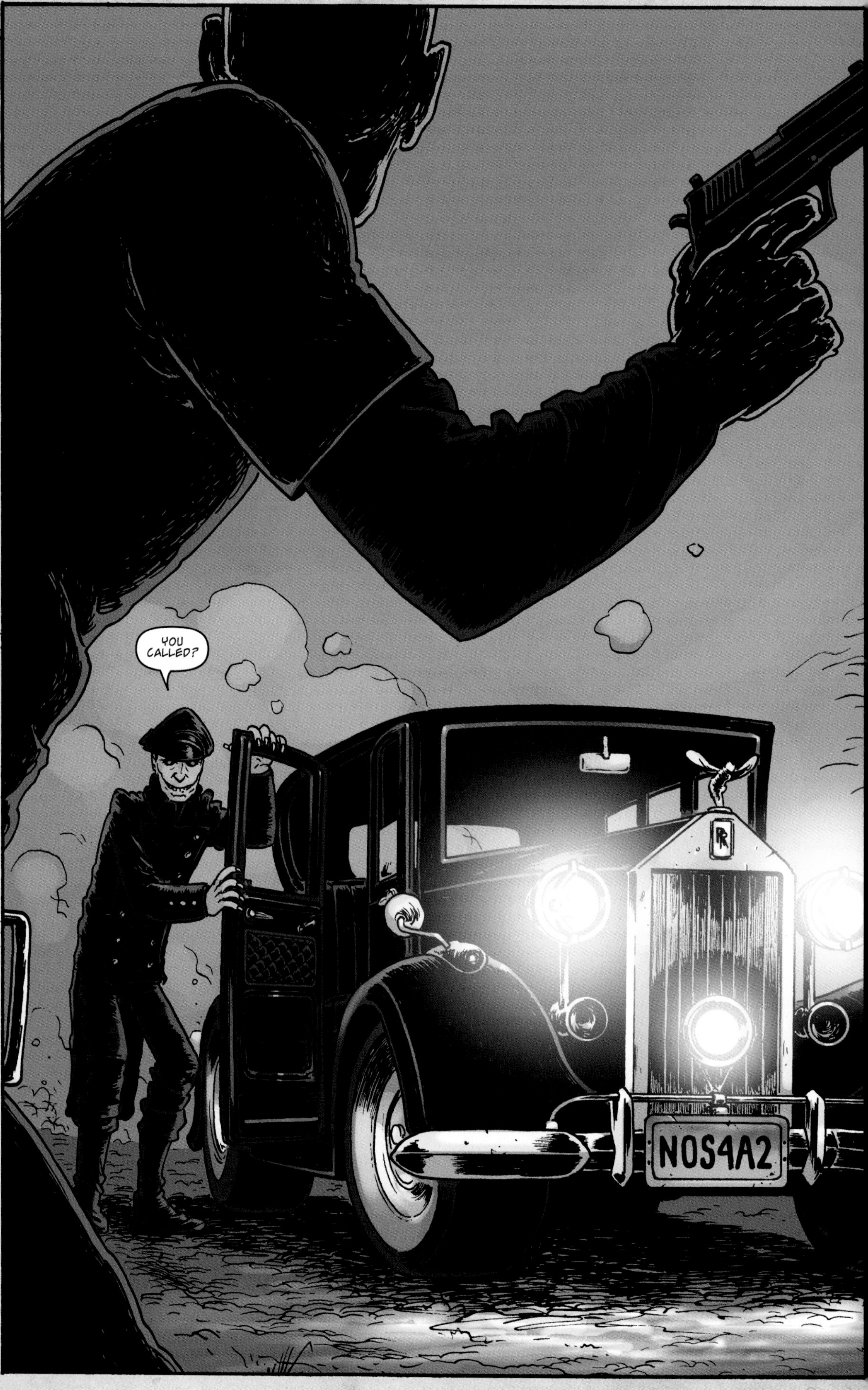

YOU CALLED?
NOS4A2

WELCOME TO CHRISTMASLAND chapter two
DARK PASSAGE

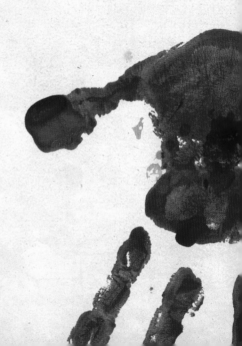

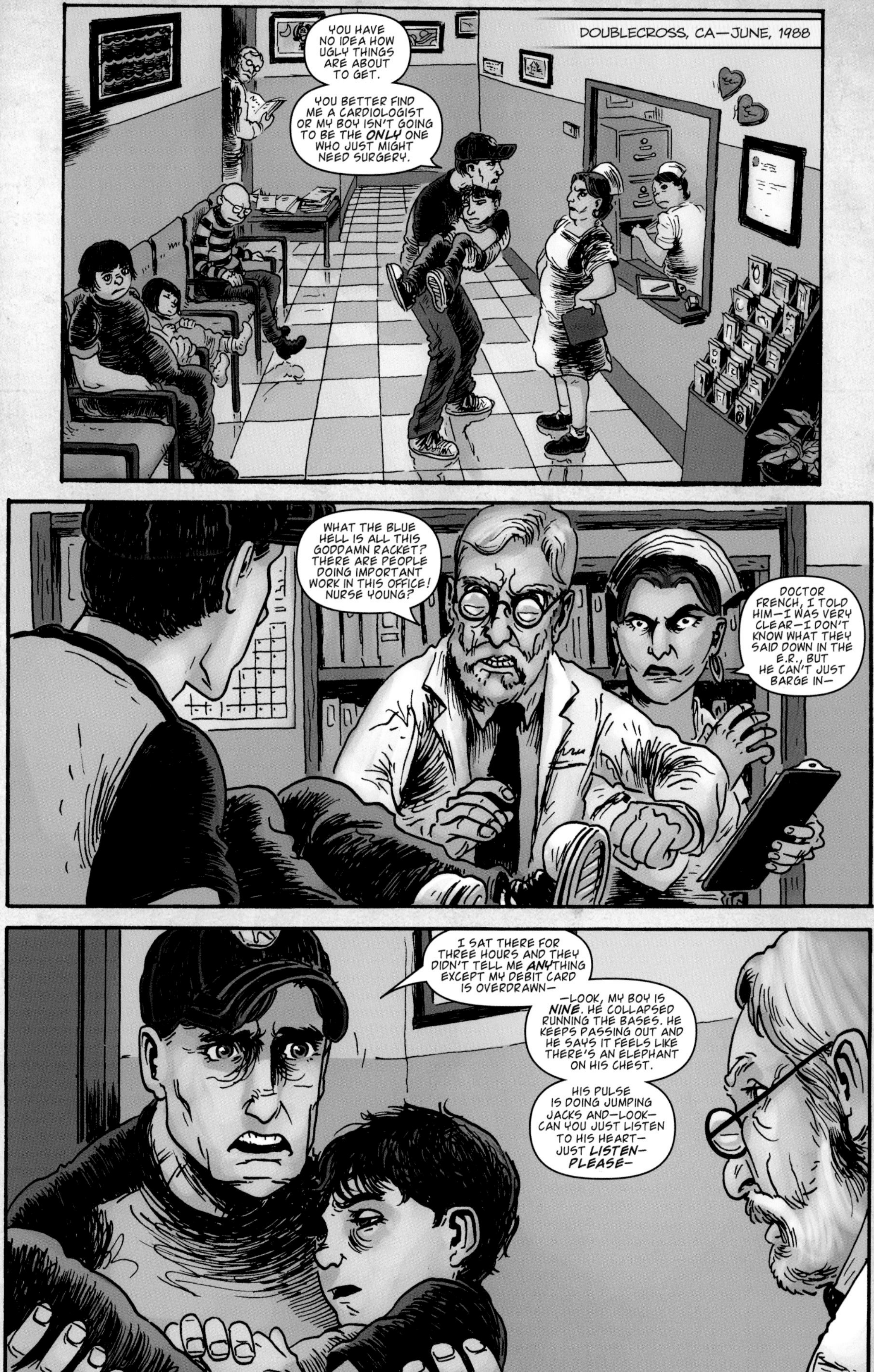
DOUBLECROSS, CA—JUNE, 1988
YOU HAVE NO IDEA HOW UGLY THINGS ARE ABOUT TO GET.
YOU BETTER FIND ME A CARDIOLOGIST OR MY BOY ISN'T GOING TO BE THE ONLY ONE WHO JUST MIGHT NEED SURGERY.
WHAT THE BLUE HELL IS ALL THIS GODDAMN RACKET? THERE ARE PEOPLE DOING IMPORTANT WORK IN THIS OFFICE! NURSE YOUNG?
DOCTOR FRENCH, I TOLD HIM—I WAS VERY CLEAR—I DON'T KNOW WHAT THEY SAID DOWN IN THE E.R., BUT HE CAN'T JUST BARGE IN—
I SAT THERE FOR THREE HOURS AND THEY DIDN'T TELL ME ANYTHING EXCEPT MY DEBIT CARD IS OVERDRAWN—
—LOOK, MY BOY IS NINE. HE COLLAPSED RUNNING THE BASES. HE KEEPS PASSING OUT AND HE SAYS IT FEELS LIKE THERE'S AN ELEPHANT ON HIS CHEST.
HIS PULSE IS DOING JUMPING JACKS AND—LOOK—CAN YOU JUST LISTEN TO HIS HEART—JUST LISTEN—PLEASE—

HOW LONG WAS HE RUNNING IN THE SUN AND WHEN DID HE LAST EAT?

ALL AFTERNOON— *CHRIST*, I HAD HIM GOING ALL AFTERNOON IN THE HEAT—LUNCH? I—I DON'T REMEMBER. I THINK—A COUPLE HOT DOGS AROUND 1? LOOK, CAN WE TAKE THIS TO AN EXAM ROOM...

HOLD YOUR HORSES, SON. NURSE YOUNG WILL HAVE TO TAKE SOME INFORMATION AND A COPY OF YOUR INSURANCE.

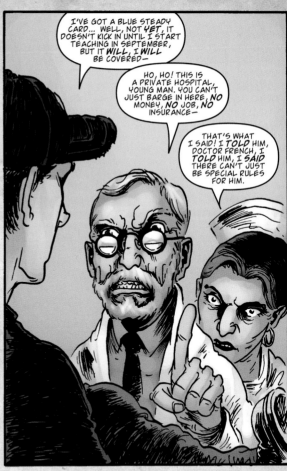

I'VE GOT A BLUE STEADY CARD... WELL, NOT *YET*, IT DOESN'T KICK IN UNTIL I START TEACHING IN SEPTEMBER, BUT IT *WILL*, I *WILL* BE COVERED—

HO, HO! THIS IS A PRIVATE HOSPITAL, YOUNG MAN. YOU CAN'T JUST BARGE IN HERE, *NO* MONEY, *NO JOB, NO* INSURANCE—

THAT'S WHAT I SAID! I *TOLD* HIM, DOCTOR FRENCH, I *TOLD* HIM, I *SAID* THERE CAN'T JUST BE SPECIAL RULES FOR HIM.

WAIT A MINUTE, I HAVE A *JOB*, I—LOOK, *PLEASE*—I THINK MY SON IS *DYING*—

SPARE US THE SOAP OPERA! HE'S PROBABLY GOT HEAT STROKE OR INDIGESTION OR BOTH! AND YOU, YOU'RE SUFFERING FROM AN ADVANCED CASE OF *FREE-LOADER-ITIS!*

I CAN'T JUST START TREATING YOUR SON FOR SOME MYSTERY AILMENT WITHOUT PROPER INSURANCE. I SO MUCH AS PUT MY STETHOSCOPE ON HIS CHEST, I OPEN MYSELF UP TO A SUIT, REVIEW BY MY BOARD, AND ENOUGH RED TAPE TO STRANGLE A PERSON!

WE DON'T TREAT *UNEMPLOYMENT* HERE—OR *POVERTY*— OR *HALF-ASSED PARENTING!* TAKE YOURSELF TO THE CITY HOSPITAL IN BARSTOW!

YOU WANT SOME MEDICAL ADVICE? DON'T LET THE DOOR HIT YOUR BUTT ON THE WAY OUT!

GO ON NOW. GO ON...

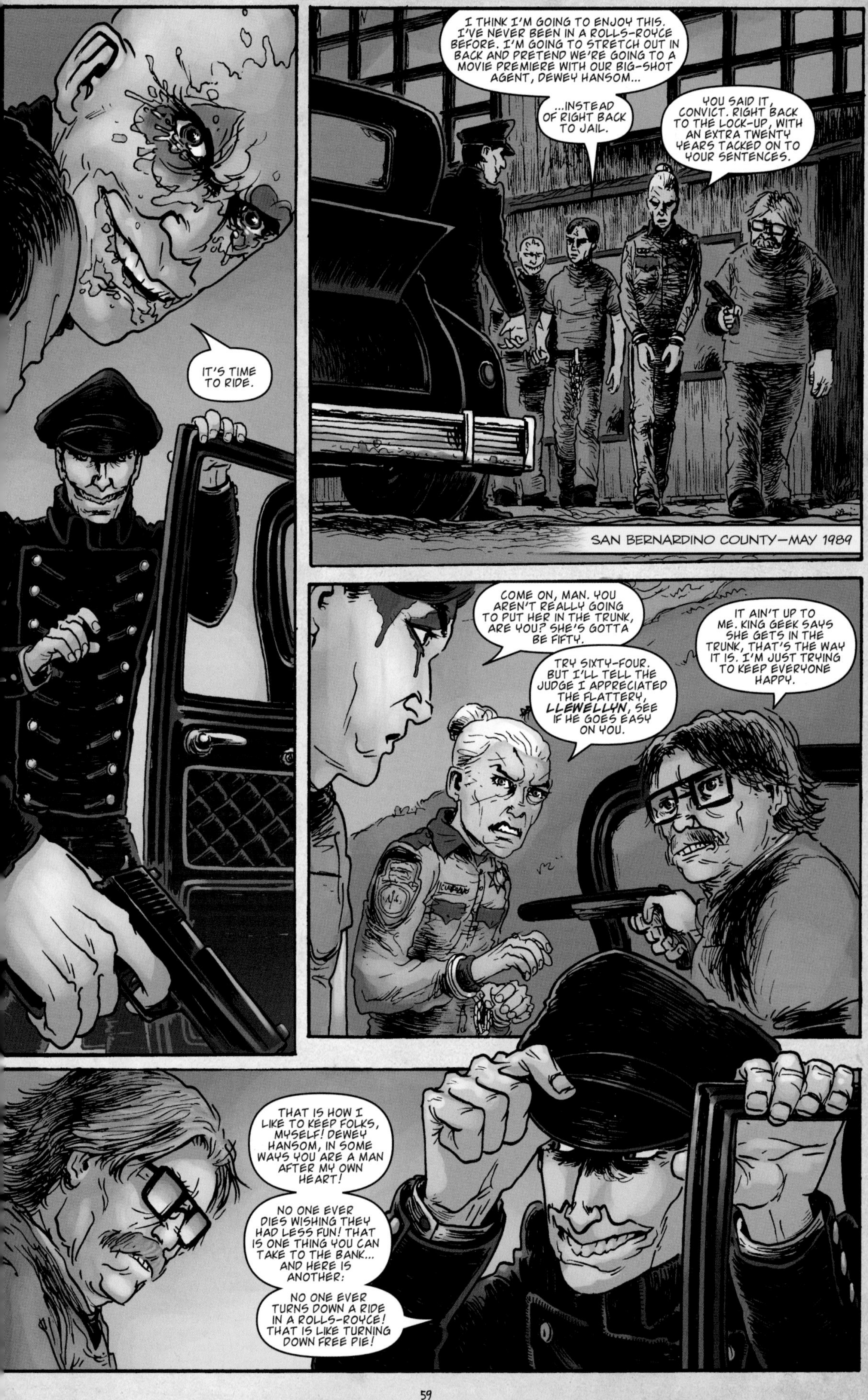
IT'S TIME TO RIDE.
I THINK I'M GOING TO ENJOY THIS. I'VE NEVER BEEN IN A ROLLS-ROYCE BEFORE. I'M GOING TO STRETCH OUT IN BACK AND PRETEND WE'RE GOING TO A MOVIE PREMIERE WITH OUR BIG-SHOT AGENT, DEWEY HANSOM...
...INSTEAD OF RIGHT BACK TO JAIL.
YOU SAID IT, CONVICT. RIGHT BACK TO THE LOCK-UP, WITH AN EXTRA TWENTY YEARS TACKED ON TO YOUR SENTENCES.
SAN BERNARDINO COUNTY—MAY 1989
COME ON, MAN. YOU AREN'T REALLY GOING TO PUT HER IN THE TRUNK, ARE YOU? SHE'S GOTTA BE FIFTY.
TRY SIXTY-FOUR. BUT I'LL TELL THE JUDGE I APPRECIATED THE FLATTERY, LLEWELLYN, SEE IF HE GOES EASY ON YOU.
IT AIN'T UP TO ME. KING GEEK SAYS SHE GETS IN THE TRUNK, THAT'S THE WAY IT IS. I'M JUST TRYING TO KEEP EVERYONE HAPPY.
THAT IS HOW I LIKE TO KEEP FOLKS, MYSELF! DEWEY HANSOM, IN SOME WAYS YOU ARE A MAN AFTER MY OWN HEART!
NO ONE EVER DIES WISHING THEY HAD LESS FUN! THAT IS ONE THING YOU CAN TAKE TO THE BANK... AND HERE IS ANOTHER:
NO ONE EVER TURNS DOWN A RIDE IN A ROLLS-ROYCE! THAT IS LIKE TURNING DOWN FREE PIE!

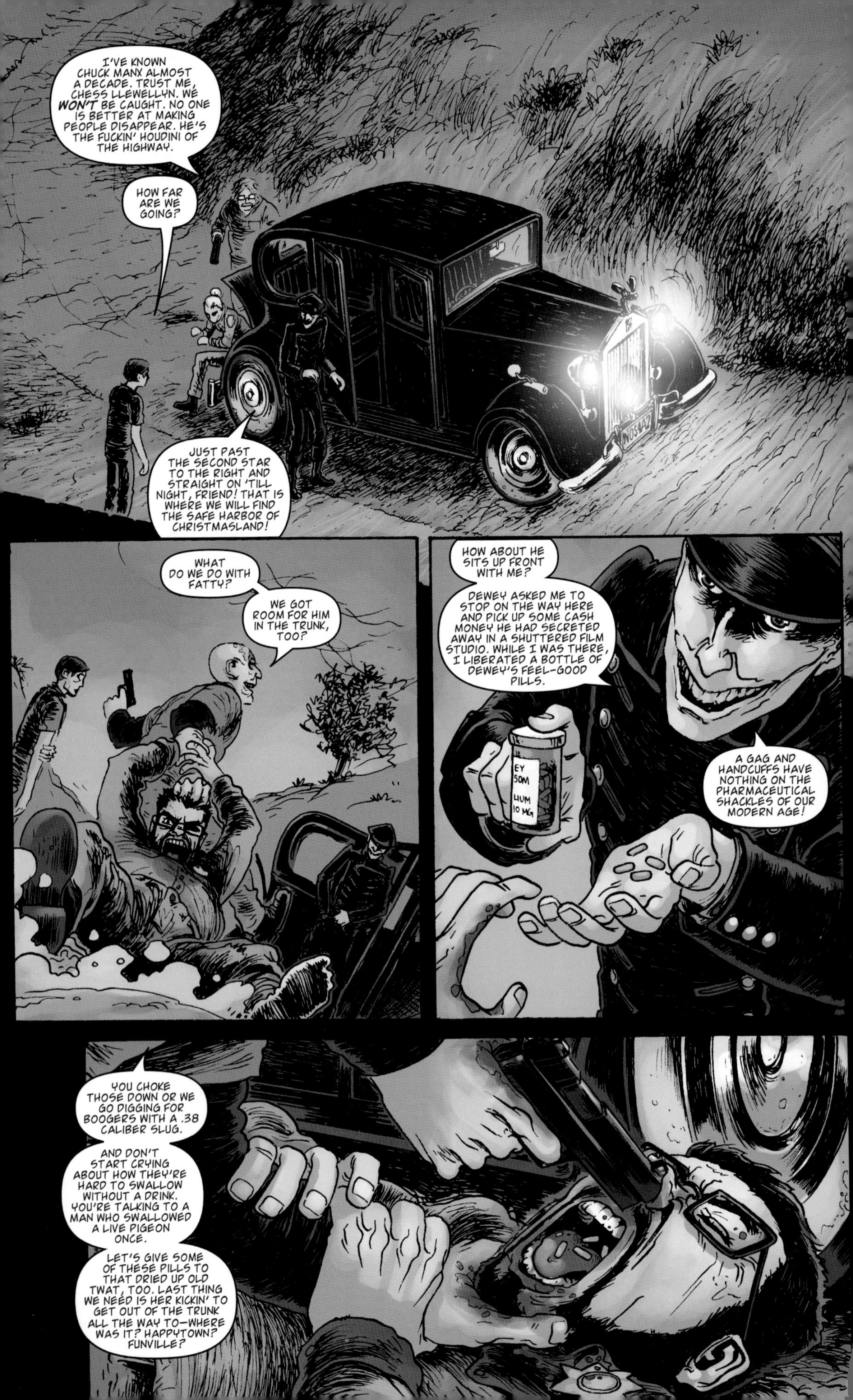
I'VE KNOWN CHUCK MANX ALMOST A DECADE. TRUST ME, CHESS LLEWELLYN. WE WON'T BE CAUGHT. NO ONE IS BETTER AT MAKING PEOPLE DISAPPEAR. HE'S THE FUCKIN' HOUDINI OF THE HIGHWAY.
HOW FAR ARE WE GOING?
JUST PAST THE SECOND STAR TO THE RIGHT AND STRAIGHT ON 'TILL NIGHT, FRIEND! THAT IS WHERE WE WILL FIND THE SAFE HARBOR OF CHRISTMASLAND!
WHAT DO WE DO WITH FATTY?
WE GOT ROOM FOR HIM IN THE TRUNK, TOO?
HOW ABOUT HE SITS UP FRONT WITH ME?
DEWEY ASKED ME TO STOP ON THE WAY HERE AND PICK UP SOME CASH MONEY HE HAD SECRETED AWAY IN A SHUTTERED FILM STUDIO. WHILE I WAS THERE, I LIBERATED A BOTTLE OF DEWEY'S FEEL-GOOD PILLS.
A GAG AND HANDCUFFS HAVE NOTHING ON THE PHARMACEUTICAL SHACKLES OF OUR MODERN AGE!
YOU CHOKE THOSE DOWN OR WE GO DIGGING FOR BOOGERS WITH A .38 CALIBER SLUG.
AND DON'T START CRYING ABOUT HOW THEY'RE HARD TO SWALLOW WITHOUT A DRINK. YOU'RE TALKING TO A MAN WHO SWALLOWED A LIVE PIGEON ONCE.
LET'S GIVE SOME OF THESE PILLS TO THAT DRIED UP OLD TWAT, TOO. LAST THING WE NEED IS HER KICKIN' TO GET OUT OF THE TRUNK ALL THE WAY TO—WHERE WAS IT? HAPPYTOWN? FUNVILLE?

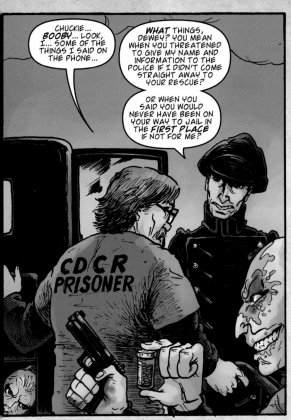

CHUCKIE... BOOBY... LOOK, I... SOME OF THE THINGS I SAID ON THE PHONE...

WHAT THINGS, DEWEY? YOU MEAN WHEN YOU THREATENED TO GIVE MY NAME AND INFORMATION TO THE POLICE IF I DIDN'T COME STRAIGHT AWAY TO YOUR RESCUE?

OR WHEN YOU SAID YOU WOULD NEVER HAVE BEEN ON YOUR WAY TO JAIL IN THE FIRST PLACE IF NOT FOR ME?

AH... CHUCK... IF YOU'RE THE MAN I THINK YOU ARE, YOU DIDN'T LISTEN TO A WORD. I'M MORE OF A GRAY-HAIRED CUNT THAN THAT PATHETIC EXTRA FROM THE GOLDEN GIRLS WE GOT STUFFED IN THE TRUNK.

DON'T FRET FOR A MOMENT, DEWEY! YOU ARE AN OLD FRIEND AND YOU ASKED IF I COULD GIVE YOU A HAND! OF COURSE I CAN... AND I TRUST ONE DAY YOU WILL DO THE SAME FOR ME!

CHUCK, IF YOU EVER NEED A HAND, IT'S YOURS! DON'T THINK TWICE!

AND YOU BROUGHT MY FAVORITE PAIR OF SUNGLASSES!

SHUT UP AND HOLD ME, YOU LOVELY MOTHERFUCKER.

61

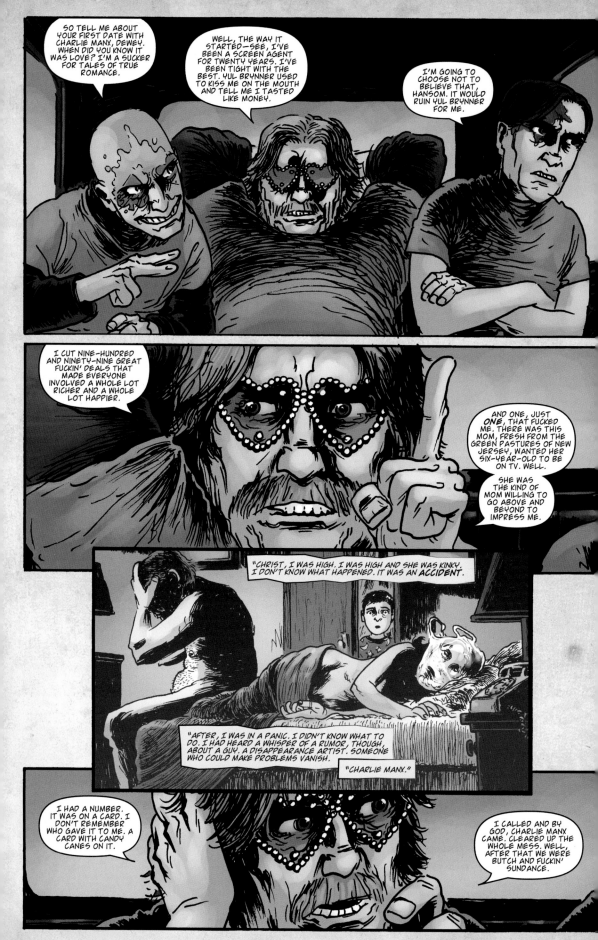

SO TELL ME ABOUT YOUR FIRST DATE WITH CHARLIE MANX, DEWEY. WHEN DID YOU KNOW IT WAS LOVE? I'M A SUCKER FOR TALES OF TRUE ROMANCE.

WELL, THE WAY IT STARTED—SEE, I'VE BEEN A SCREEN AGENT FOR TWENTY YEARS. I'VE BEEN TIGHT WITH THE BEST. YUL BRYNNER USED TO KISS ME ON THE MOUTH AND TELL ME I TASTED LIKE MONEY.

I'M GOING TO CHOOSE NOT TO BELIEVE THAT, HANSOM. IT WOULD RUIN YUL BRYNNER FOR ME.

I CUT NINE-HUNDRED AND NINETY-NINE GREAT FUCKIN' DEALS THAT MADE EVERYONE INVOLVED A WHOLE LOT RICHER AND A WHOLE LOT HAPPIER.

AND ONE, JUST ONE, THAT FUCKED ME. THERE WAS THIS MOM, FRESH FROM THE GREEN PASTURES OF NEW JERSEY, WANTED HER SIX-YEAR-OLD TO BE ON TV. WELL.

SHE WAS THE KIND OF MOM WILLING TO GO ABOVE AND BEYOND TO IMPRESS ME.

"CHRIST, I WAS HIGH. I WAS HIGH AND SHE WAS KINKY. I DON'T KNOW WHAT HAPPENED. IT WAS AN ACCIDENT.

"AFTER, I WAS IN A PANIC. I DIDN'T KNOW WHAT TO DO. I HAD HEARD A WHISPER OF A RUMOR, THOUGH, ABOUT A GUY. A DISAPPEARANCE ARTIST. SOMEONE WHO COULD MAKE PROBLEMS VANISH.

"CHARLIE MANX."

I HAD A NUMBER. IT WAS ON A CARD. I DON'T REMEMBER WHO GAVE IT TO ME. A CARD WITH CANDY CANES ON IT.

I CALLED AND BY GOD, CHARLIE MANX CAME. CLEARED UP THE WHOLE MESS. WELL, AFTER THAT WE WERE BUTCH AND FUCKIN' SUNDANCE.

62

WHAT ABOUT THE KID? THE SIX-YEAR-OLD?

HE WENT WITH CHARLIE.

HE—*WHAT?*

COOL OFF. WE ALL HAVE COMMON CAUSE HERE, FRIEND! LET'S NOT GET UGLY WITH EACH OTHER. ANYWAY—THE KID IS FINE! I SWEAR!

WHAT THE FUCK DOES THAT MEAN?

YES, I AM GLAD TO REPORT YOUNG ROBIN ROBARDS IS BETTER THAN FINE! HE IS HAPPIER THAN HE EVER WAS WITH HIS MOTHER, A DRUG ADDICT WHO SAW HIM AS A MEAL TICKET AND NOT A CHILD!

YOU WILL MEET HIM SOON ENOUGH. HE WILL BE WAITING FOR US IN CHRISTMASLAND! YOU NEVER ENCOUNTERED A SIX-YEAR-OLD WITH A BETTER SENSE OF FUN.

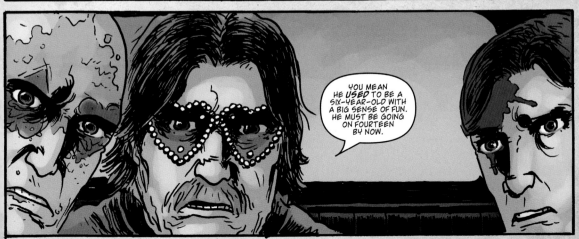

YOU MEAN HE *USED* TO BE A SIX-YEAR-OLD WITH A BIG SENSE OF FUN. HE MUST BE GOING ON FOURTEEN BY NOW.

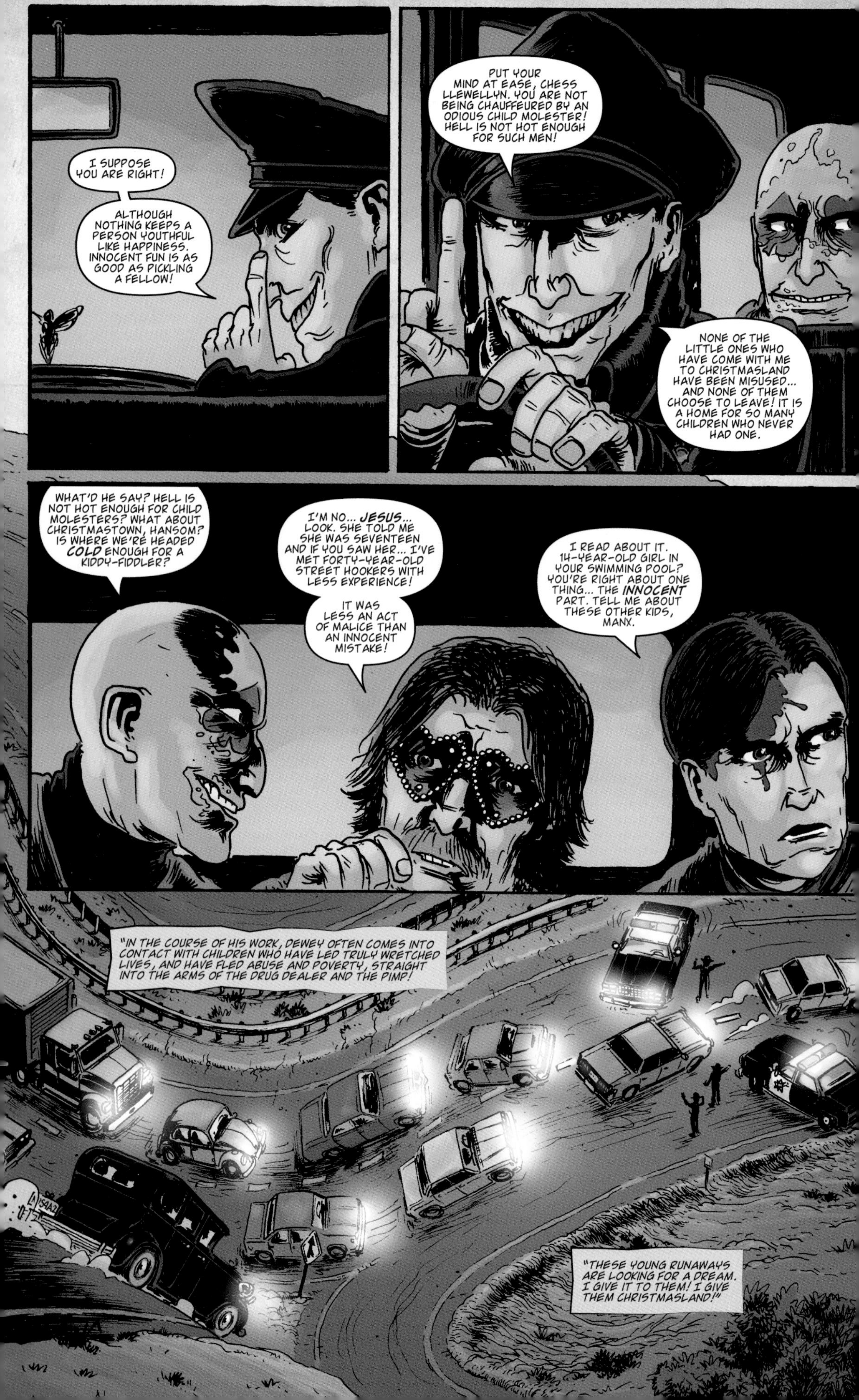
I SUPPOSE YOU ARE RIGHT!
ALTHOUGH NOTHING KEEPS A PERSON YOUTHFUL LIKE HAPPINESS. INNOCENT FUN IS AS GOOD AS PICKLING A FELLOW!
PUT YOUR MIND AT EASE, CHESS LLEWELLYN. YOU ARE NOT BEING CHAUFFEURED BY AN ODIOUS CHILD MOLESTER! HELL IS NOT HOT ENOUGH FOR SUCH MEN!
NONE OF THE LITTLE ONES WHO HAVE COME WITH ME TO CHRISTMASLAND HAVE BEEN MISUSED... AND NONE OF THEM CHOOSE TO LEAVE! IT IS A HOME FOR SO MANY CHILDREN WHO NEVER HAD ONE.
WHAT'D HE SAY? HELL IS NOT HOT ENOUGH FOR CHILD MOLESTERS? WHAT ABOUT CHRISTMASTOWN, HANSOM? IS WHERE WE'RE HEADED COLD ENOUGH FOR A KIDDY-FIDDLER?
I'M NO... JESUS... LOOK. SHE TOLD ME SHE WAS SEVENTEEN AND IF YOU SAW HER... I'VE MET FORTY-YEAR-OLD STREET HOOKERS WITH LESS EXPERIENCE!
IT WAS LESS AN ACT OF MALICE THAN AN INNOCENT MISTAKE!
I READ ABOUT IT. 14-YEAR-OLD GIRL IN YOUR SWIMMING POOL? YOU'RE RIGHT ABOUT ONE THING... THE INNOCENT PART. TELL ME ABOUT THESE OTHER KIDS, MANX.
"IN THE COURSE OF HIS WORK, DEWEY OFTEN COMES INTO CONTACT WITH CHILDREN WHO HAVE LED TRULY WRETCHED LIVES, AND HAVE FLED ABUSE AND POVERTY, STRAIGHT INTO THE ARMS OF THE DRUG DEALER AND THE PIMP!
"THESE YOUNG RUNAWAYS ARE LOOKING FOR A DREAM. I GIVE IT TO THEM! I GIVE THEM CHRISTMASLAND!"

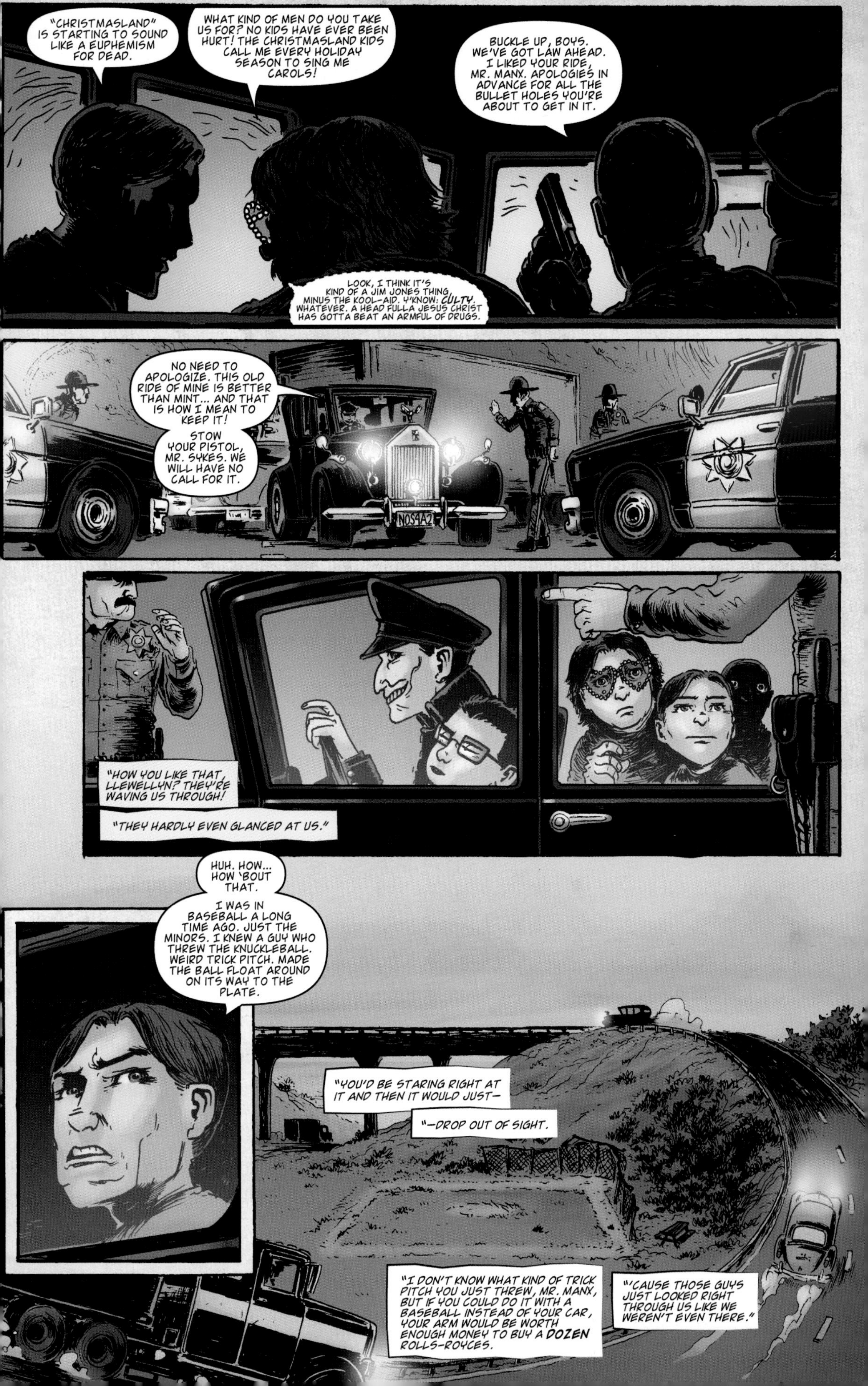
"CHRISTMASLAND" IS STARTING TO SOUND LIKE A EUPHEMISM FOR DEAD.
WHAT KIND OF MEN DO YOU TAKE US FOR? NO KIDS HAVE EVER BEEN HURT! THE CHRISTMASLAND KIDS CALL ME EVERY HOLIDAY SEASON TO SING ME CAROLS!
BUCKLE UP, BOYS. WE'VE GOT LAW AHEAD. I LIKED YOUR RIDE, MR. MANX. APOLOGIES IN ADVANCE FOR ALL THE BULLET HOLES YOU'RE ABOUT TO GET IN IT.
LOOK, I THINK IT'S KIND OF A JIM JONES THING, MINUS THE KOOL-AID. Y'KNOW: CULTY. WHATEVER. A HEAD FULLA JESUS CHRIST HAS GOTTA BEAT AN ARMFUL OF DRUGS.
NO NEED TO APOLOGIZE. THIS OLD RIDE OF MINE IS BETTER THAN MINT... AND THAT IS HOW I MEAN TO KEEP IT!
STOW YOUR PISTOL, MR. SYKES. WE WILL HAVE NO CALL FOR IT.
NOS4A2
"HOW YOU LIKE THAT, LLEWELLYN? THEY'RE WAVING US THROUGH!
"THEY HARDLY EVEN GLANCED AT US."
HUH. HOW... HOW 'BOUT THAT.
I WAS IN BASEBALL A LONG TIME AGO. JUST THE MINORS. I KNEW A GUY WHO THREW THE KNUCKLEBALL. WEIRD TRICK PITCH. MADE THE BALL FLOAT AROUND ON ITS WAY TO THE PLATE.
"YOU'D BE STARING RIGHT AT IT AND THEN IT WOULD JUST—
"—DROP OUT OF SIGHT.
"I DON'T KNOW WHAT KIND OF TRICK PITCH YOU JUST THREW, MR. MANX, BUT IF YOU COULD DO IT WITH A BASEBALL INSTEAD OF YOUR CAR, YOUR ARM WOULD BE WORTH ENOUGH MONEY TO BUY A DOZEN ROLLS-ROYCES.
"'CAUSE THOSE GUYS JUST LOOKED RIGHT THROUGH US LIKE WE WEREN'T EVEN THERE."

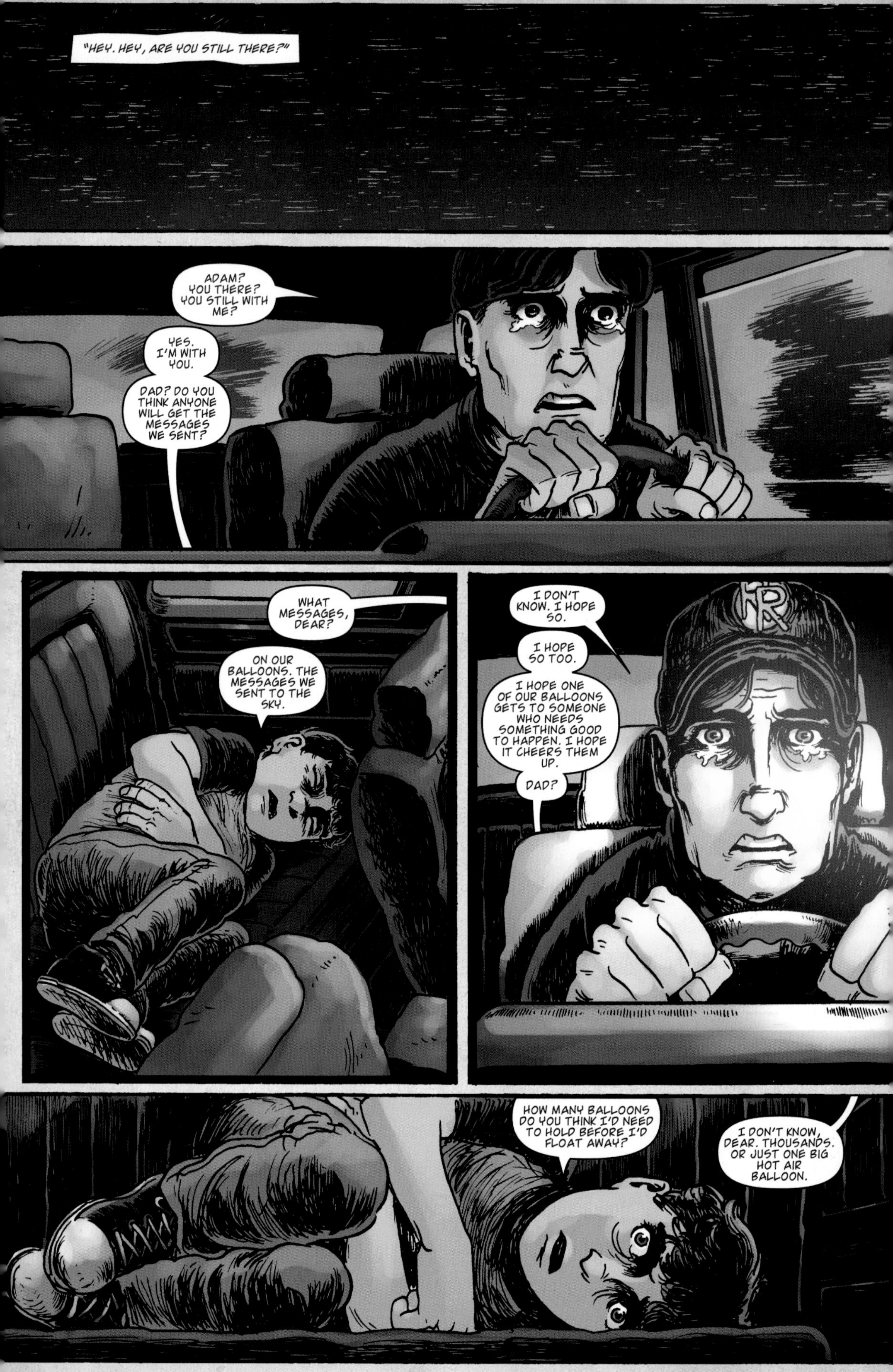
"HEY. HEY, ARE YOU STILL THERE?"
ADAM? YOU THERE? YOU STILL WITH ME?
YES. I'M WITH YOU.
DAD? DO YOU THINK ANYONE WILL GET THE MESSAGES WE SENT?
WHAT MESSAGES, DEAR?
ON OUR BALLOONS. THE MESSAGES WE SENT TO THE SKY.
I DON'T KNOW. I HOPE SO.
I HOPE SO TOO.
I HOPE ONE OF OUR BALLOONS GETS TO SOMEONE WHO NEEDS SOMETHING GOOD TO HAPPEN. I HOPE IT CHEERS THEM UP.
DAD?
HOW MANY BALLOONS DO YOU THINK I'D NEED TO HOLD BEFORE I'D FLOAT AWAY?
I DON'T KNOW, DEAR. THOUSANDS. OR JUST ONE BIG HOT AIR BALLOON.

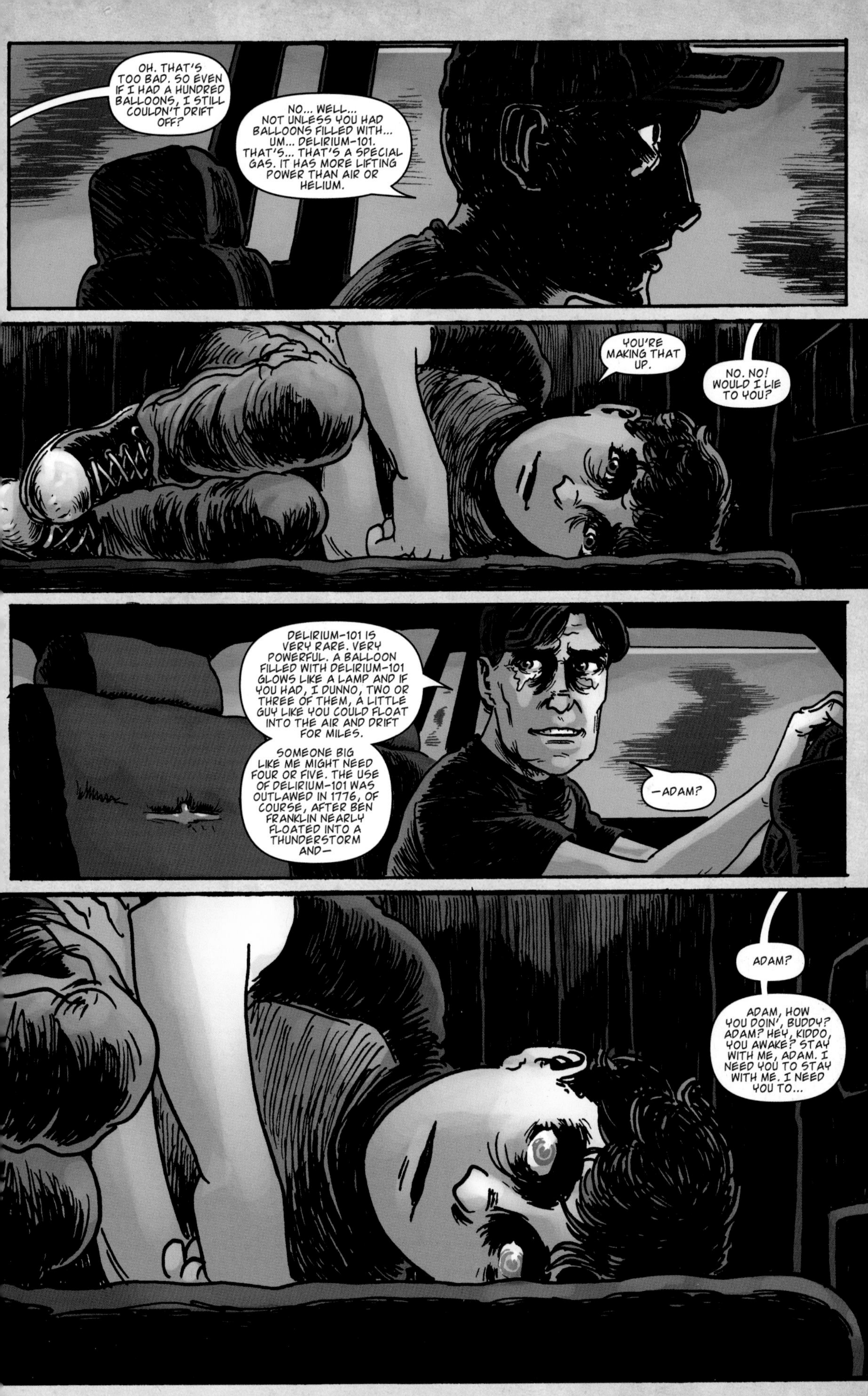
OH. THAT'S TOO BAD. SO EVEN IF I HAD A HUNDRED BALLOONS, I STILL COULDN'T DRIFT OFF?
NO... WELL... NOT UNLESS YOU HAD BALLOONS FILLED WITH... UM... DELIRIUM-101. THAT'S... THAT'S A SPECIAL GAS. IT HAS MORE LIFTING POWER THAN AIR OR HELIUM.
YOU'RE MAKING THAT UP.
NO. NO! WOULD I LIE TO YOU?
DELIRIUM-101 IS VERY RARE. VERY POWERFUL. A BALLOON FILLED WITH DELIRIUM-101 GLOWS LIKE A LAMP AND IF YOU HAD, I DUNNO, TWO OR THREE OF THEM, A LITTLE GUY LIKE YOU COULD FLOAT INTO THE AIR AND DRIFT FOR MILES.
SOMEONE BIG LIKE ME MIGHT NEED FOUR OR FIVE. THE USE OF DELIRIUM-101 WAS OUTLAWED IN 1776, OF COURSE, AFTER BEN FRANKLIN NEARLY FLOATED INTO A THUNDERSTORM AND—
—ADAM?
ADAM?
ADAM, HOW YOU DOIN', BUDDY? ADAM? HEY, KIDDO, YOU AWAKE? STAY WITH ME, ADAM. I NEED YOU TO STAY WITH ME. I NEED YOU TO...

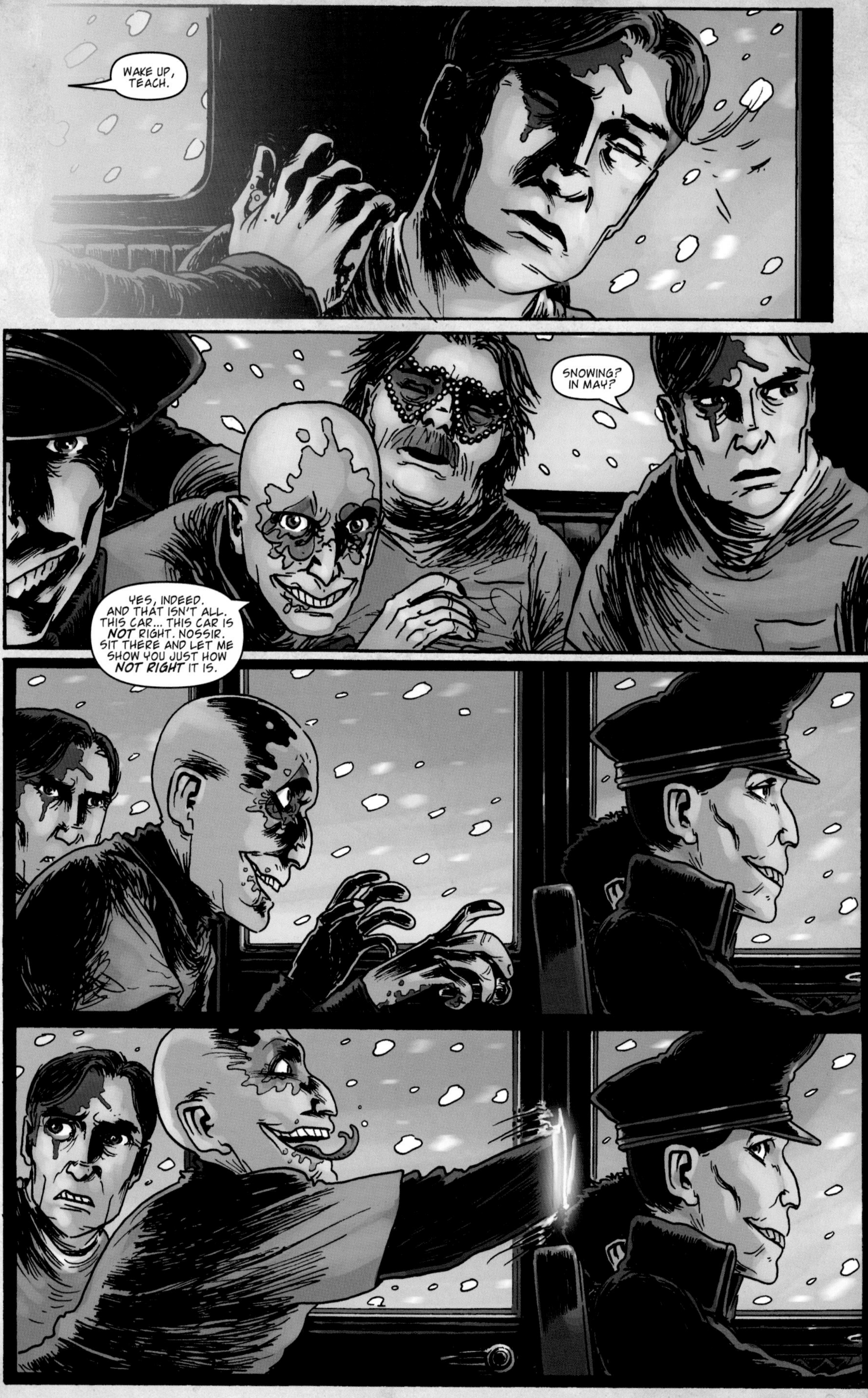
WAKE UP, TEACH.
SNOWING? IN MAY?
YES, INDEED. AND THAT ISN'T ALL. THIS CAR... THIS CAR IS **NOT** RIGHT. NOSSIR. SIT THERE AND LET ME SHOW YOU JUST HOW **NOT RIGHT** IT IS.

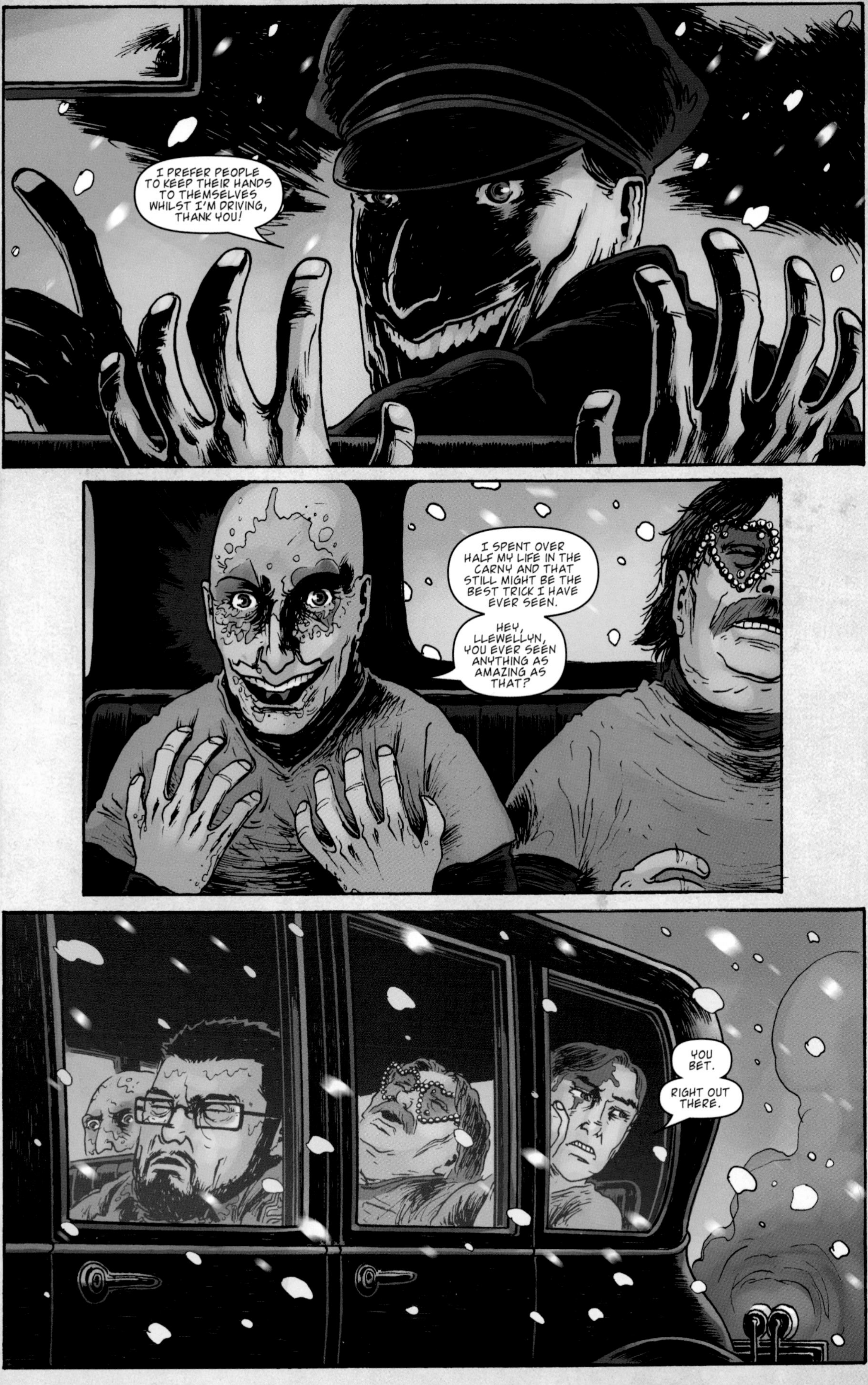
I PREFER PEOPLE TO KEEP THEIR HANDS TO THEMSELVES WHILST I'M DRIVING, THANK YOU!
I SPENT OVER HALF MY LIFE IN THE CARNY AND THAT STILL MIGHT BE THE BEST TRICK I HAVE EVER SEEN.
HEY, LLEWELLYN, YOU EVER SEEN ANYTHING AS AMAZING AS THAT?
YOU BET.
RIGHT OUT THERE.

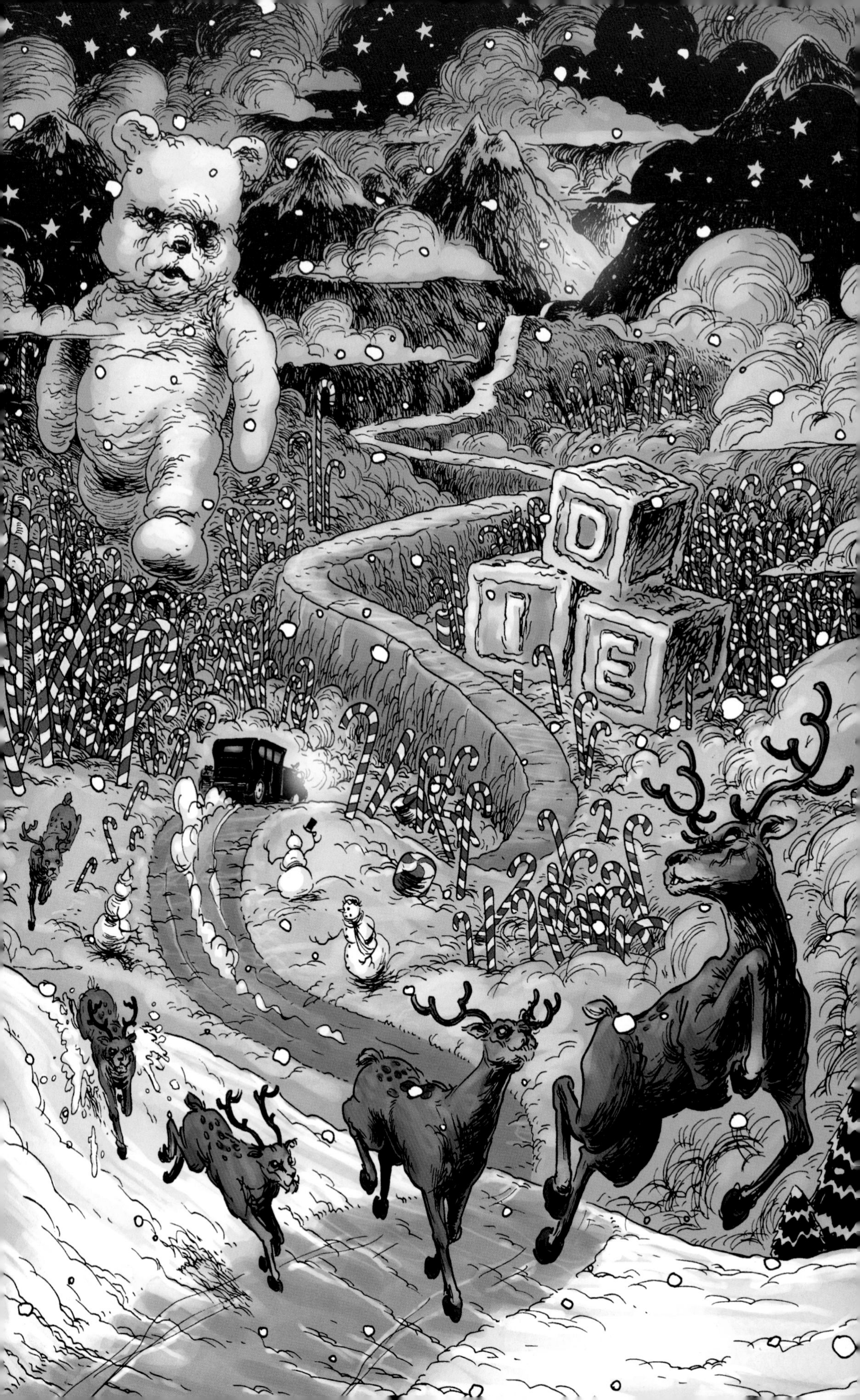
D
I
E

I... TAKE IT FROM YOUR CALM DEMEANOR THAT YOU MEAN TO TELL ME I AM DREAMING.

NO, MAN. I MEAN TO TELL YOU *I'M* DREAMING.

THERE IS ONLY ONE WAY TO SETTLE THIS ARGUMENT! YOU WILL BOTH HAVE TO GO BACK TO SLEEP AND ARGUE ABOUT IT WHEN YOU WAKE UP!

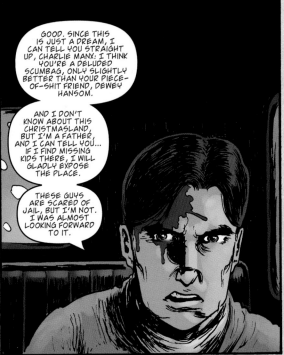

GOOD. SINCE THIS IS JUST A DREAM, I CAN TELL YOU STRAIGHT UP, CHARLIE MANX: I THINK YOU'RE A DELUDED SCUMBAG, ONLY SLIGHTLY BETTER THAN YOUR PIECE-OF-SHIT FRIEND, DEWEY HANSOM.

AND I DON'T KNOW ABOUT THIS CHRISTMASLAND, BUT I'M A FATHER, AND I CAN TELL YOU... IF I FIND MISSING KIDS THERE, I WILL GLADLY EXPOSE THE PLACE.

THESE GUYS ARE SCARED OF JAIL, BUT I'M NOT. I WAS ALMOST LOOKING FORWARD TO IT.

YOU AREN'T A FATHER ANY MORE, CHESS LLEWELLYN.

YOUR BOY DIED WHILE YOU RAN AROUND LIKE A CHICKEN WITH HER HEAD CUT OFF. IT WOULD'VE BEEN BETTER IF THE CHILD WAS WITH *ME*, IN CHRISTMASLAND.

IF HE HAD BEEN ONE OF *MY* CHILDREN, HE WOULDN'T HAVE DIED.

71

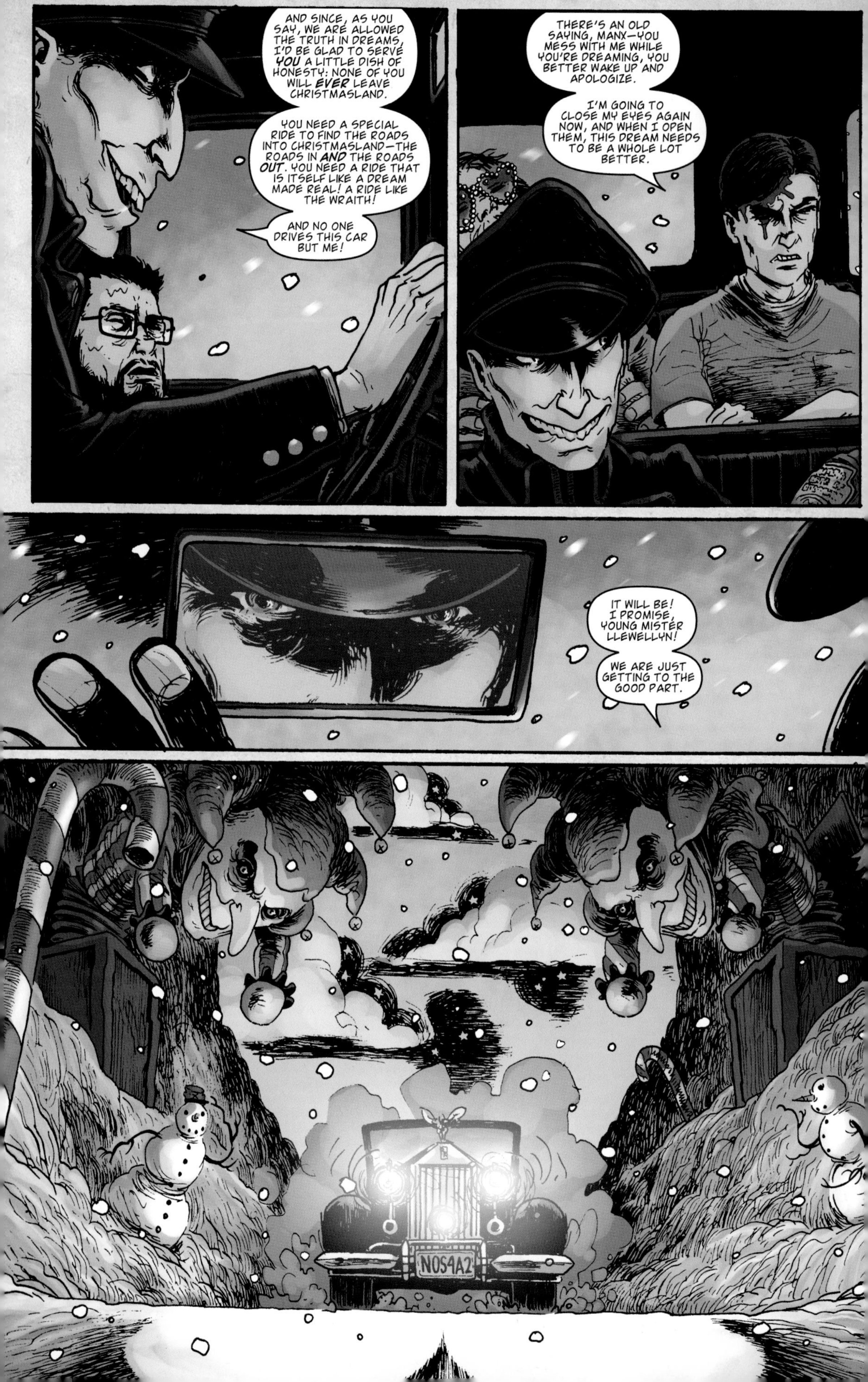
AND SINCE, AS YOU SAY, WE ARE ALLOWED THE TRUTH IN DREAMS, I'D BE GLAD TO SERVE YOU A LITTLE DISH OF HONESTY: NONE OF YOU WILL EVER LEAVE CHRISTMASLAND.
YOU NEED A SPECIAL RIDE TO FIND THE ROADS INTO CHRISTMASLAND—THE ROADS IN AND THE ROADS OUT. YOU NEED A RIDE THAT IS ITSELF LIKE A DREAM MADE REAL! A RIDE LIKE THE WRAITH!
AND NO ONE DRIVES THIS CAR BUT ME!
THERE'S AN OLD SAYING, MANX—YOU MESS WITH ME WHILE YOU'RE DREAMING, YOU BETTER WAKE UP AND APOLOGIZE.
I'M GOING TO CLOSE MY EYES AGAIN NOW, AND WHEN I OPEN THEM, THIS DREAM NEEDS TO BE A WHOLE LOT BETTER.
IT WILL BE! I PROMISE, YOUNG MISTER LLEWELLYN!
WE ARE JUST GETTING TO THE GOOD PART.
NOS4A2

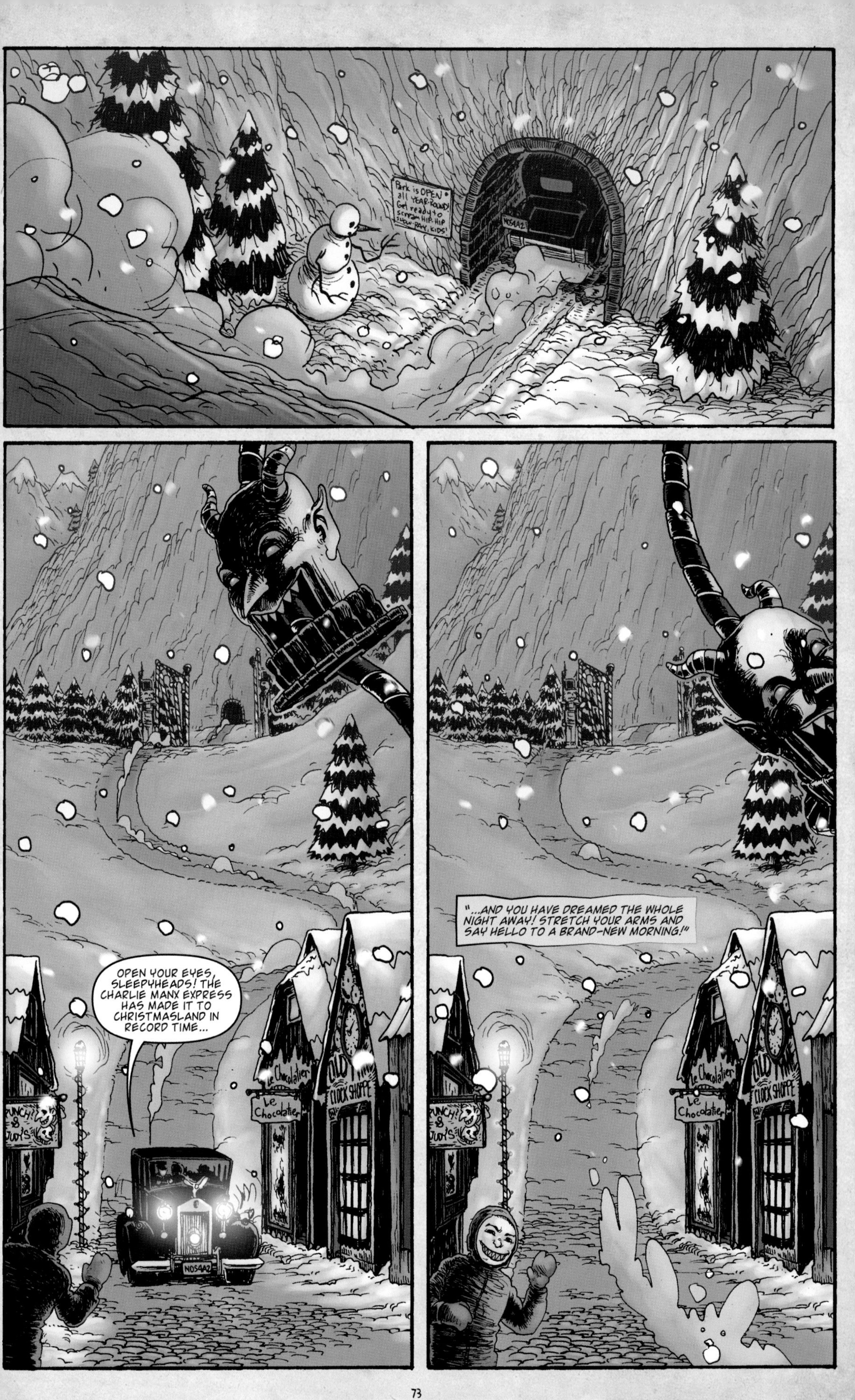

Park is OPEN all YEAR-ROUND! Get ready to scream HIP-HIP SNOW-RAY, KIDS!
NOS4A2
OPEN YOUR EYES, SLEEPYHEADS! THE CHARLIE MANX EXPRESS HAS MADE IT TO CHRISTMASLAND IN RECORD TIME...
PUNCH! & JUDY'S
Le Chocolatier
Le Chocolatier
OLD TIME CLOCK SHOPPE
NOS4A2
"...AND YOU HAVE DREAMED THE WHOLE NIGHT AWAY! STRETCH YOUR ARMS AND SAY HELLO TO A BRAND-NEW MORNING!"

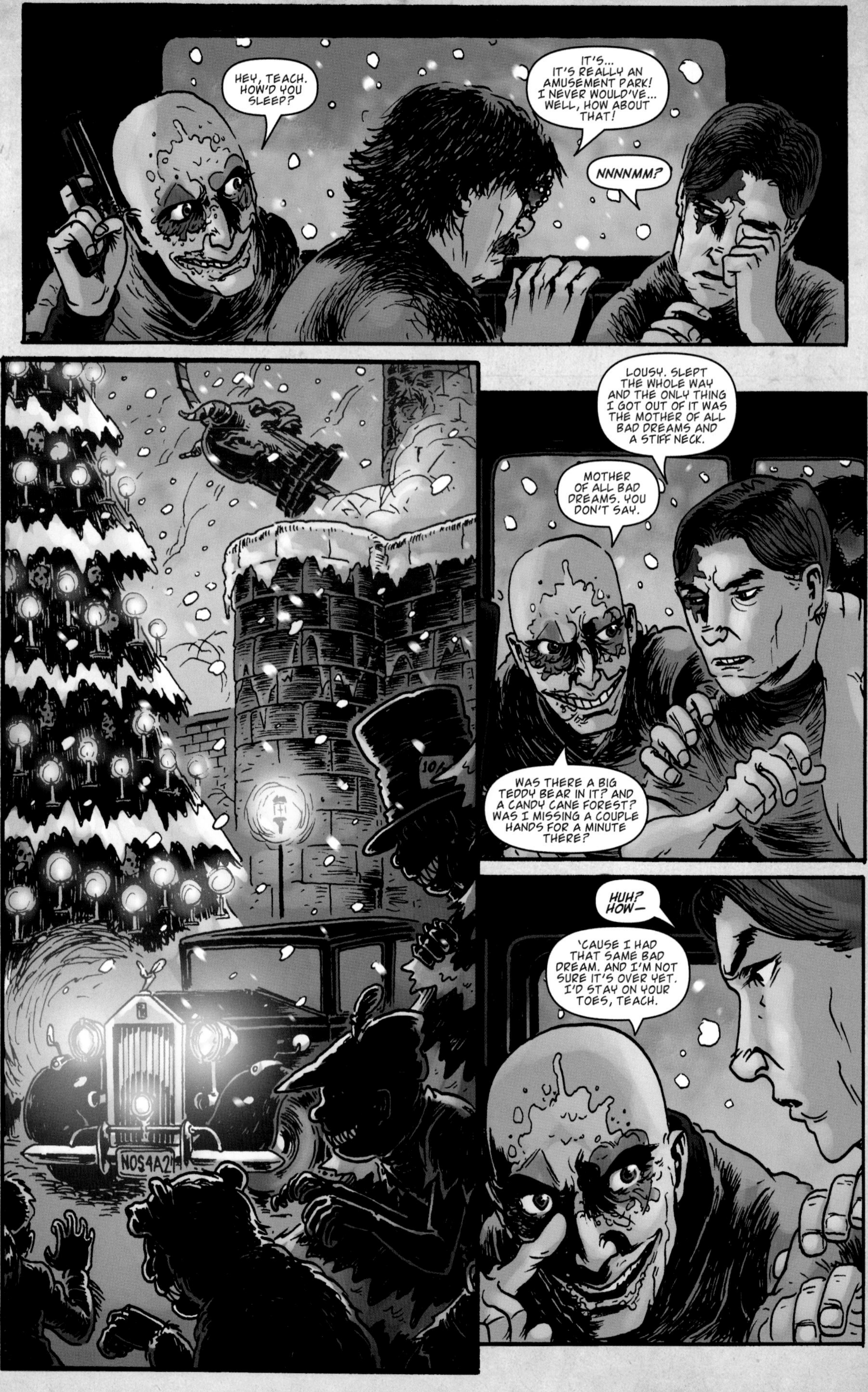
HEY, TEACH. HOW'D YOU SLEEP?
IT'S... IT'S REALLY AN AMUSEMENT PARK! I NEVER WOULD'VE... WELL, HOW ABOUT THAT!
NNNNMM?
LOUSY. SLEPT THE WHOLE WAY AND THE ONLY THING I GOT OUT OF IT WAS THE MOTHER OF ALL BAD DREAMS AND A STIFF NECK.
MOTHER OF ALL BAD DREAMS. YOU DON'T SAY.
WAS THERE A BIG TEDDY BEAR IN IT? AND A CANDY CANE FOREST? WAS I MISSING A COUPLE HANDS FOR A MINUTE THERE?
NOS4A2
HUH? HOW—
'CAUSE I HAD THAT SAME BAD DREAM. AND I'M NOT SURE IT'S OVER YET. I'D STAY ON YOUR TOES, TEACH.

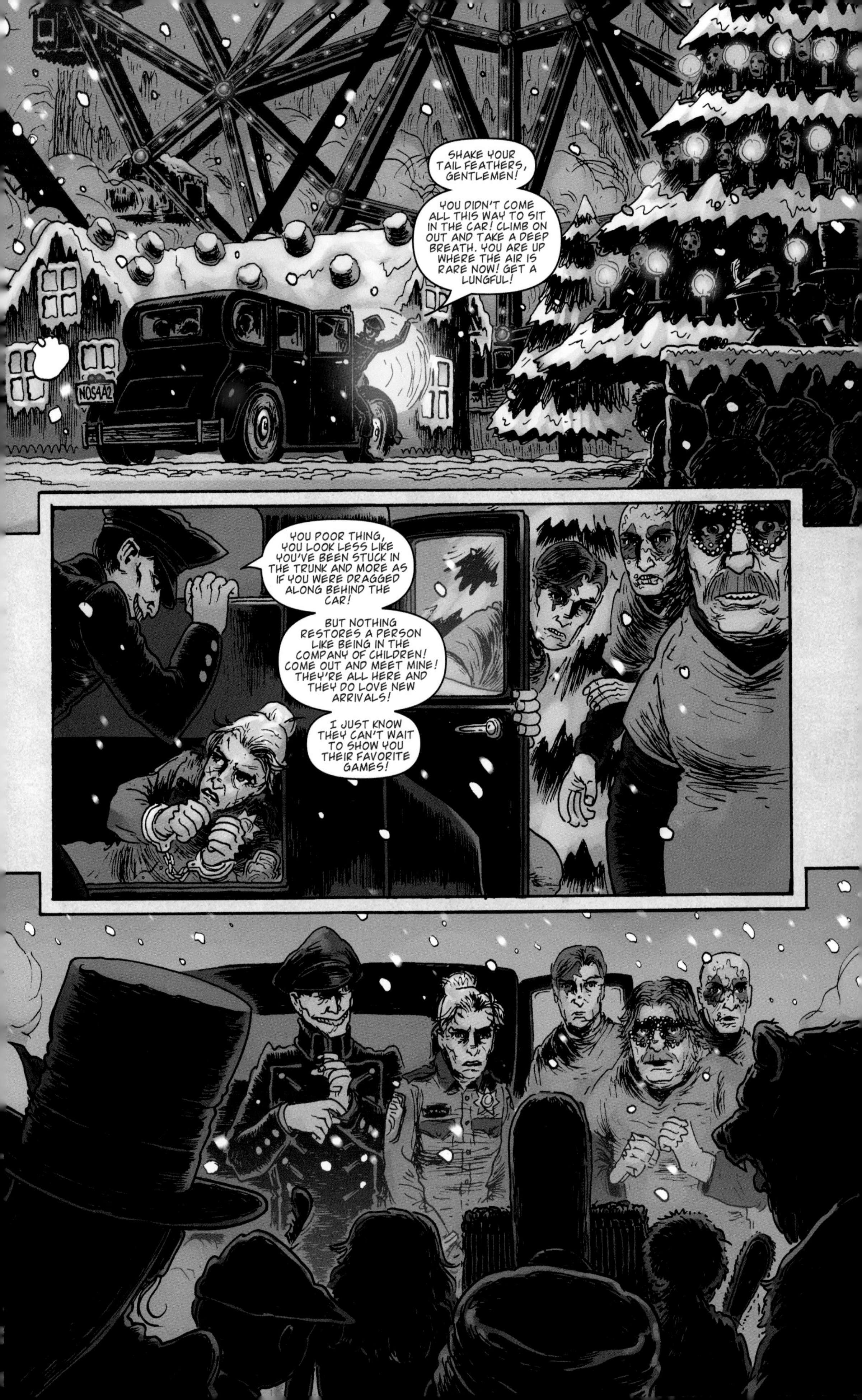
SHAKE YOUR TAIL FEATHERS, GENTLEMEN!
YOU DIDN'T COME ALL THIS WAY TO SIT IN THE CAR! CLIMB ON OUT AND TAKE A DEEP BREATH. YOU ARE UP WHERE THE AIR IS RARE NOW! GET A LUNGFUL!
NOS4A2
YOU POOR THING, YOU LOOK LESS LIKE YOU'VE BEEN STUCK IN THE TRUNK AND MORE AS IF YOU WERE DRAGGED ALONG BEHIND THE CAR!
BUT NOTHING RESTORES A PERSON LIKE BEING IN THE COMPANY OF CHILDREN! COME OUT AND MEET MINE! THEY'RE ALL HERE AND THEY DO LOVE NEW ARRIVALS!
I JUST KNOW THEY CAN'T WAIT TO SHOW YOU THEIR FAVORITE GAMES!

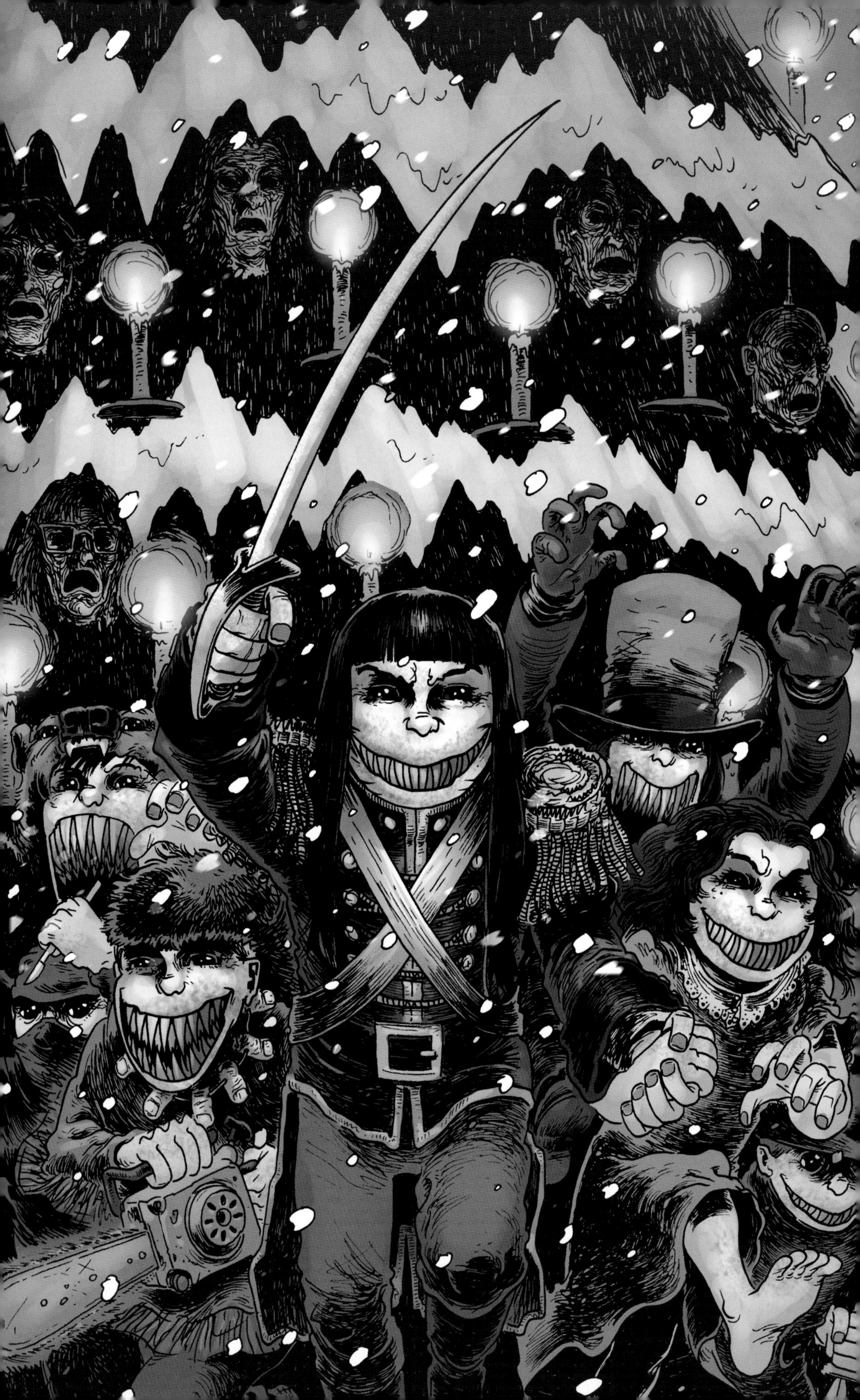

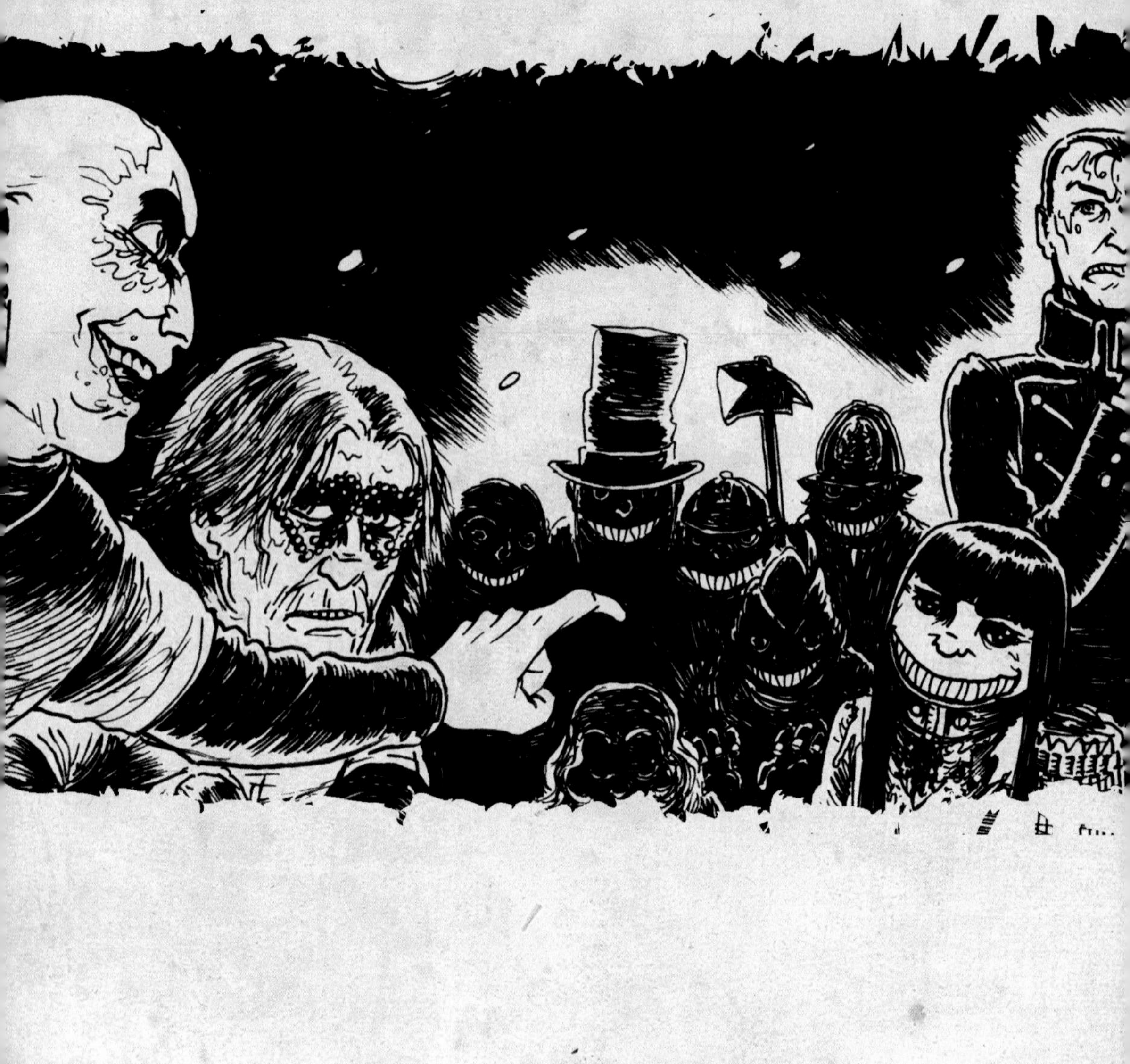

WELCOME TO CHRISTMASLAND chapter three

FASTBALL

MY PRETTIES!

NOS4A2

WHO HAS SOME SUGAR FOR DADDY?!?

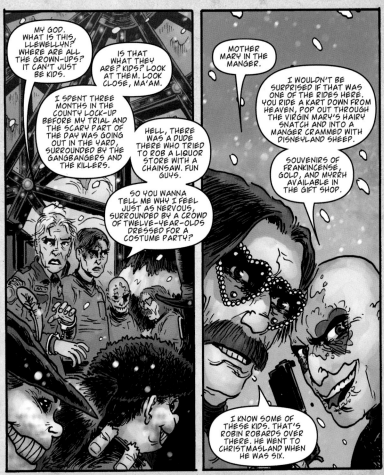

MY GOD. WHAT IS THIS, LLEWELLYN? WHERE ARE ALL THE GROWN-UPS? IT CAN'T JUST BE KIDS.

IS THAT WHAT THEY ARE? KIDS? LOOK AT THEM. LOOK CLOSE, MA'AM.

I SPENT THREE MONTHS IN THE COUNTY LOCK-UP BEFORE MY TRIAL AND THE SCARY PART OF THE DAY WAS GOING OUT IN THE YARD, SURROUNDED BY THE GANGBANGERS AND THE KILLERS.

HELL, THERE WAS A DUDE THERE WHO TRIED TO ROB A LIQUOR STORE WITH A CHAINSAW. FUN GUYS.

SO YOU WANNA TELL ME WHY I FEEL JUST AS NERVOUS, SURROUNDED BY A CROWD OF TWELVE-YEAR-OLDS DRESSED FOR A COSTUME PARTY?

MOTHER MARY IN THE MANGER.

I WOULDN'T BE SURPRISED IF THAT WAS ONE OF THE RIDES HERE. YOU RIDE A KART DOWN FROM HEAVEN, POP OUT THROUGH THE VIRGIN MARY'S HAIRY SNATCH AND INTO A MANGER CRAMMED WITH DISNEYLAND SHEEP.

SOUVENIRS OF FRANKINCENSE, GOLD, AND MYRRH AVAILABLE IN THE GIFT SHOP.

I KNOW SOME OF THESE KIDS. THAT'S ROBIN ROBARDS OVER THERE. HE WENT TO CHRISTMASLAND WHEN HE WAS SIX.

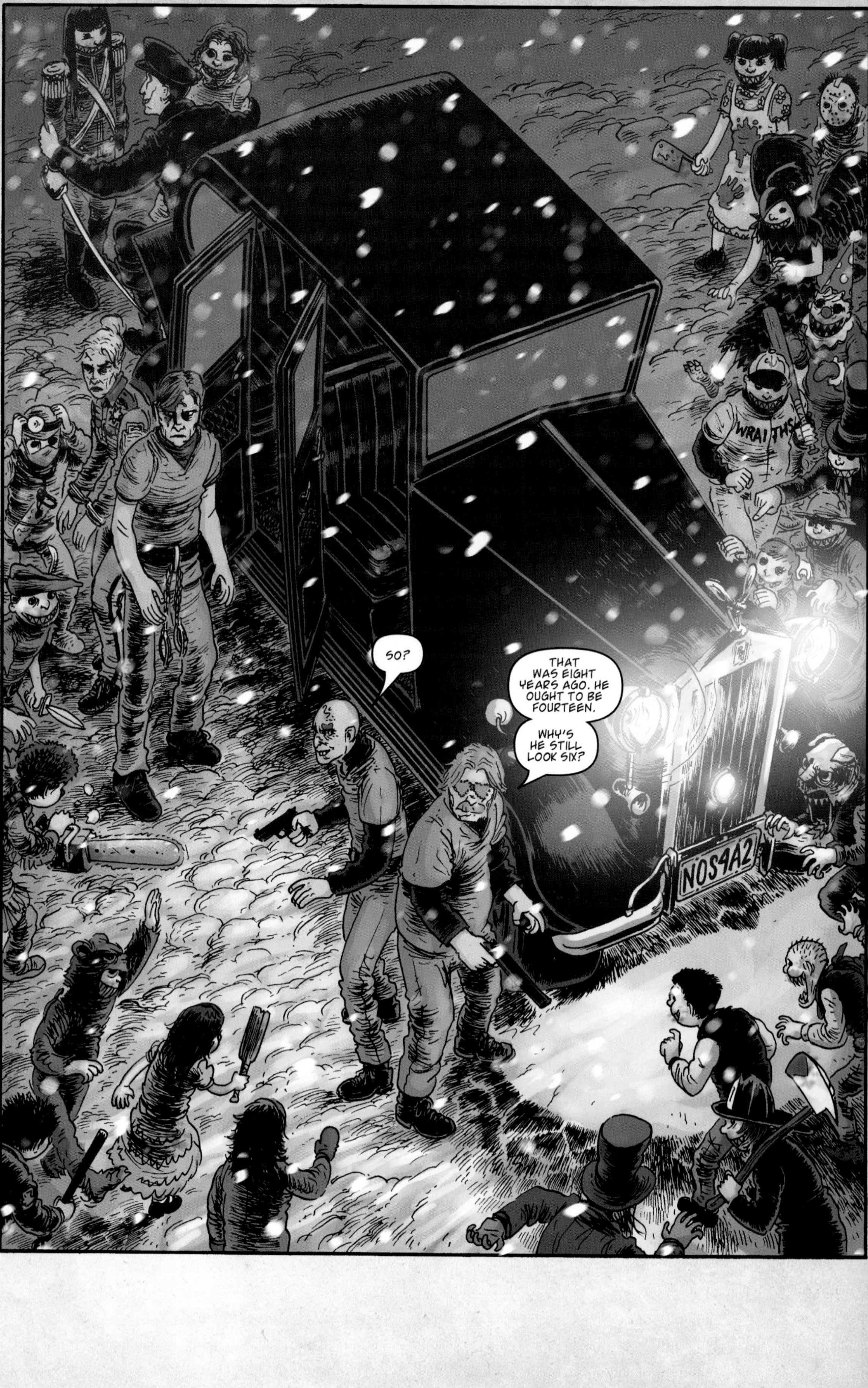
WRAITHS
SO?
THAT WAS EIGHT YEARS AGO. HE OUGHT TO BE FOURTEEN.
WHY'S HE STILL LOOK SIX?
NOS4A2

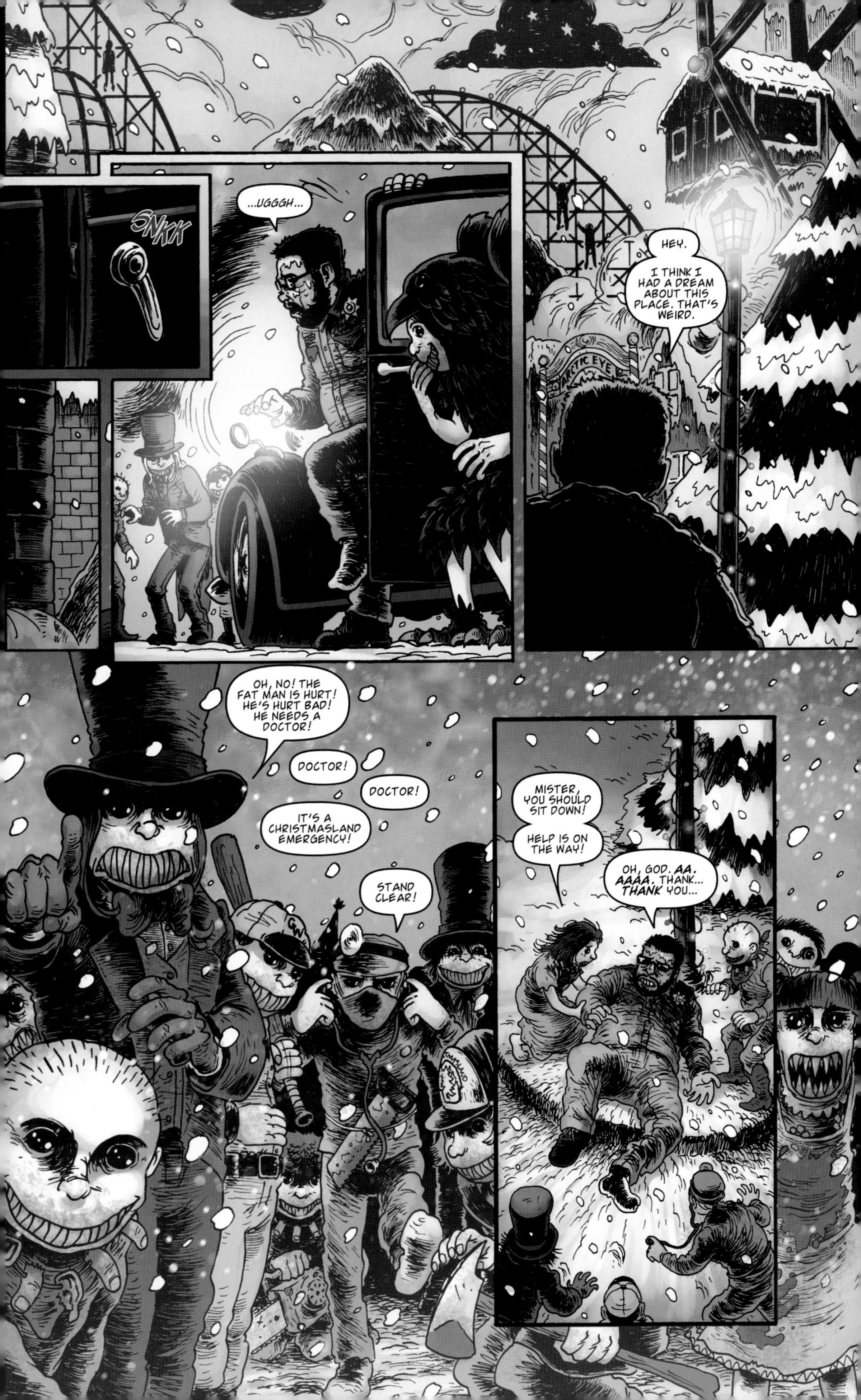
SNKK
...UGGGH...
HEY.
I THINK I HAD A DREAM ABOUT THIS PLACE. THAT'S WEIRD.
ARCTIC EYE
OH, NO! THE FAT MAN IS HURT! HE'S HURT BAD! HE NEEDS A DOCTOR!
DOCTOR!
DOCTOR!
IT'S A CHRISTMASLAND EMERGENCY!
STAND CLEAR!
MISTER, YOU SHOULD SIT DOWN!
HELP IS ON THE WAY!
OH, GOD. **AA. AAAA.** THANK... **THANK** YOU...

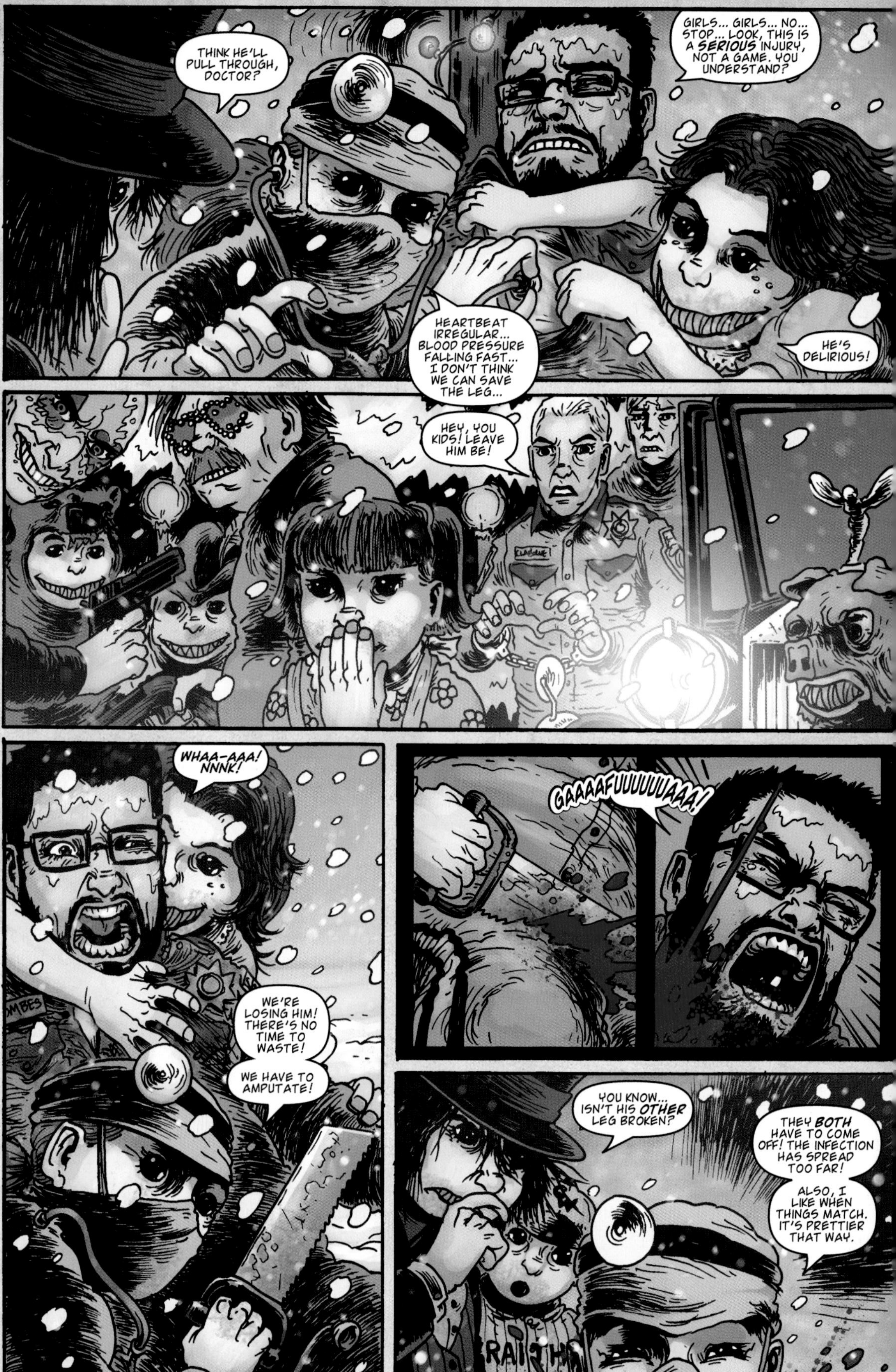
THINK HE'LL PULL THROUGH, DOCTOR?
GIRLS... GIRLS... NO... STOP... LOOK, THIS IS A SERIOUS INJURY, NOT A GAME. YOU UNDERSTAND?
HEARTBEAT IRREGULAR... BLOOD PRESSURE FALLING FAST... I DON'T THINK WE CAN SAVE THE LEG...
HE'S DELIRIOUS!
HEY, YOU KIDS! LEAVE HIM BE!
WHAA-AAA! NNNK!
WE'RE LOSING HIM! THERE'S NO TIME TO WASTE!
WE HAVE TO AMPUTATE!
GAAAAFUUUUUUAAA!
YOU KNOW... ISN'T HIS OTHER LEG BROKEN?
THEY BOTH HAVE TO COME OFF! THE INFECTION HAS SPREAD TOO FAR!
ALSO, I LIKE WHEN THINGS MATCH. IT'S PRETTIER THAT WAY.

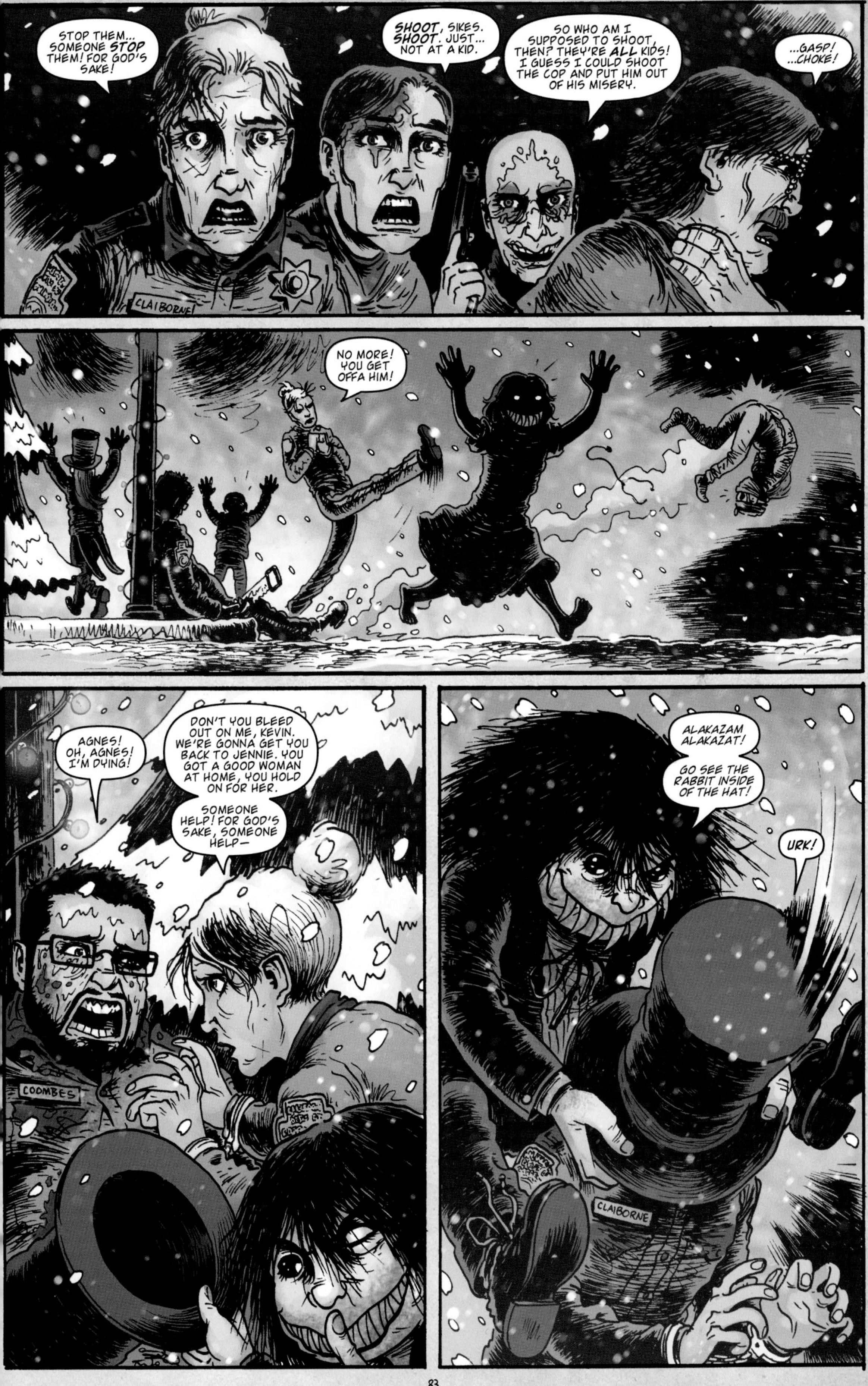
STOP THEM... SOMEONE STOP THEM! FOR GOD'S SAKE!
SHOOT, SIKES. SHOOT. JUST... NOT AT A KID.
SO WHO AM I SUPPOSED TO SHOOT, THEN? THEY'RE ALL KIDS! I GUESS I COULD SHOOT THE COP AND PUT HIM OUT OF HIS MISERY.
...GASP! ...CHOKE!
CLAIBORNE
NO MORE! YOU GET OFFA HIM!
AGNES! OH, AGNES! I'M DYING!
DON'T YOU BLEED OUT ON ME, KEVIN. WE'RE GONNA GET YOU BACK TO JENNIE. YOU GOT A GOOD WOMAN AT HOME, YOU HOLD ON FOR HER.
SOMEONE HELP! FOR GOD'S SAKE, SOMEONE HELP—
COOMBES
ALAKAZAM ALAKAZAT!
GO SEE THE RABBIT INSIDE OF THE HAT!
URK!
CLAIBORNE

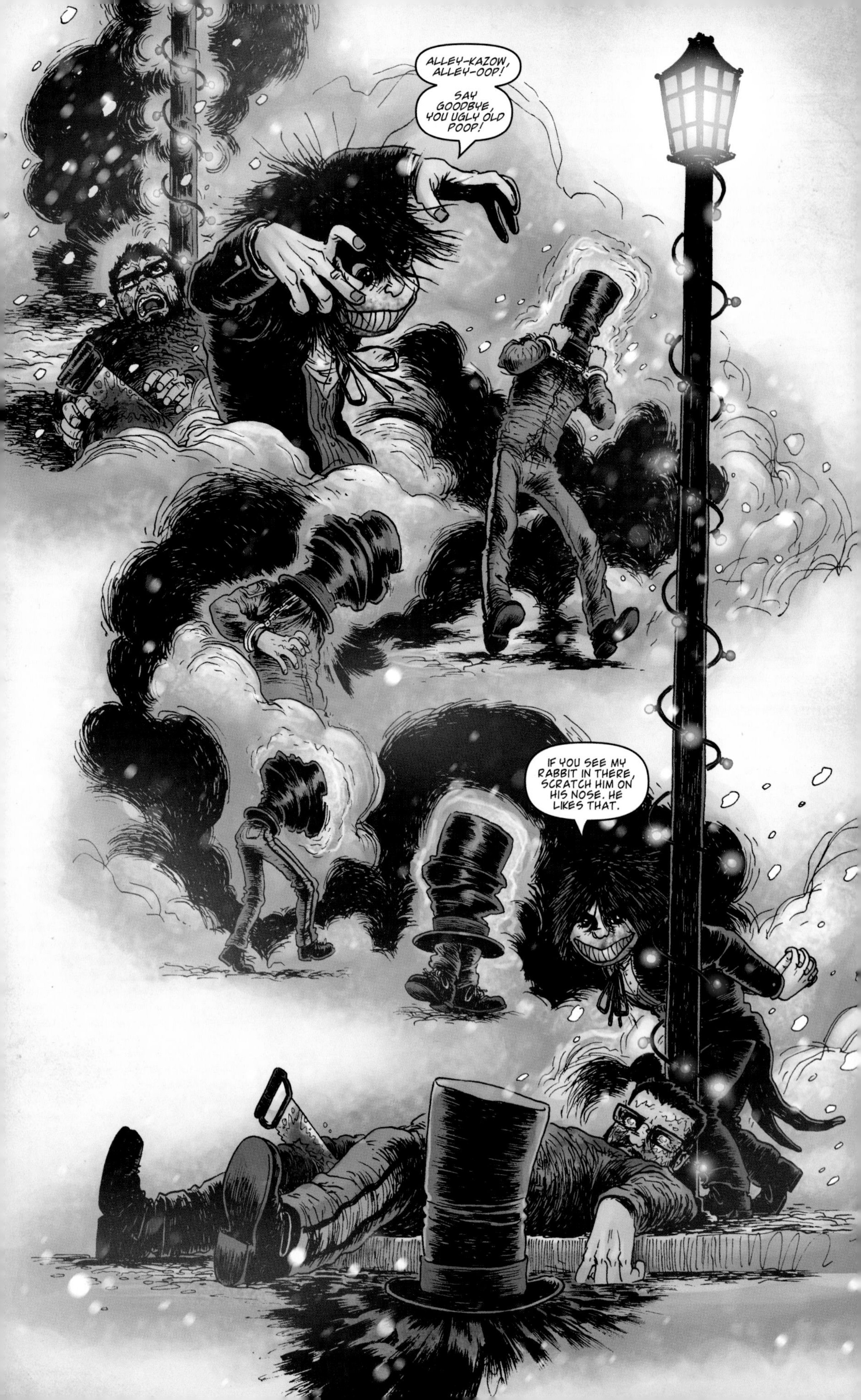
ALLEY-KAZOW, ALLEY-OOP!
SAY GOODBYE, YOU UGLY OLD POOP!
IF YOU SEE MY RABBIT IN THERE, SCRATCH HIM ON HIS NOSE. HE LIKES THAT.

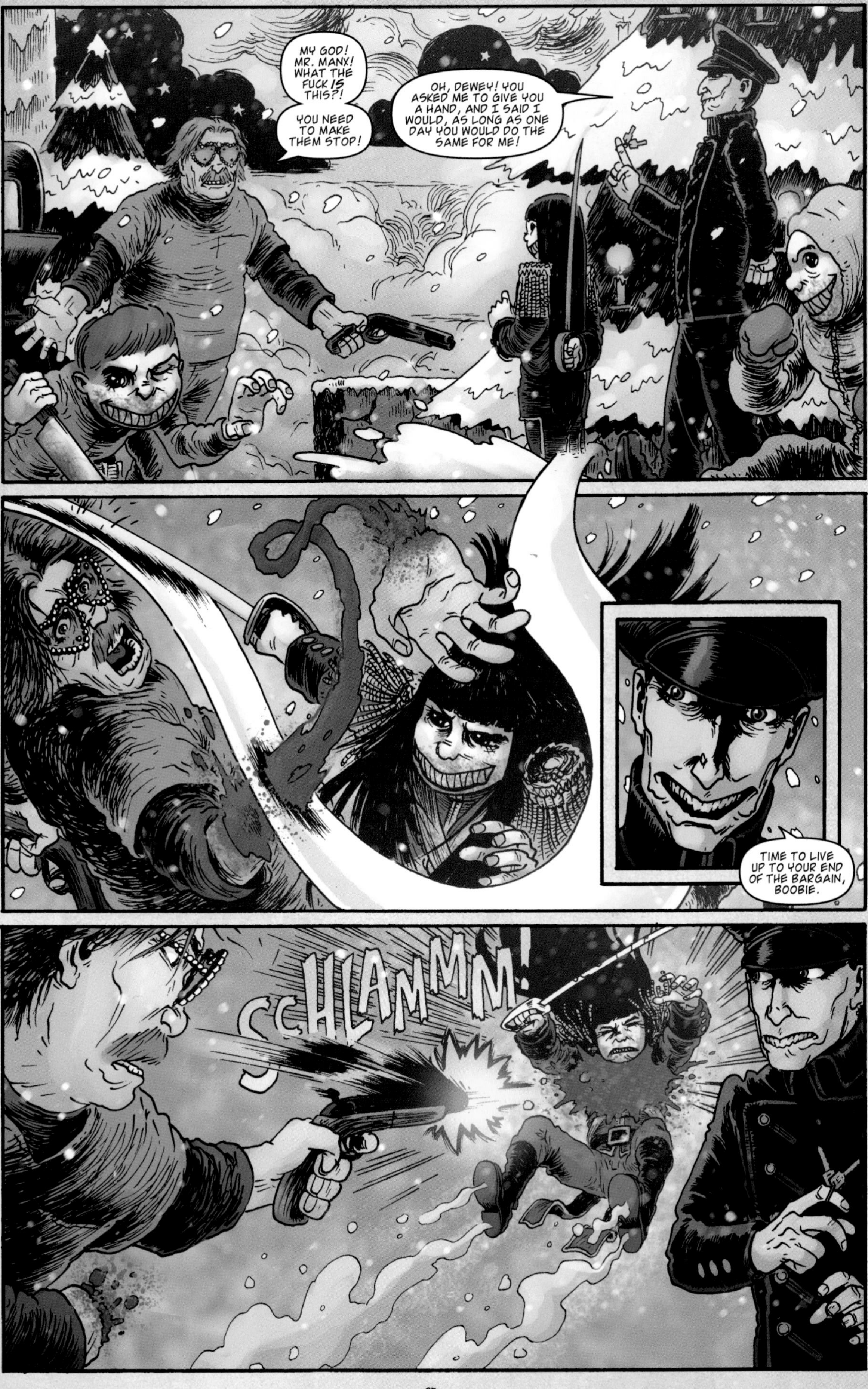
MY GOD! MR. MANX! WHAT THE FUCK IS THIS?!
YOU NEED TO MAKE THEM STOP!
OH, DEWEY! YOU ASKED ME TO GIVE YOU A HAND, AND I SAID I WOULD, AS LONG AS ONE DAY YOU WOULD DO THE SAME FOR ME!
TIME TO LIVE UP TO YOUR END OF THE BARGAIN, BOOBIE.
SCHLAMMM!

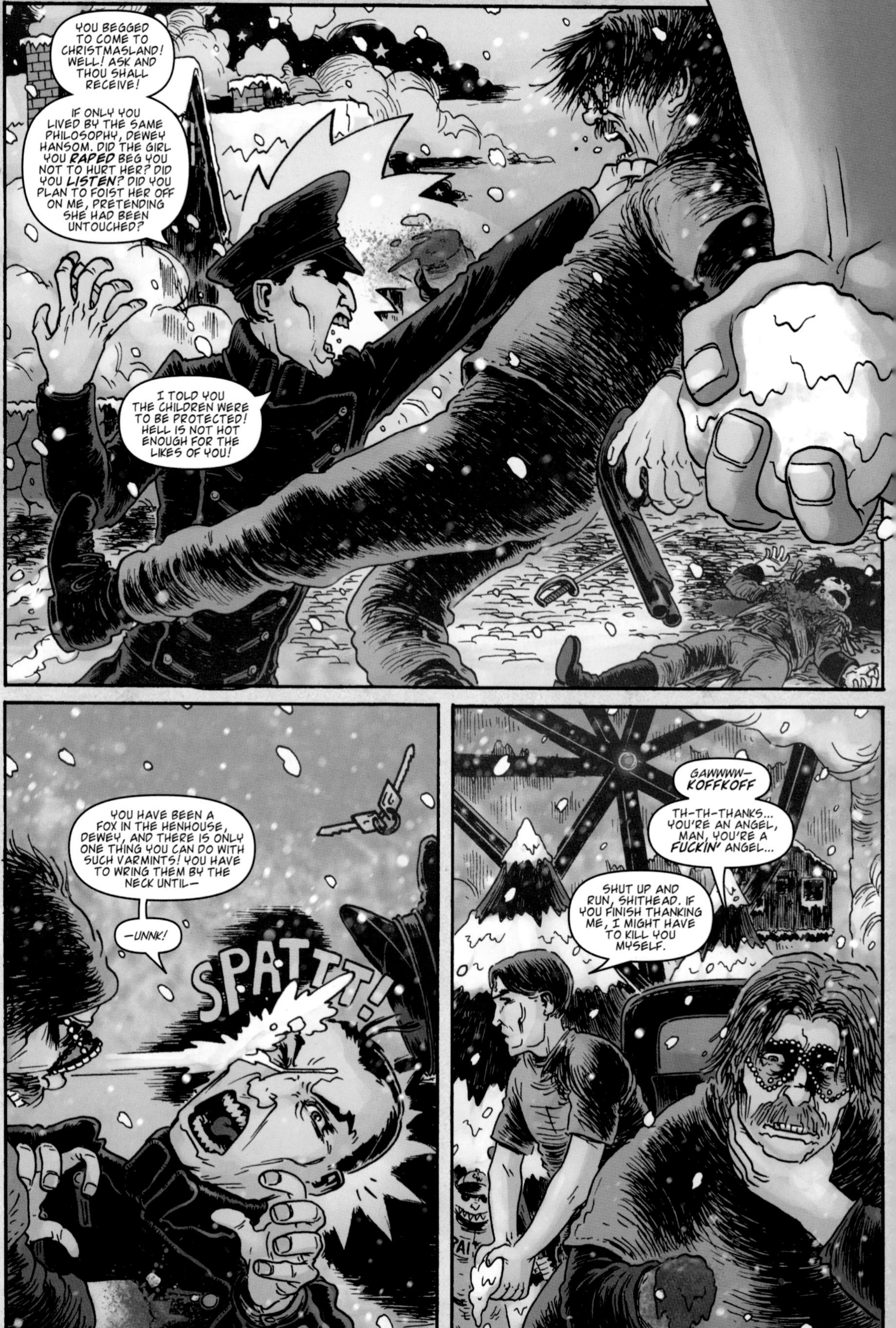
YOU BEGGED TO COME TO CHRISTMASLAND! WELL! ASK AND THOU SHALL RECEIVE!
IF ONLY YOU LIVED BY THE SAME PHILOSOPHY, DEWEY HANSOM. DID THE GIRL YOU RAPED BEG YOU NOT TO HURT HER? DID YOU LISTEN? DID YOU PLAN TO FOIST HER OFF ON ME, PRETENDING SHE HAD BEEN UNTOUCHED?
I TOLD YOU THE CHILDREN WERE TO BE PROTECTED! HELL IS NOT HOT ENOUGH FOR THE LIKES OF YOU!
YOU HAVE BEEN A FOX IN THE HENHOUSE, DEWEY, AND THERE IS ONLY ONE THING YOU CAN DO WITH SUCH VARMINTS! YOU HAVE TO WRING THEM BY THE NECK UNTIL—
—UNNK!
SPATTT!
GAWWWW— KOFFKOFF
TH-TH-THANKS... YOU'RE AN ANGEL, MAN, YOU'RE A FUCKIN' ANGEL...
SHUT UP AND RUN, SHITHEAD. IF YOU FINISH THANKING ME, I MIGHT HAVE TO KILL YOU MYSELF.

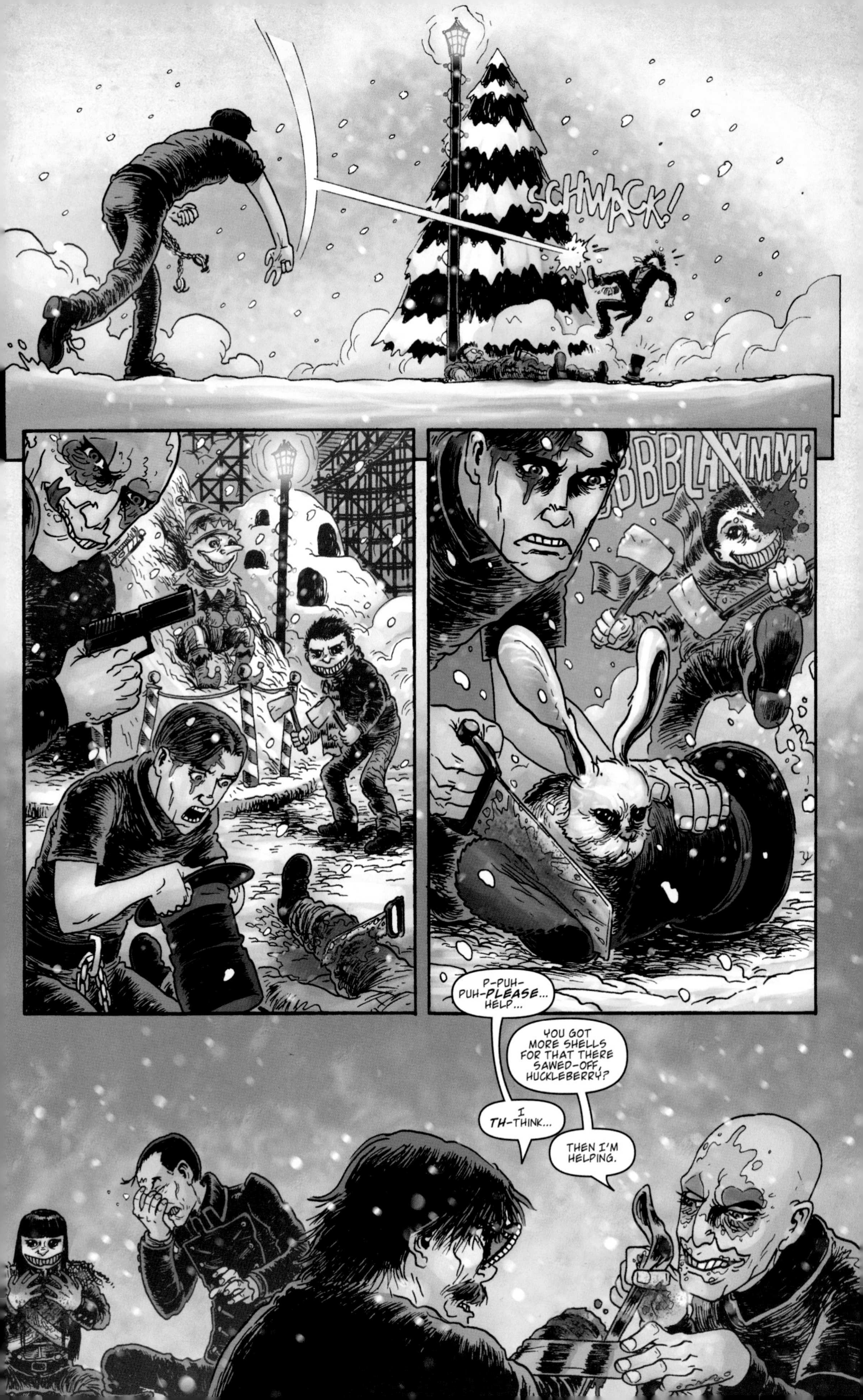
SCHWACK!
BBBLAMMM!
P-PUH-PUH-PLEASE... HELP...
YOU GOT MORE SHELLS FOR THAT THERE SAWED-OFF, HUCKLEBERRY?
I TH-THINK...
THEN I'M HELPING.

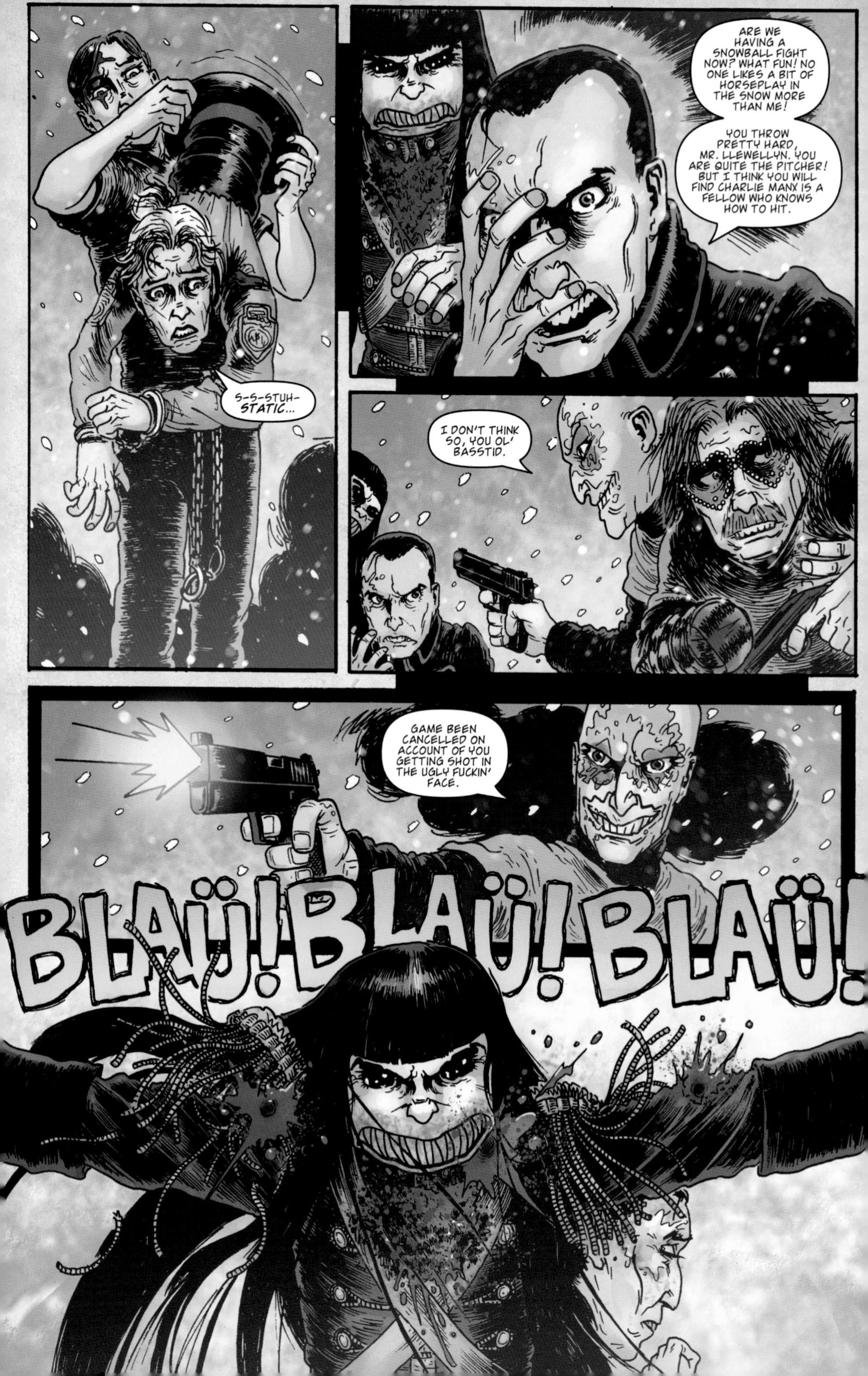
S-S-STUH-STATIC...
ARE WE HAVING A SNOWBALL FIGHT NOW? WHAT FUN! NO ONE LIKES A BIT OF HORSEPLAY IN THE SNOW MORE THAN ME!
YOU THROW PRETTY HARD, MR. LLEWELLYN. YOU ARE QUITE THE PITCHER! BUT I THINK YOU WILL FIND CHARLIE MANX IS A FELLOW WHO KNOWS HOW TO HIT.
I DON'T THINK SO, YOU OL' BASSTID.
GAME BEEN CANCELLED ON ACCOUNT OF YOU GETTING SHOT IN THE UGLY FUCKIN' FACE.
BLAÜ! BLAÜ! BLAÜ!

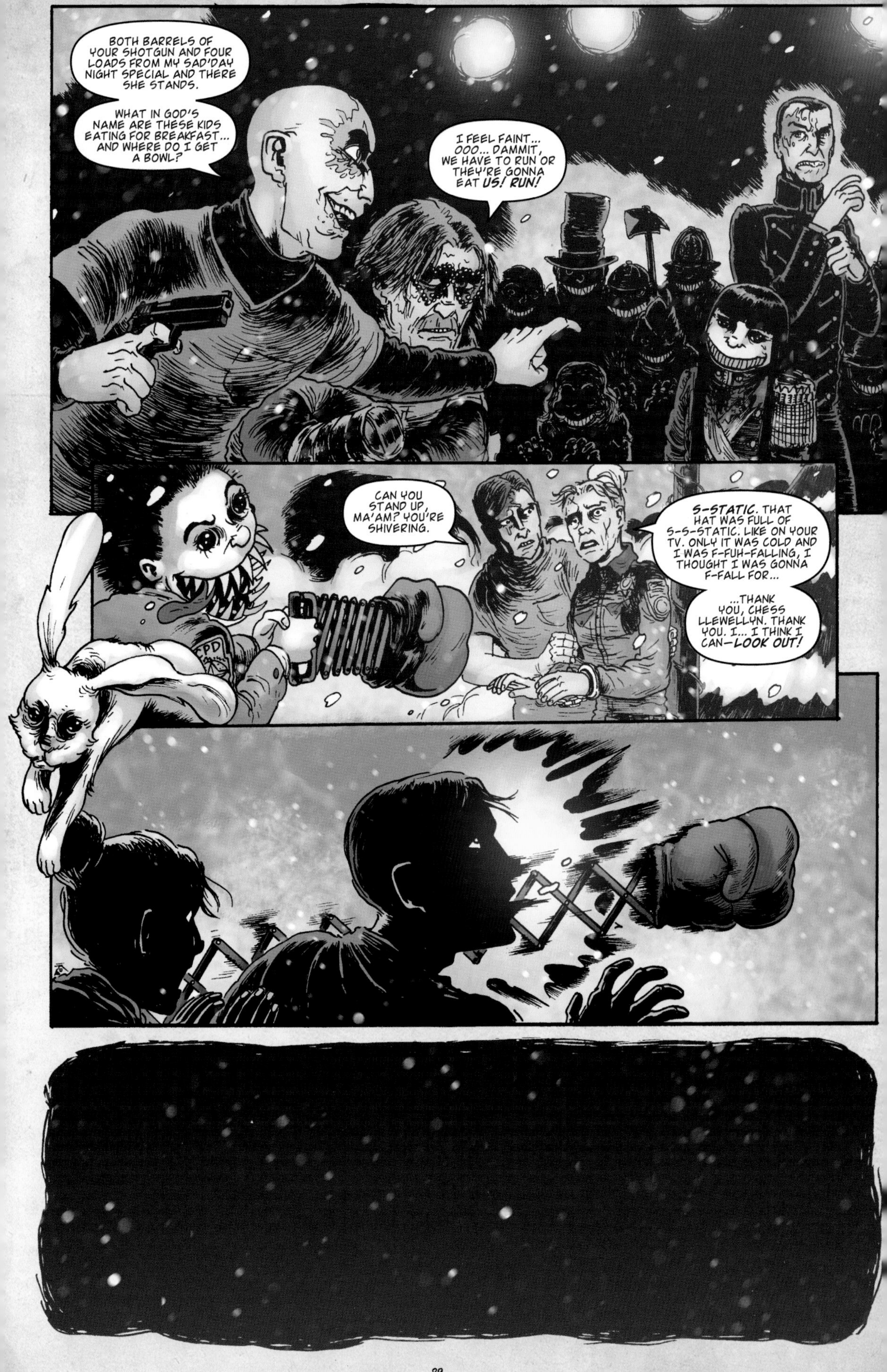
BOTH BARRELS OF YOUR SHOTGUN AND FOUR LOADS FROM MY SAD'DAY NIGHT SPECIAL AND THERE SHE STANDS.
WHAT IN GOD'S NAME ARE THESE KIDS EATING FOR BREAKFAST... AND WHERE DO I GET A BOWL?
I FEEL FAINT... OOO... DAMMIT, WE HAVE TO RUN OR THEY'RE GONNA EAT US! RUN!
CAN YOU STAND UP, MA'AM? YOU'RE SHIVERING.
S-STATIC. THAT HAT WAS FULL OF S-S-STATIC. LIKE ON YOUR TV. ONLY IT WAS COLD AND I WAS F-FUH-FALLING, I THOUGHT I WAS GONNA F-FALL FOR...
...THANK YOU, CHESS LLEWELLYN. THANK YOU. I... I THINK I CAN—LOOK OUT!

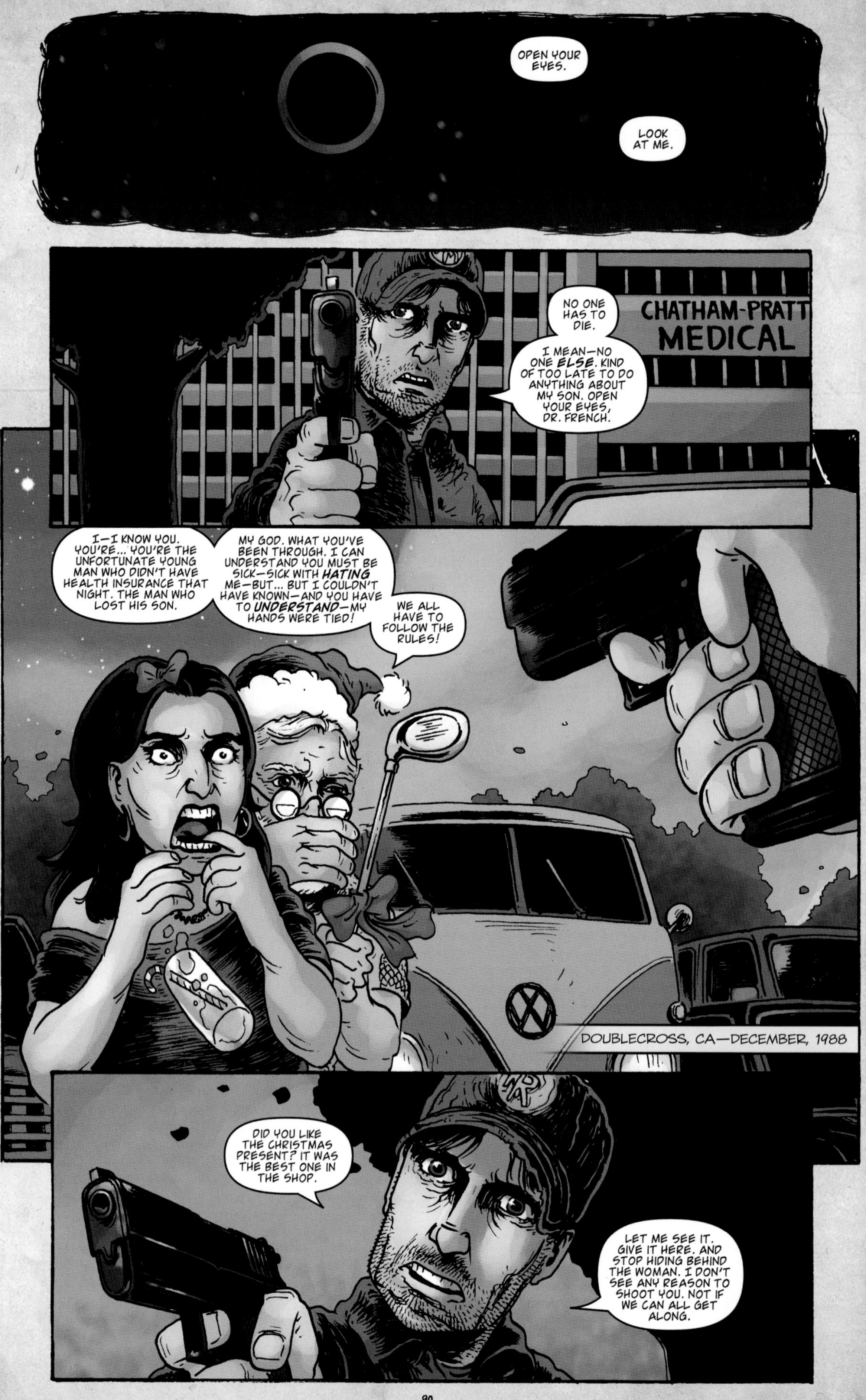
OPEN YOUR EYES.
LOOK AT ME.
NO ONE HAS TO DIE.
CHATHAM-PRATT MEDICAL
I MEAN—NO ONE ELSE. KIND OF TOO LATE TO DO ANYTHING ABOUT MY SON. OPEN YOUR EYES, DR. FRENCH.
I—I KNOW YOU. YOU'RE... YOU'RE THE UNFORTUNATE YOUNG MAN WHO DIDN'T HAVE HEALTH INSURANCE THAT NIGHT. THE MAN WHO LOST HIS SON.
MY GOD. WHAT YOU'VE BEEN THROUGH. I CAN UNDERSTAND YOU MUST BE SICK—SICK WITH HATING ME—BUT... BUT I COULDN'T HAVE KNOWN—AND YOU HAVE TO UNDERSTAND—MY HANDS WERE TIED!
WE ALL HAVE TO FOLLOW THE RULES!
DOUBLECROSS, CA—DECEMBER, 1988
DID YOU LIKE THE CHRISTMAS PRESENT? IT WAS THE BEST ONE IN THE SHOP.
LET ME SEE IT. GIVE IT HERE. AND STOP HIDING BEHIND THE WOMAN. I DON'T SEE ANY REASON TO SHOOT YOU. NOT IF WE CAN ALL GET ALONG.

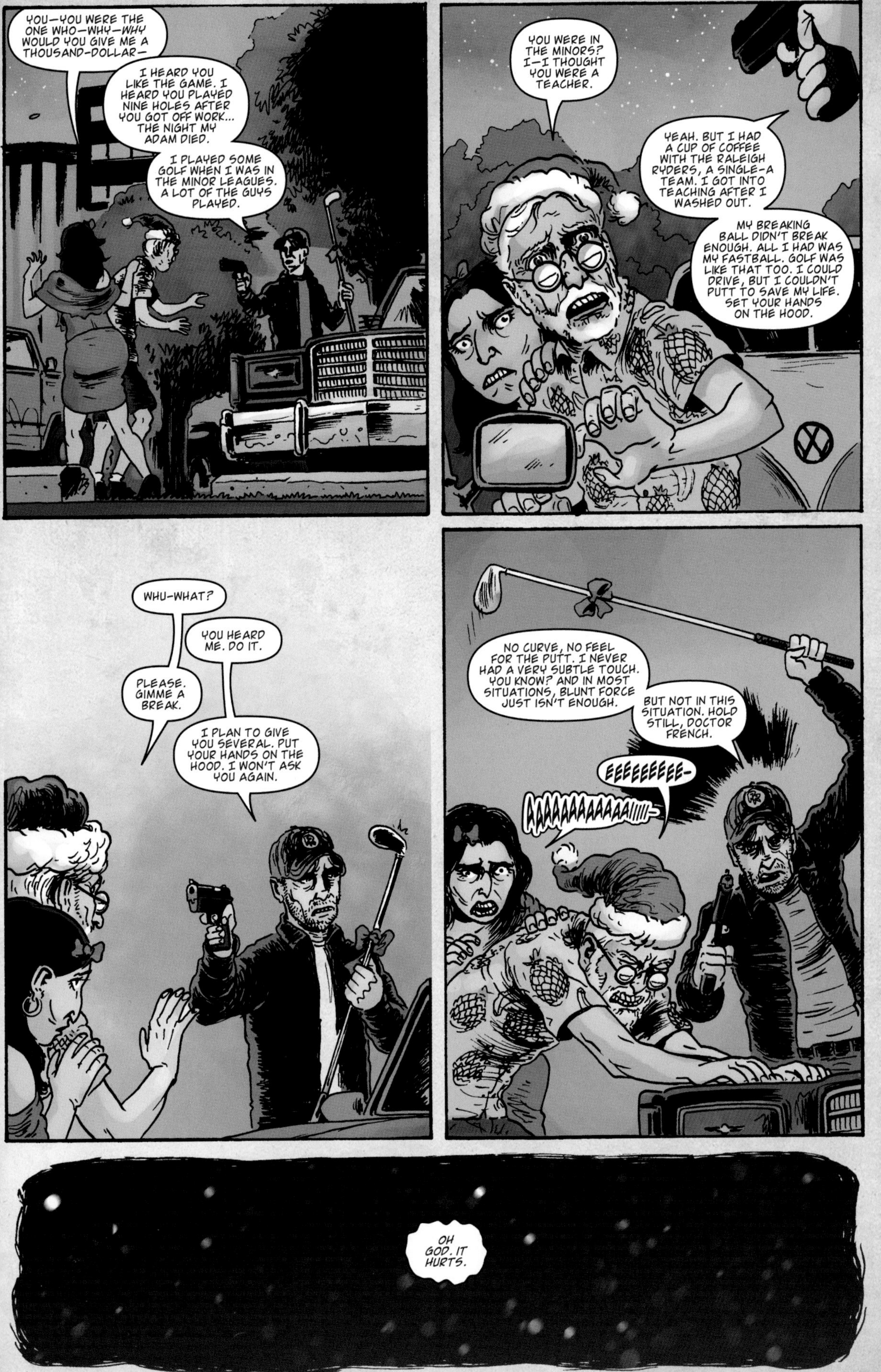
YOU—YOU WERE THE ONE WHO—WHY—WHY WOULD YOU GIVE ME A THOUSAND-DOLLAR—
I HEARD YOU LIKE THE GAME. I HEARD YOU PLAYED NINE HOLES AFTER YOU GOT OFF WORK... THE NIGHT MY ADAM DIED.
I PLAYED SOME GOLF WHEN I WAS IN THE MINOR LEAGUES. A LOT OF THE GUYS PLAYED.
YOU WERE IN THE MINORS? I—I THOUGHT YOU WERE A TEACHER.
YEAH. BUT I HAD A CUP OF COFFEE WITH THE RALEIGH RYDERS, A SINGLE-A TEAM. I GOT INTO TEACHING AFTER I WASHED OUT.
MY BREAKING BALL DIDN'T BREAK ENOUGH. ALL I HAD WAS MY FASTBALL. GOLF WAS LIKE THAT TOO. I COULD DRIVE, BUT I COULDN'T PUTT TO SAVE MY LIFE. SET YOUR HANDS ON THE HOOD.
WHU-WHAT?
YOU HEARD ME. DO IT.
PLEASE. GIMME A BREAK.
I PLAN TO GIVE YOU SEVERAL. PUT YOUR HANDS ON THE HOOD. I WON'T ASK YOU AGAIN.
NO CURVE, NO FEEL FOR THE PUTT. I NEVER HAD A VERY SUBTLE TOUCH. YOU KNOW? AND IN MOST SITUATIONS, BLUNT FORCE JUST ISN'T ENOUGH.
BUT NOT IN THIS SITUATION. HOLD STILL, DOCTOR FRENCH.
EEEEEEEEE-
AAAAAAAAAAAI!!!-
OH GOD. IT HURTS.

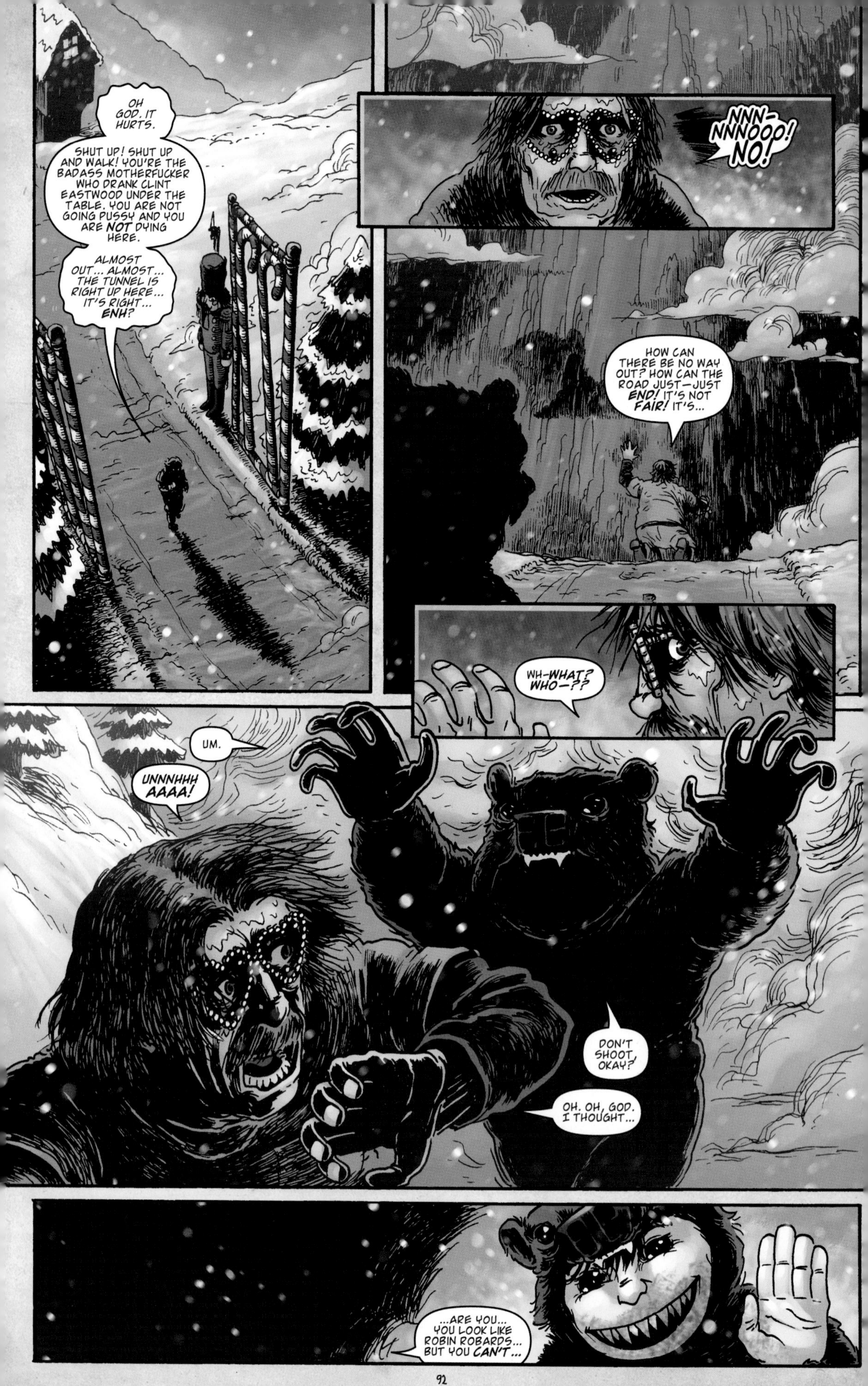

OH GOD. IT HURTS.
SHUT UP! SHUT UP AND WALK! YOU'RE THE BADASS MOTHERFUCKER WHO DRANK CLINT EASTWOOD UNDER THE TABLE. YOU ARE NOT GOING PUSSY AND YOU ARE **NOT** DYING HERE.
ALMOST OUT... ALMOST... THE TUNNEL IS RIGHT UP HERE... IT'S RIGHT... **ENH?**
NNN-NNNOOO! NO!
HOW CAN THERE BE NO WAY OUT? HOW CAN THE ROAD JUST—JUST **END!** IT'S NOT **FAIR!** IT'S...
WH-**WHAT?** **WHO—??**
UM.
UNNNHHH AAAA!
DON'T SHOOT, OKAY?
OH. OH, GOD. I THOUGHT...
...ARE YOU... YOU LOOK LIKE ROBIN ROBARDS... BUT YOU **CAN'T**...

YES, MR. HANSOM! IT'S ME! IT'S ROBIN! YOU BROUGHT ME HERE A LONG TIME AGO! YOU SAVED ME!

OH. AH. I DID?

YOU SURE DID! FROM MY MOTHER. SHE WAS A *BAD* PERSON. SHE DID ALL KINDS OF *BAD* THINGS TO ME. DID YOU LOSE YOUR GUN?

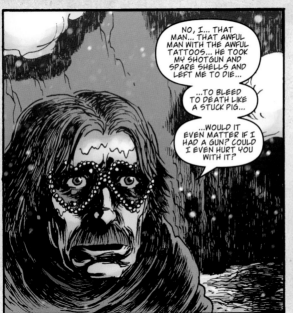

NO, I... THAT MAN... THAT AWFUL MAN WITH THE AWFUL TATTOOS... HE TOOK MY SHOTGUN AND SPARE SHELLS AND LEFT ME TO DIE...

...TO BLEED TO DEATH LIKE A STUCK PIG...

...WOULD IT EVEN MATTER IF I HAD A GUN? COULD I EVEN HURT YOU WITH IT?

UM. IT WOULD PUT HOLES IN MY BEAR COSTUME. I REALLY LIKE MY BEAR COSTUME.

YOU CAN'T GET OUT OF HERE THIS WAY. NOT WITHOUT A SPECIAL VEHICLE, LIKE THE WRAITH. THAT'S ONE OF THE RULES.

THERE MIGHT BE ANOTHER WAY TO LEAVE BUT YOU HAVE TO PROMISE SOMETHING BEFORE I SHOW YOU.

SOME OF US ARE TIRED OF ALL THE RIDES IN CHRISTMASLAND. SOME OF MY FRIENDS WANT TO DO SOMETHING DIFFERENT. SOMETHING *NEW*. WE COULD HELP YOU AND—AND YOU COULD HELP *US*. WILL YOU *PROMISE* TO HELP US?

DOES A BEAR SHIT IN THE... UH... YEAH. YOU KNOW IT. YOU SHOW ME THE FASTEST WAY OUT OF THIS PLACE I'LL DO ANYTHING YOU WANT.

OH. OH THAT'S GOOD. NOW CAN YOU STAND UP? CAN YOU GO A LITTLE FURTHER? I KNOW YOU'RE AWFUL HURT, BUT I THINK YOU'RE GOING TO LIVE A LITTLE WHILE LONGER. I *THINK*.

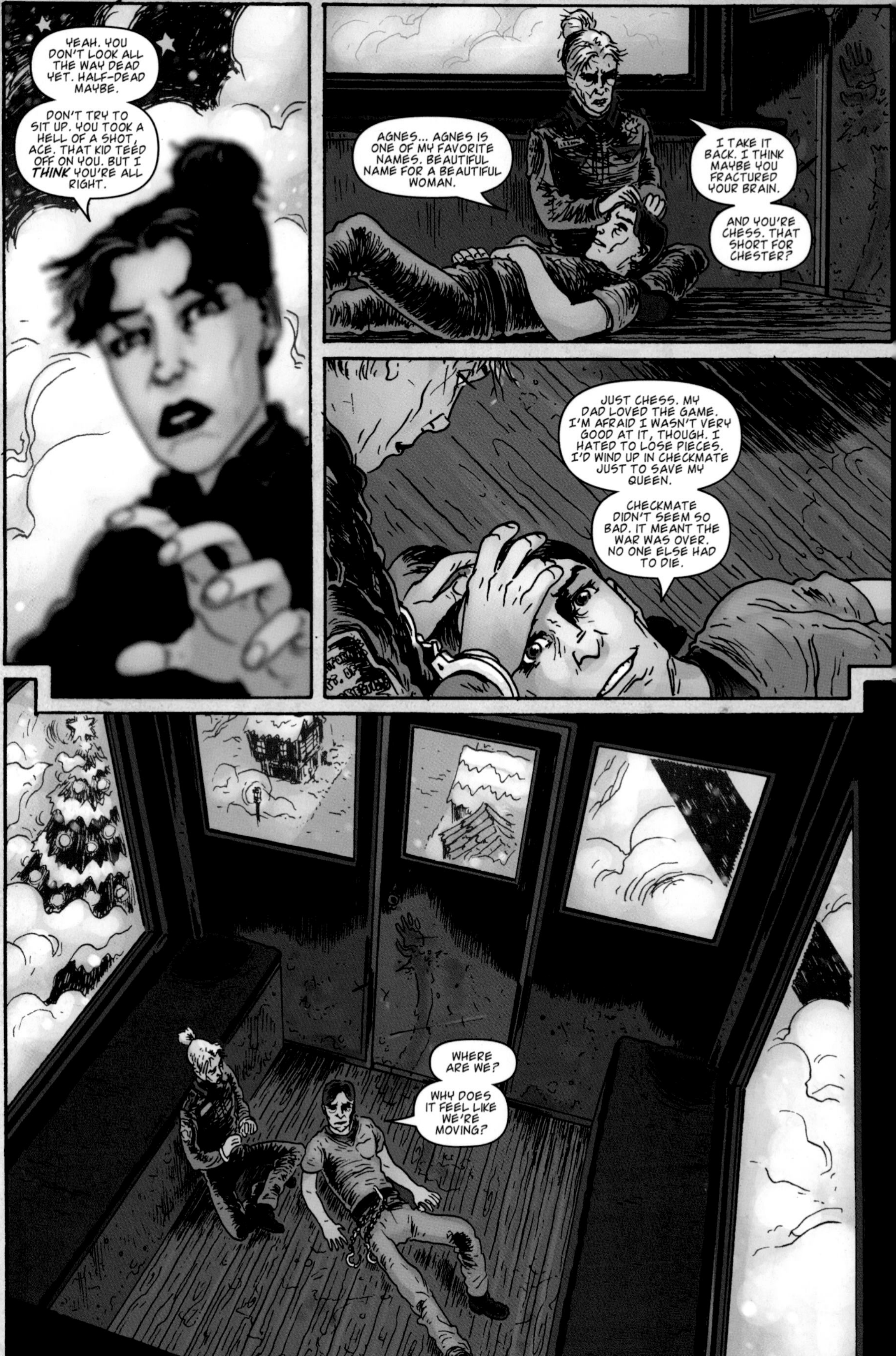
YEAH. YOU DON'T LOOK ALL THE WAY DEAD YET. HALF-DEAD MAYBE.
DON'T TRY TO SIT UP. YOU TOOK A HELL OF A SHOT, ACE. THAT KID TEED OFF ON YOU. BUT I **THINK** YOU'RE ALL RIGHT.
AGNES... AGNES IS ONE OF MY FAVORITE NAMES. BEAUTIFUL NAME FOR A BEAUTIFUL WOMAN.
I TAKE IT BACK. I THINK MAYBE YOU FRACTURED YOUR BRAIN.
AND YOU'RE CHESS. THAT SHORT FOR CHESTER?
JUST CHESS. MY DAD LOVED THE GAME. I'M AFRAID I WASN'T VERY GOOD AT IT, THOUGH. I HATED TO LOSE PIECES. I'D WIND UP IN CHECKMATE JUST TO SAVE MY QUEEN.
CHECKMATE DIDN'T SEEM SO BAD. IT MEANT THE WAR WAS OVER. NO ONE ELSE HAD TO DIE.
WHERE ARE WE?
WHY DOES IT FEEL LIKE WE'RE MOVING?

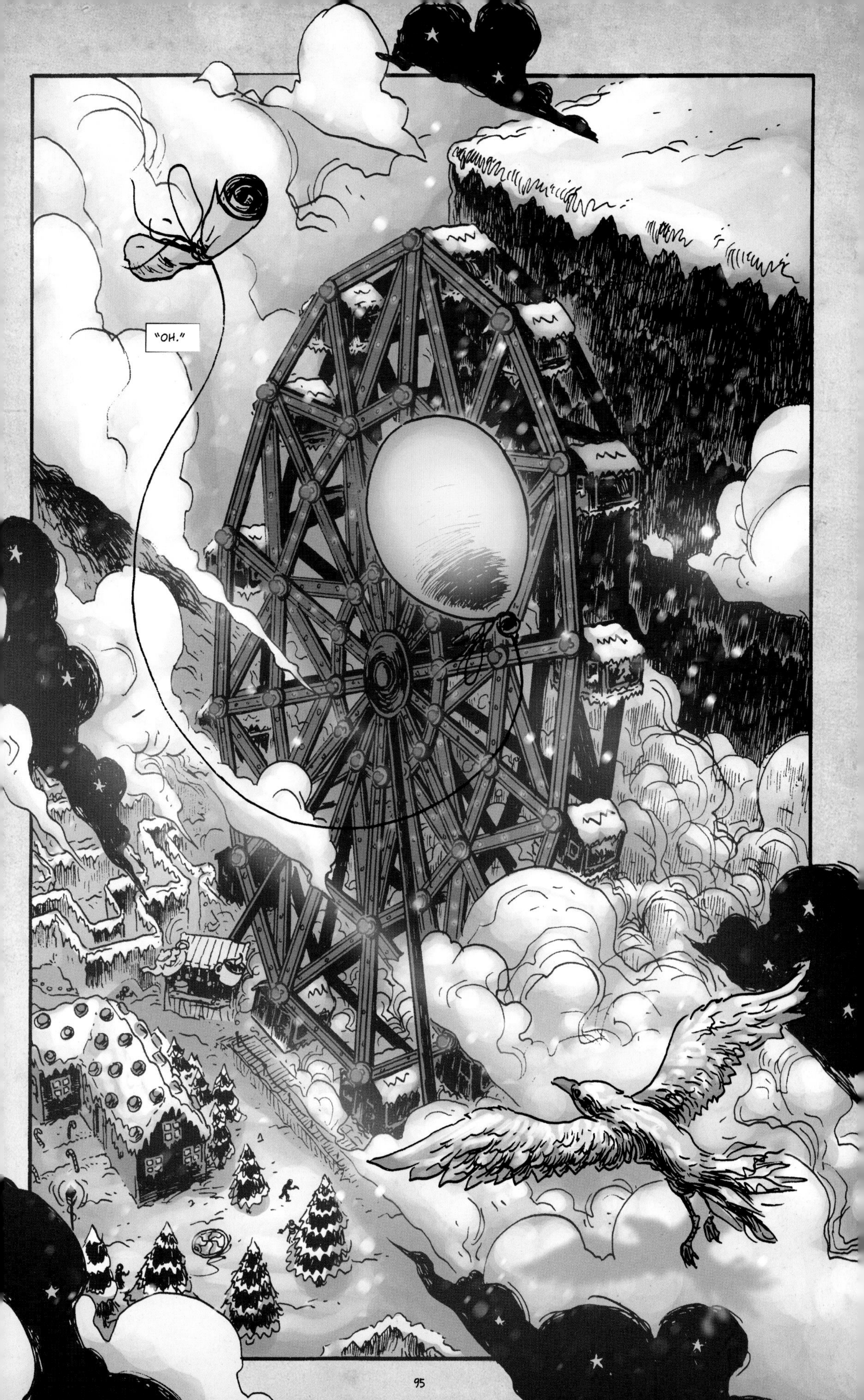
"OH."

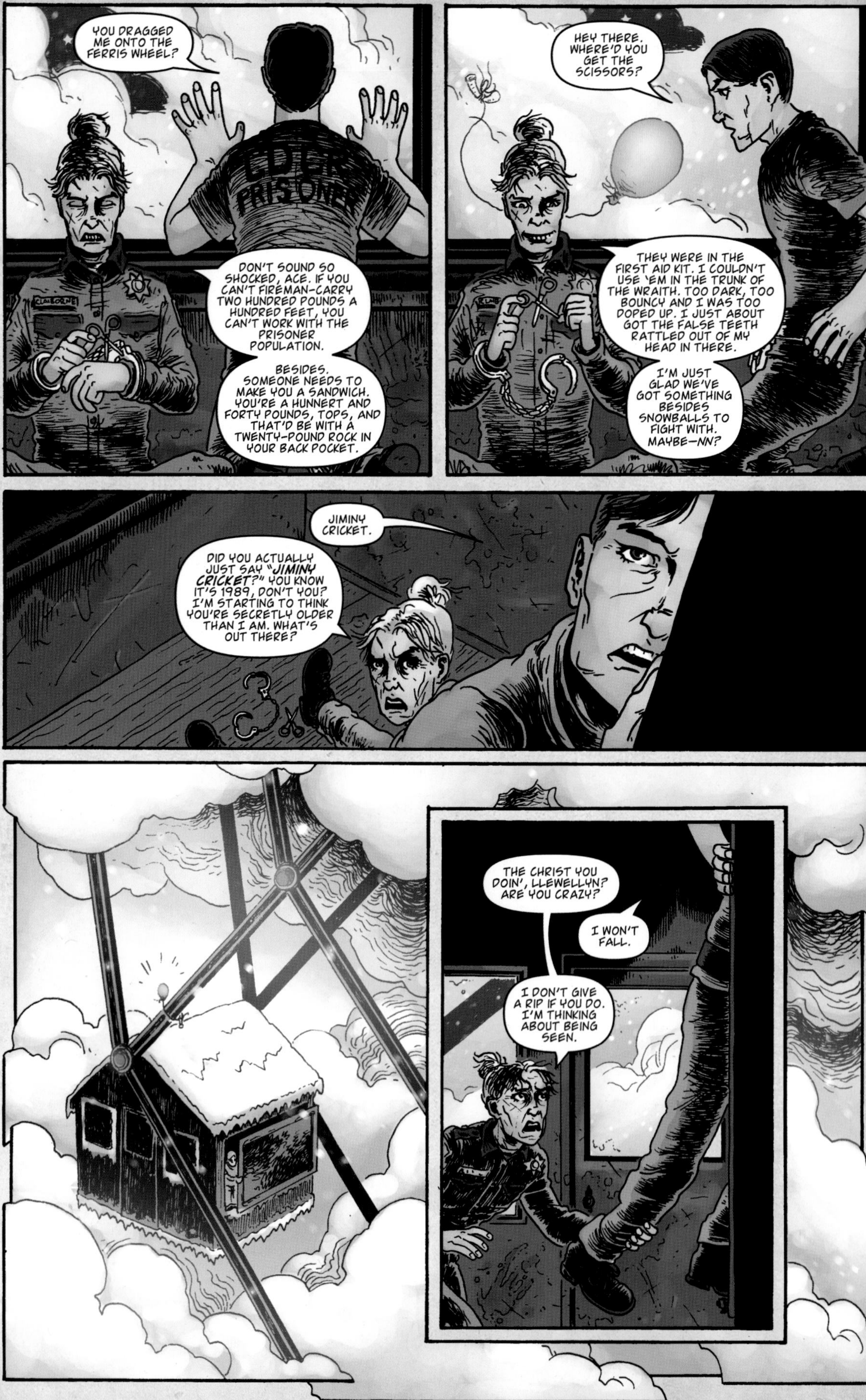
YOU DRAGGED ME ONTO THE FERRIS WHEEL?
DON'T SOUND SO SHOCKED, ACE. IF YOU CAN'T FIREMAN-CARRY TWO HUNDRED POUNDS A HUNDRED FEET, YOU CAN'T WORK WITH THE PRISONER POPULATION.
BESIDES. SOMEONE NEEDS TO MAKE YOU A SANDWICH. YOU'RE A HUNNERT AND FORTY POUNDS, TOPS, AND THAT'D BE WITH A TWENTY-POUND ROCK IN YOUR BACK POCKET.
PRISONER
HEY THERE. WHERE'D YOU GET THE SCISSORS?
THEY WERE IN THE FIRST AID KIT. I COULDN'T USE 'EM IN THE TRUNK OF THE WRAITH. TOO DARK, TOO BOUNCY AND I WAS TOO DOPED UP. I JUST ABOUT GOT THE FALSE TEETH RATTLED OUT OF MY HEAD IN THERE.
I'M JUST GLAD WE'VE GOT SOMETHING BESIDES SNOWBALLS TO FIGHT WITH. MAYBE—NN?
JIMINY CRICKET.
DID YOU ACTUALLY JUST SAY "JIMINY CRICKET?" YOU KNOW IT'S 1989, DON'T YOU? I'M STARTING TO THINK YOU'RE SECRETLY OLDER THAN I AM. WHAT'S OUT THERE?
THE CHRIST YOU DOIN', LLEWELLYN? ARE YOU CRAZY?
I WON'T FALL.
I DON'T GIVE A RIP IF YOU DO. I'M THINKING ABOUT BEING SEEN.

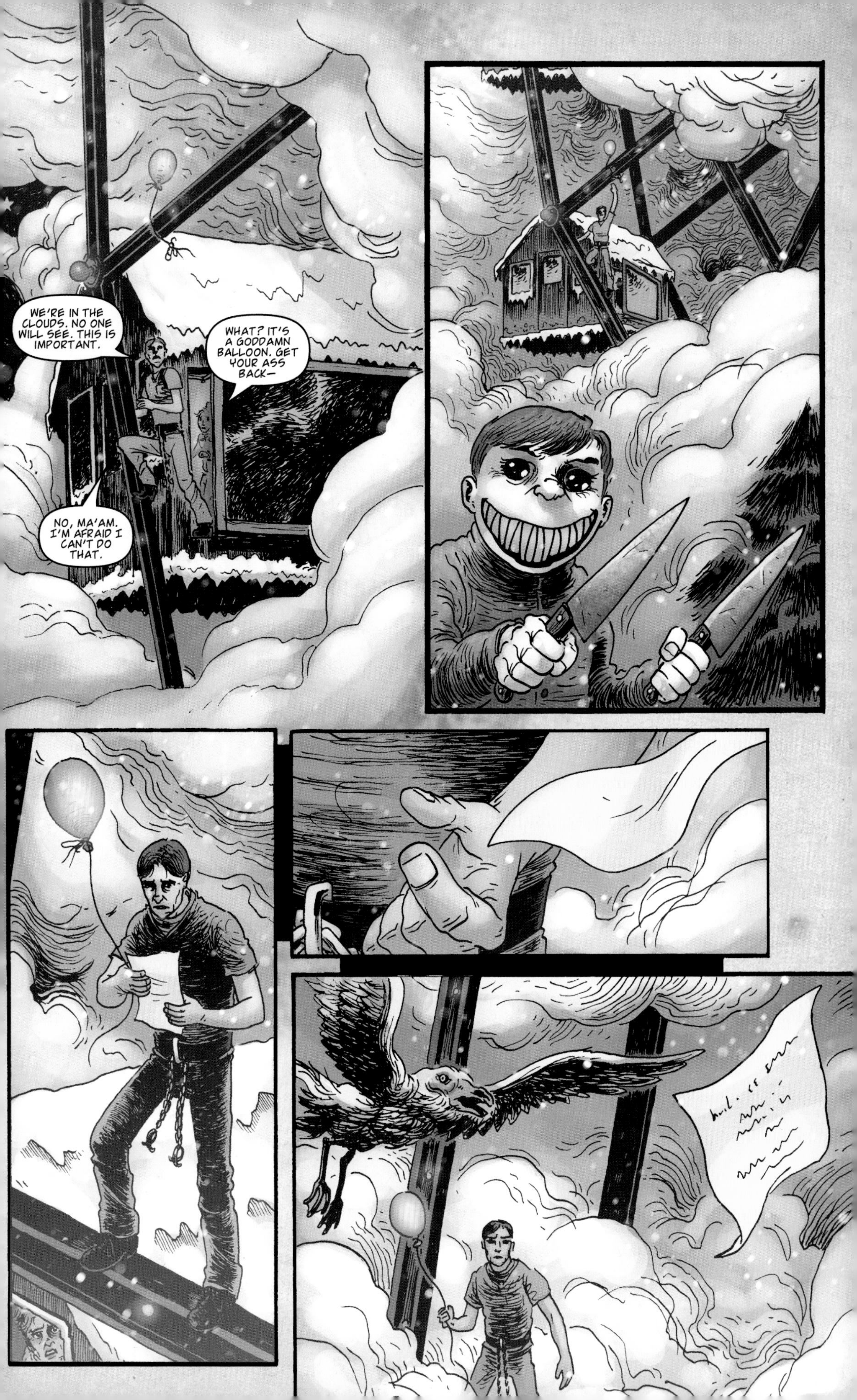
WE'RE IN THE CLOUDS. NO ONE WILL SEE. THIS IS IMPORTANT.
WHAT? IT'S A GODDAMN BALLOON. GET YOUR ASS BACK—
NO, MA'AM. I'M AFRAID I CAN'T DO THAT.

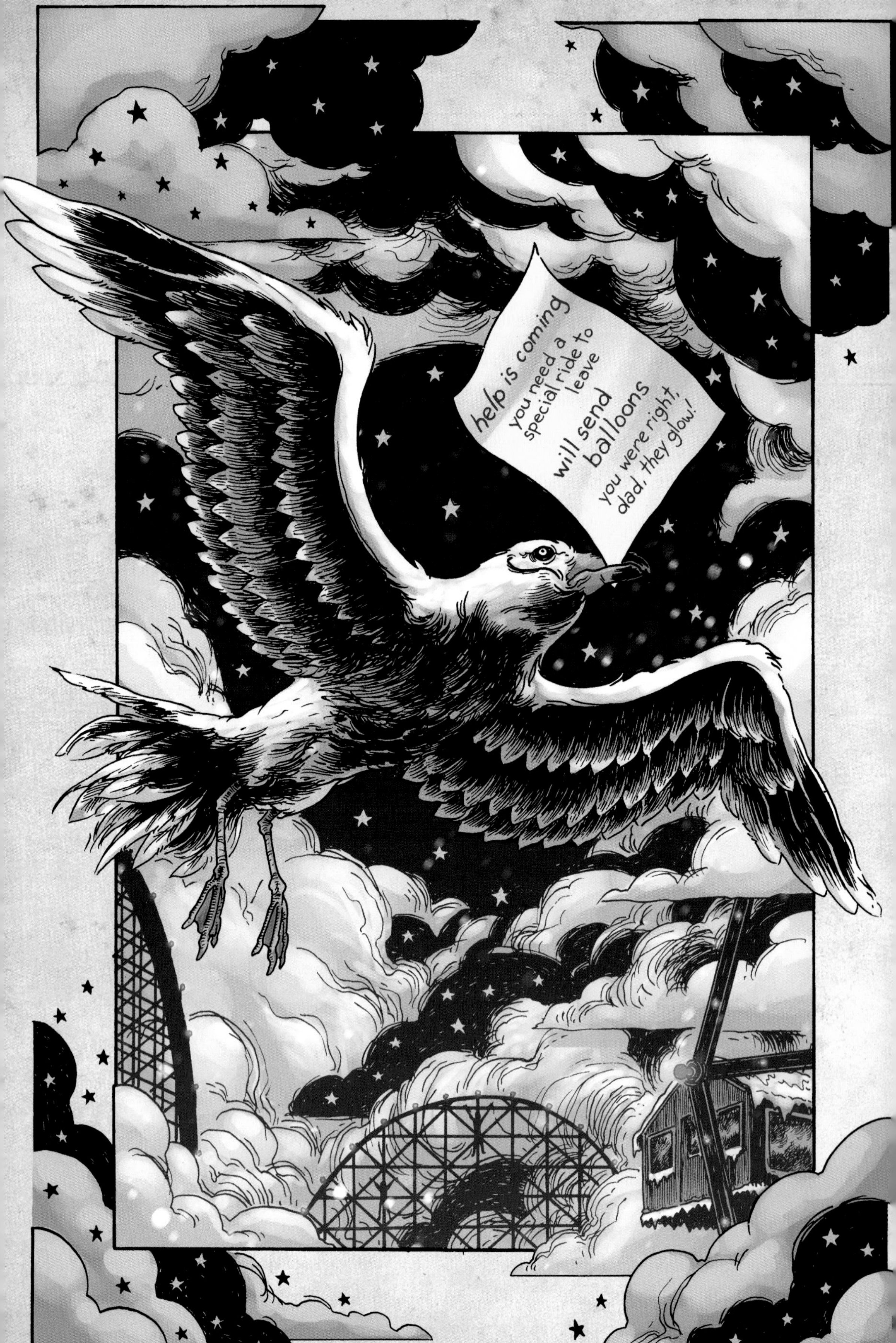
help is coming
you need a special ride to leave
will send balloons
you were right, dad, they glow!

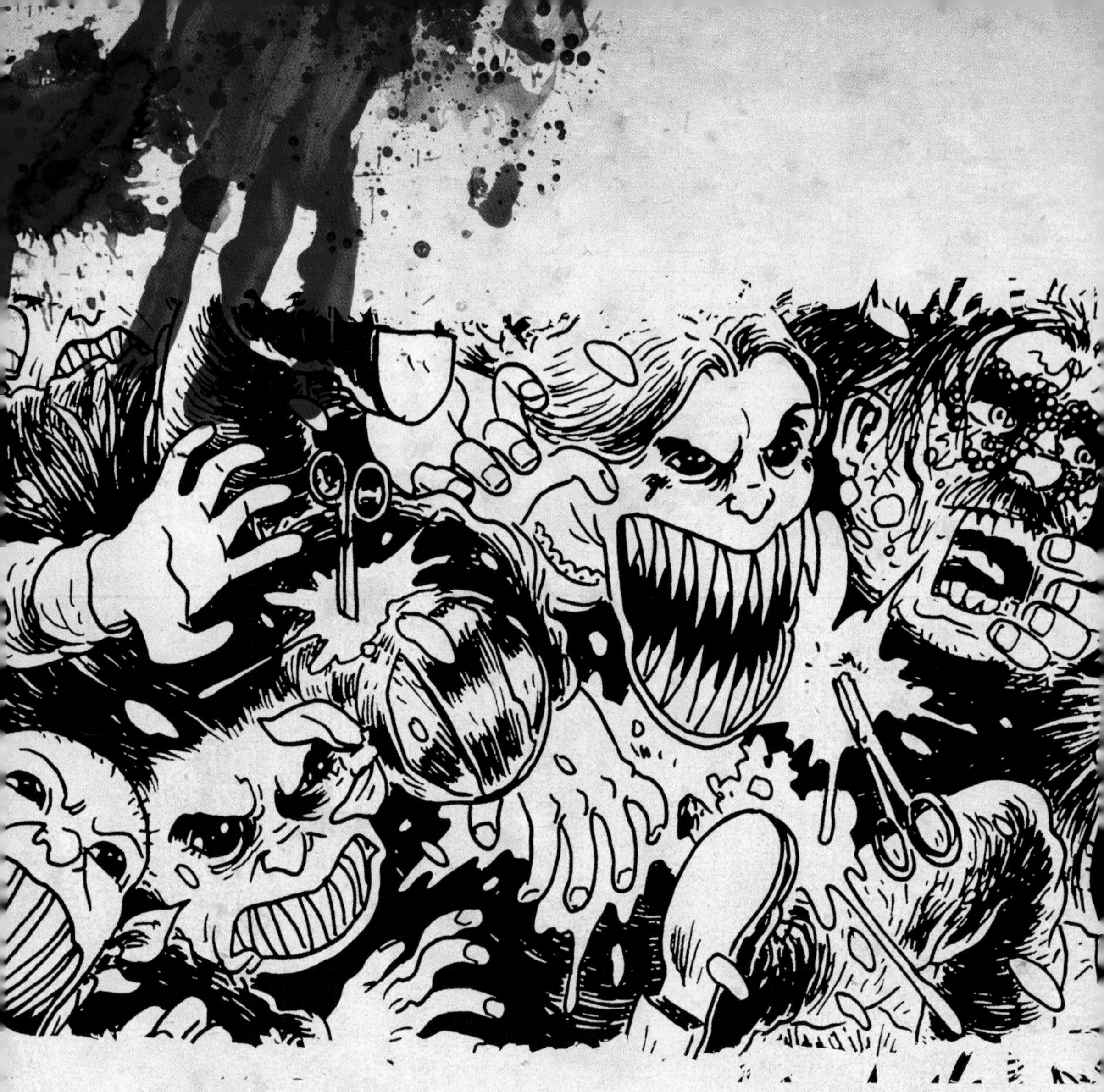

WELCOME TO CHRISTMASLAND chapter four

RULES OF THE GAME

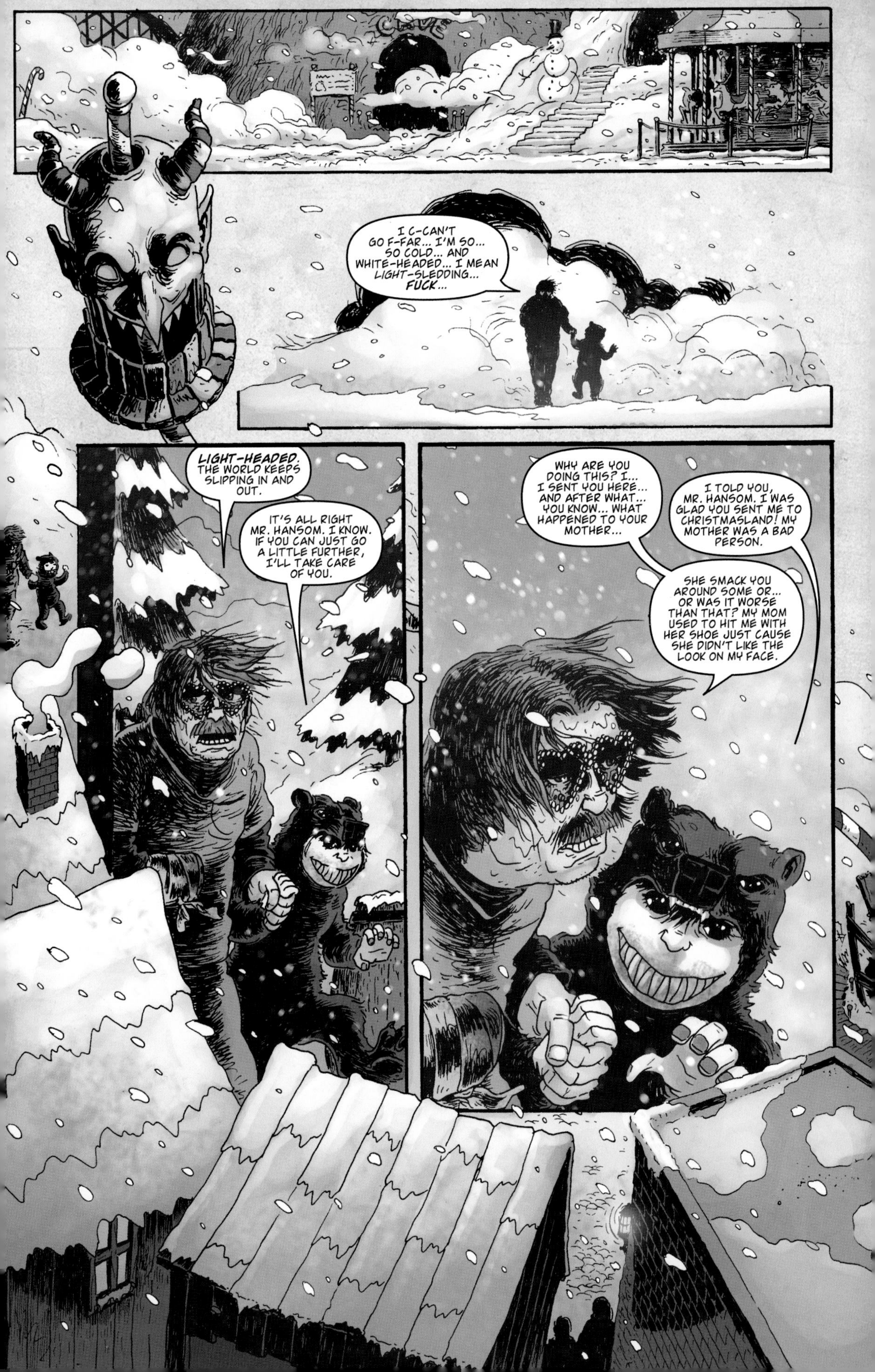
I C-CAN'T GO F-FAR... I'M SO... SO COLD... AND WHITE-HEADED... I MEAN LIGHT-SLEDDING... FUCK...
LIGHT-HEADED. THE WORLD KEEPS SLIPPING IN AND OUT.
IT'S ALL RIGHT MR. HANSOM. I KNOW. IF YOU CAN JUST GO A LITTLE FURTHER, I'LL TAKE CARE OF YOU.
WHY ARE YOU DOING THIS? I... I SENT YOU HERE... AND AFTER WHAT... YOU KNOW... WHAT HAPPENED TO YOUR MOTHER...
I TOLD YOU, MR. HANSOM. I WAS GLAD YOU SENT ME TO CHRISTMASLAND! MY MOTHER WAS A BAD PERSON.
SHE SMACK YOU AROUND SOME OR... OR WAS IT WORSE THAN THAT? MY MOM USED TO HIT ME WITH HER SHOE JUST CAUSE SHE DIDN'T LIKE THE LOOK ON MY FACE.

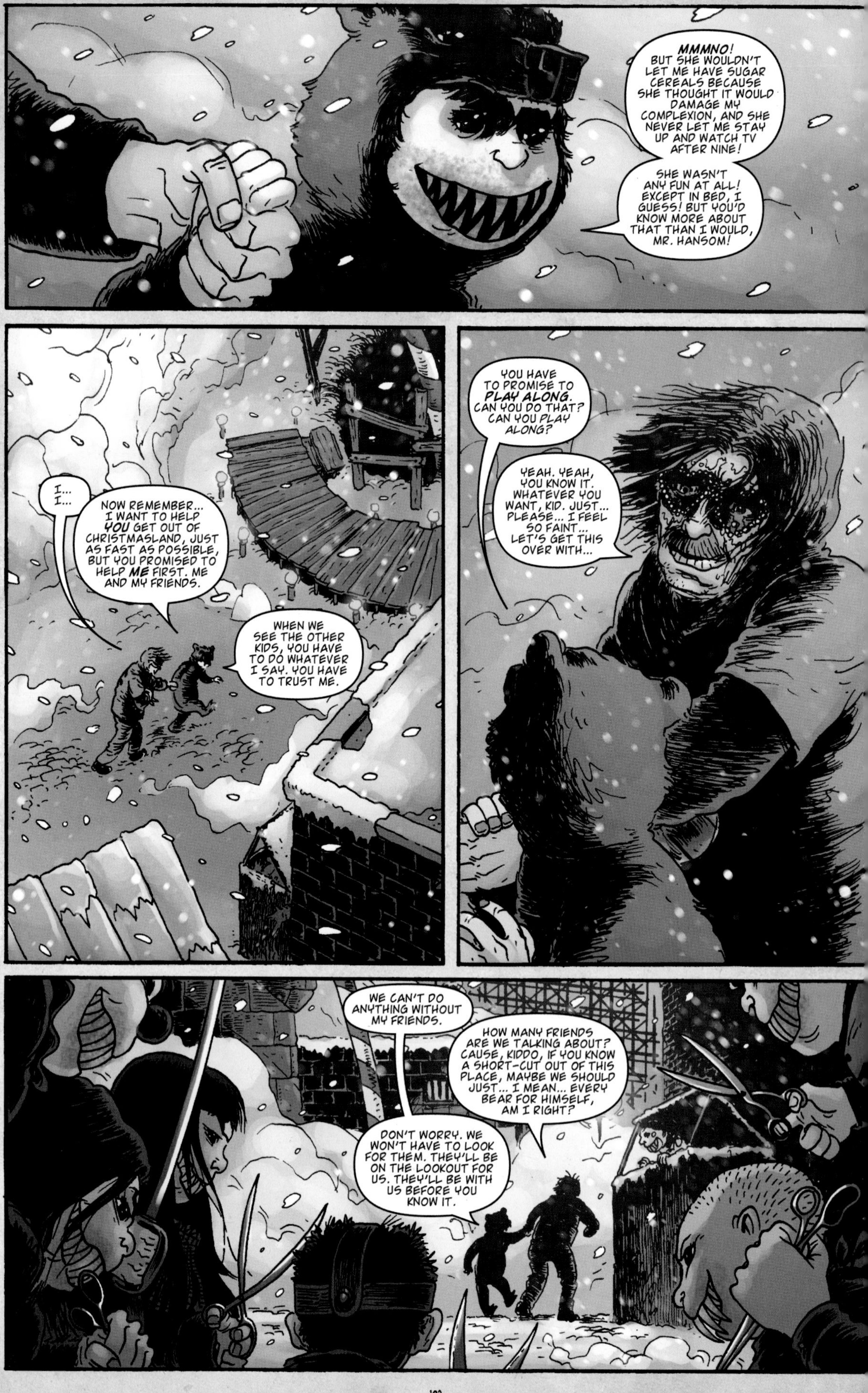
MMMNO! BUT SHE WOULDN'T LET ME HAVE SUGAR CEREALS BECAUSE SHE THOUGHT IT WOULD DAMAGE MY COMPLEXION, AND SHE NEVER LET ME STAY UP AND WATCH TV AFTER NINE!
SHE WASN'T ANY FUN AT ALL! EXCEPT IN BED, I GUESS! BUT YOU'D KNOW MORE ABOUT THAT THAN I WOULD, MR. HANSOM!
I... I...
NOW REMEMBER... I WANT TO HELP YOU GET OUT OF CHRISTMASLAND, JUST AS FAST AS POSSIBLE, BUT YOU PROMISED TO HELP ME FIRST. ME AND MY FRIENDS.
WHEN WE SEE THE OTHER KIDS, YOU HAVE TO DO WHATEVER I SAY. YOU HAVE TO TRUST ME.
YOU HAVE TO PROMISE TO PLAY ALONG. CAN YOU DO THAT? CAN YOU PLAY ALONG?
YEAH. YEAH, YOU KNOW IT. WHATEVER YOU WANT, KID. JUST... PLEASE... I FEEL SO FAINT... LET'S GET THIS OVER WITH...
WE CAN'T DO ANYTHING WITHOUT MY FRIENDS.
HOW MANY FRIENDS ARE WE TALKING ABOUT? CAUSE, KIDDO, IF YOU KNOW A SHORT-CUT OUT OF THIS PLACE, MAYBE WE SHOULD JUST... I MEAN... EVERY BEAR FOR HIMSELF, AM I RIGHT?
DON'T WORRY. WE WON'T HAVE TO LOOK FOR THEM. THEY'LL BE ON THE LOOKOUT FOR US. THEY'LL BE WITH US BEFORE YOU KNOW IT.

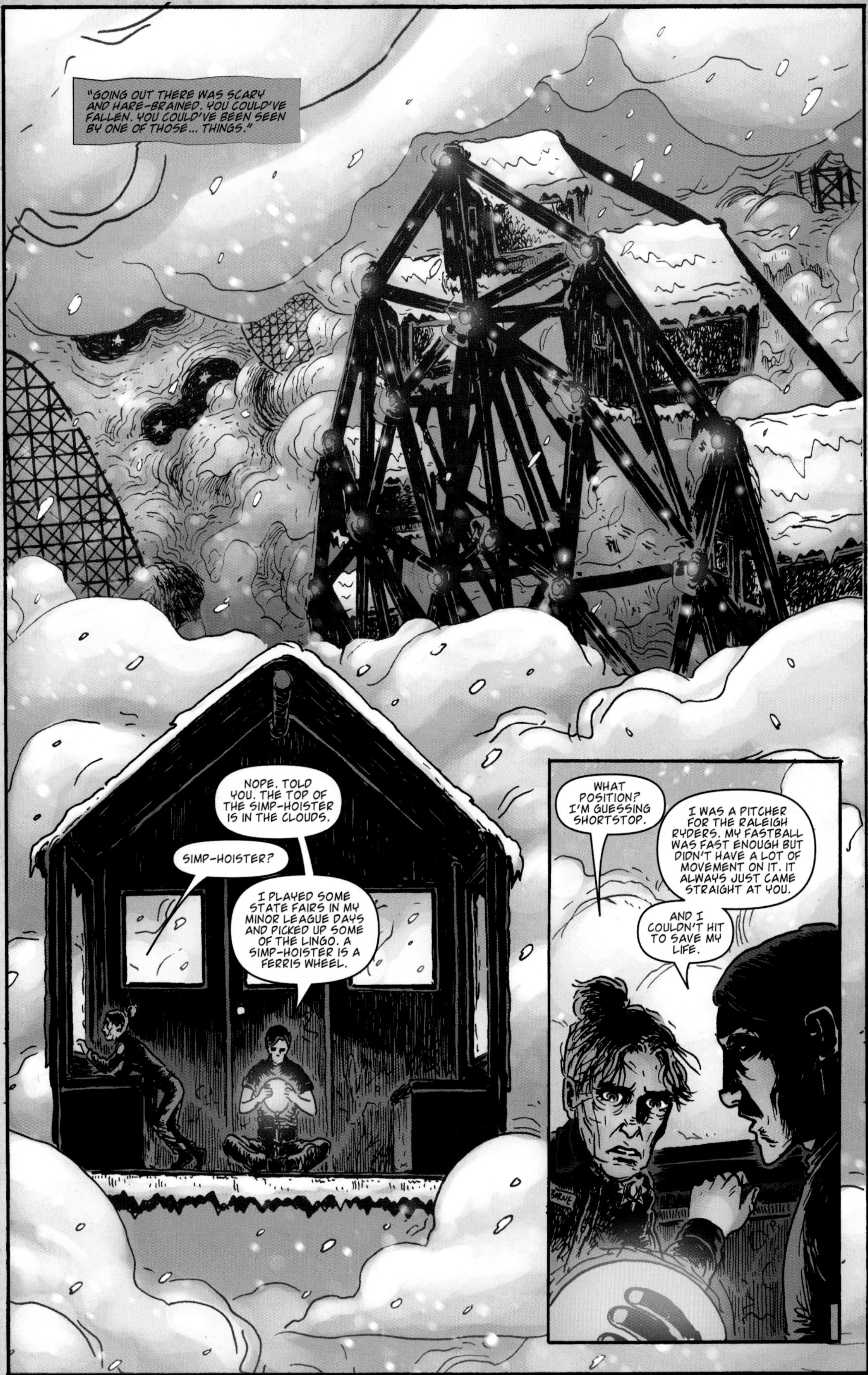
"GOING OUT THERE WAS SCARY AND HARE-BRAINED. YOU COULD'VE FALLEN. YOU COULD'VE BEEN SEEN BY ONE OF THOSE... THINGS."
NOPE. TOLD YOU. THE TOP OF THE SIMP-HOISTER IS IN THE CLOUDS.
SIMP-HOISTER?
I PLAYED SOME STATE FAIRS IN MY MINOR LEAGUE DAYS AND PICKED UP SOME OF THE LINGO. A SIMP-HOISTER IS A FERRIS WHEEL.
WHAT POSITION? I'M GUESSING SHORTSTOP.
I WAS A PITCHER FOR THE RALEIGH RYDERS. MY FASTBALL WAS FAST ENOUGH BUT DIDN'T HAVE A LOT OF MOVEMENT ON IT. IT ALWAYS JUST CAME STRAIGHT AT YOU.
AND I COULDN'T HIT TO SAVE MY LIFE.

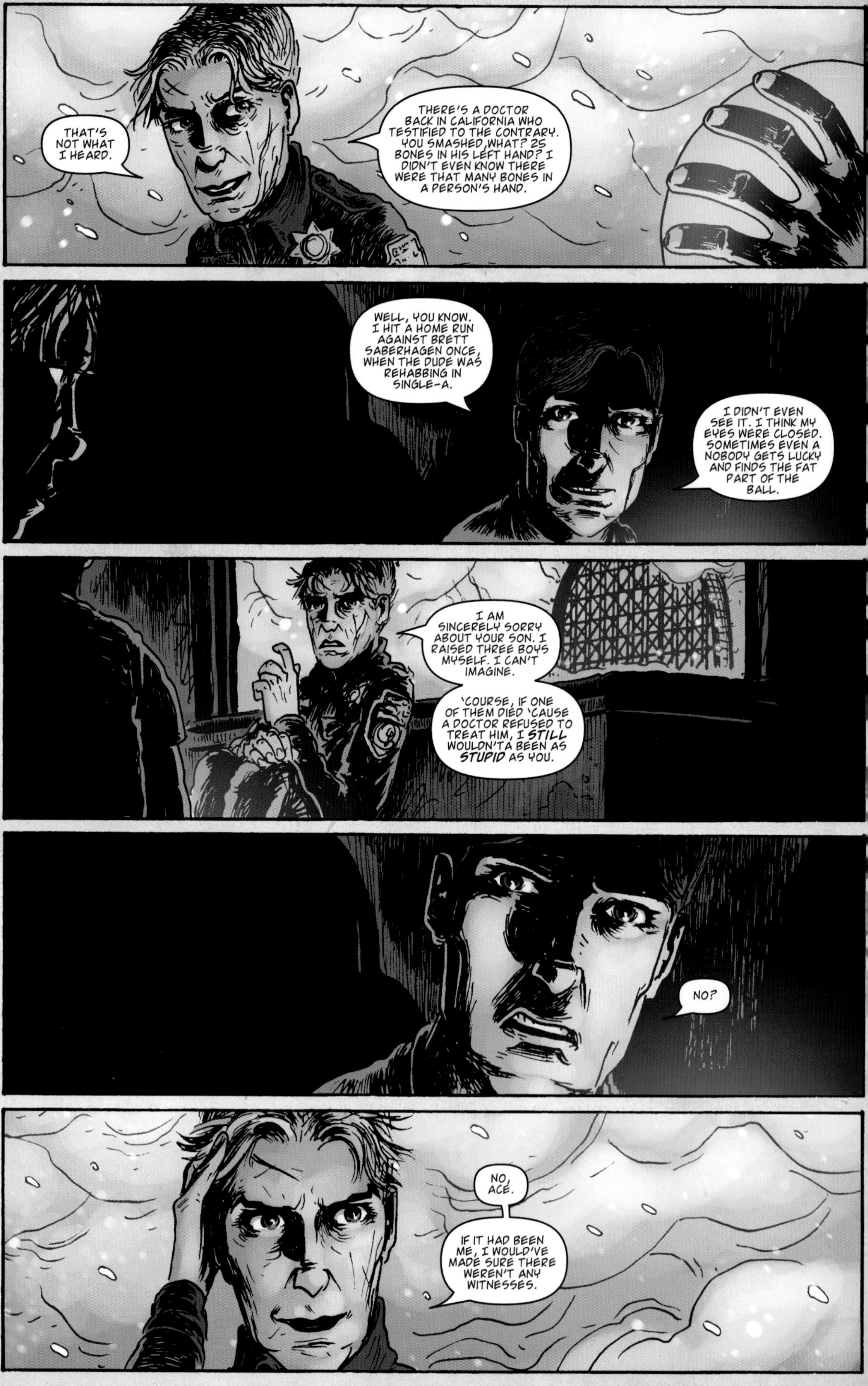
THAT'S NOT WHAT I HEARD.
THERE'S A DOCTOR BACK IN CALIFORNIA WHO TESTIFIED TO THE CONTRARY. YOU SMASHED, WHAT? 25 BONES IN HIS LEFT HAND? I DIDN'T EVEN KNOW THERE WERE THAT MANY BONES IN A PERSON'S HAND.
WELL, YOU KNOW. I HIT A HOME RUN AGAINST BRETT SABERHAGEN ONCE, WHEN THE DUDE WAS REHABBING IN SINGLE-A.
I DIDN'T EVEN SEE IT. I THINK MY EYES WERE CLOSED. SOMETIMES EVEN A NOBODY GETS LUCKY AND FINDS THE FAT PART OF THE BALL.
I AM SINCERELY SORRY ABOUT YOUR SON. I RAISED THREE BOYS MYSELF. I CAN'T IMAGINE.
'COURSE, IF ONE OF THEM DIED 'CAUSE A DOCTOR REFUSED TO TREAT HIM, I STILL WOULDN'T'A BEEN AS STUPID AS YOU.
NO?
NO, ACE.
IF IT HAD BEEN ME, I WOULD'VE MADE SURE THERE WEREN'T ANY WITNESSES.

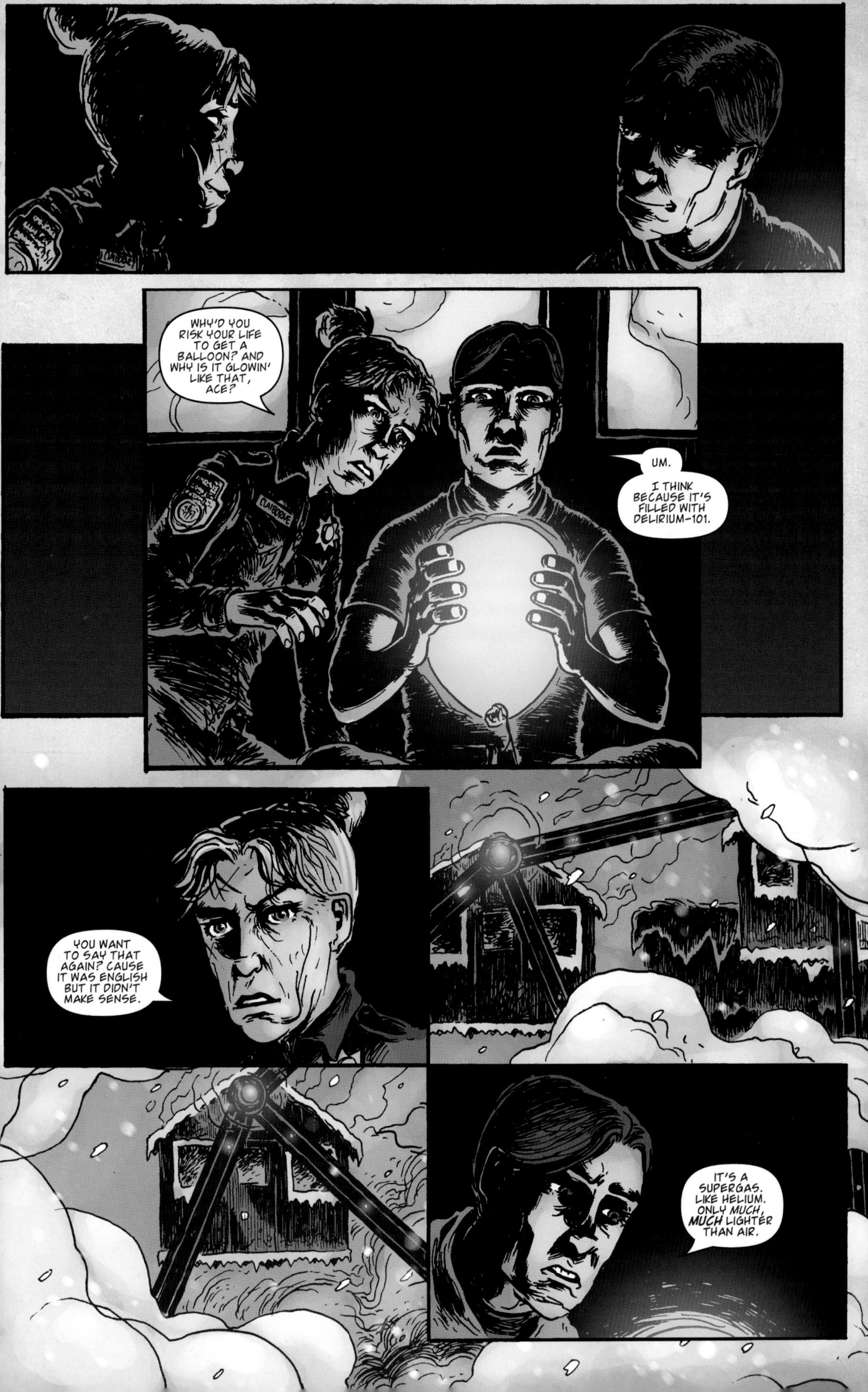
WHY'D YOU RISK YOUR LIFE TO GET A BALLOON? AND WHY IS IT GLOWIN' LIKE THAT, ACE?
UM.
I THINK BECAUSE IT'S FILLED WITH DELIRIUM-101.
YOU WANT TO SAY THAT AGAIN? CAUSE IT WAS ENGLISH BUT IT DIDN'T MAKE SENSE.
IT'S A SUPERGAS. LIKE HELIUM. ONLY MUCH, MUCH LIGHTER THAN AIR.

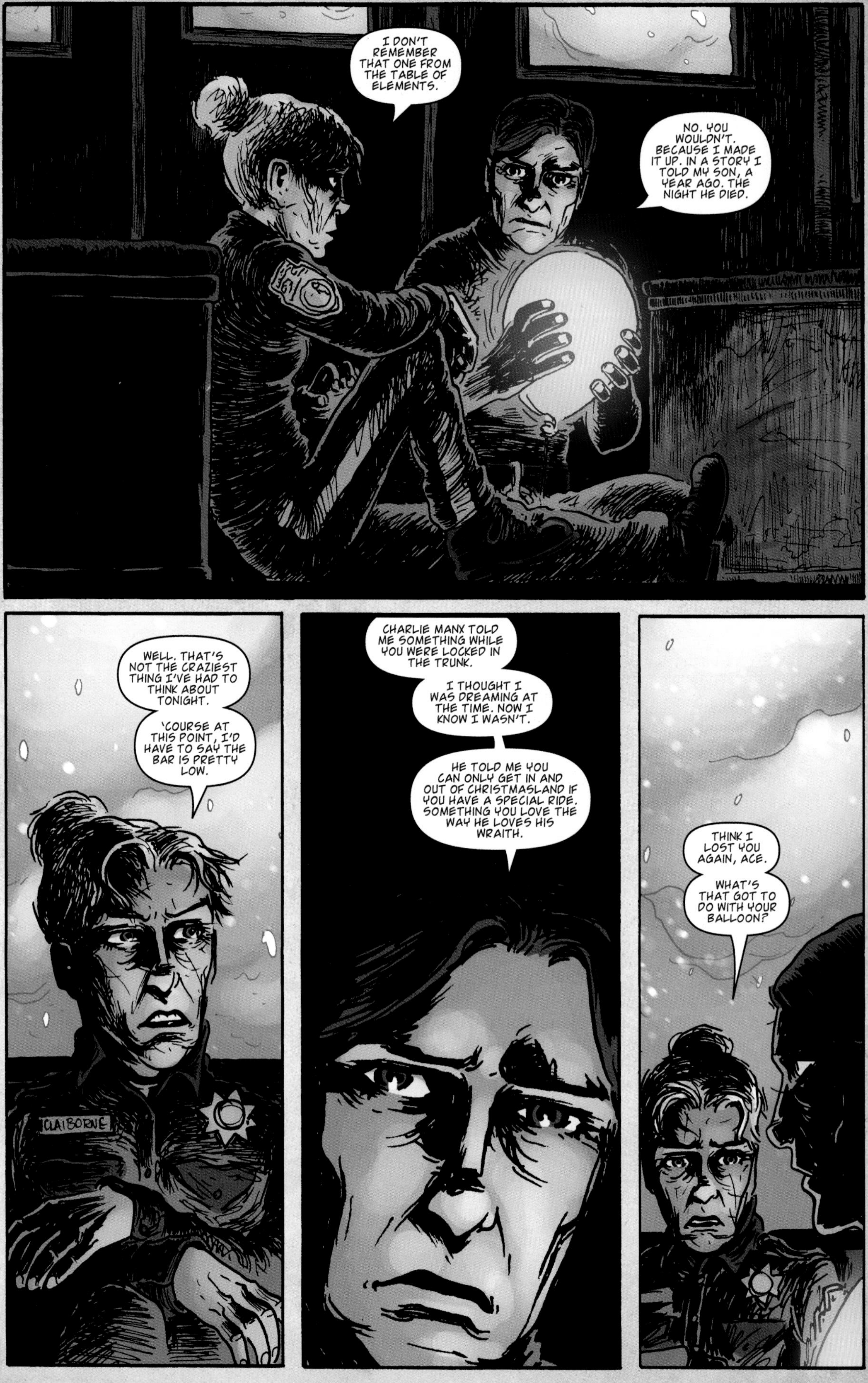
I DON'T REMEMBER THAT ONE FROM THE TABLE OF ELEMENTS.
NO. YOU WOULDN'T. BECAUSE I MADE IT UP. IN A STORY I TOLD MY SON, A YEAR AGO. THE NIGHT HE DIED.
WELL. THAT'S NOT THE CRAZIEST THING I'VE HAD TO THINK ABOUT TONIGHT.
'COURSE AT THIS POINT, I'D HAVE TO SAY THE BAR IS PRETTY LOW.
CLAIBORNE
CHARLIE MANX TOLD ME SOMETHING WHILE YOU WERE LOCKED IN THE TRUNK.
I THOUGHT I WAS DREAMING AT THE TIME. NOW I KNOW I WASN'T.
HE TOLD ME YOU CAN ONLY GET IN AND OUT OF CHRISTMASLAND IF YOU HAVE A SPECIAL RIDE. SOMETHING YOU LOVE THE WAY HE LOVES HIS WRAITH.
THINK I LOST YOU AGAIN, ACE.
WHAT'S THAT GOT TO DO WITH YOUR BALLOON?

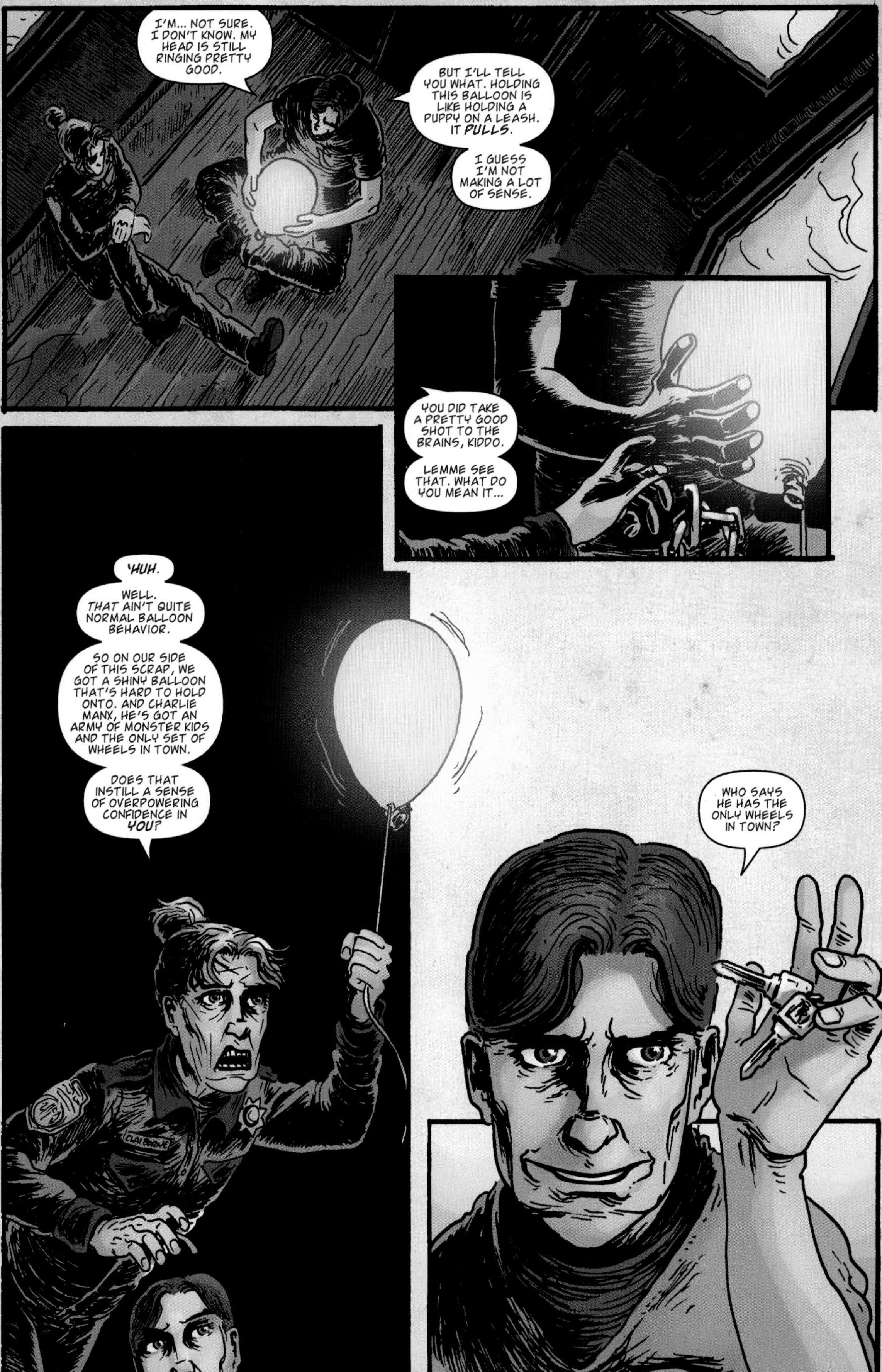
I'M... NOT SURE. I DON'T KNOW. MY HEAD IS STILL RINGING PRETTY GOOD.
BUT I'LL TELL YOU WHAT. HOLDING THIS BALLOON IS LIKE HOLDING A PUPPY ON A LEASH. IT PULLS.
I GUESS I'M NOT MAKING A LOT OF SENSE.
YOU DID TAKE A PRETTY GOOD SHOT TO THE BRAINS, KIDDO.
LEMME SEE THAT. WHAT DO YOU MEAN IT...
'HUH.
WELL. THAT AIN'T QUITE NORMAL BALLOON BEHAVIOR.
SO ON OUR SIDE OF THIS SCRAP, WE GOT A SHINY BALLOON THAT'S HARD TO HOLD ONTO. AND CHARLIE MANX, HE'S GOT AN ARMY OF MONSTER KIDS AND THE ONLY SET OF WHEELS IN TOWN.
DOES THAT INSTILL A SENSE OF OVERPOWERING CONFIDENCE IN YOU?
WHO SAYS HE HAS THE ONLY WHEELS IN TOWN?
CLAIBORNE

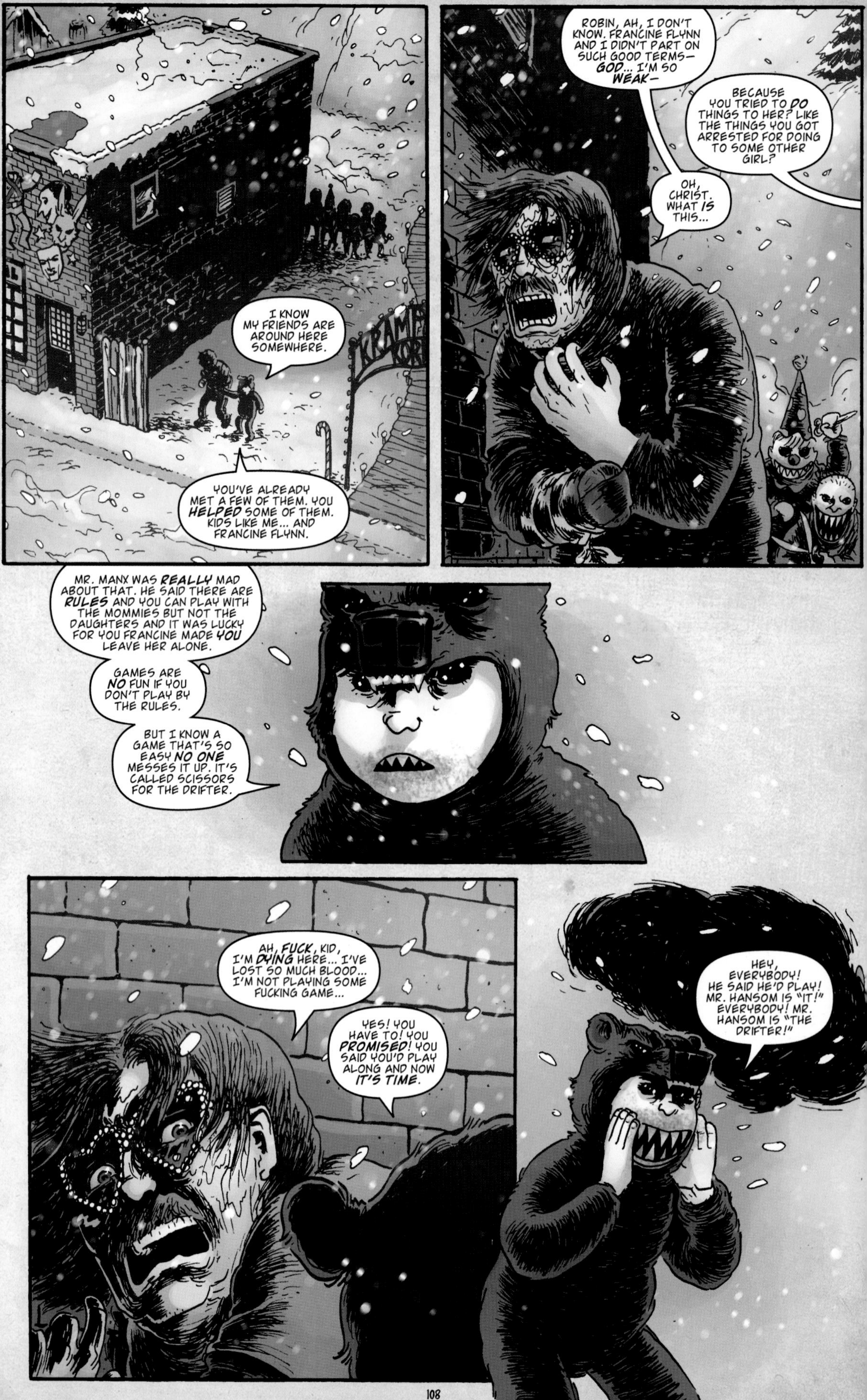
I KNOW MY FRIENDS ARE AROUND HERE SOMEWHERE.
YOU'VE ALREADY MET A FEW OF THEM. YOU HELPED SOME OF THEM. KIDS LIKE ME... AND FRANCINE FLYNN.
ROBIN, AH, I DON'T KNOW. FRANCINE FLYNN AND I DIDN'T PART ON SUCH GOOD TERMS— GOD... I'M SO WEAK—
BECAUSE YOU TRIED TO DO THINGS TO HER? LIKE THE THINGS YOU GOT ARRESTED FOR DOING TO SOME OTHER GIRL?
OH, CHRIST. WHAT IS THIS...
MR. MANX WAS REALLY MAD ABOUT THAT. HE SAID THERE ARE RULES AND YOU CAN PLAY WITH THE MOMMIES BUT NOT THE DAUGHTERS AND IT WAS LUCKY FOR YOU FRANCINE MADE YOU LEAVE HER ALONE.
GAMES ARE NO FUN IF YOU DON'T PLAY BY THE RULES.
BUT I KNOW A GAME THAT'S SO EASY NO ONE MESSES IT UP. IT'S CALLED SCISSORS FOR THE DRIFTER.
AH, FUCK, KID, I'M DYING HERE... I'VE LOST SO MUCH BLOOD... I'M NOT PLAYING SOME FUCKING GAME...
YES! YOU HAVE TO! YOU PROMISED! YOU SAID YOU'D PLAY ALONG AND NOW IT'S TIME.
HEY, EVERYBODY! HE SAID HE'D PLAY! MR. HANSOM IS "IT!" EVERYBODY! MR. HANSOM IS "THE DRIFTER!"

WHAAA—NNNNNOOOO!

NNNG!

CHARGE! FOR CHRISTMASLAND!

CHARGE!!

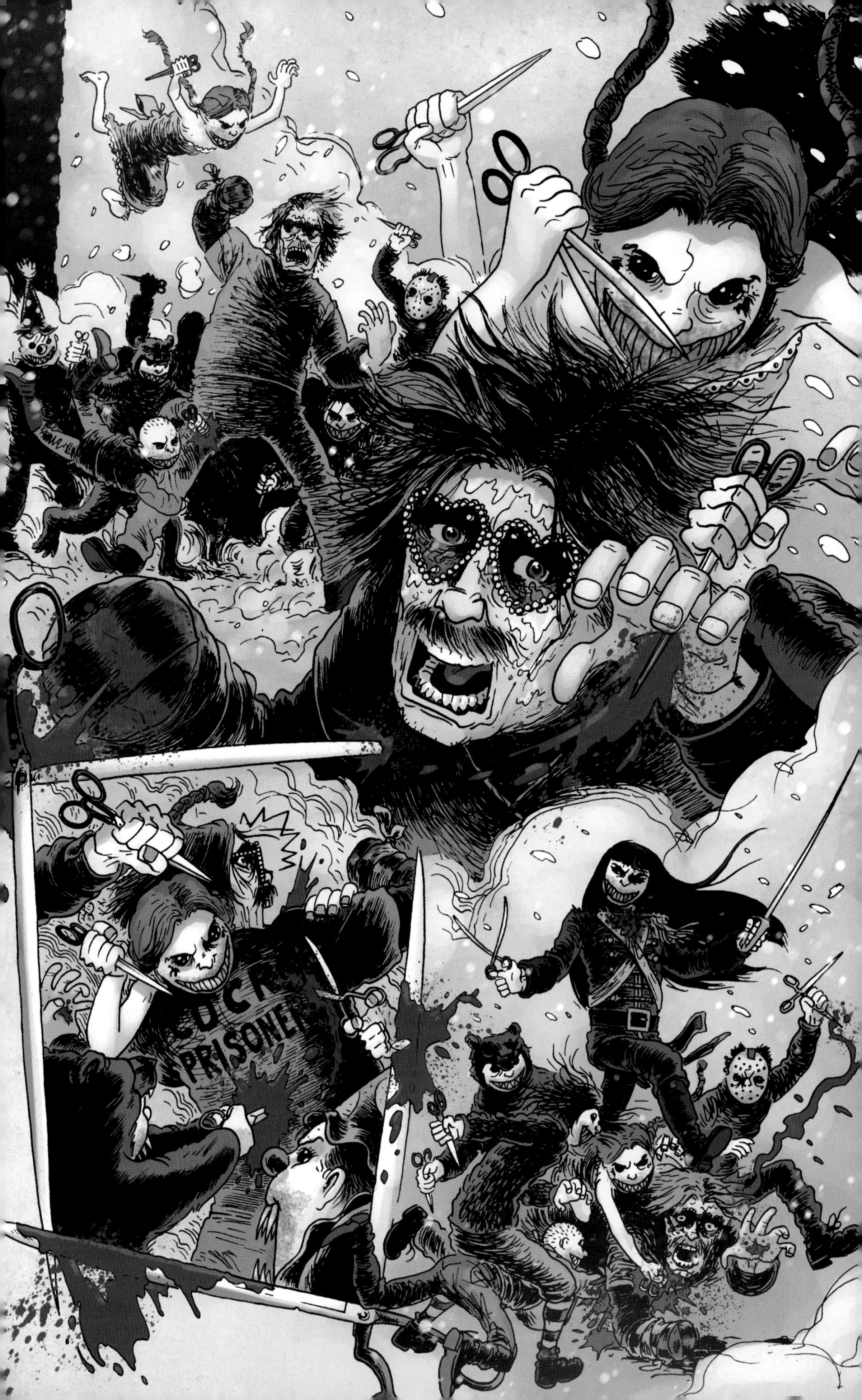

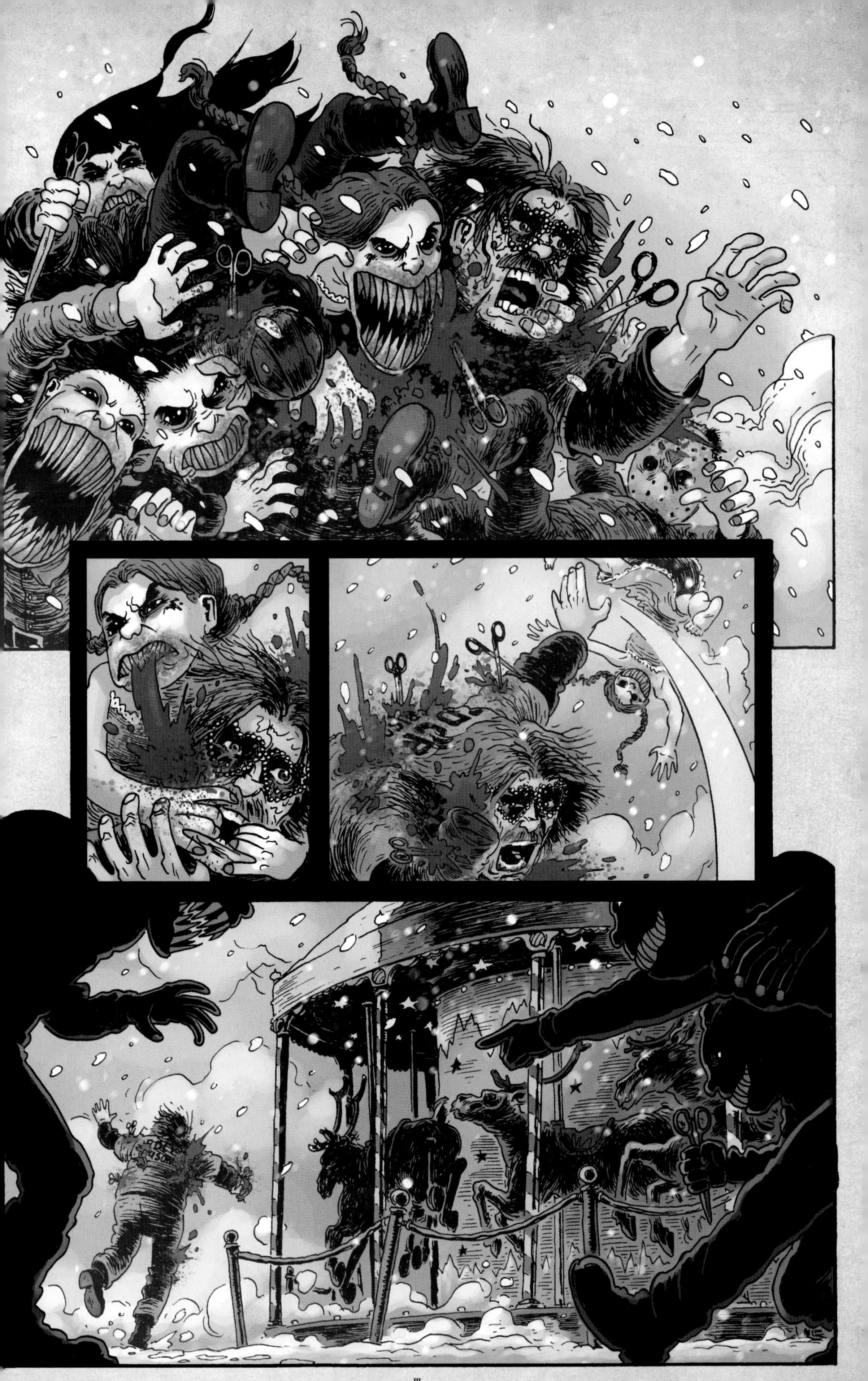

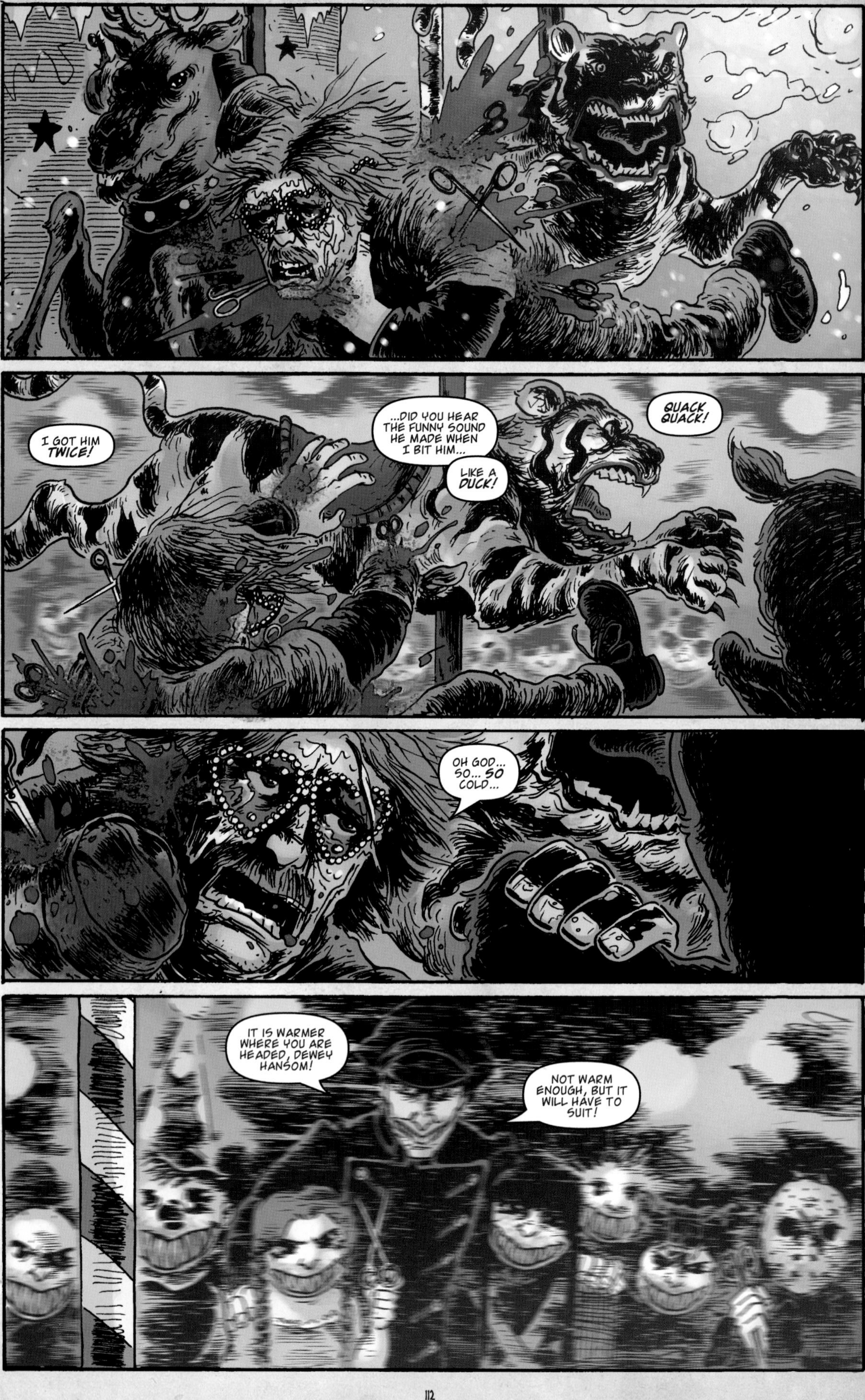
I GOT HIM TWICE!
...DID YOU HEAR THE FUNNY SOUND HE MADE WHEN I BIT HIM...
LIKE A DUCK!
QUACK QUACK!
OH GOD... SO... SO COLD...
IT IS WARMER WHERE YOU ARE HEADED, DEWEY HANSOM!
NOT WARM ENOUGH, BUT IT WILL HAVE TO SUIT!

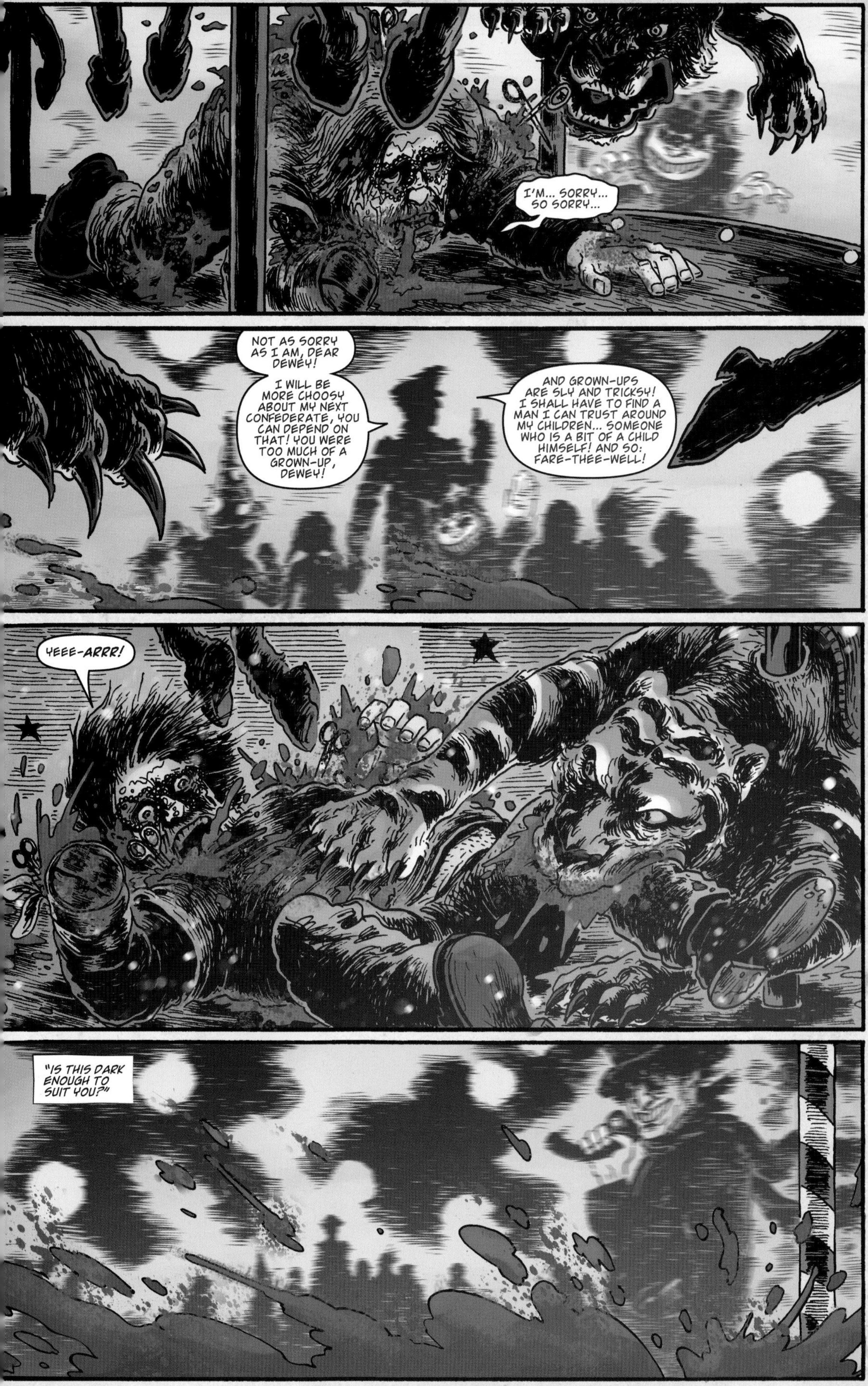
I'M... SORRY... SO SORRY...
NOT AS SORRY AS I AM, DEAR DEWEY!
I WILL BE MORE CHOOSY ABOUT MY NEXT CONFEDERATE, YOU CAN DEPEND ON THAT! YOU WERE TOO MUCH OF A GROWN-UP, DEWEY!
AND GROWN-UPS ARE SLY AND TRICKSY! I SHALL HAVE TO FIND A MAN I CAN TRUST AROUND MY CHILDREN... SOMEONE WHO IS A BIT OF A CHILD HIMSELF! AND SO: FARE-THEE-WELL!
YEEE-ARRR!
"IS THIS DARK ENOUGH TO SUIT YOU?"

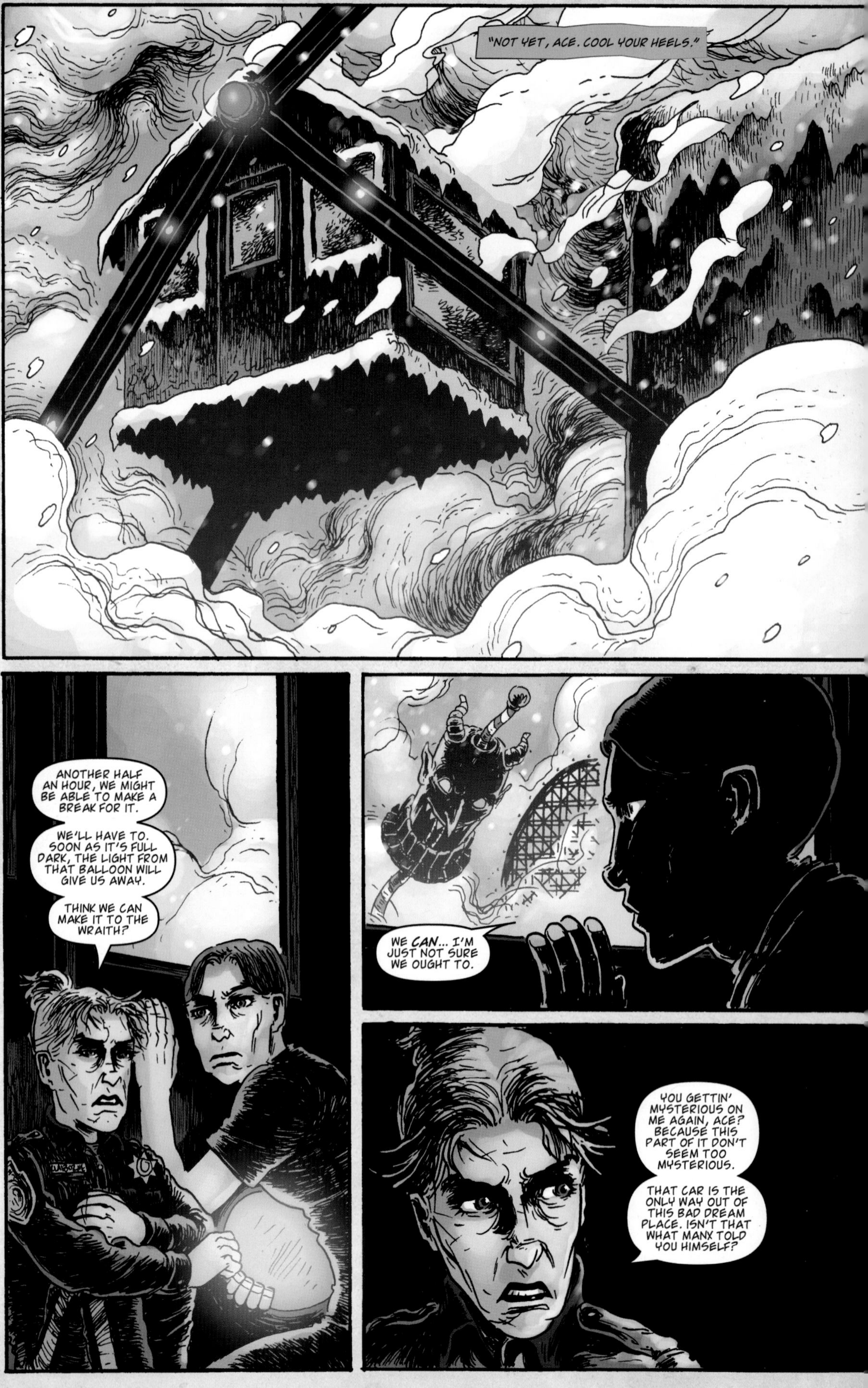
"NOT YET, ACE. COOL YOUR HEELS."
ANOTHER HALF AN HOUR, WE MIGHT BE ABLE TO MAKE A BREAK FOR IT.
WE'LL HAVE TO. SOON AS IT'S FULL DARK, THE LIGHT FROM THAT BALLOON WILL GIVE US AWAY.
THINK WE CAN MAKE IT TO THE WRAITH?
WE CAN... I'M JUST NOT SURE WE OUGHT TO.
YOU GETTIN' MYSTERIOUS ON ME AGAIN, ACE? BECAUSE THIS PART OF IT DON'T SEEM TOO MYSTERIOUS.
THAT CAR IS THE ONLY WAY OUT OF THIS BAD DREAM PLACE. ISN'T THAT WHAT MANX TOLD YOU HIMSELF?

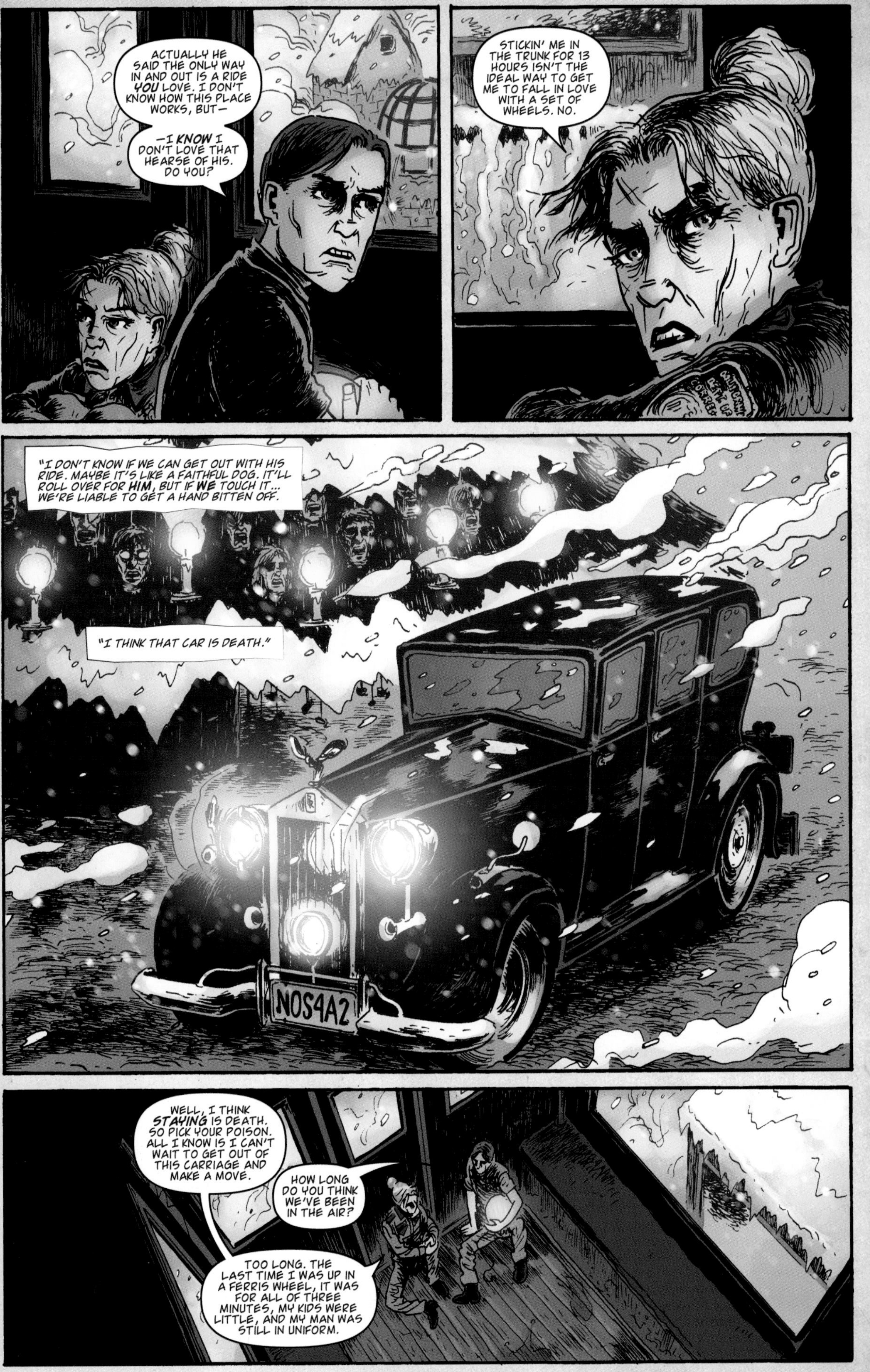
ACTUALLY HE SAID THE ONLY WAY IN AND OUT IS A RIDE YOU LOVE. I DON'T KNOW HOW THIS PLACE WORKS, BUT—
—I KNOW I DON'T LOVE THAT HEARSE OF HIS. DO YOU?
STICKIN' ME IN THE TRUNK FOR 13 HOURS ISN'T THE IDEAL WAY TO GET ME TO FALL IN LOVE WITH A SET OF WHEELS. NO.
"I DON'T KNOW IF WE CAN GET OUT WITH HIS RIDE. MAYBE IT'S LIKE A FAITHFUL DOG. IT'LL ROLL OVER FOR HIM, BUT IF WE TOUCH IT... WE'RE LIABLE TO GET A HAND BITTEN OFF.
"I THINK THAT CAR IS DEATH."
NOS4A2
WELL, I THINK STAYING IS DEATH. SO PICK YOUR POISON. ALL I KNOW IS I CAN'T WAIT TO GET OUT OF THIS CARRIAGE AND MAKE A MOVE.
HOW LONG DO YOU THINK WE'VE BEEN IN THE AIR?
TOO LONG. THE LAST TIME I WAS UP IN A FERRIS WHEEL, IT WAS FOR ALL OF THREE MINUTES, MY KIDS WERE LITTLE, AND MY MAN WAS STILL IN UNIFORM.

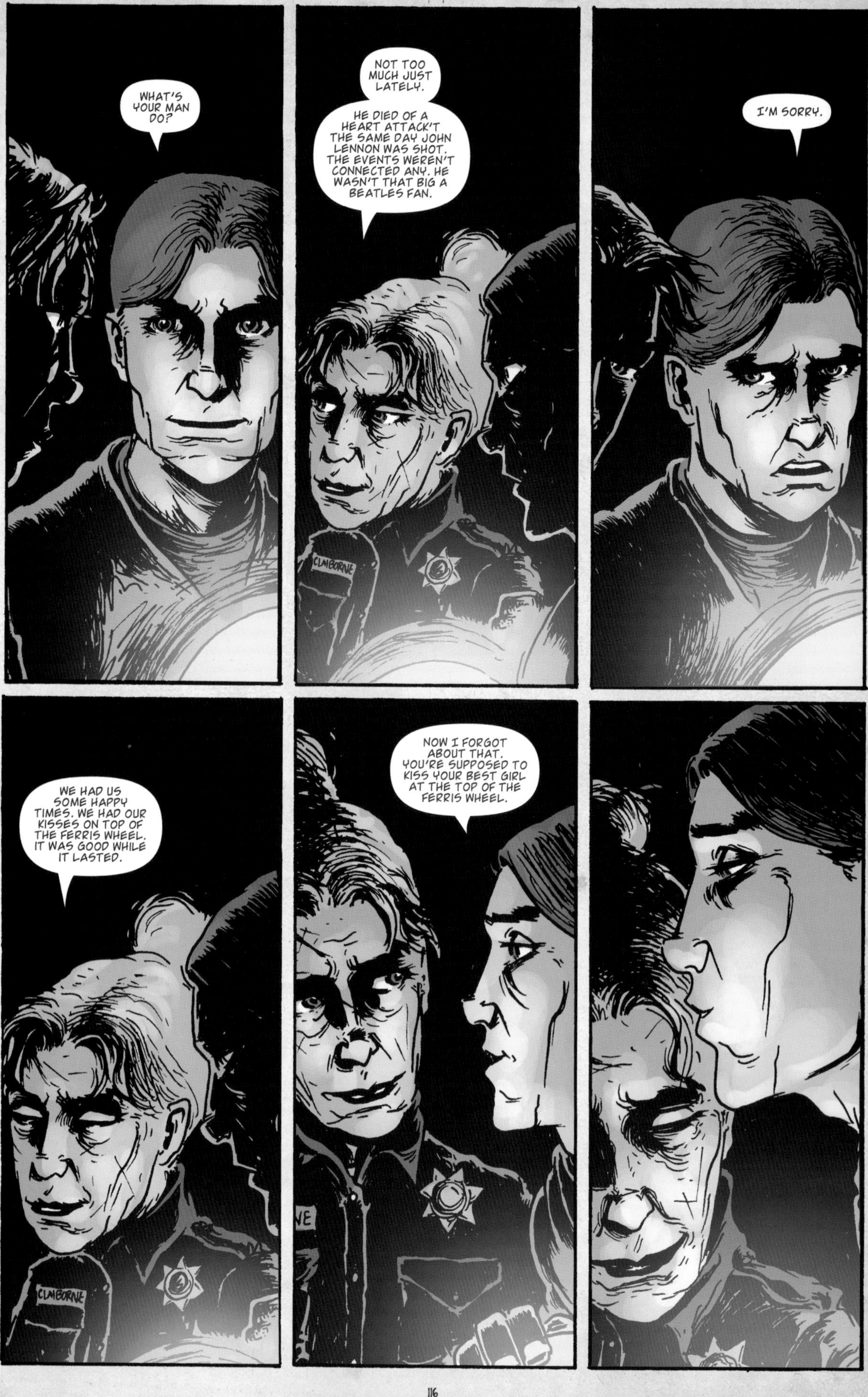
WHAT'S YOUR MAN DO?
NOT TOO MUCH JUST LATELY.
HE DIED OF A HEART ATTACK'T THE SAME DAY JOHN LENNON WAS SHOT. THE EVENTS WEREN'T CONNECTED ANY. HE WASN'T THAT BIG A BEATLES FAN.
CLAIBORNE
I'M SORRY.
WE HAD US SOME HAPPY TIMES. WE HAD OUR KISSES ON TOP OF THE FERRIS WHEEL. IT WAS GOOD WHILE IT LASTED.
CLAIBORNE
NOW I FORGOT ABOUT THAT. YOU'RE SUPPOSED TO KISS YOUR BEST GIRL AT THE TOP OF THE FERRIS WHEEL.

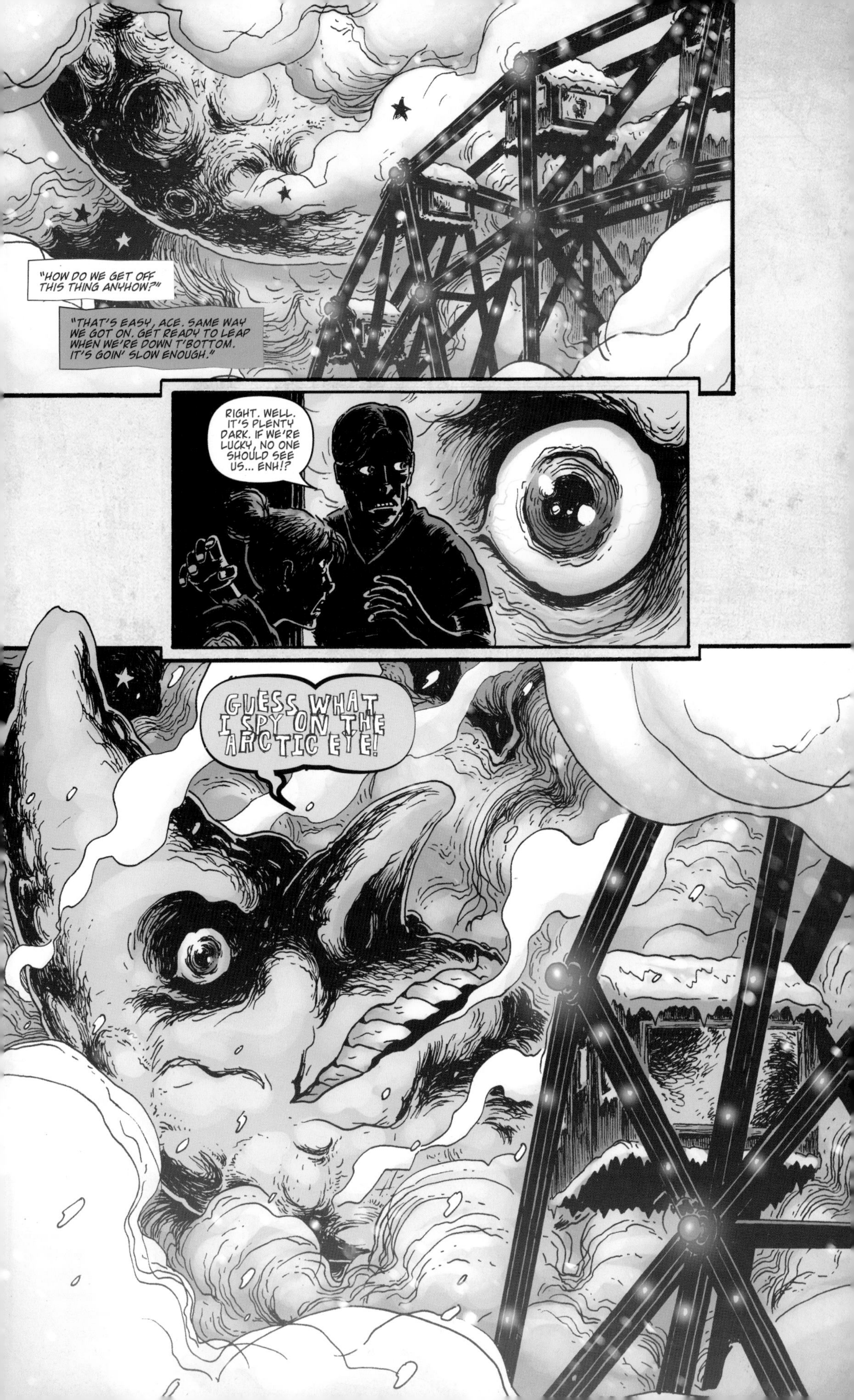
"HOW DO WE GET OFF THIS THING ANYHOW?"
"THAT'S EASY, ACE. SAME WAY WE GOT ON. GET READY TO LEAP WHEN WE'RE DOWN T'BOTTOM. IT'S GOIN' SLOW ENOUGH."
RIGHT. WELL. IT'S PLENTY DARK. IF WE'RE LUCKY, NO ONE SHOULD SEE US... ENH!?
GUESS WHAT I SPY ON THE ARCTIC EYE!

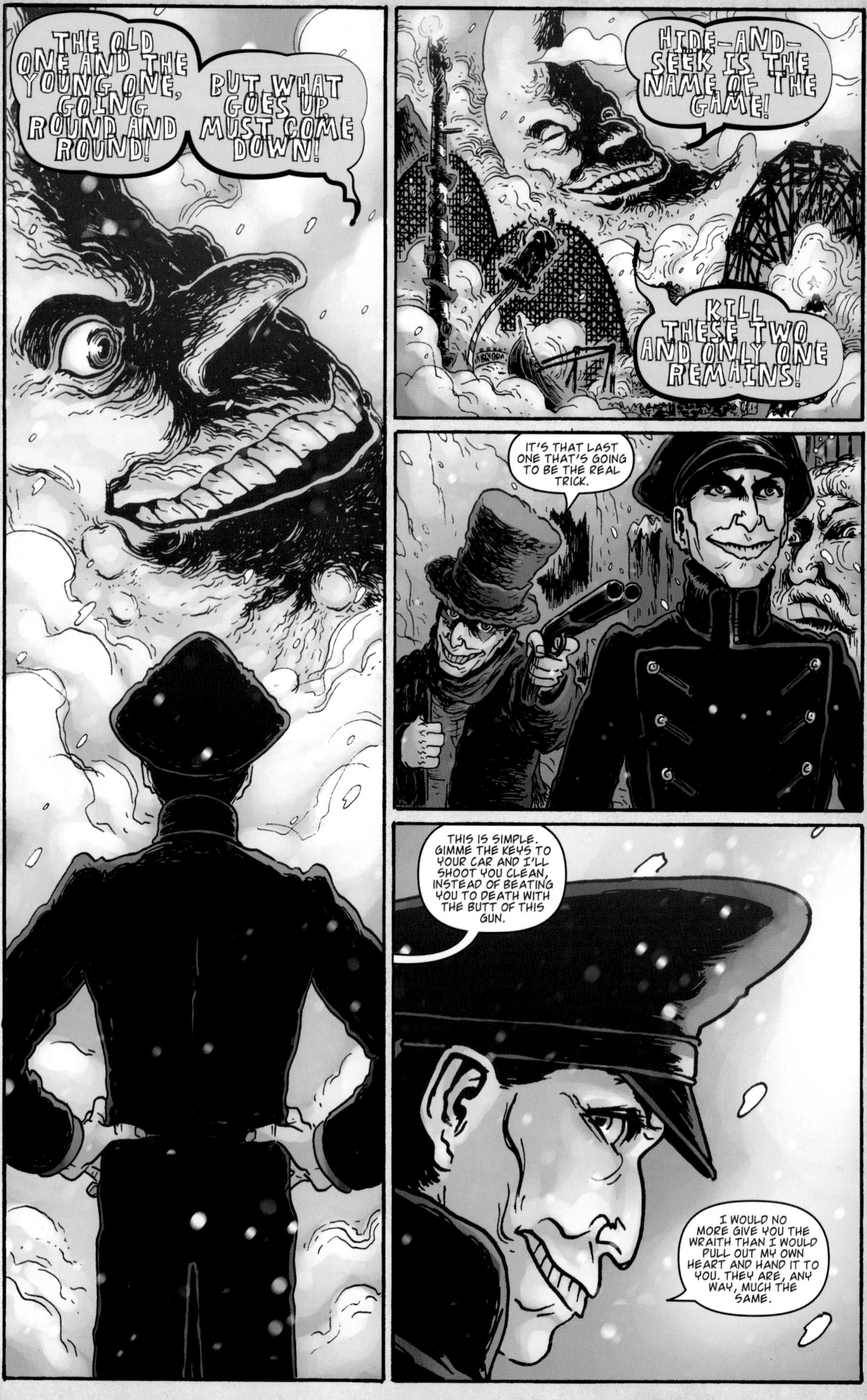
THE OLD ONE AND THE YOUNG ONE, GOING ROUND AND ROUND!
BUT WHAT GOES UP, MUST COME DOWN!
HIDE-AND-SEEK IS THE NAME OF THE GAME!
KILL THESE TWO AND ONLY ONE REMAINS!
IT'S THAT LAST ONE THAT'S GOING TO BE THE REAL TRICK.
THIS IS SIMPLE. GIMME THE KEYS TO YOUR CAR AND I'LL SHOOT YOU CLEAN, INSTEAD OF BEATING YOU TO DEATH WITH THE BUTT OF THIS GUN.
I WOULD NO MORE GIVE YOU THE WRAITH THAN I WOULD PULL OUT MY OWN HEART AND HAND IT TO YOU. THEY ARE, ANY WAY, MUCH THE SAME.

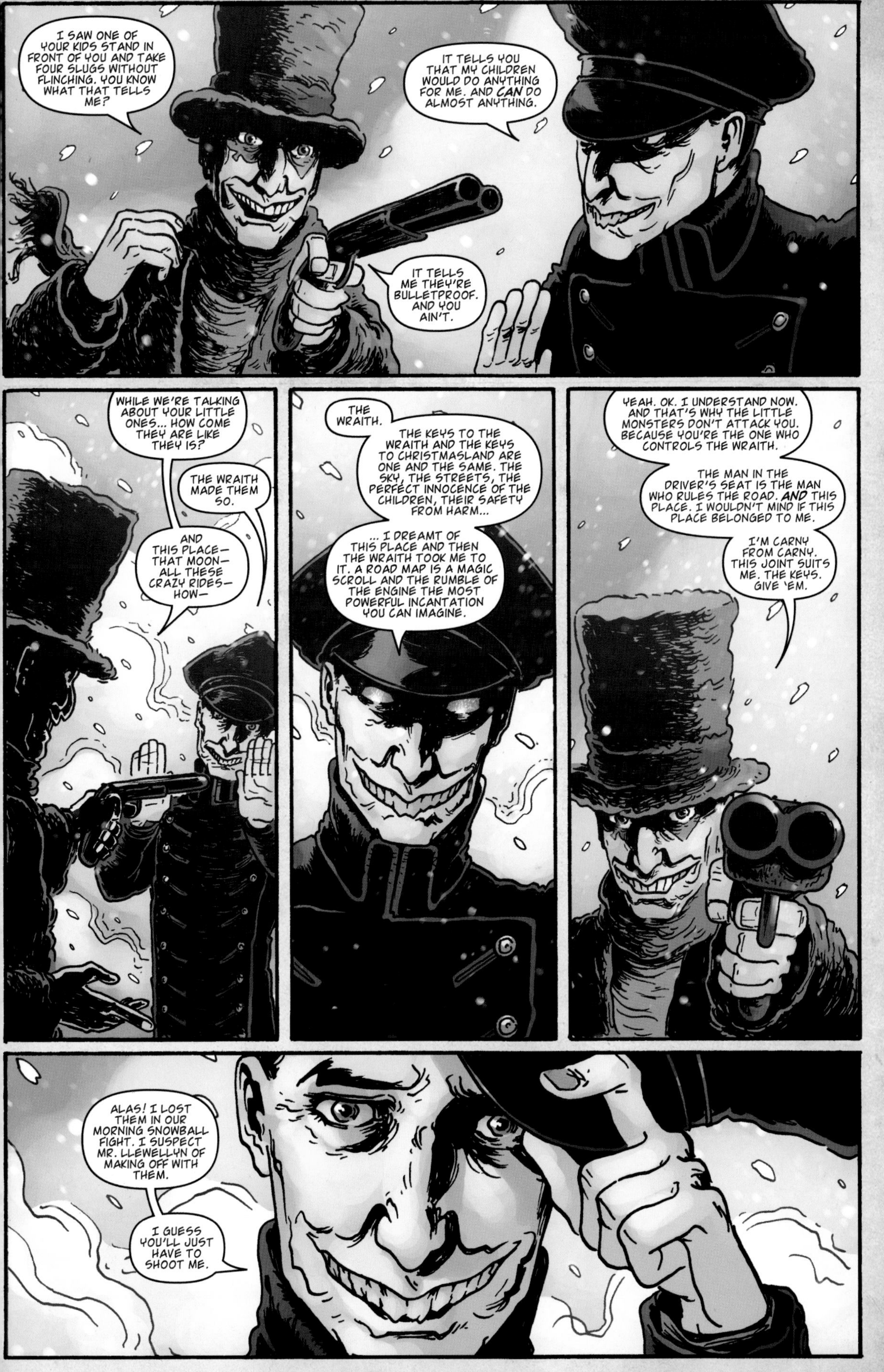
I SAW ONE OF YOUR KIDS STAND IN FRONT OF YOU AND TAKE FOUR SLUGS WITHOUT FLINCHING. YOU KNOW WHAT THAT TELLS ME?
IT TELLS YOU THAT MY CHILDREN WOULD DO ANYTHING FOR ME. AND CAN DO ALMOST ANYTHING.
IT TELLS ME THEY'RE BULLETPROOF. AND YOU AIN'T.
WHILE WE'RE TALKING ABOUT YOUR LITTLE ONES... HOW COME THEY ARE LIKE THEY IS?
THE WRAITH MADE THEM SO.
AND THIS PLACE— THAT MOON— ALL THESE CRAZY RIDES— HOW—
THE WRAITH.
THE KEYS TO THE WRAITH AND THE KEYS TO CHRISTMASLAND ARE ONE AND THE SAME. THE SKY, THE STREETS, THE PERFECT INNOCENCE OF THE CHILDREN, THEIR SAFETY FROM HARM...
... I DREAMT OF THIS PLACE AND THEN THE WRAITH TOOK ME TO IT. A ROAD MAP IS A MAGIC SCROLL AND THE RUMBLE OF THE ENGINE THE MOST POWERFUL INCANTATION YOU CAN IMAGINE.
YEAH. OK. I UNDERSTAND NOW. AND THAT'S WHY THE LITTLE MONSTERS DON'T ATTACK YOU. BECAUSE YOU'RE THE ONE WHO CONTROLS THE WRAITH.
THE MAN IN THE DRIVER'S SEAT IS THE MAN WHO RULES THE ROAD. AND THIS PLACE. I WOULDN'T MIND IF THIS PLACE BELONGED TO ME.
I'M CARNY FROM CARNY. THIS JOINT SUITS ME. THE KEYS. GIVE 'EM.
ALAS! I LOST THEM IN OUR MORNING SNOWBALL FIGHT. I SUSPECT MR. LLEWELLYN OF MAKING OFF WITH THEM.
I GUESS YOU'LL JUST HAVE TO SHOOT ME.

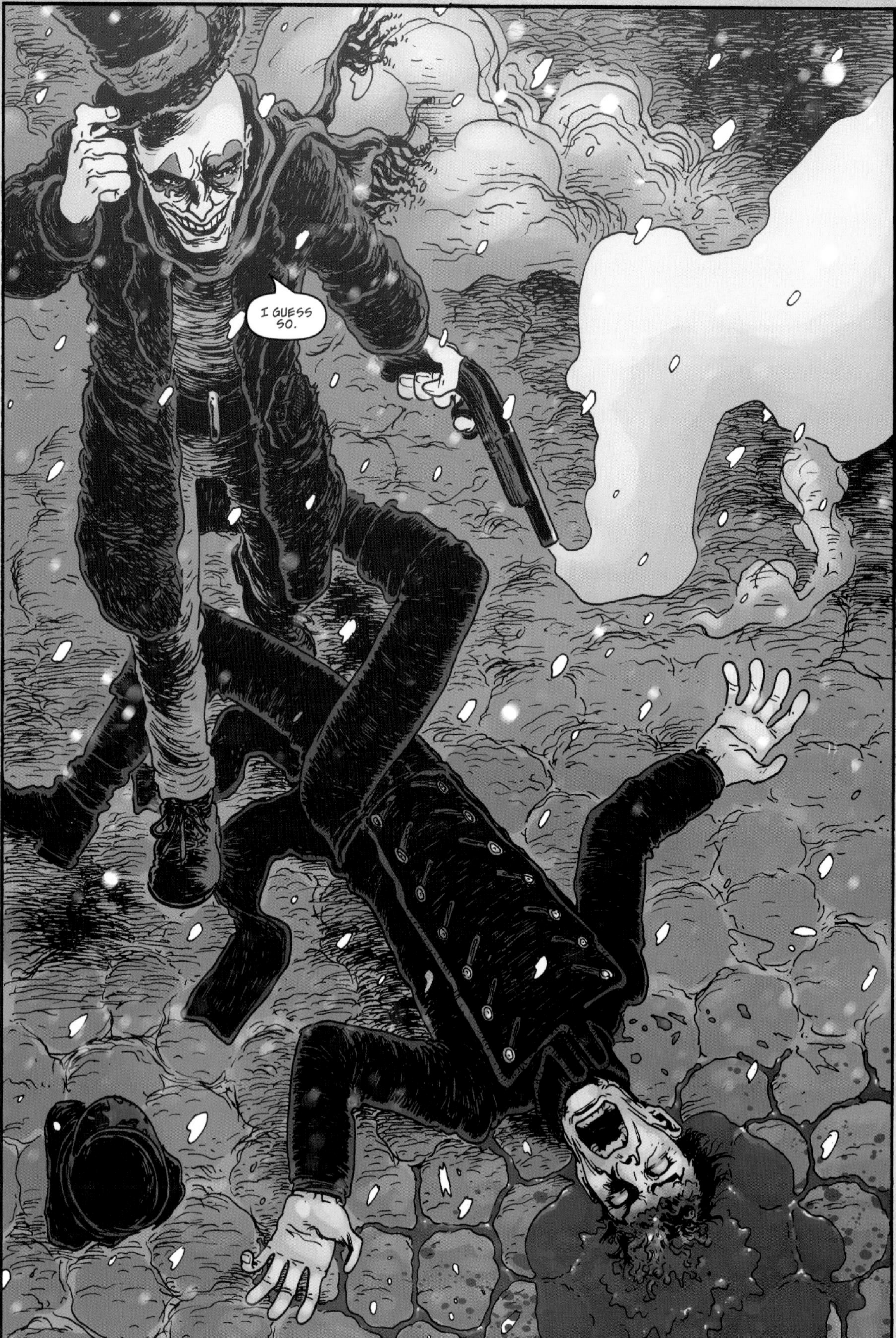
I GUESS SO.

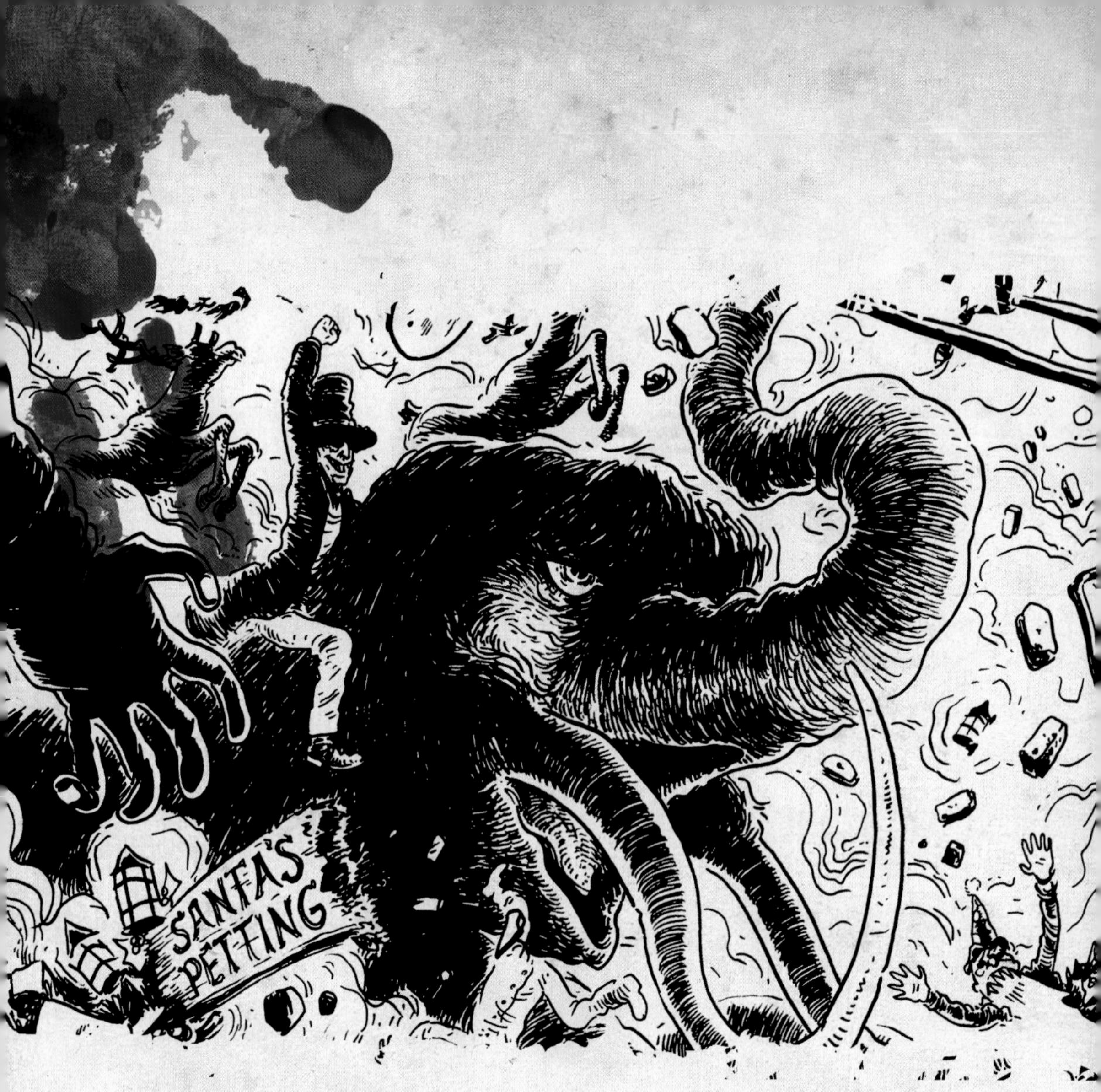
SANTA'S
PETTING

WELCOME TO CHRISTMASLAND chapter five

SHOOT THE MOON

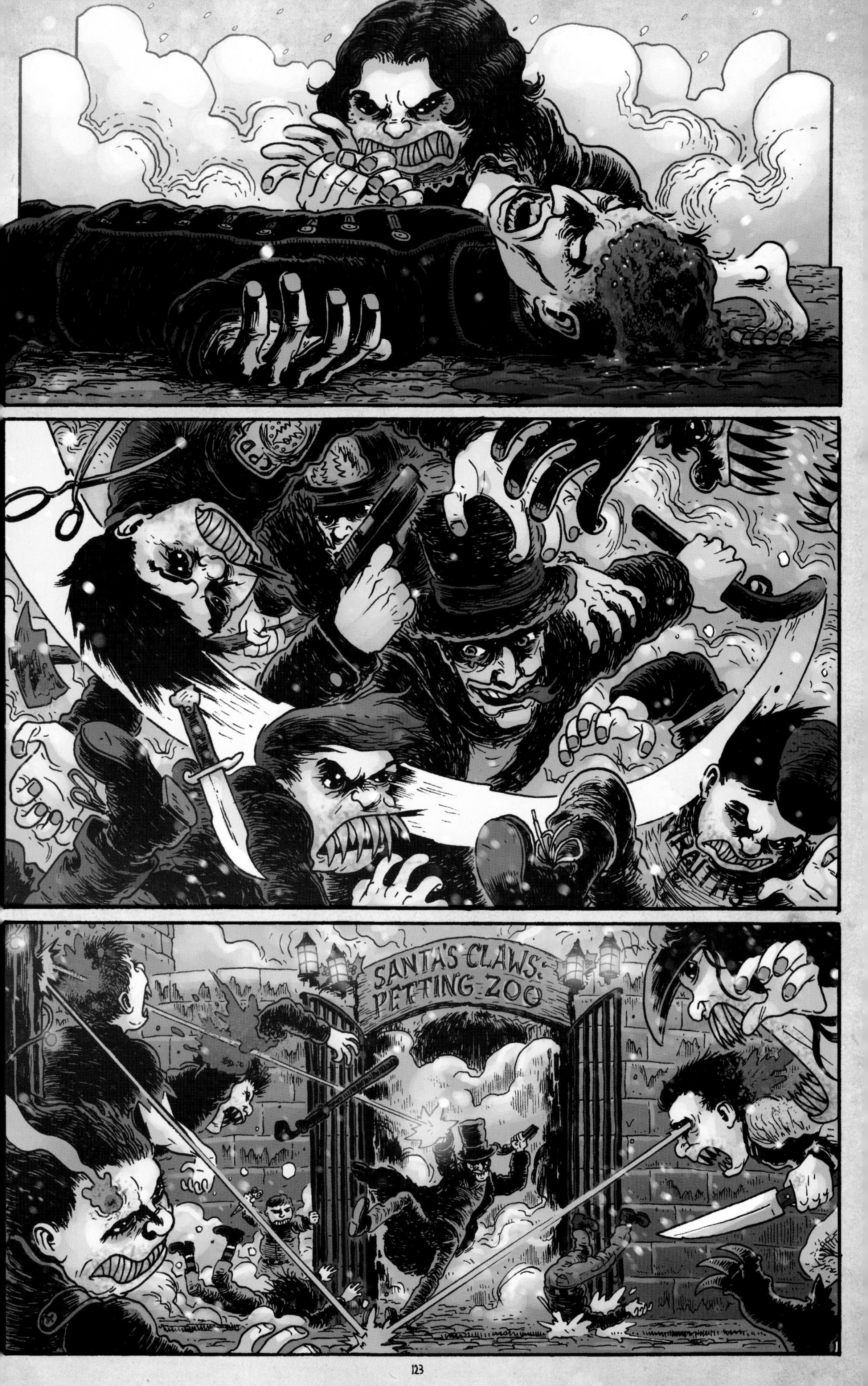
SANTA'S CLAWS PETTING ZOO

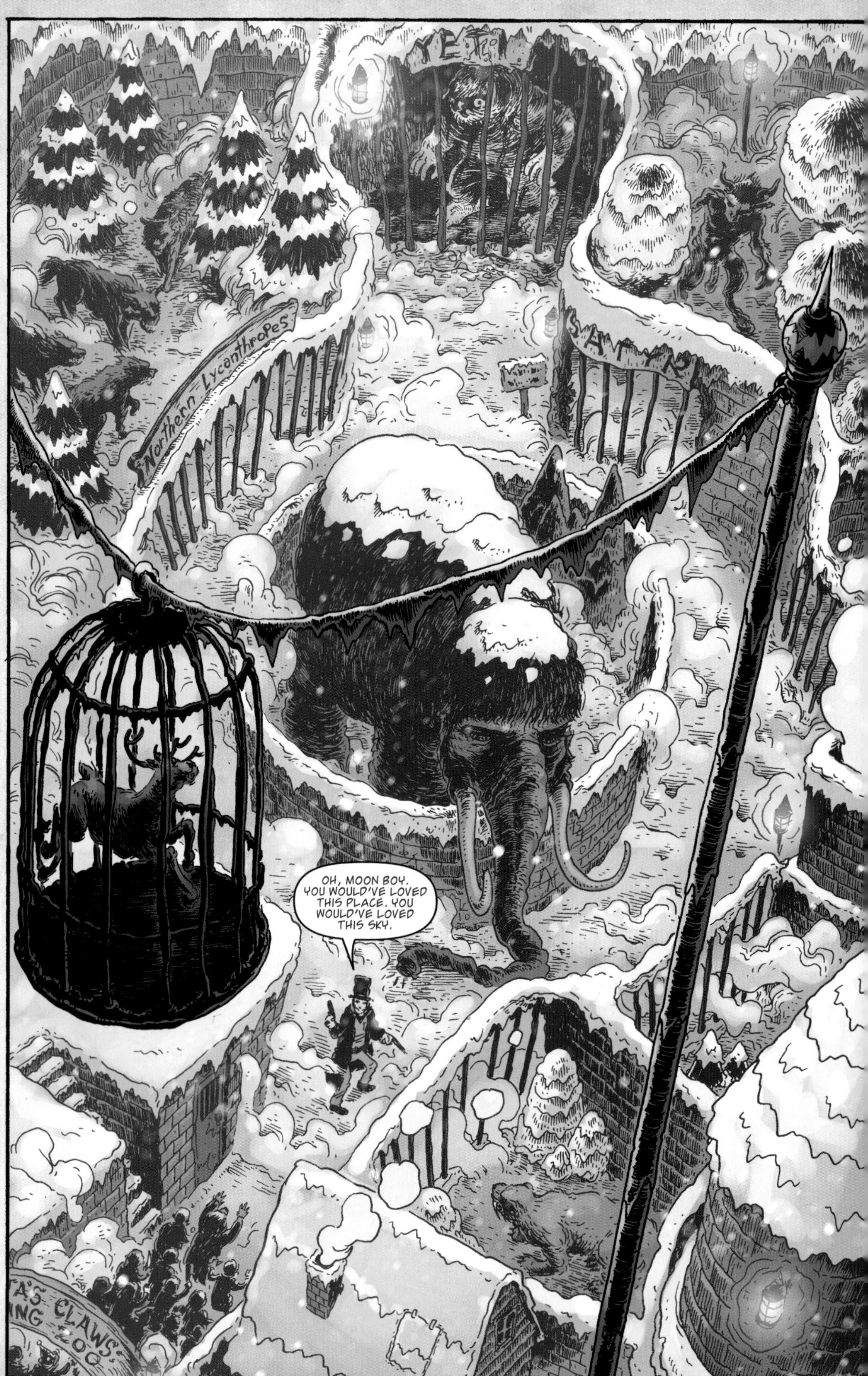
YETI
Northern Lycanthropes
SATYR
OH, MOON BOY. YOU WOULD'VE LOVED THIS PLACE. YOU WOULD'VE LOVED THIS SKY.

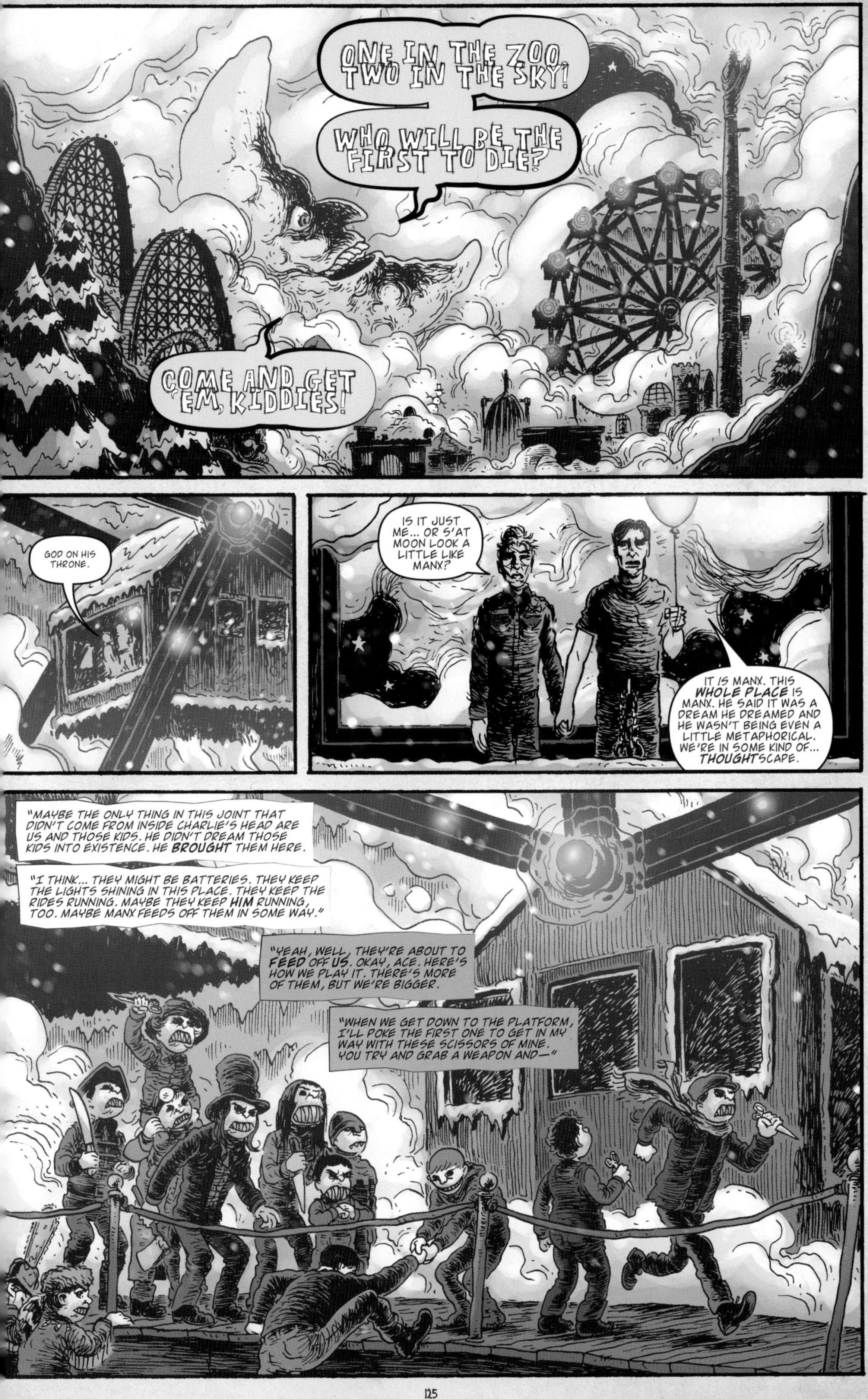

ONE IN THE ZOO, TWO IN THE SKY!
WHO WILL BE THE FIRST TO DIE?
COME AND GET 'EM, KIDDIES!
GOD ON HIS THRONE.
IS IT JUST ME... OR S'AT MOON LOOK A LITTLE LIKE MANX?
IT IS MANX. THIS WHOLE PLACE IS MANX. HE SAID IT WAS A DREAM HE DREAMED AND HE WASN'T BEING EVEN A LITTLE METAPHORICAL. WE'RE IN SOME KIND OF... THOUGHTSCAPE.
"MAYBE THE ONLY THING IN THIS JOINT THAT DIDN'T COME FROM INSIDE CHARLIE'S HEAD ARE US AND THOSE KIDS. HE DIDN'T DREAM THOSE KIDS INTO EXISTENCE. HE BROUGHT THEM HERE.
"I THINK... THEY MIGHT BE BATTERIES. THEY KEEP THE LIGHTS SHINING IN THIS PLACE. THEY KEEP THE RIDES RUNNING. MAYBE THEY KEEP HIM RUNNING, TOO. MAYBE MANX FEEDS OFF THEM IN SOME WAY."
"YEAH, WELL, THEY'RE ABOUT TO FEED OFF US. OKAY, ACE. HERE'S HOW WE PLAY IT. THERE'S MORE OF THEM, BUT WE'RE BIGGER.
"WHEN WE GET DOWN TO THE PLATFORM, I'LL POKE THE FIRST ONE TO GET IN MY WAY WITH THESE SCISSORS OF MINE. YOU TRY AND GRAB A WEAPON AND—"

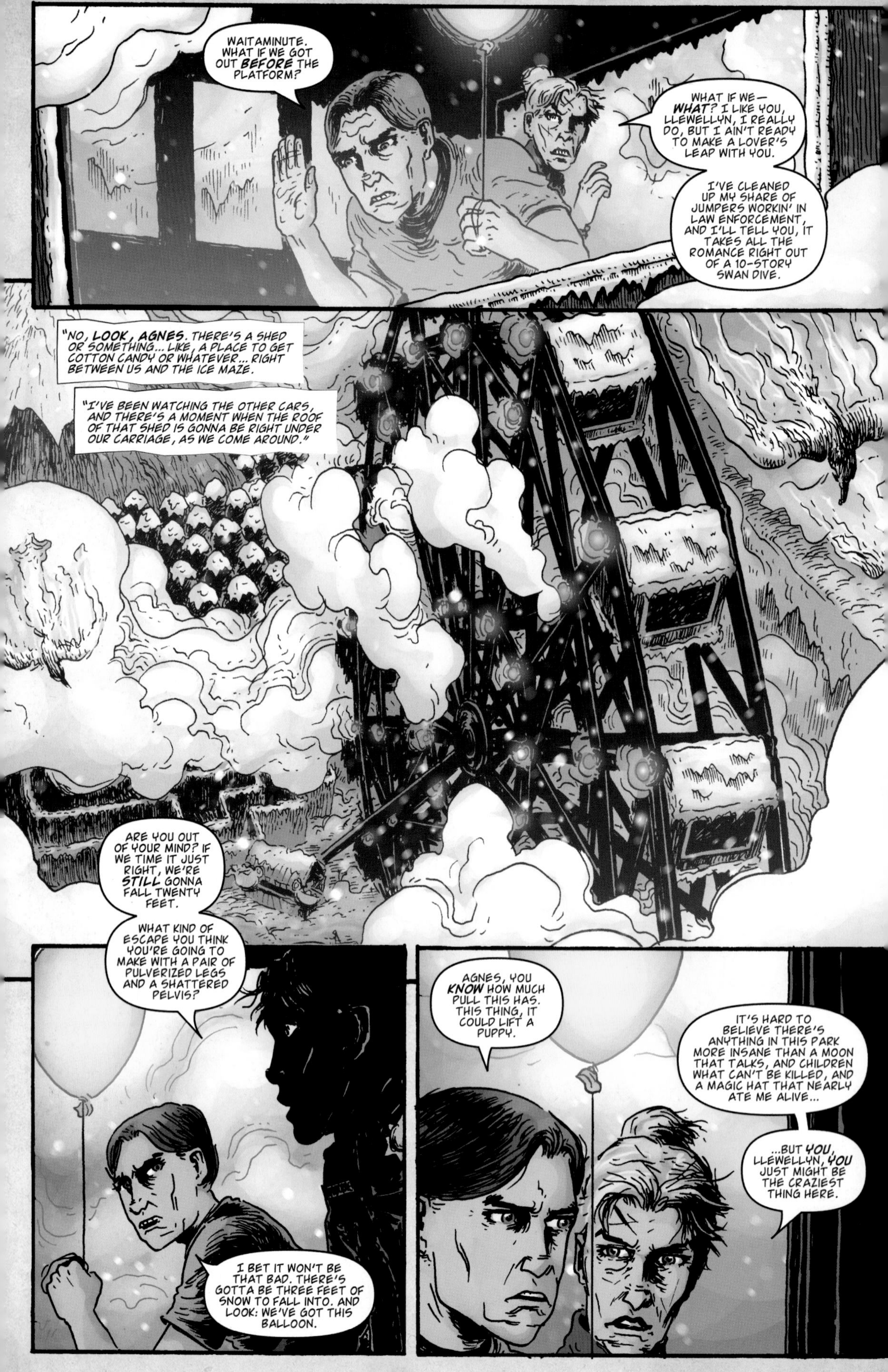

WAITAMINUTE. WHAT IF WE GOT OUT BEFORE THE PLATFORM?
WHAT IF WE— WHAT? I LIKE YOU, LLEWELLYN, I REALLY DO, BUT I AIN'T READY TO MAKE A LOVER'S LEAP WITH YOU.
I'VE CLEANED UP MY SHARE OF JUMPERS WORKIN' IN LAW ENFORCEMENT, AND I'LL TELL YOU, IT TAKES ALL THE ROMANCE RIGHT OUT OF A 10-STORY SWAN DIVE.
"NO, LOOK, AGNES. THERE'S A SHED OR SOMETHING... LIKE, A PLACE TO GET COTTON CANDY OR WHATEVER... RIGHT BETWEEN US AND THE ICE MAZE.
"I'VE BEEN WATCHING THE OTHER CARS, AND THERE'S A MOMENT WHEN THE ROOF OF THAT SHED IS GONNA BE RIGHT UNDER OUR CARRIAGE, AS WE COME AROUND."
ARE YOU OUT OF YOUR MIND? IF WE TIME IT JUST RIGHT, WE'RE STILL GONNA FALL TWENTY FEET.
WHAT KIND OF ESCAPE YOU THINK YOU'RE GOING TO MAKE WITH A PAIR OF PULVERIZED LEGS AND A SHATTERED PELVIS?
I BET IT WON'T BE THAT BAD. THERE'S GOTTA BE THREE FEET OF SNOW TO FALL INTO. AND LOOK: WE'VE GOT THIS BALLOON.
AGNES, YOU KNOW HOW MUCH PULL THIS HAS. THIS THING, IT COULD LIFT A PUPPY.
IT'S HARD TO BELIEVE THERE'S ANYTHING IN THIS PARK MORE INSANE THAN A MOON THAT TALKS, AND CHILDREN WHAT CAN'T BE KILLED, AND A MAGIC HAT THAT NEARLY ATE ME ALIVE...
...BUT YOU, LLEWELLYN, YOU JUST MIGHT BE THE CRAZIEST THING HERE.

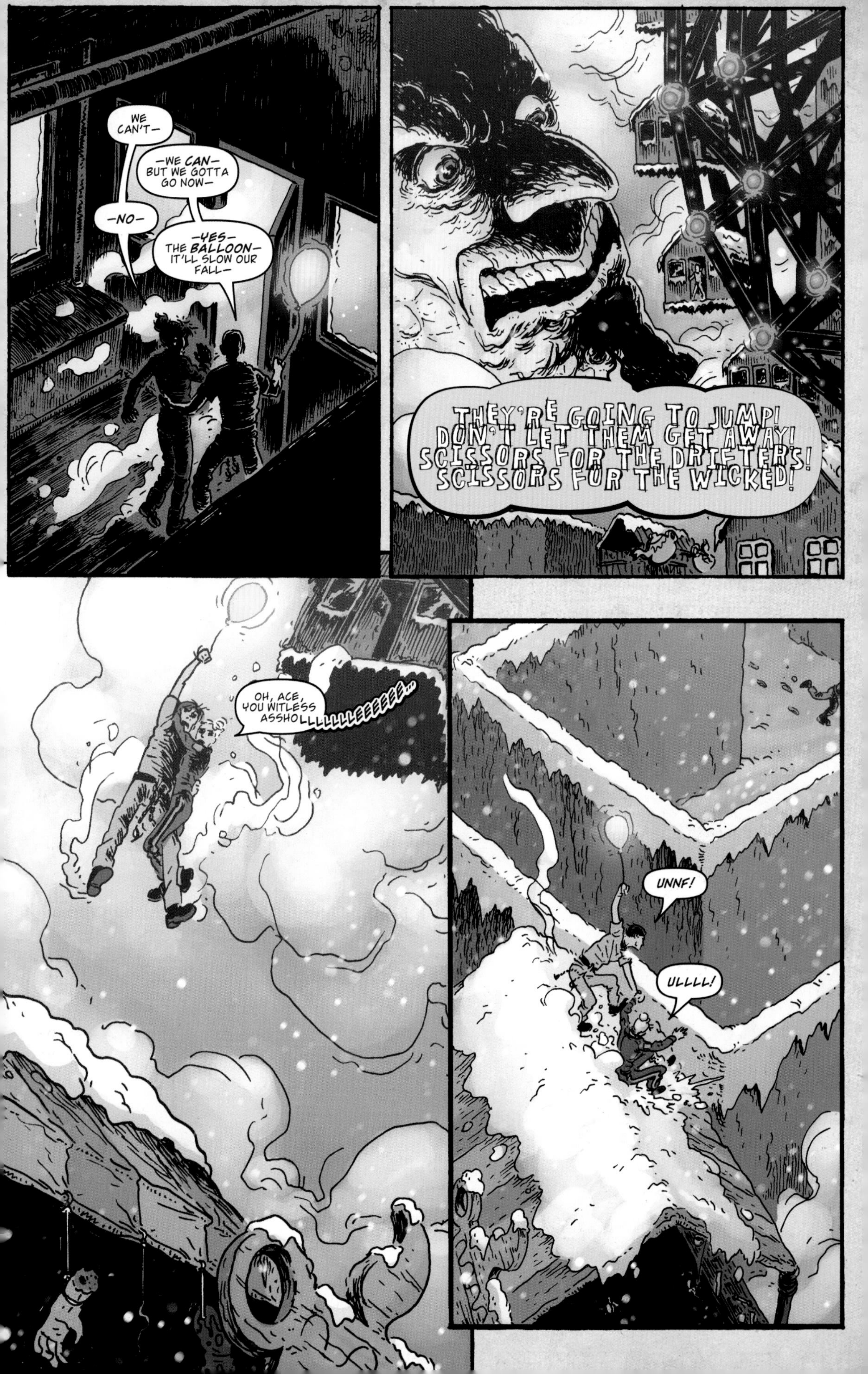
WE CAN'T—
—WE CAN—
BUT WE GOTTA GO NOW—
—NO—
—YES—
THE BALLOON—
IT'LL SLOW OUR FALL—
THEY'RE GOING TO JUMP!
DON'T LET THEM GET AWAY!
SCISSORS FOR THE DRIFTERS!
SCISSORS FOR THE WICKED!
OH, ACE, YOU WITLESS ASSHOLLLLLLLEEEEEE...
UNNF!
ULLLL!

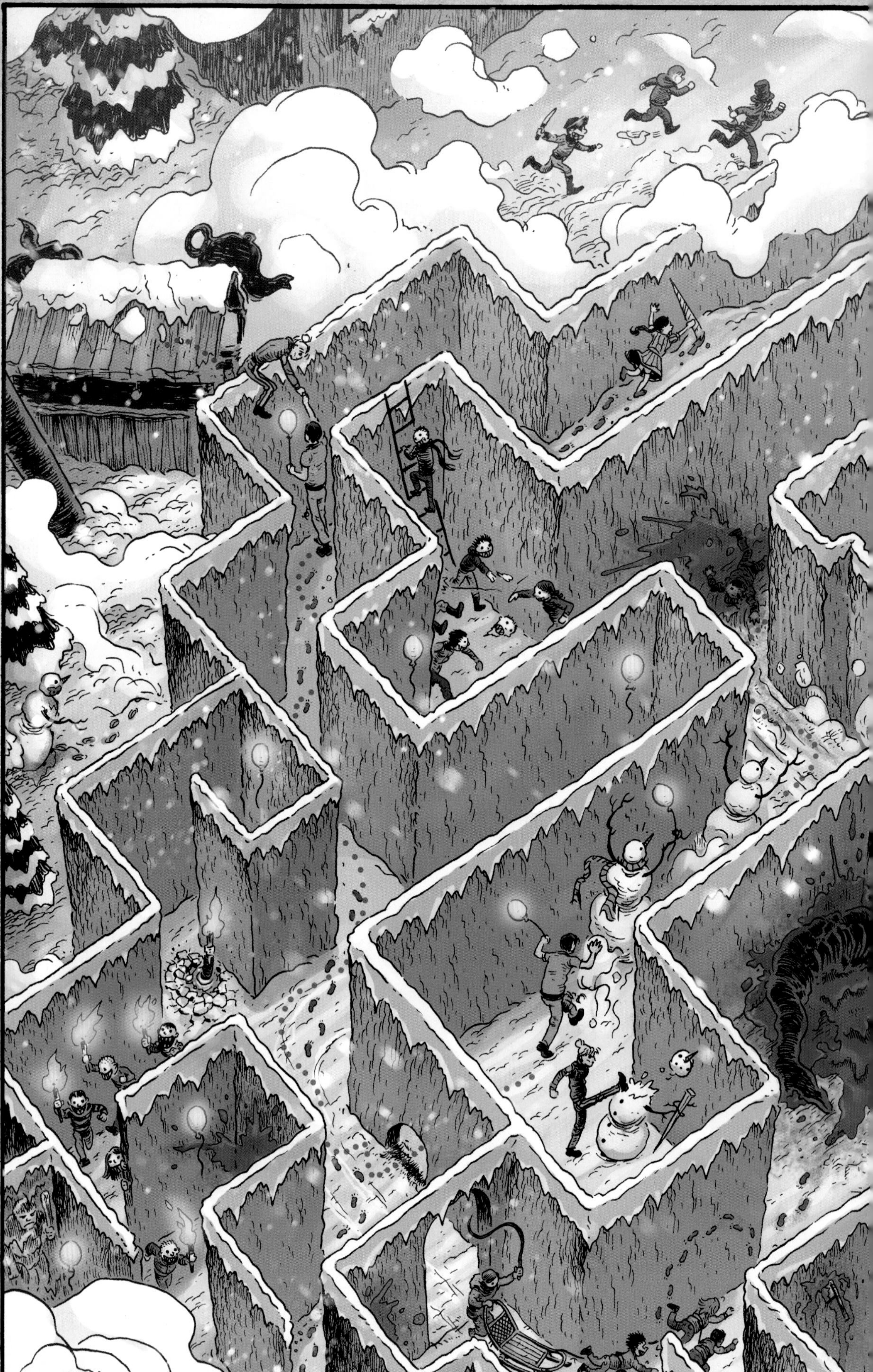

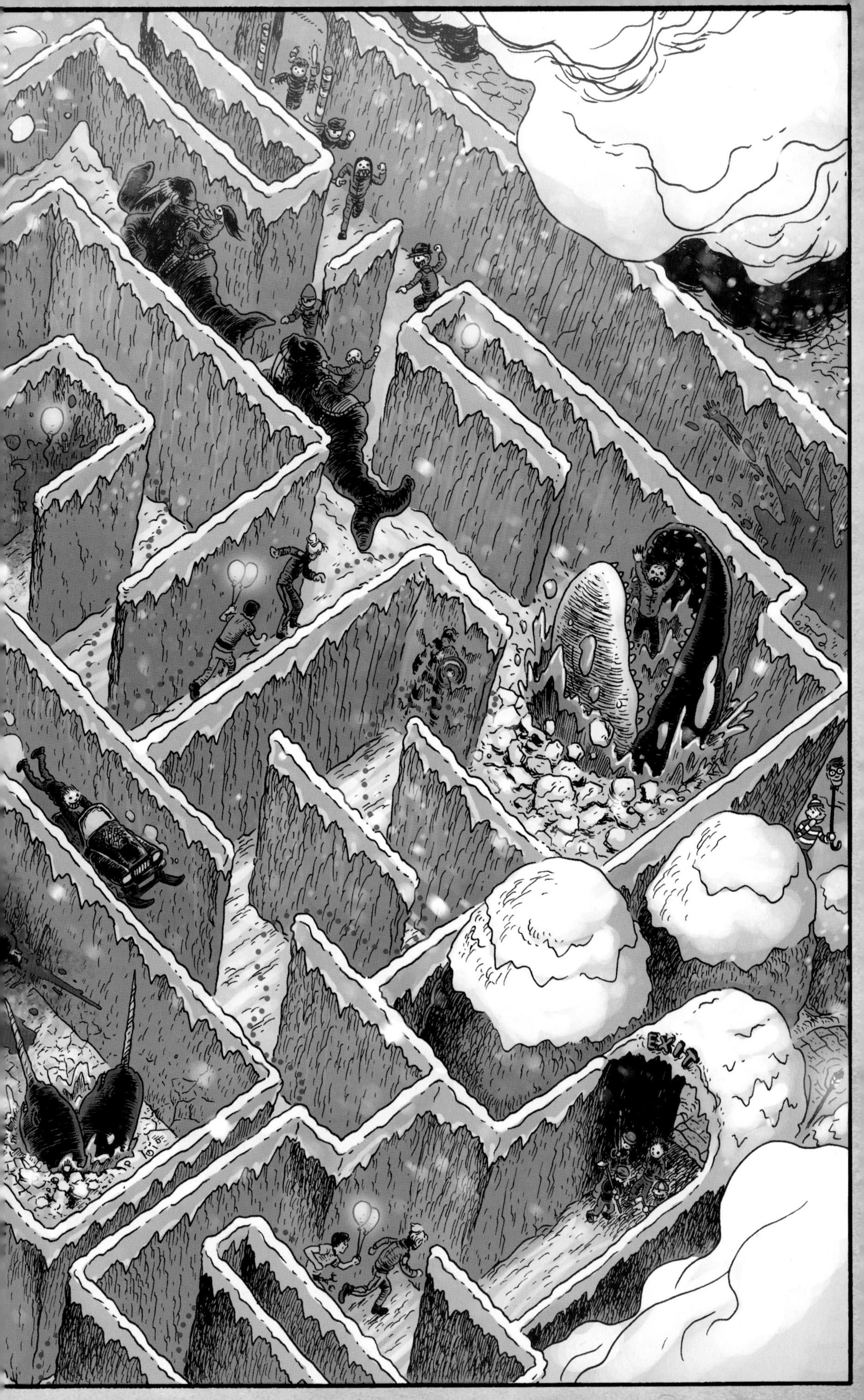
EXIT

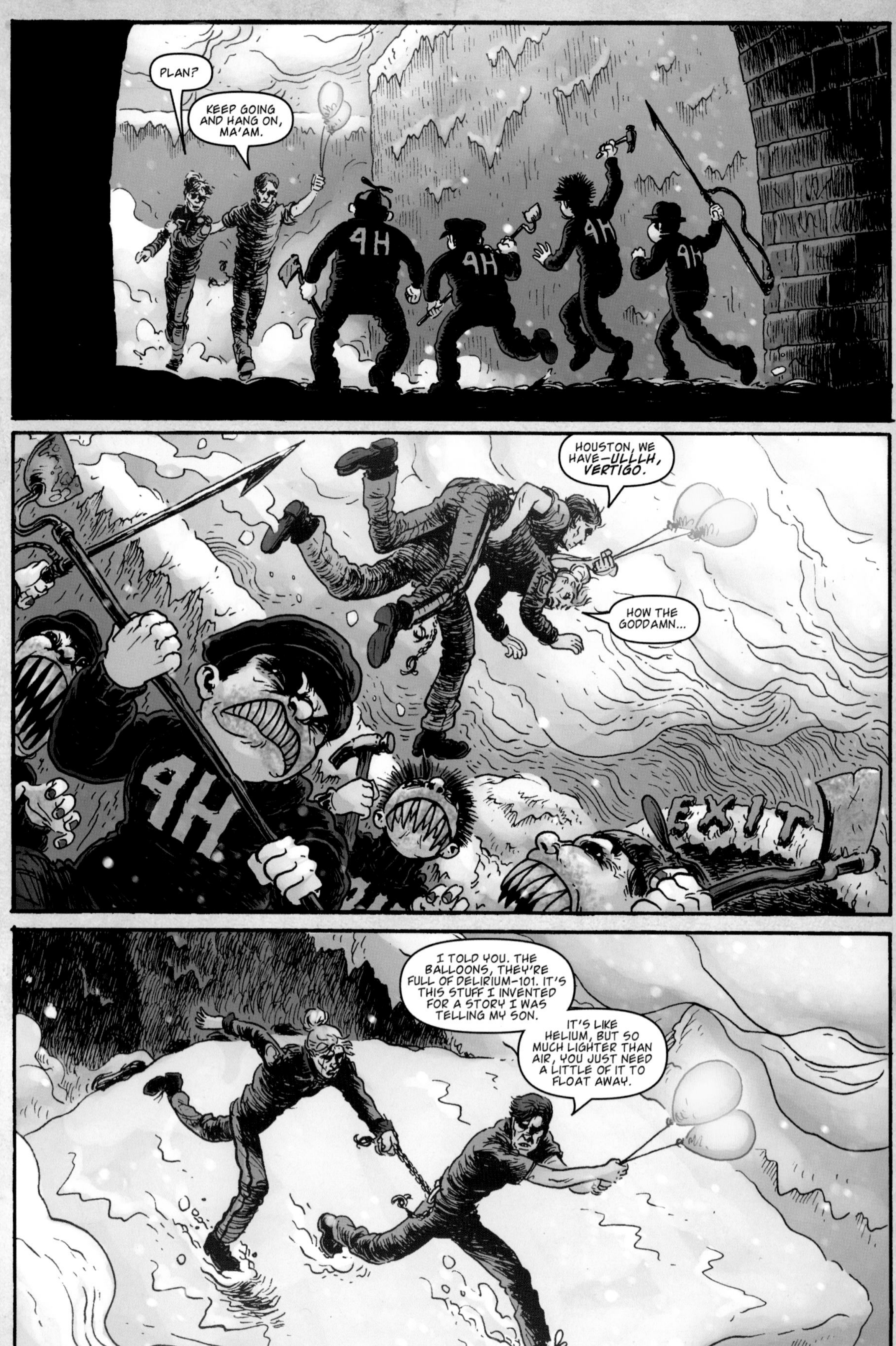
PLAN?
KEEP GOING AND HANG ON, MA'AM.
4H
HOUSTON, WE HAVE—ULLLH, VERTIGO.
HOW THE GODDAMN...
EXIT
I TOLD YOU. THE BALLOONS, THEY'RE FULL OF DELIRIUM-101. IT'S THIS STUFF I INVENTED FOR A STORY I WAS TELLING MY SON.
IT'S LIKE HELIUM, BUT SO MUCH LIGHTER THAN AIR, YOU JUST NEED A LITTLE OF IT TO FLOAT AWAY.

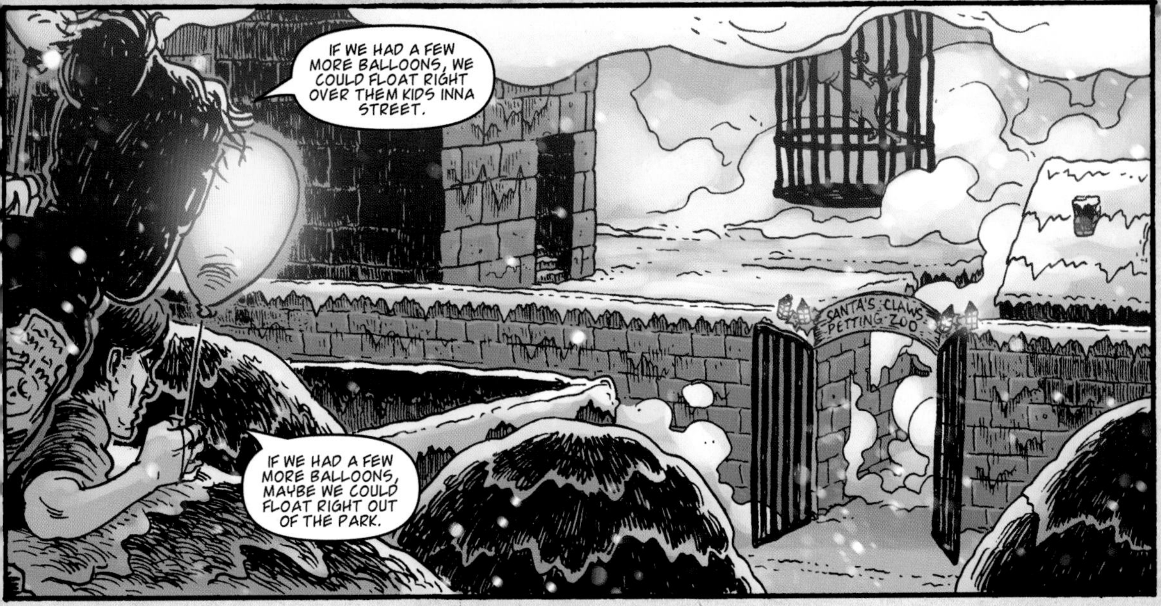
IF WE HAD A FEW MORE BALLOONS, WE COULD FLOAT RIGHT OVER THEM KIDS INNA STREET.
IF WE HAD A FEW MORE BALLOONS, MAYBE WE COULD FLOAT RIGHT OUT OF THE PARK.
SANTA'S CLAWS PETTING ZOO

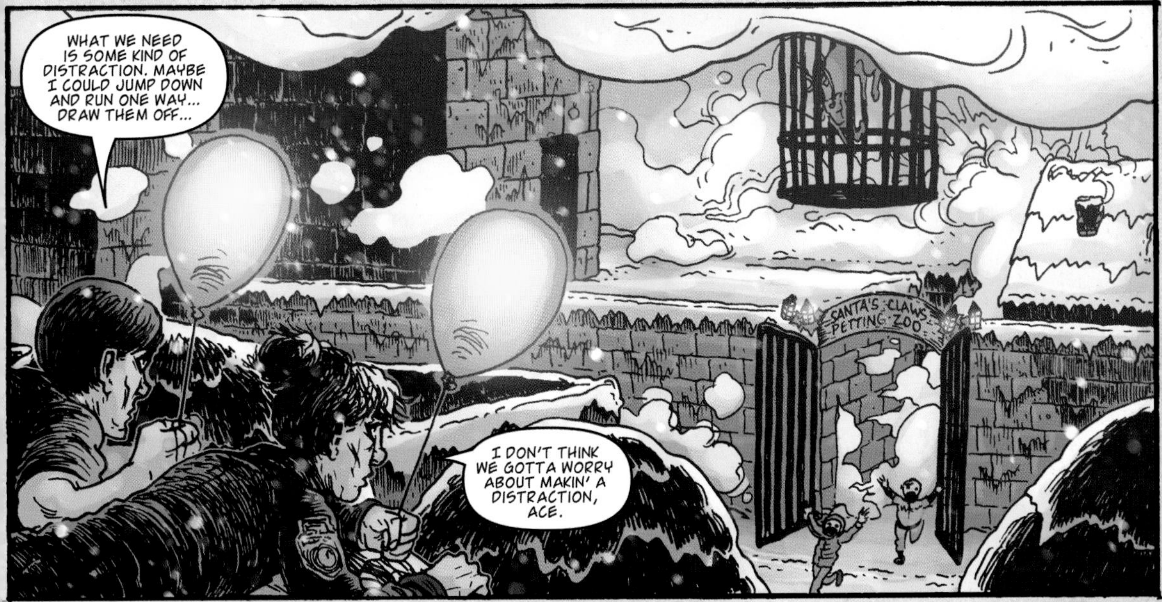
WHAT WE NEED IS SOME KIND OF DISTRACTION. MAYBE I COULD JUMP DOWN AND RUN ONE WAY... DRAW THEM OFF...
SANTA'S CLAWS PETTING ZOO
I DON'T THINK WE GOTTA WORRY ABOUT MAKIN' A DISTRACTION, ACE.

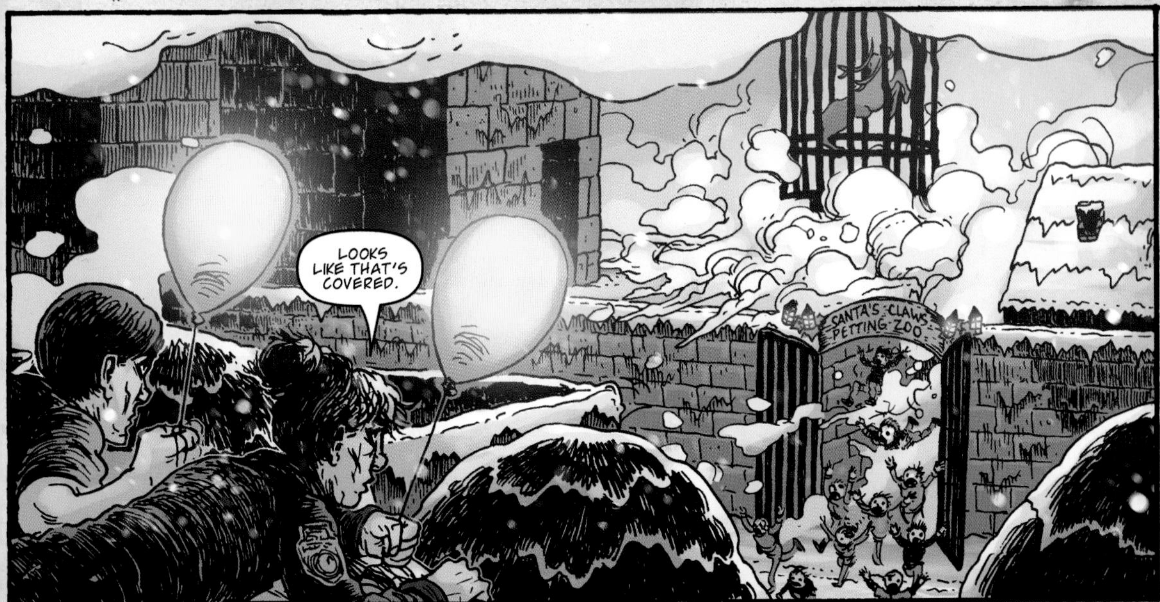
LOOKS LIKE THAT'S COVERED.
SANTA'S CLAWS PETTING ZOO

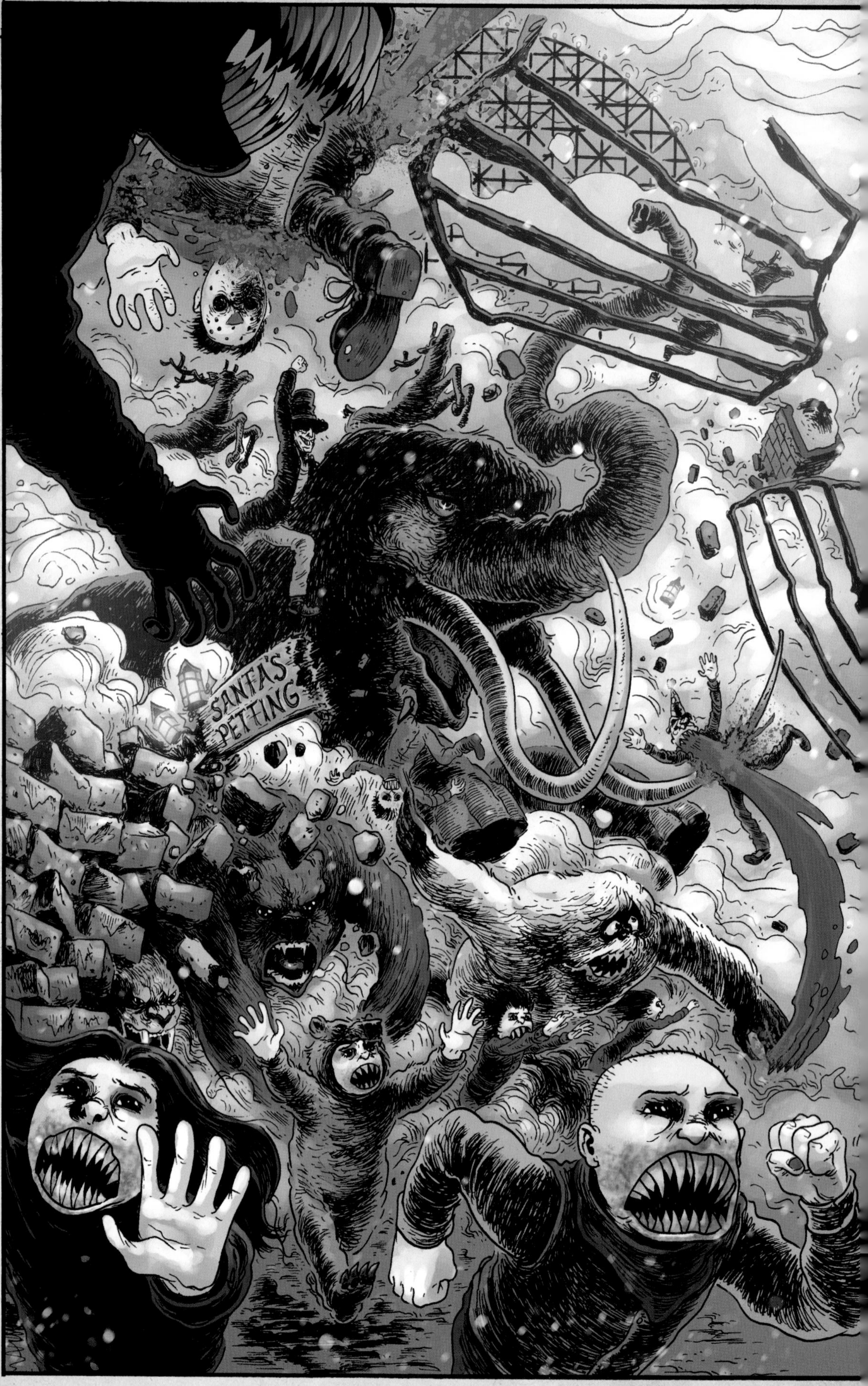
SANTA'S PETTING

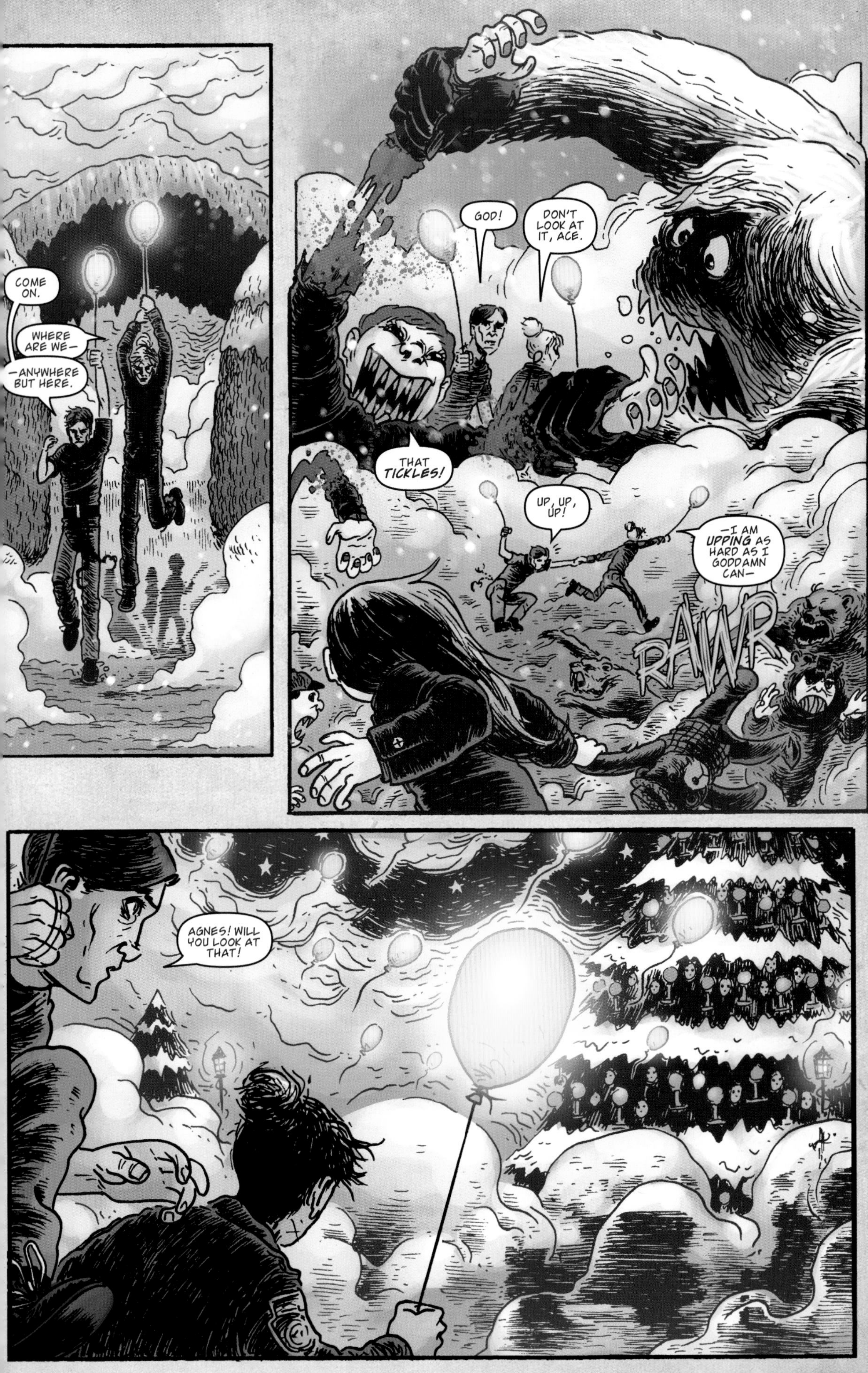
COME ON.
WHERE ARE WE—
—ANYWHERE BUT HERE.
GOD!
DON'T LOOK AT IT, ACE.
THAT TICKLES!
UP, UP, UP!
—I AM UPPING AS HARD AS I GODDAMN CAN—
RAWR
AGNES! WILL YOU LOOK AT THAT!

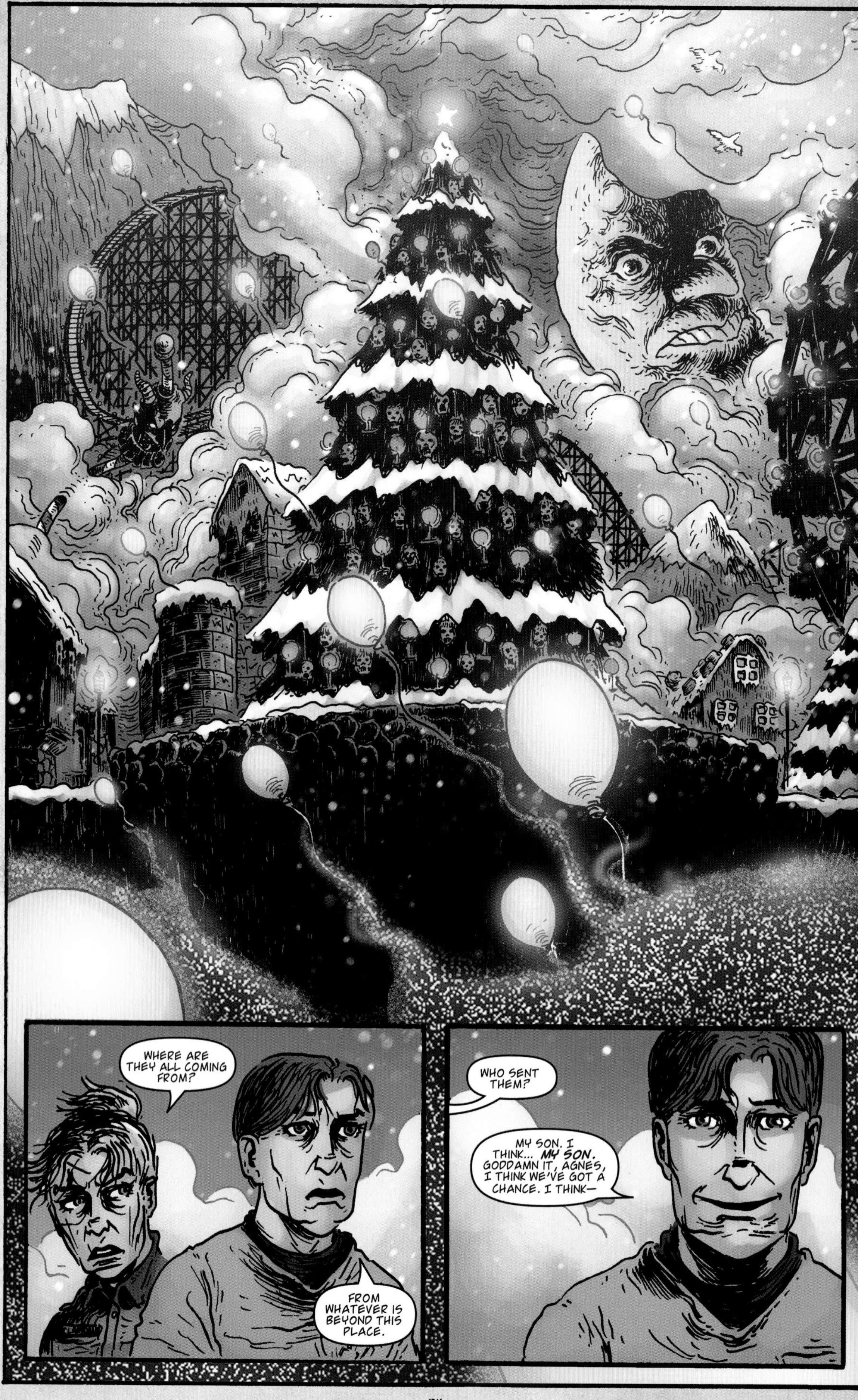
WHERE ARE THEY ALL COMING FROM?
FROM WHATEVER IS BEYOND THIS PLACE.
WHO SENT THEM?
MY SON. I THINK... MY SON. GODDAMN IT, AGNES, I THINK WE'VE GOT A CHANCE. I THINK—

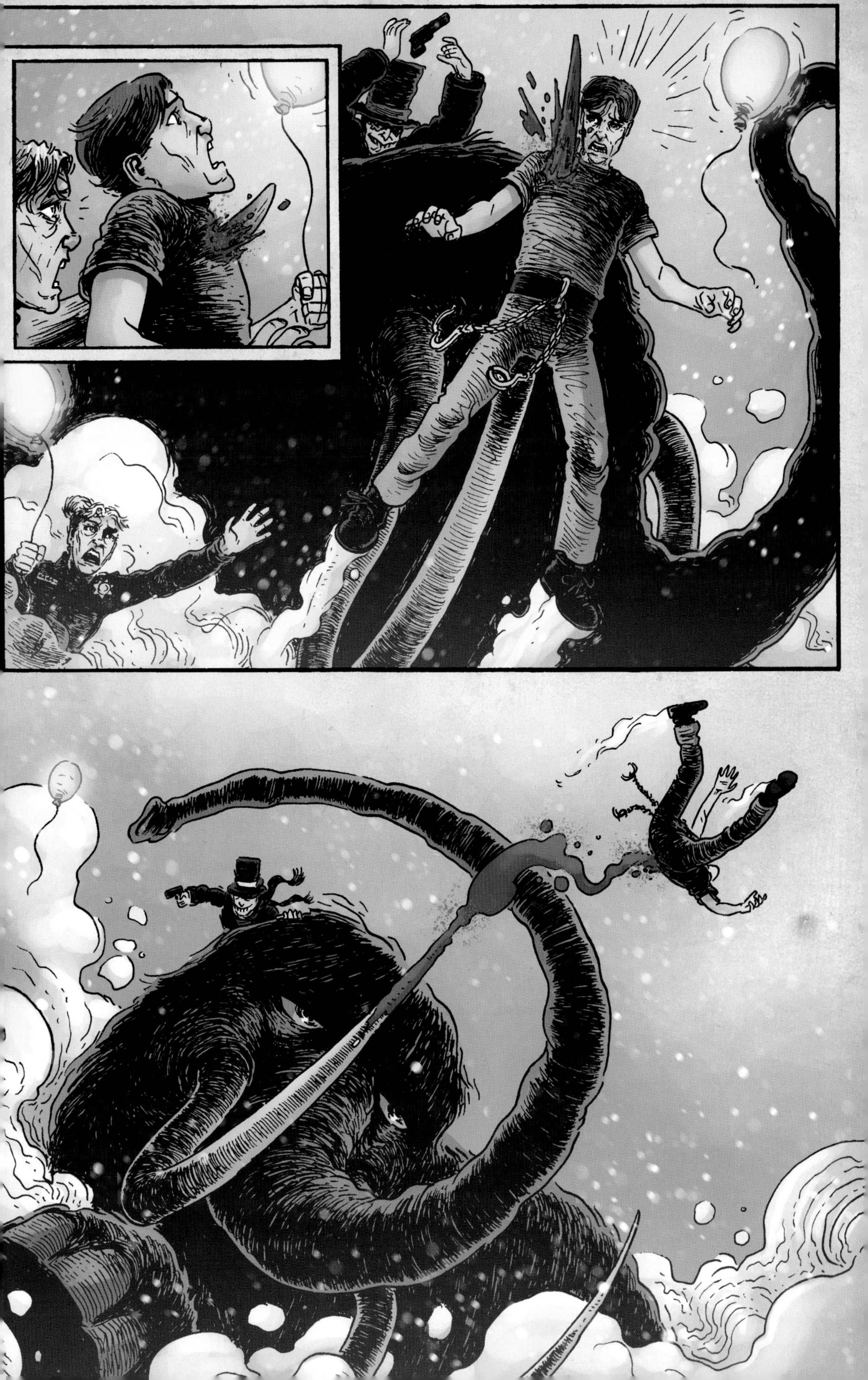

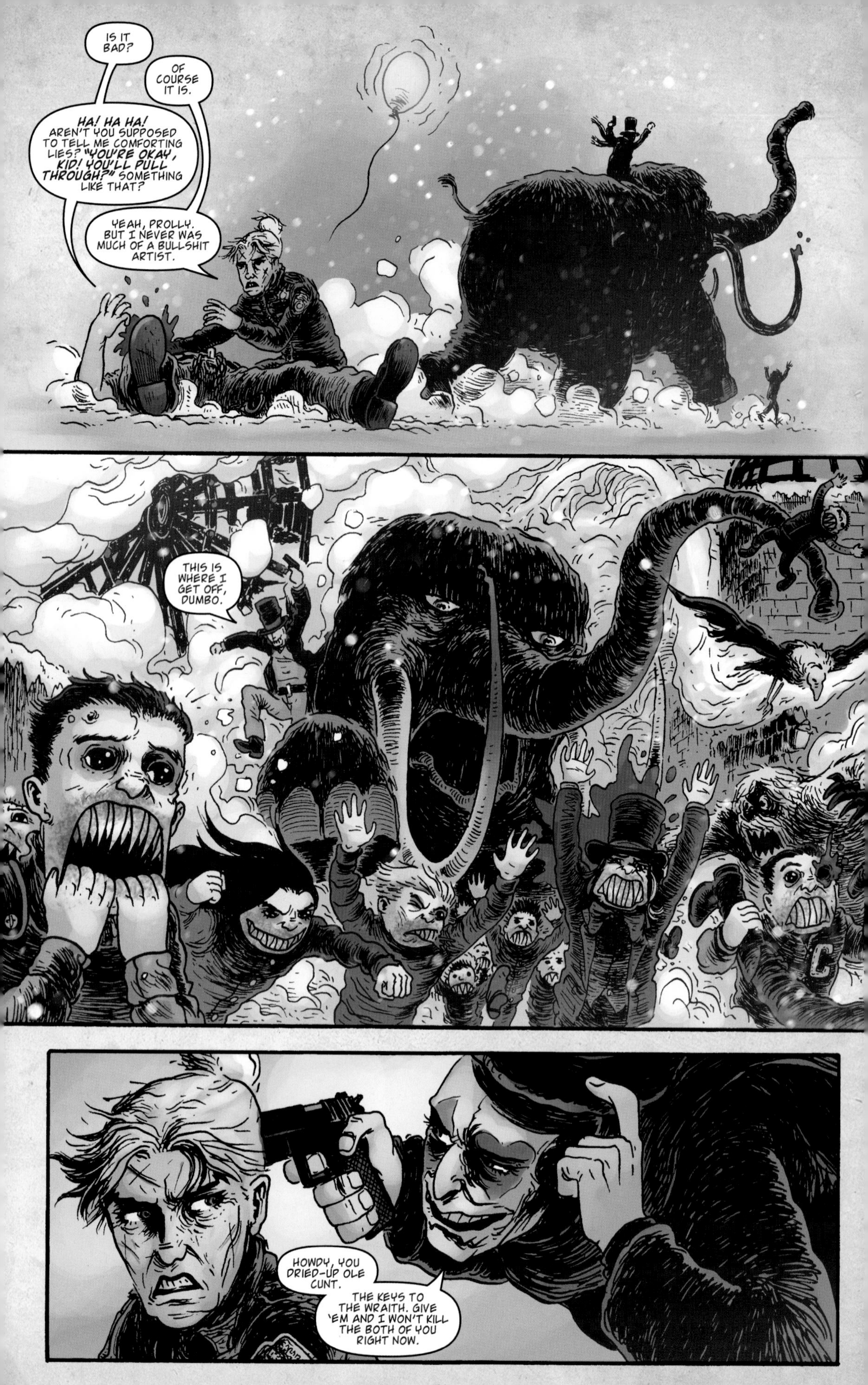
IS IT BAD?
OF COURSE IT IS.
HA! HA HA! AREN'T YOU SUPPOSED TO TELL ME COMFORTING LIES? "YOU'RE OKAY, KID! YOU'LL PULL THROUGH?" SOMETHING LIKE THAT?
YEAH, PROLLY. BUT I NEVER WAS MUCH OF A BULLSHIT ARTIST.
THIS IS WHERE I GET OFF, DUMBO.
HOWDY, YOU DRIED-UP OLE CUNT.
THE KEYS TO THE WRAITH. GIVE 'EM AND I WON'T KILL THE BOTH OF YOU RIGHT NOW.

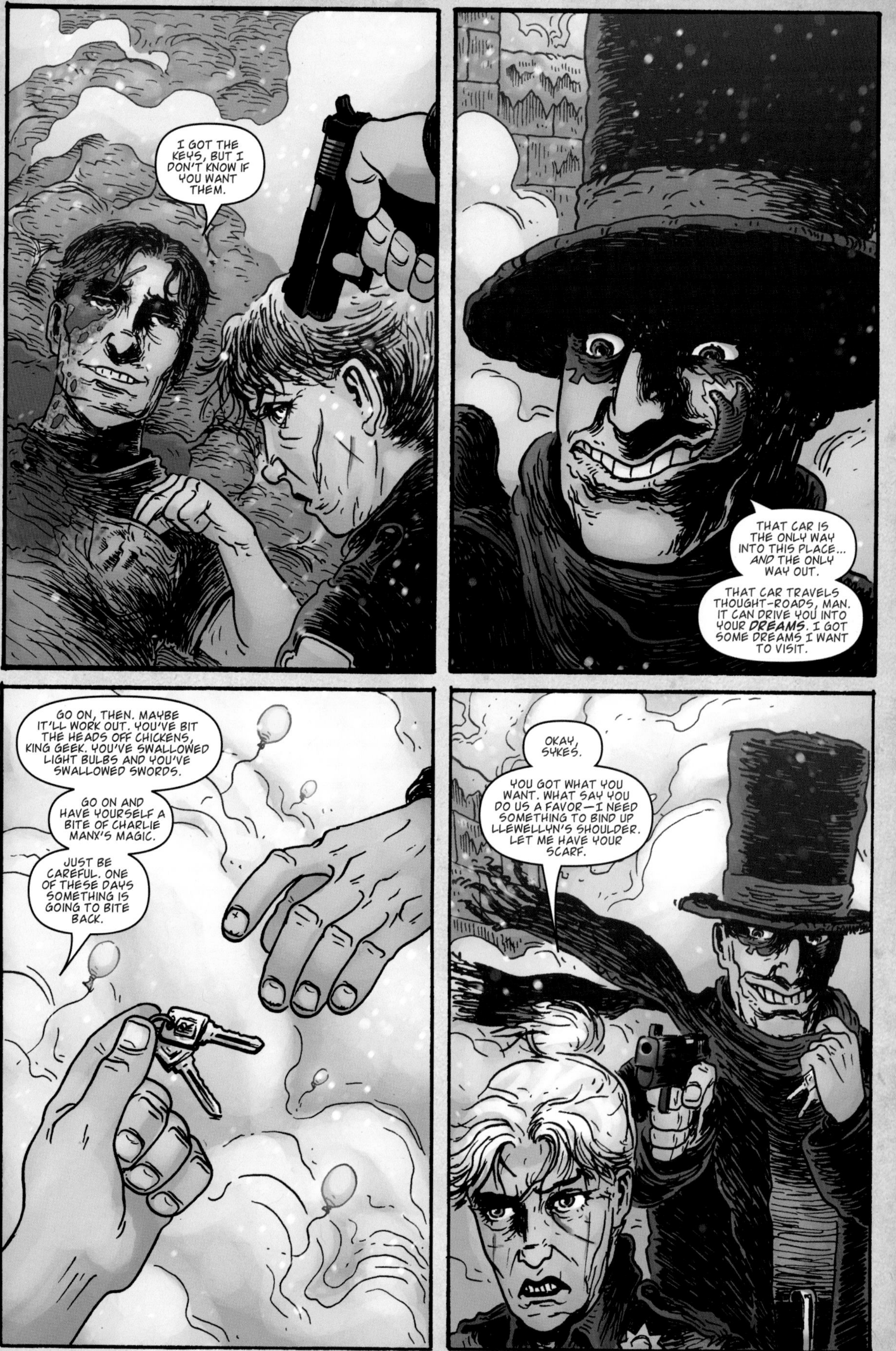
I GOT THE KEYS, BUT I DON'T KNOW IF YOU WANT THEM.
THAT CAR IS THE ONLY WAY INTO THIS PLACE... *AND* THE ONLY WAY OUT.
THAT CAR TRAVELS THOUGHT-ROADS, MAN. IT CAN DRIVE YOU INTO YOUR ***DREAMS***. I GOT SOME DREAMS I WANT TO VISIT.
GO ON, THEN. MAYBE IT'LL WORK OUT. YOU'VE BIT THE HEADS OFF CHICKENS, KING GEEK. YOU'VE SWALLOWED LIGHT BULBS AND YOU'VE SWALLOWED SWORDS.
GO ON AND HAVE YOURSELF A BITE OF CHARLIE MANX'S MAGIC.
JUST BE CAREFUL. ONE OF THESE DAYS SOMETHING IS GOING TO BITE BACK.
OKAY, SYKES.
YOU GOT WHAT YOU WANT. WHAT SAY YOU DO US A FAVOR—I NEED SOMETHING TO BIND UP LLEWELLYN'S SHOULDER. LET ME HAVE YOUR SCARF.

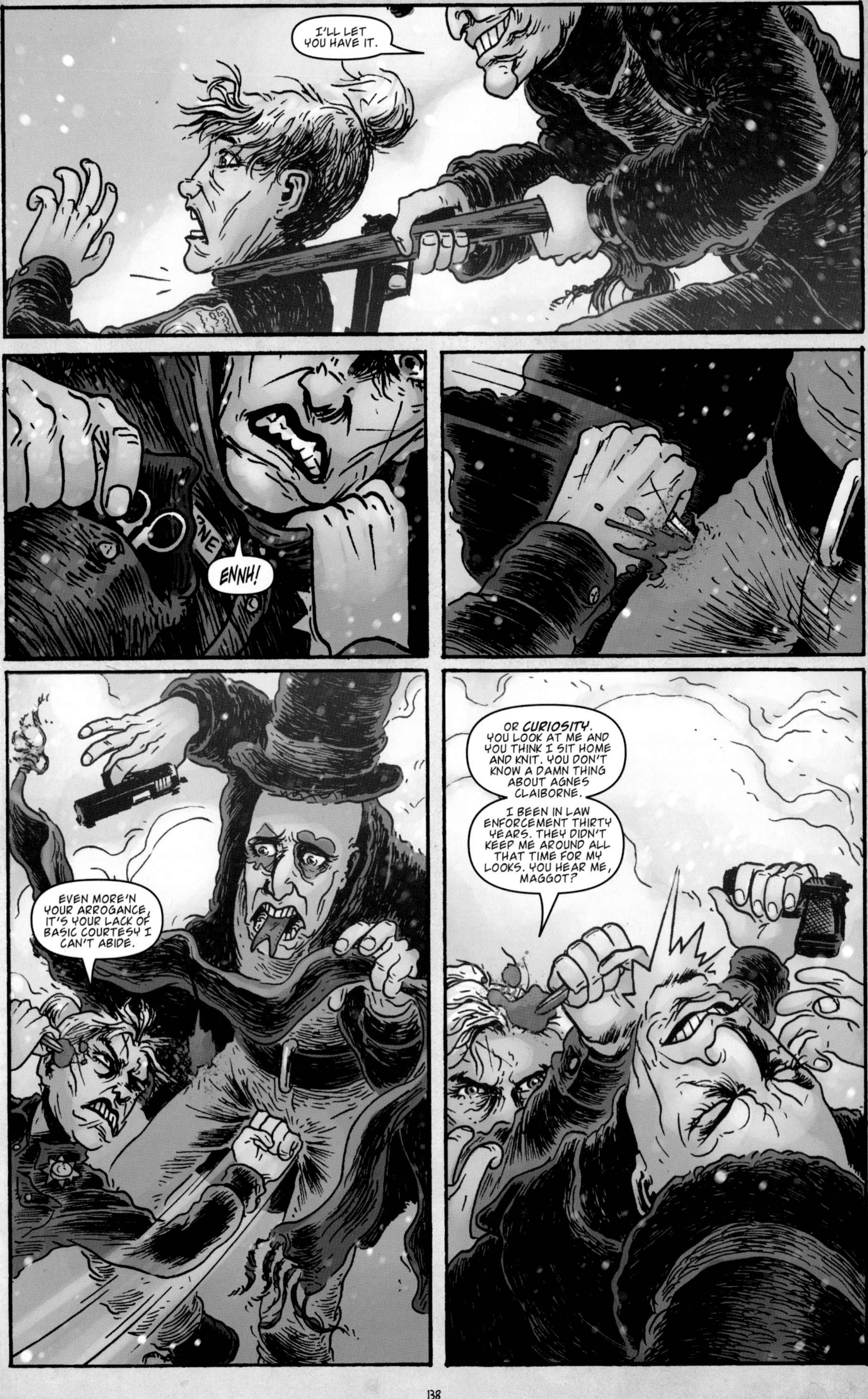

I'LL LET YOU HAVE IT.
ENNH!
EVEN MORE'N YOUR ARROGANCE, IT'S YOUR LACK OF BASIC COURTESY I CAN'T ABIDE.
OR CURIOSITY. YOU LOOK AT ME AND YOU THINK I SIT HOME AND KNIT. YOU DON'T KNOW A DAMN THING ABOUT AGNES CLAIBORNE.
I BEEN IN LAW ENFORCEMENT THIRTY YEARS. THEY DIDN'T KEEP ME AROUND ALL THAT TIME FOR MY LOOKS. YOU HEAR ME, MAGGOT?

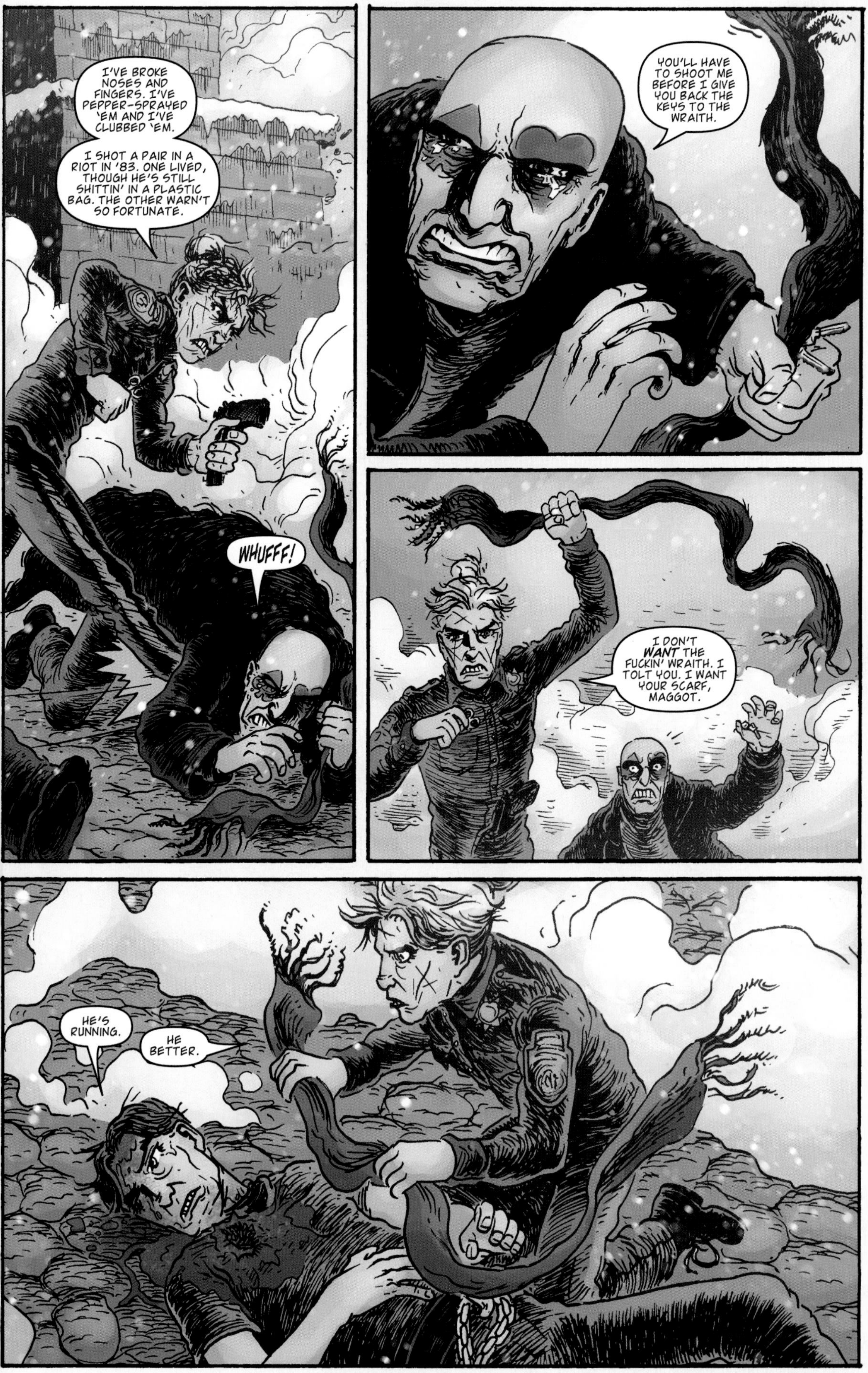
I'VE BROKE NOSES AND FINGERS. I'VE PEPPER-SPRAYED 'EM AND I'VE CLUBBED 'EM.
I SHOT A PAIR IN A RIOT IN '83. ONE LIVED, THOUGH HE'S STILL SHITTIN' IN A PLASTIC BAG. THE OTHER WARN'T SO FORTUNATE.
WHUFFF!
YOU'LL HAVE TO SHOOT ME BEFORE I GIVE YOU BACK THE KEYS TO THE WRAITH.
I DON'T WANT THE FUCKIN' WRAITH. I TOLT YOU. I WANT YOUR SCARF, MAGGOT.
HE'S RUNNING.
HE BETTER.

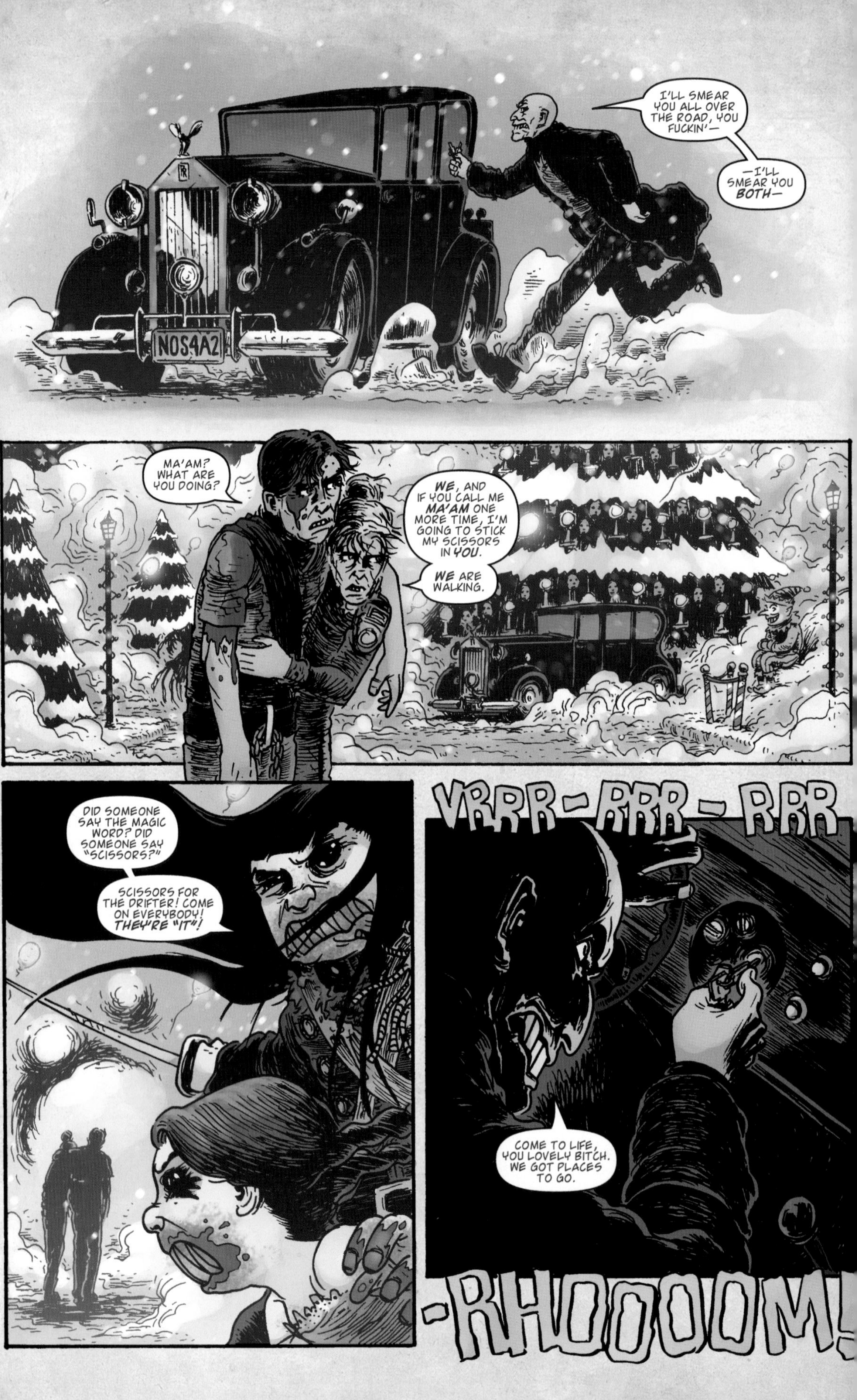
I'LL SMEAR YOU ALL OVER THE ROAD, YOU FUCKIN'—
—I'LL SMEAR YOU BOTH—
NOS4A2
MA'AM? WHAT ARE YOU DOING?
WE, AND IF YOU CALL ME MA'AM ONE MORE TIME, I'M GOING TO STICK MY SCISSORS IN YOU.
WE ARE WALKING.
DID SOMEONE SAY THE MAGIC WORD? DID SOMEONE SAY "SCISSORS?"
SCISSORS FOR THE DRIFTER! COME ON EVERYBODY! THEY'RE "IT"!
VRRR-RRR-RRR
COME TO LIFE, YOU LOVELY BITCH. WE GOT PLACES TO GO.
-RHOOOOM!

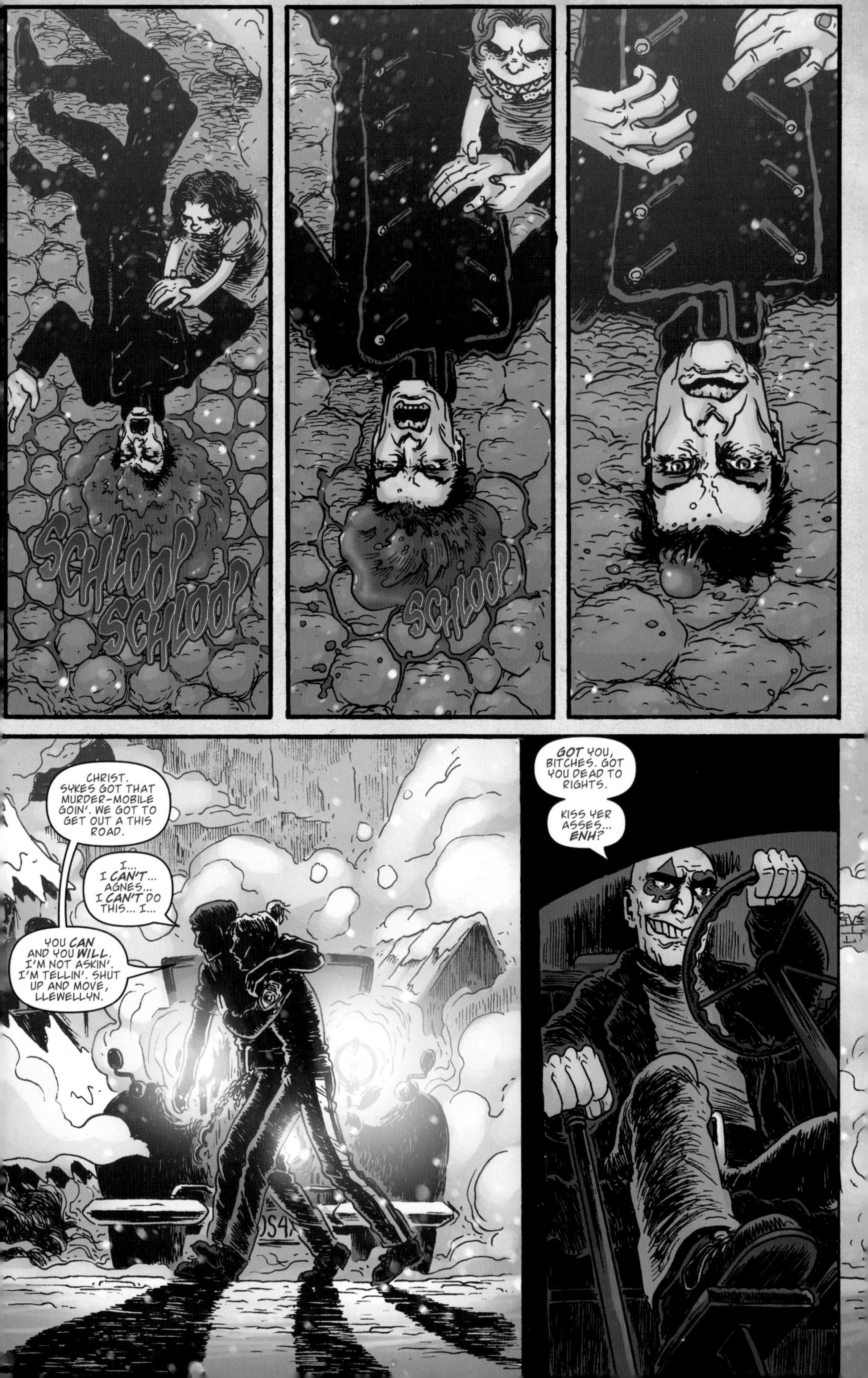
SCHLOOP
SCHLOOP
SCHLOOP
CHRIST. SYKES GOT THAT MURDER-MOBILE GOIN'. WE GOT TO GET OUT A THIS ROAD.
I... I CAN'T... AGNES... I CAN'T DO THIS... I...
YOU CAN AND YOU WILL. I'M NOT ASKIN'. I'M TELLIN'. SHUT UP AND MOVE, LLEWELLYN.
GOT YOU, BITCHES. GOT YOU DEAD TO RIGHTS.
KISS YER ASSES... ENH?

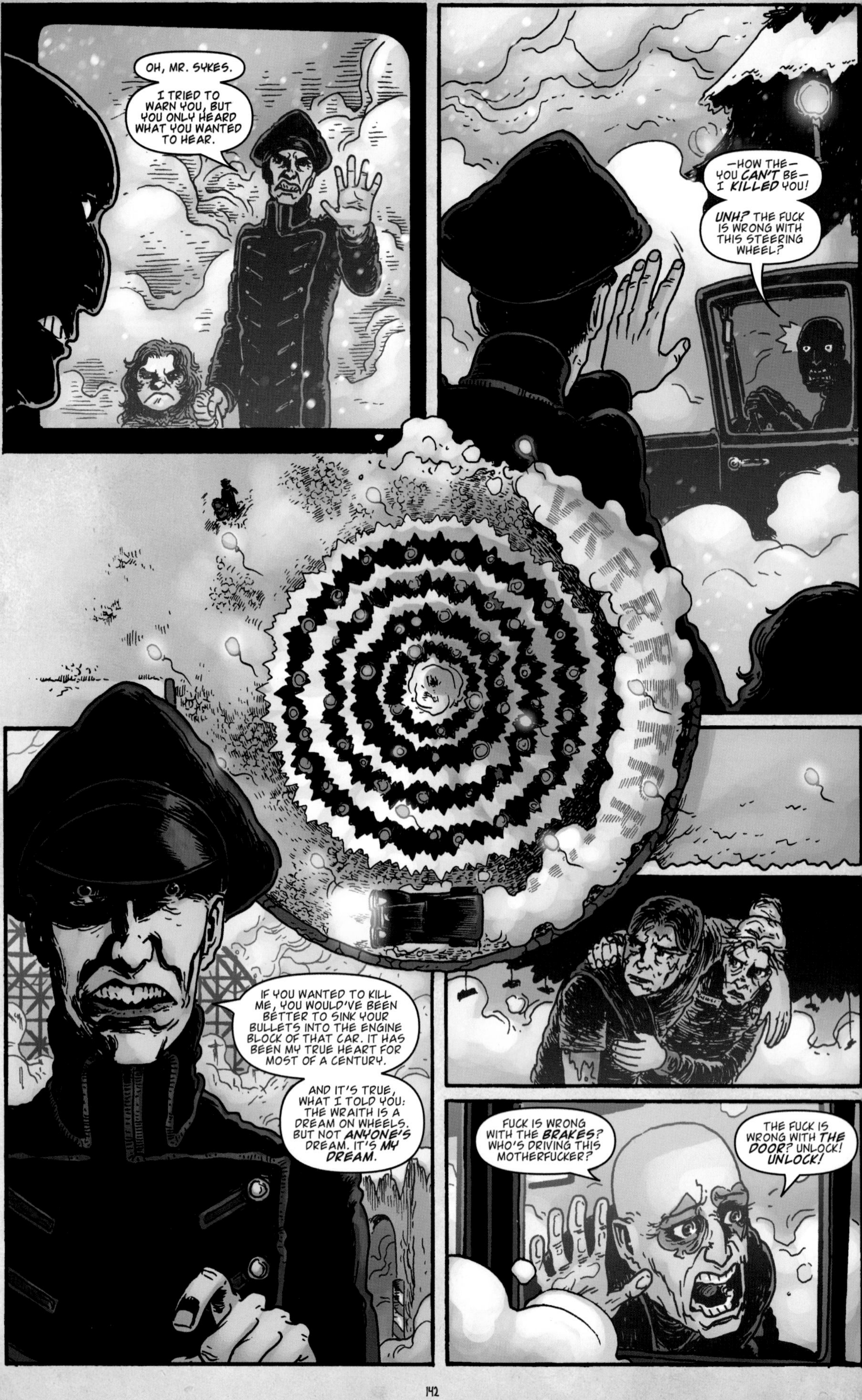
OH, MR. SYKES.
I TRIED TO WARN YOU, BUT YOU ONLY HEARD WHAT YOU WANTED TO HEAR.
—HOW THE— YOU CAN'T BE— I KILLED YOU!
UNH? THE FUCK IS WRONG WITH THIS STEERING WHEEL?
IF YOU WANTED TO KILL ME, YOU WOULD'VE BEEN BETTER TO SINK YOUR BULLETS INTO THE ENGINE BLOCK OF THAT CAR. IT HAS BEEN MY TRUE HEART FOR MOST OF A CENTURY.
AND IT'S TRUE, WHAT I TOLD YOU: THE WRAITH IS A DREAM ON WHEELS. BUT NOT ANYONE'S DREAM. IT'S MY DREAM.
FUCK IS WRONG WITH THE BRAKES? WHO'S DRIVING THIS MOTHERFUCKER?
THE FUCK IS WRONG WITH THE DOOR? UNLOCK! UNLOCK!

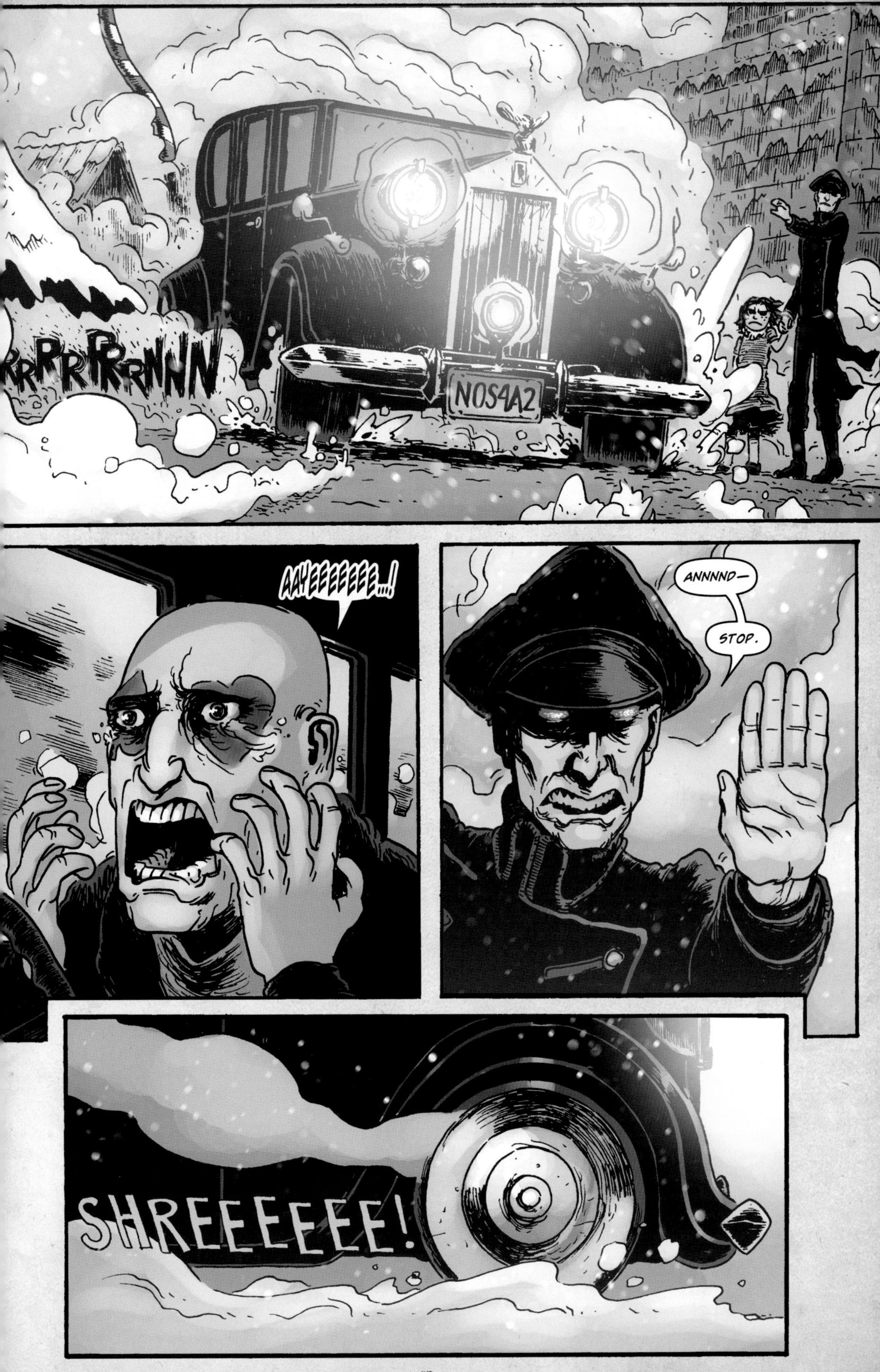
RRRRRRRRNNN
NOS4A2
AAYEEEEEEE...!
ANNNND—
STOP.
SHREEEEEEE!

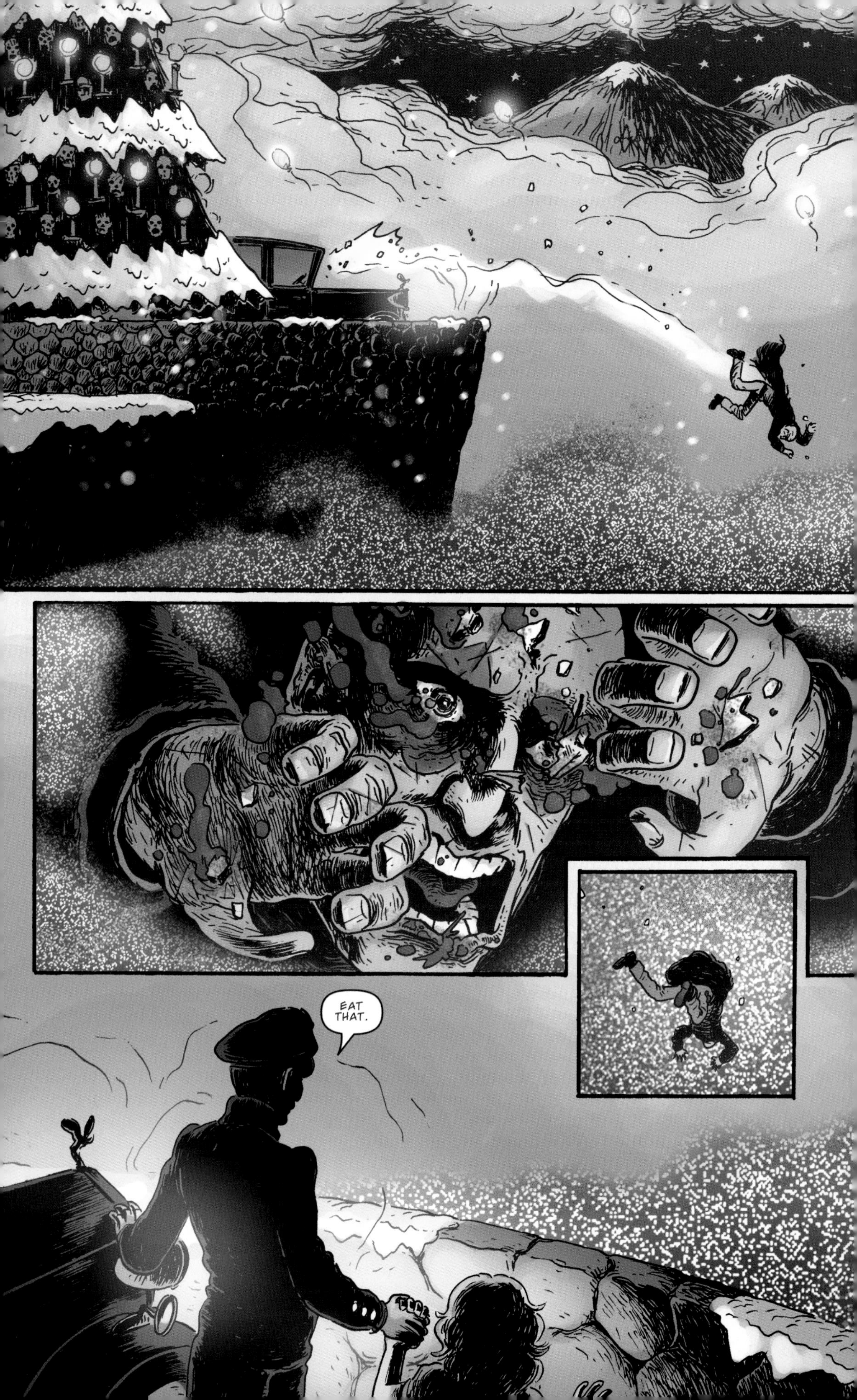
EAT THAT.

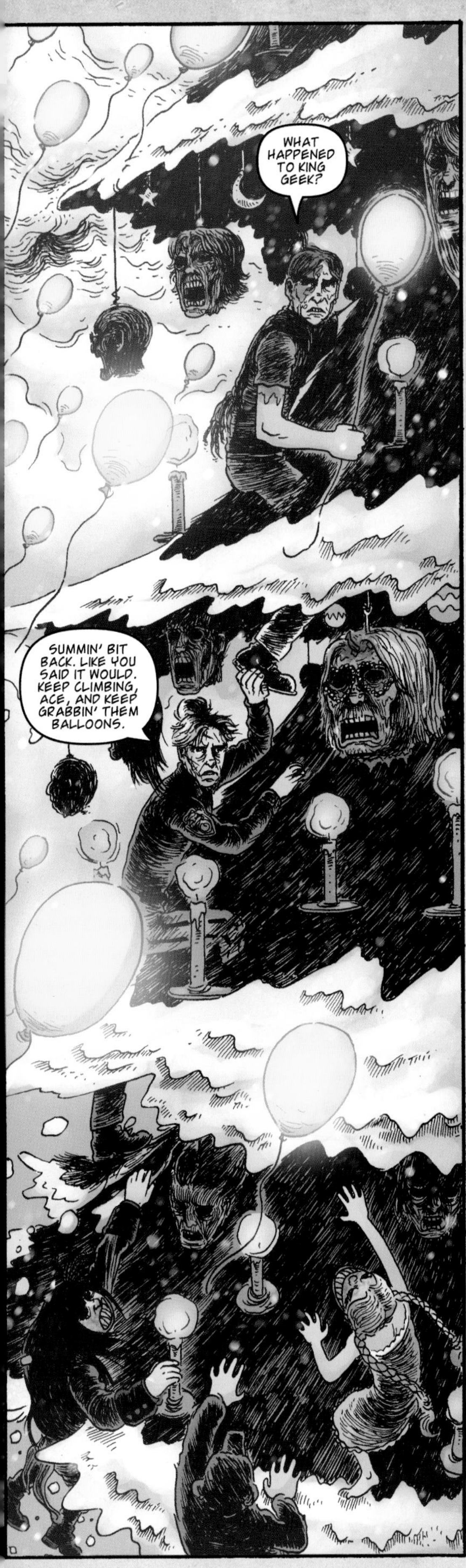
WHAT HAPPENED TO KING GEEK?
SUMMIN' BIT BACK. LIKE YOU SAID IT WOULD. KEEP CLIMBING, ACE, AND KEEP GRABBIN' THEM BALLOONS.

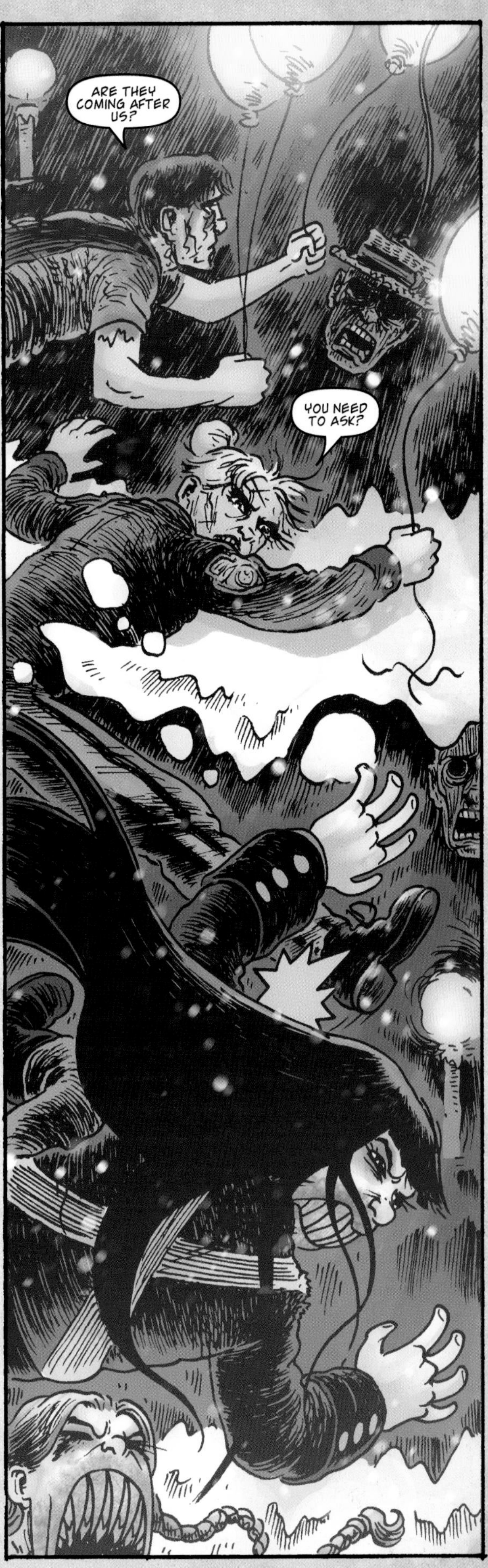
ARE THEY COMING AFTER US?
YOU NEED TO ASK?

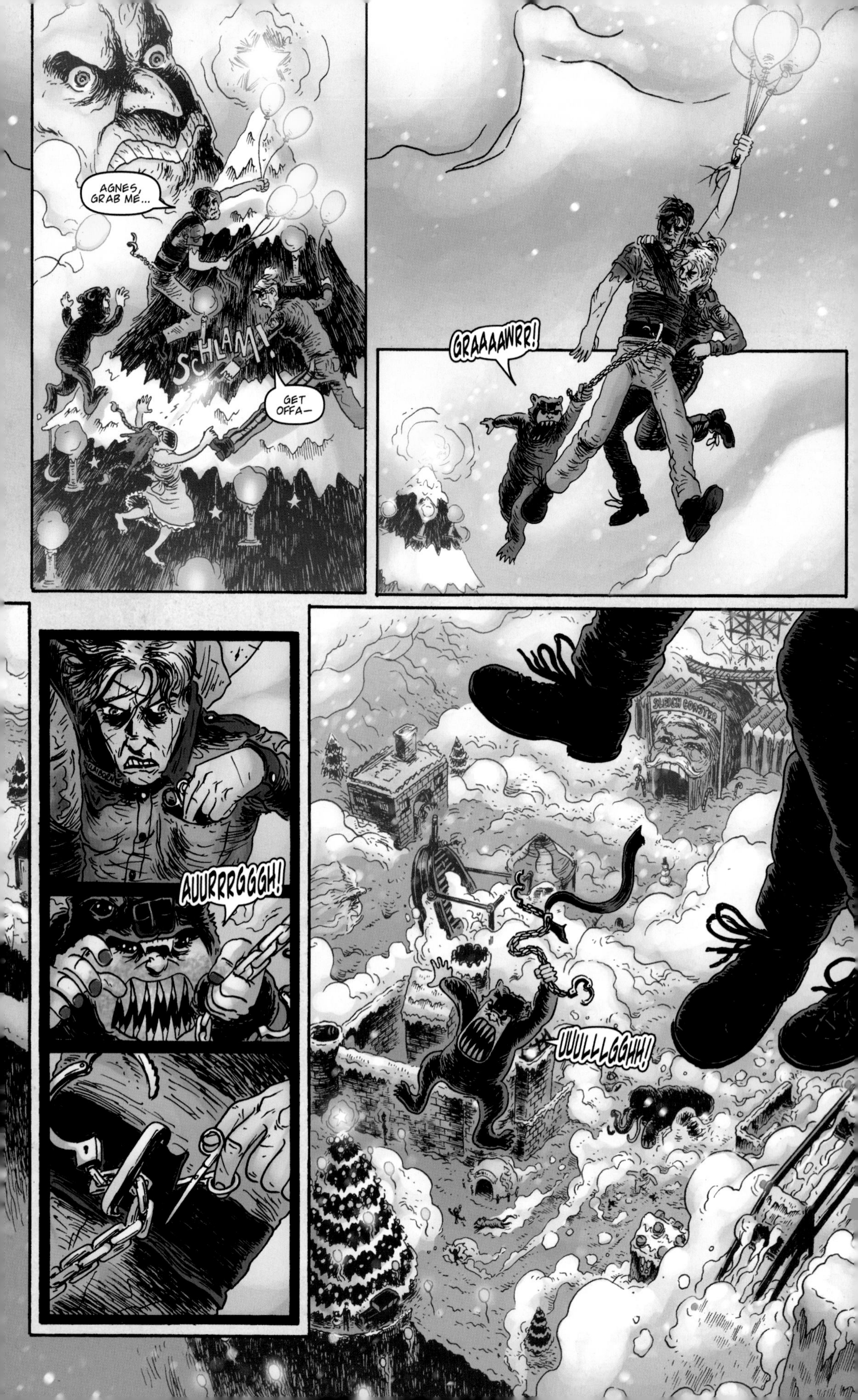
AGNES, GRAB ME...
SCHLAM!
GET OFFA—
GRAAAAWRR!
AUURRRGGGH!
SLEIGH COASTER
UUULLLGGHH!

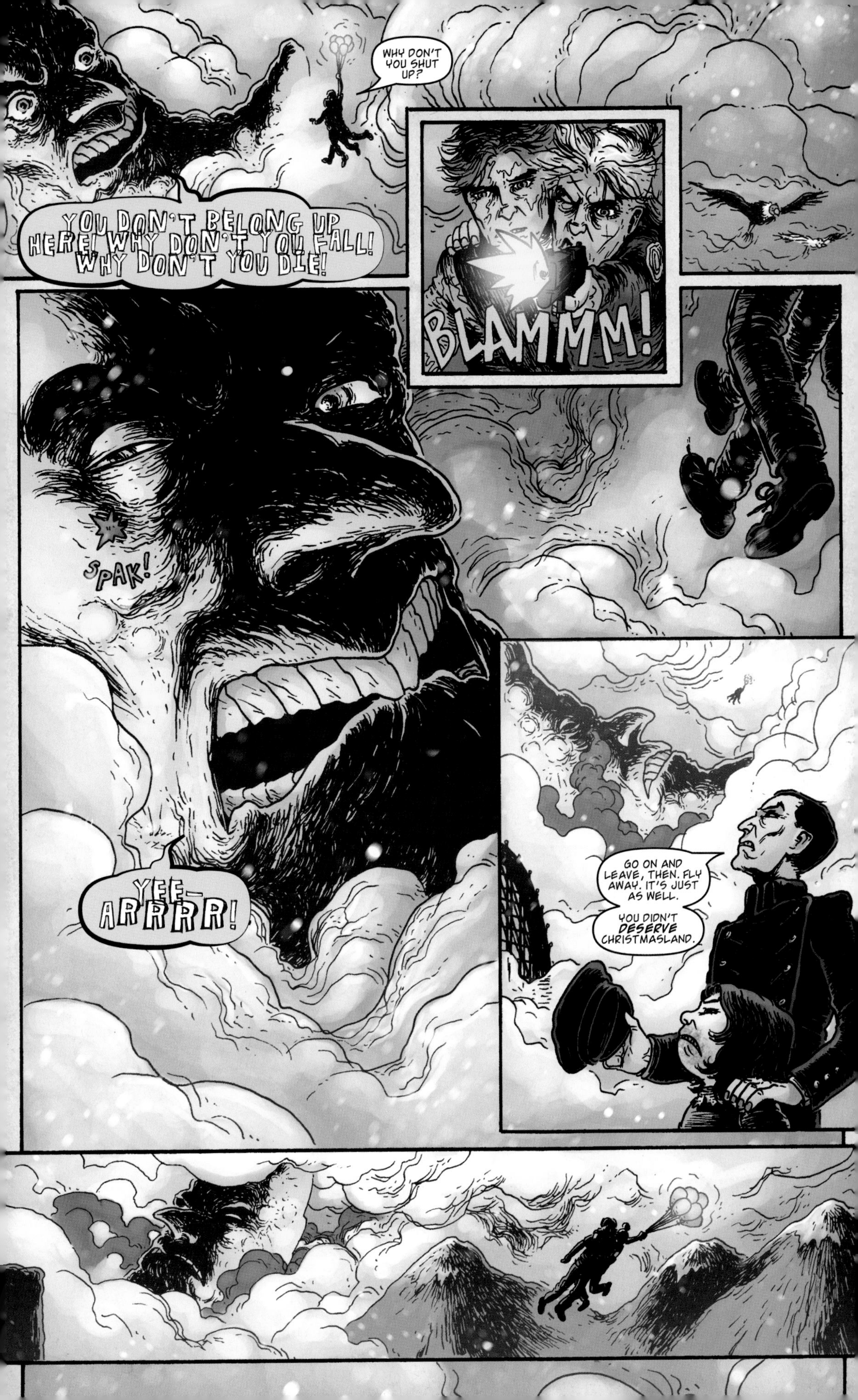
WHY DON'T YOU SHUT UP?
YOU DON'T BELONG UP HERE! WHY DON'T YOU FALL! WHY DON'T YOU DIE!
BLAMMM!
SPAK!
YEE-ARRRRR!
GO ON AND LEAVE, THEN. FLY AWAY. IT'S JUST AS WELL.
YOU DIDN'T DESERVE CHRISTMASLAND.

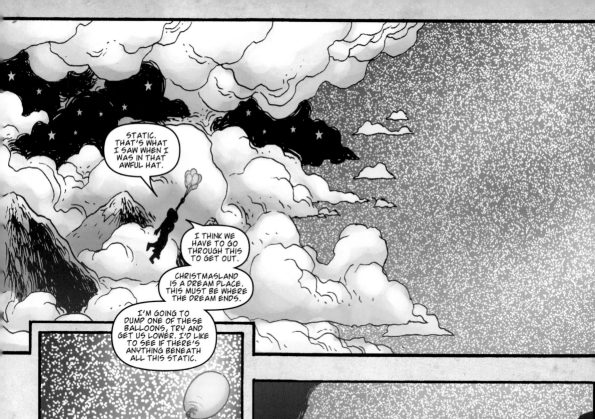

STATIC. THAT'S WHAT I SAW WHEN I WAS IN THAT AWFUL HAT.

I THINK WE HAVE TO GO THROUGH THIS TO GET OUT.

CHRISTMASLAND IS A DREAM PLACE. THIS MUST BE WHERE THE DREAM ENDS.

I'M GOING TO DUMP ONE OF THESE BALLOONS, TRY AND GET US LOWER. I'D LIKE TO SEE IF THERE'S ANYTHING BENEATH ALL THIS STATIC.

YOU AREN'T GOING TO DIE ON ME, ARE YOU, ACE?

NO PROMISES.

DESOLATION CANYON
Colorado 20 mi

I DON'T KNOW WHERE THIS IS, BUT IT DOESN'T LOOK LIKE CHRISTMASLAND.

I THINK IT'S UTAH. NOT QUITE AS BAD.

HEY— WHAT ARE YOU DOING, ACE?

148

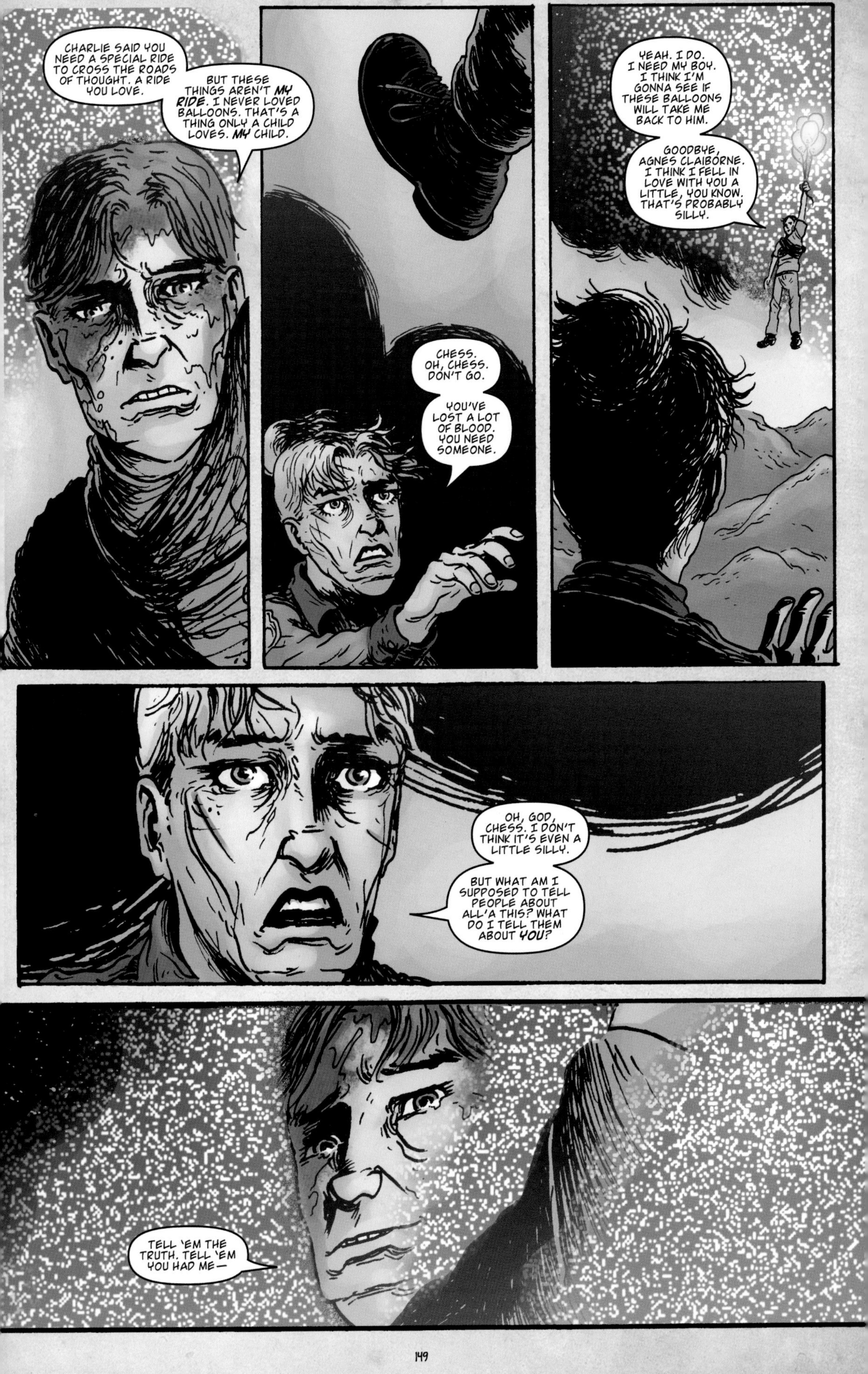
CHARLIE SAID YOU NEED A SPECIAL RIDE TO CROSS THE ROADS OF THOUGHT. A RIDE YOU LOVE.
BUT THESE THINGS AREN'T MY RIDE. I NEVER LOVED BALLOONS. THAT'S A THING ONLY A CHILD LOVES. MY CHILD.
CHESS. OH, CHESS. DON'T GO.
YOU'VE LOST A LOT OF BLOOD. YOU NEED SOMEONE.
YEAH. I DO. I NEED MY BOY. I THINK I'M GONNA SEE IF THESE BALLOONS WILL TAKE ME BACK TO HIM.
GOODBYE, AGNES CLAIBORNE. I THINK I FELL IN LOVE WITH YOU A LITTLE, YOU KNOW. THAT'S PROBABLY SILLY.
OH, GOD, CHESS. I DON'T THINK IT'S EVEN A LITTLE SILLY.
BUT WHAT AM I SUPPOSED TO TELL PEOPLE ABOUT ALL'A THIS? WHAT DO I TELL THEM ABOUT YOU?
TELL 'EM THE TRUTH. TELL 'EM YOU HAD ME—

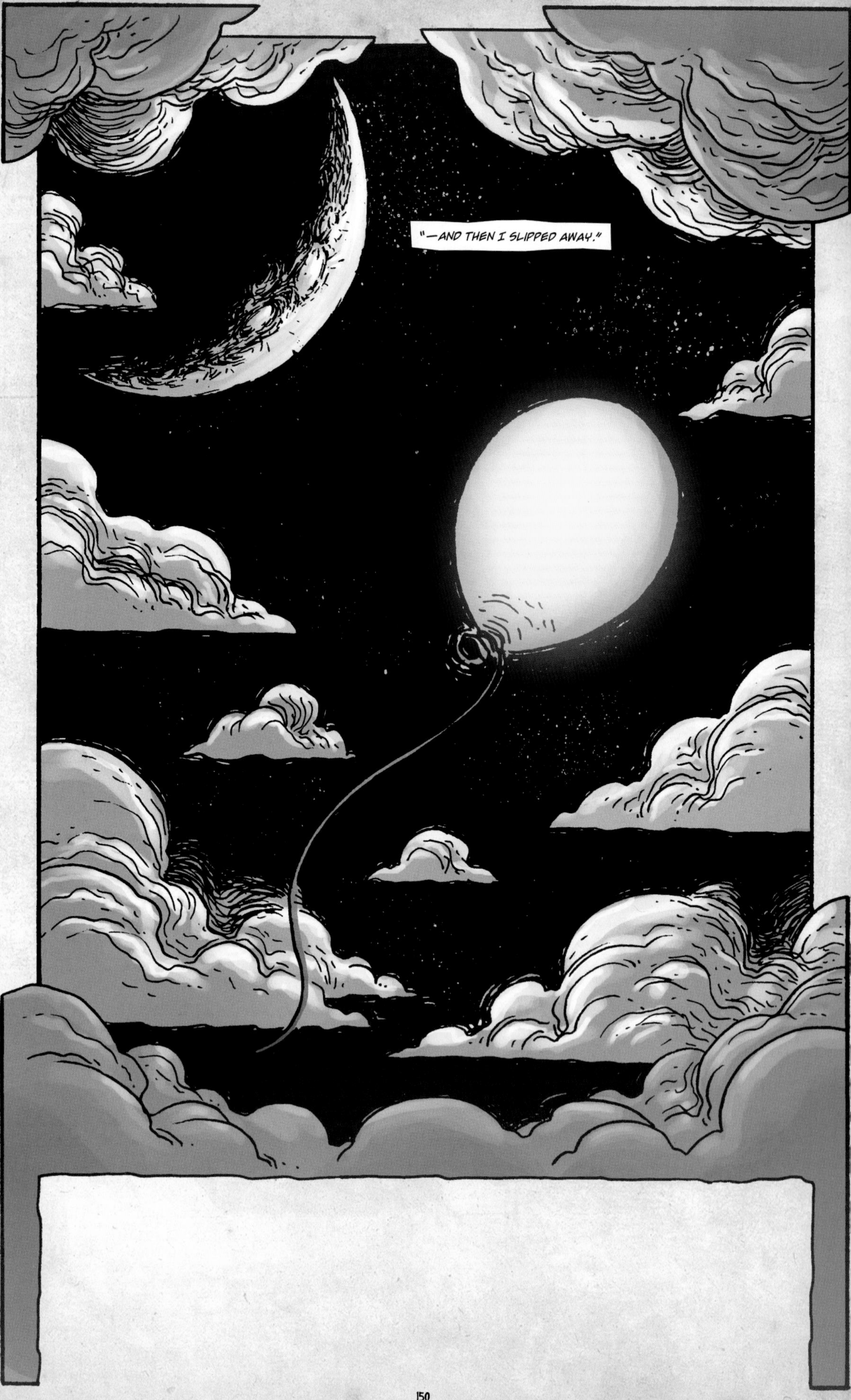
"—AND THEN I SLIPPED AWAY."

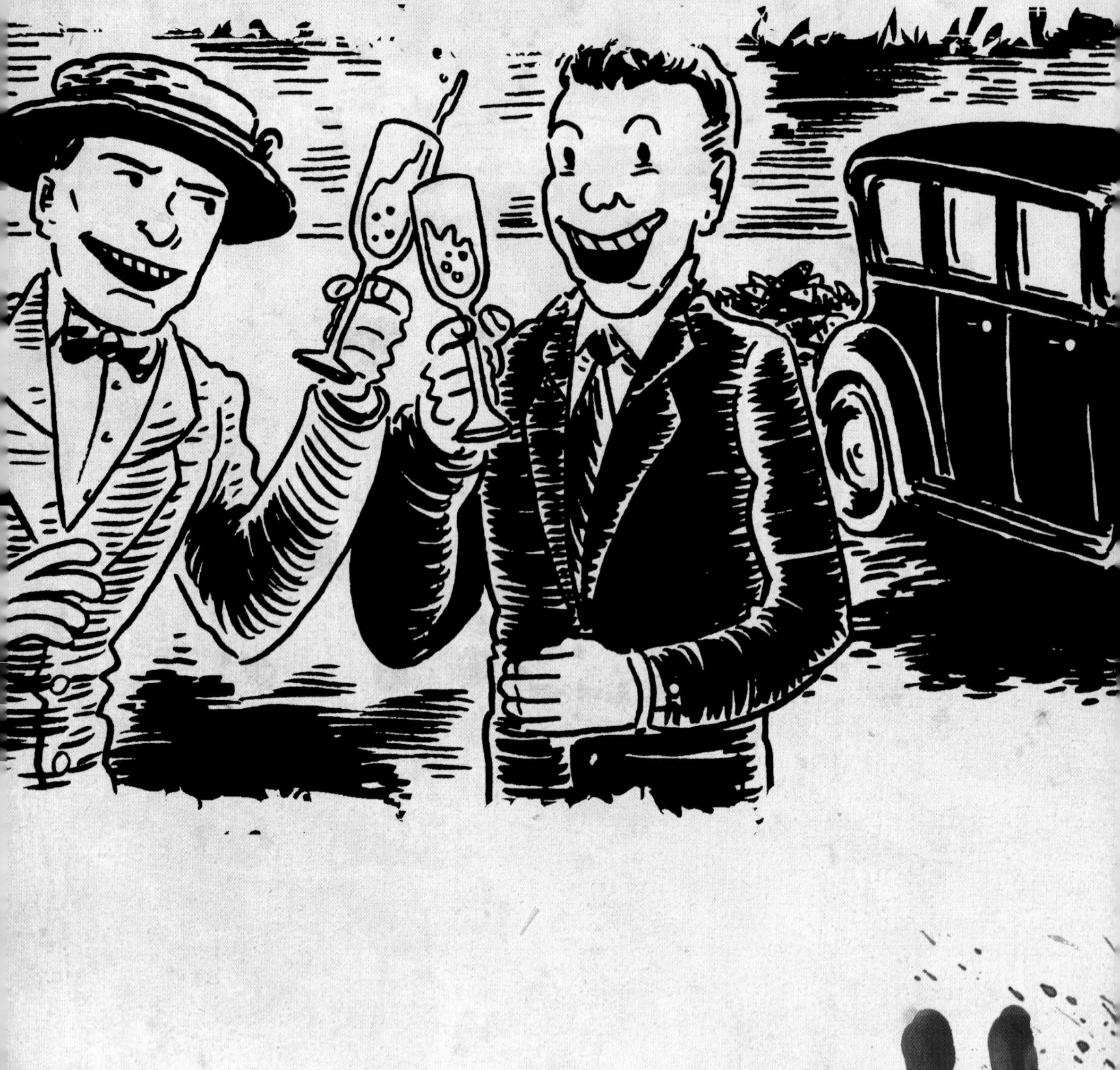

WELCOME TO CHRISTMASLAND epilogue

PHANTOMS

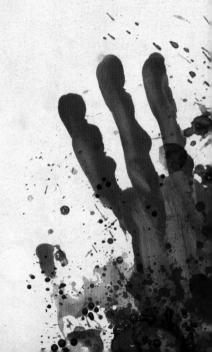

In McCarthy, Illinois, you cop a heel when a Huckleberry comes back from the send with a dozen pals lugging baseball bats.

The only reason you get away is Soapy Porter's bad bladder.

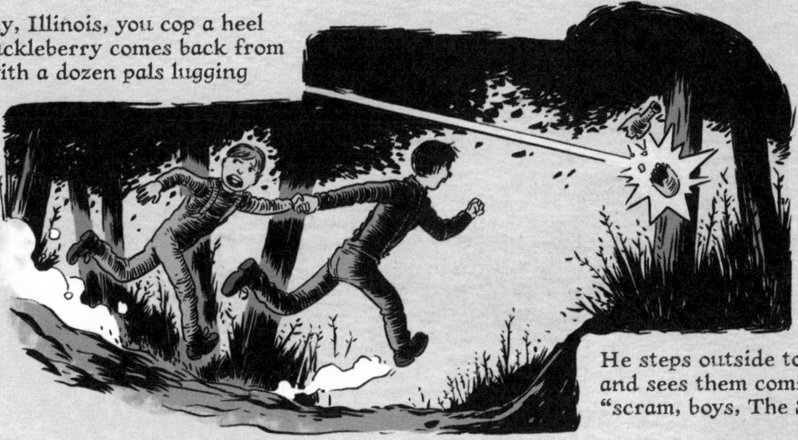

He steps outside to take a piss and sees them coming and yells, "scram, boys, The Steam is here!"

But Old Soap has it wrong. It isn't The Steam. They aren't cops. No one is going to jail tonight.

The last you see of Soapy, he's crawling in the dirt with four men clubbing at him. Their baseball bats flash up and down, and the blood stains the white pine pink.

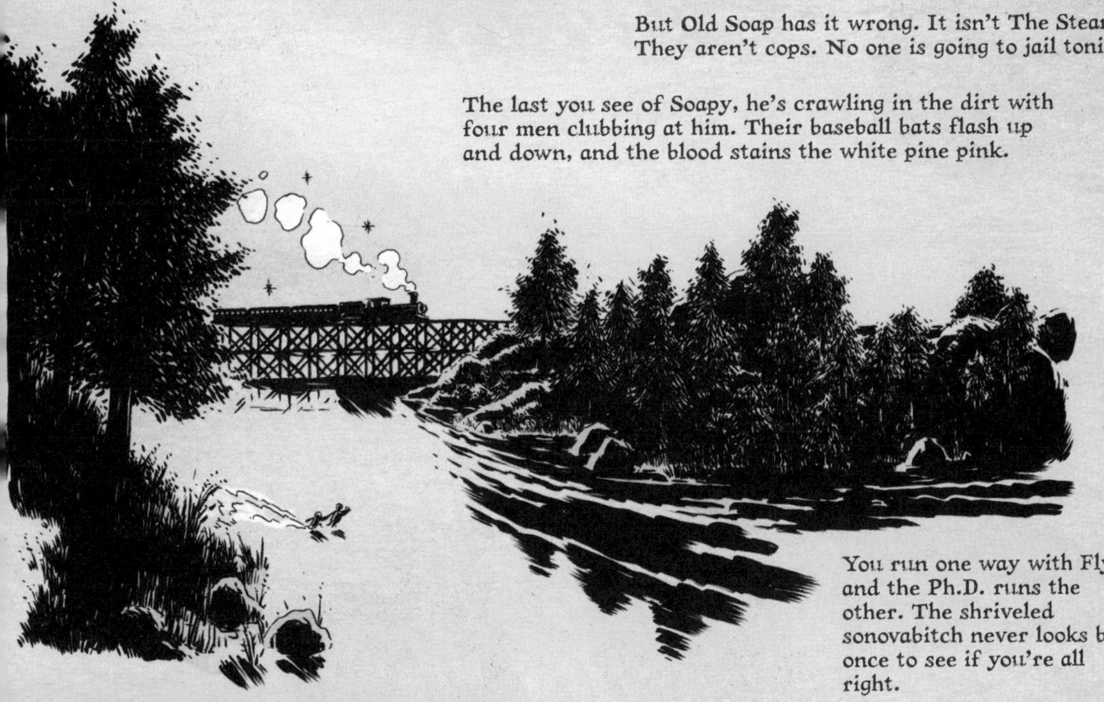

You run one way with Flynn, and the Ph.D. runs the other. The shriveled sonovabitch never looks back once to see if you're all right.

The Ph.D. doesn't hold a degree in nothing except looking out for his own self.

You are six steps into the water before Flynn begins screaming.

"Too deep, too deep! I can't make it! We have to go back!"

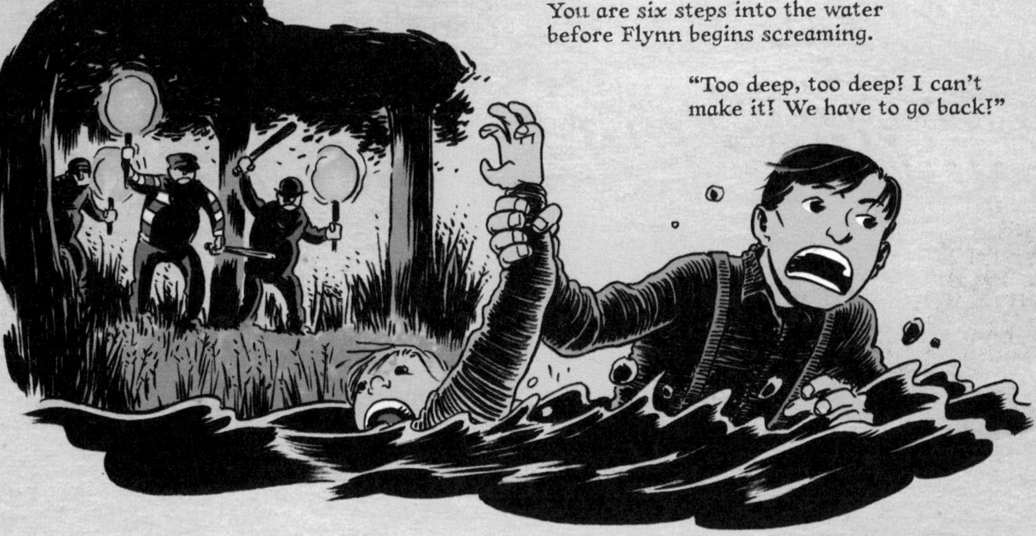

You know how to swim.
Flynn doesn't.

Halfway across the Fox River, his hand slips out of yours and your younger brother is sucked away in a black rush.

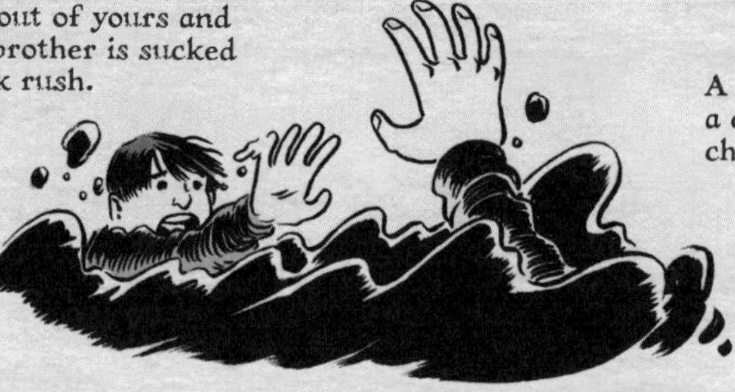

A fast river will swallow a child as easily as a child may swallow water.

The Ph.D.~who is some sort of uncle~raised you and Flynn up from little, but for all practical purposes, you were Flynn's father and mother both.

You shared a bedroll and you shared meals. When there was not enough, you gave Flynn what was on your plate and made do with hot tea.

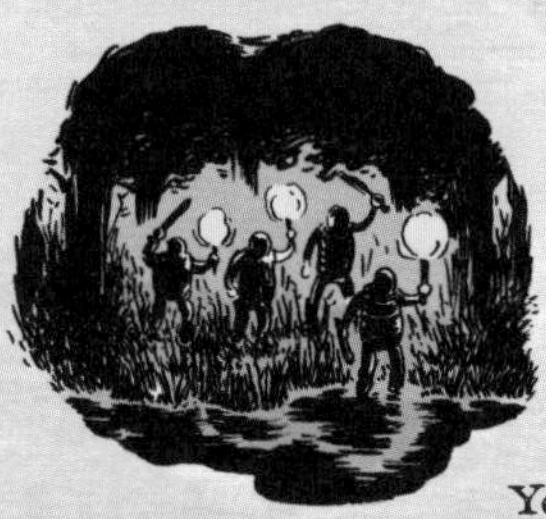

After the Ph.D. beat him, you would tell Flynn stories to make him stop crying. You told him about all the money you'd both have when you were older, described the mansion you would own on Lake Michigan, the Rolls~Royce you would gallivant around in.

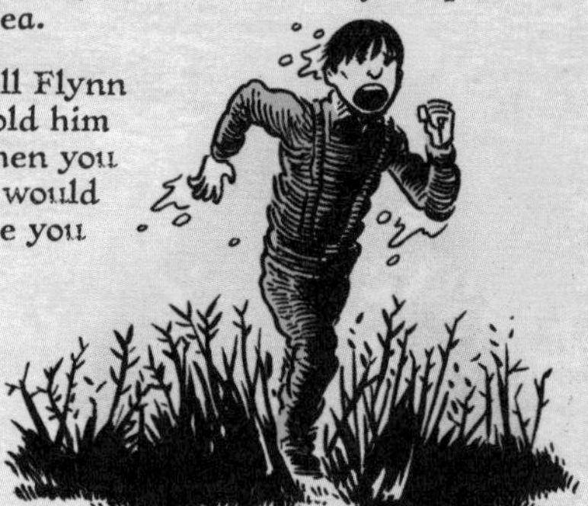

You told him how every day would be like Christmas.

It is mind~boggling to think a boy you loved and looked after~whose hair you combed and shoes you tied~could be taken away like that. Could just be lost.

You meet up with the Ph.D. at a juke joint in Peru, Indiana, called the Hully Gully.

He accepts the loss of Flynn with his typical equanimity, assuring you that the current will have brushed him back in to shore, where he was undoubtedly snapped up and hauled to the reformatory.

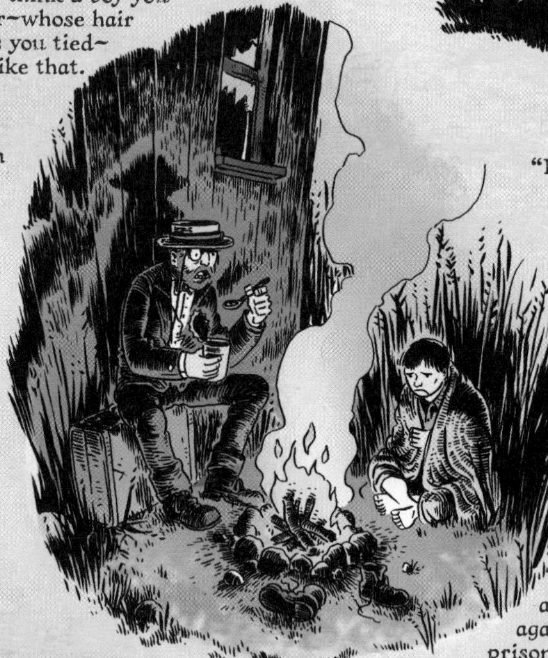

"He is better off than the likes of us, lad!" the Ph.D. tells you. "He is having fried eggs in the morning and fried chicken at night in the Barnavelt orphanage!

"A cute little dickens like him will be adopted in the blink of an eye. It is just a matter of time before a couple of Huckleberries open their homes to him... and their wallets!"

Nothing is said of Soapy and nothing is heard of him again. Not on this side of the prison walls or the other.

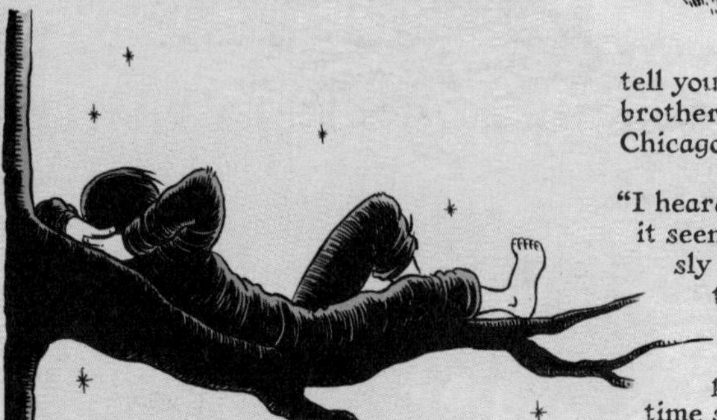

In the years to come, though, the Ph.D. will tell you~usually after a few drinks~that a friend saw your little brother in a tailored suit, walking into a private school in Chicago, hand in hand with a busty nanny in her teens.

"I heard when she hugged Flynn goodbye, there was a moment it seemed like he might smother in those titties of hers! The sly rascal! She is tucking him in at night now but it will be the other way around soon enough!"

The Ph.D. can no more hold in a lie than a person can hold in a sneeze, but it has been a long time since he could fool you. He couldn't put one over on you if his life depended on it.

Flynn isn't waking up in a four~poster bed somewhere. He's in the bed of the Fox River and he's never leaving it.

The next few years, you work the Stonewall Jackson scam around Indiana and Illinois. You play it in bus stations and bars, libraries and luncheonettes.

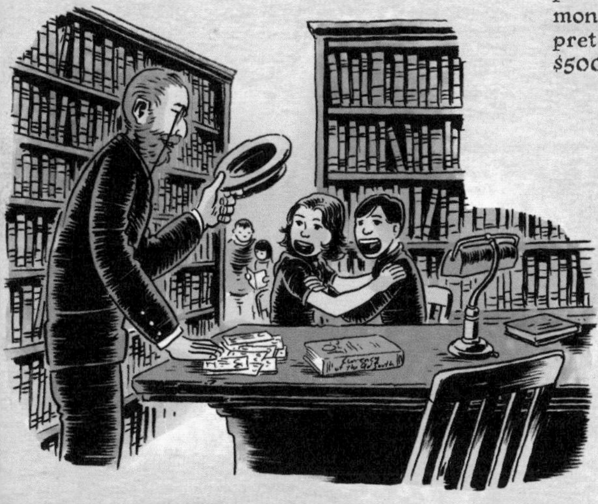

Here is the game: you strike up a conversation with a Huckleberry, someone looking for a good time, preferably a doll your own age, with plenty of spending money and not enough sense to hold onto it. Then you pretend to spot a folder full of Confederate cash, mostly $500 bills, next to a book on Southern Currency.

Before either of you can react, the Ph.D. wanders over and pretends to discover the money himself. For the grift to work, you and the Ph.D. have to play it like you've never met before.

You, the girl, and the Ph.D. look over the secessionist money together, trying to figure out what to do with it. The Ph.D. says he thinks it might belong to an elderly Southern gentleman he met earlier in the day, who was on his way to Atlanta. The Ph.D. tells you both that he saw this old man spit on the feet of a pregnant black woman mopping a floor.

That's a nice touch. It never fails to make the girl, inevitably a sweet kid at heart, indignant.

You all determine, using the book, that the pile of Confederate dough is worth $6,000... and that a bitter old racist has no right to get it back.

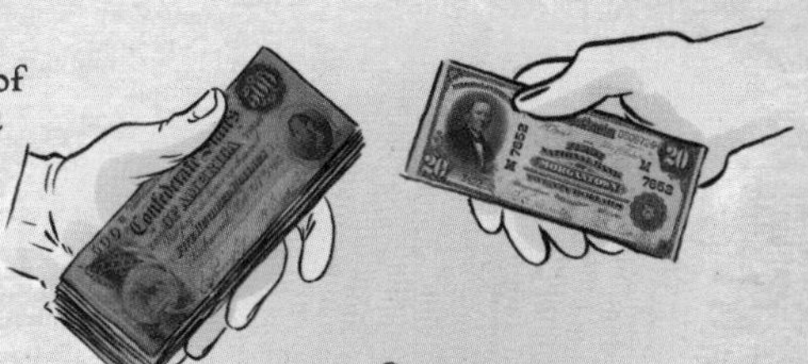

The Ph.D. pretends great amusement at the moral lesson being taught, and agrees to sell his share in the find for whatever money you and the mark have in your pockets.

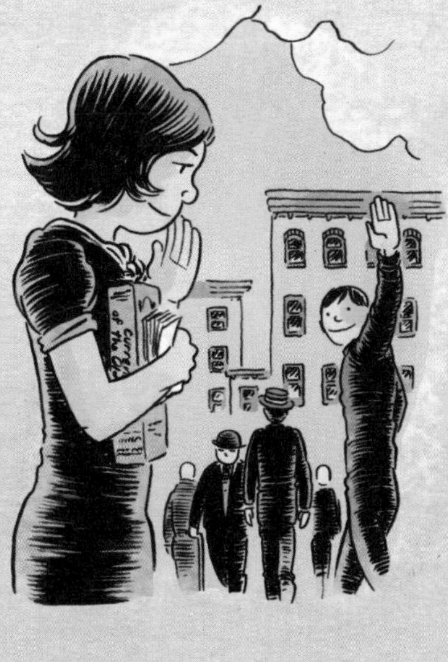

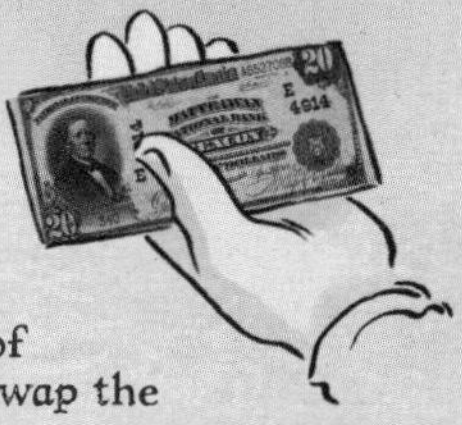

The Ph.D. takes off to make a train. You tell the doll you want to call your parents about what just happened, and you'll be back in five minutes. Then the both of you will find a place where you can swap the Stonewall Jacksons for the six grand.

You tell her not to go anywhere and leave her with a kiss and a folder full of worthless queer. Who knows how long the dames stand around, before they realize you're never coming back? That the Confederate bills are funny, and they've been cleaned out?

It's a shitty short con and you can only run it a few times before you have to blow town. Sometimes you take the girls for less than $75. The Ph.D. can drink that in a couple days.

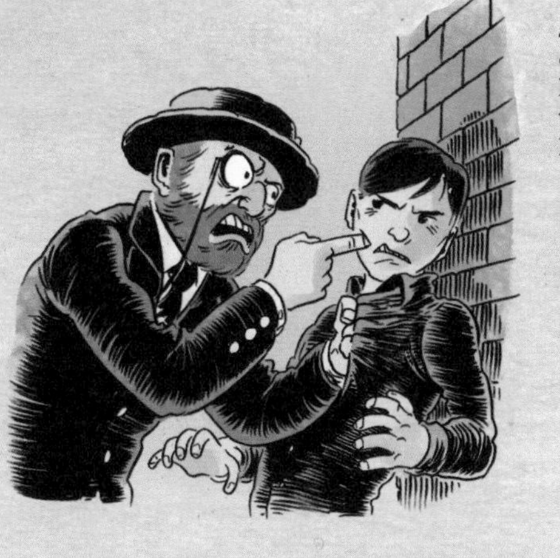

But in Vandalia, the girl you took for a preacher's daughter is sly to the grift and plays a game of her own. The sweet little twist has fast hands and helps herself to the Ph.D.'s wallet when she hugs him goodbye.

The Ph.D. screams at you for not sniffing her out, but he doesn't belt you. You note this fact with cold interest. There was a time when he would've worked you over for a fuck-up of these dimensions.

When did he become afraid to use his hands on you?

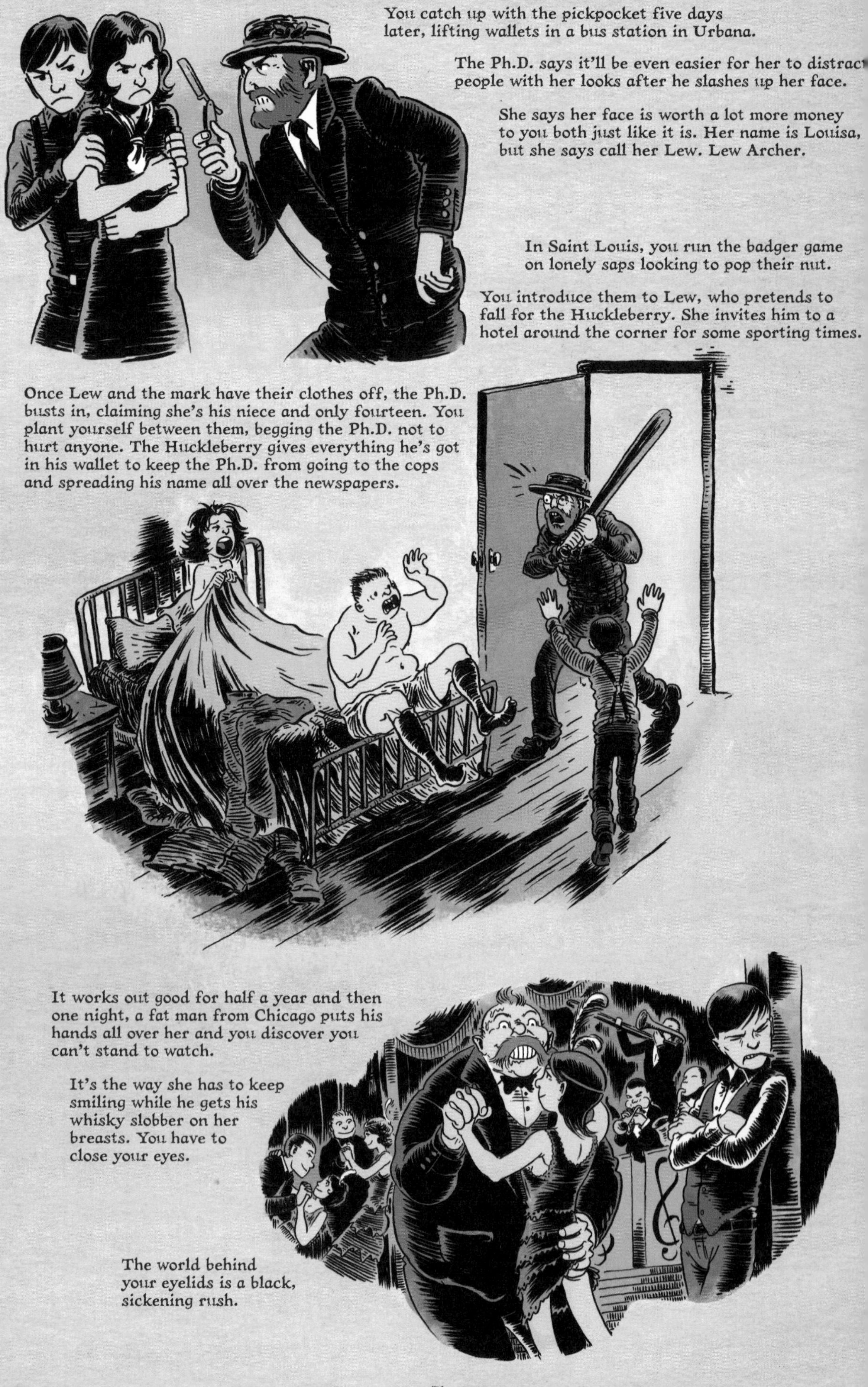
You catch up with the pickpocket five days later, lifting wallets in a bus station in Urbana.
The Ph.D. says it'll be even easier for her to distract people with her looks after he slashes up her face.
She says her face is worth a lot more money to you both just like it is. Her name is Louisa, but she says call her Lew. Lew Archer.
In Saint Louis, you run the badger game on lonely saps looking to pop their nut.
You introduce them to Lew, who pretends to fall for the Huckleberry. She invites him to a hotel around the corner for some sporting times.
Once Lew and the mark have their clothes off, the Ph.D. busts in, claiming she's his niece and only fourteen. You plant yourself between them, begging the Ph.D. not to hurt anyone. The Huckleberry gives everything he's got in his wallet to keep the Ph.D. from going to the cops and spreading his name all over the newspapers.
It works out good for half a year and then one night, a fat man from Chicago puts his hands all over her and you discover you can't stand to watch.
It's the way she has to keep smiling while he gets his whisky slobber on her breasts. You have to close your eyes.
The world behind your eyelids is a black, sickening rush.

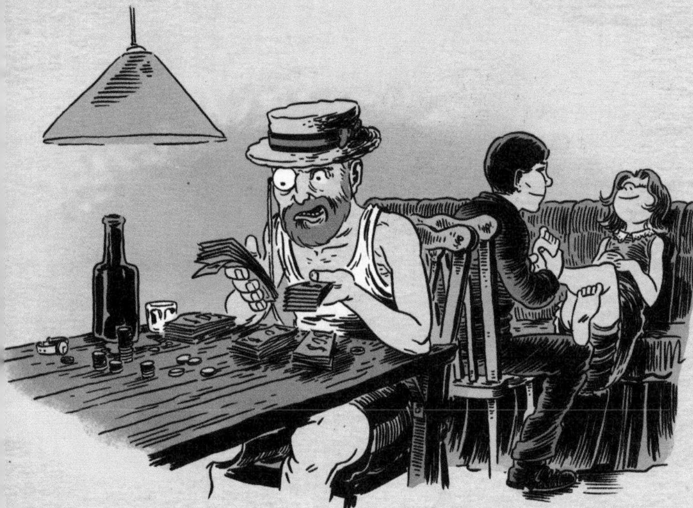

The next night, you tell the Ph.D. it's time to run a new game.

The Ph.D. says you don't leave the table when the dice are hot. "We aren't gonna make five C-Notes a week off *your* ass, Tommy."

The Ph.D. asks Lew if *she* wants to switch things up. Lew says no and the Ph.D. says good thing, because if she isn't helping them screw the marks, the next best thing would be letting the marks screw *her*.

The Ph.D. says there's no way to ever get too much of a good thing, but one rainy night in March proves him wrong.

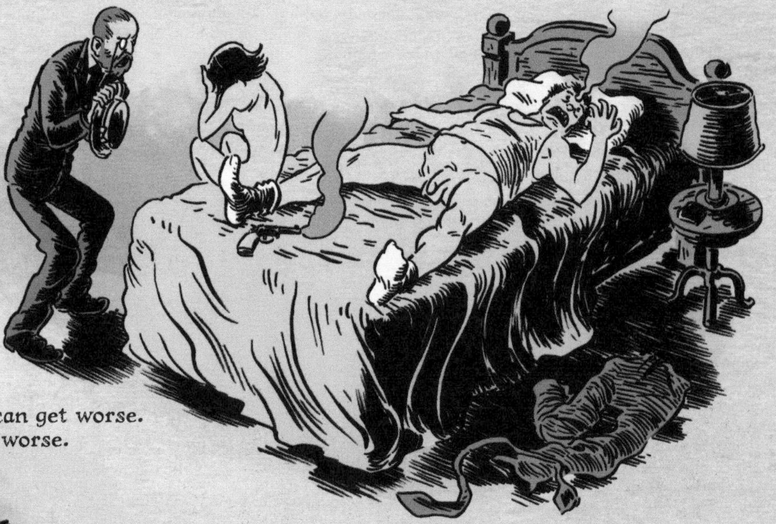

The shot goes off about three minutes after Lew and the mark disappear into the hotel room, well before the Ph.D. is due to bust in.

She says, "He was choking me. I couldn't breathe. He said I'd like it, but I got scared. The gun was under his pillow and I~I just meant to frighten him with it... I just meant~"

Never ask if things can get worse. They can always get worse.

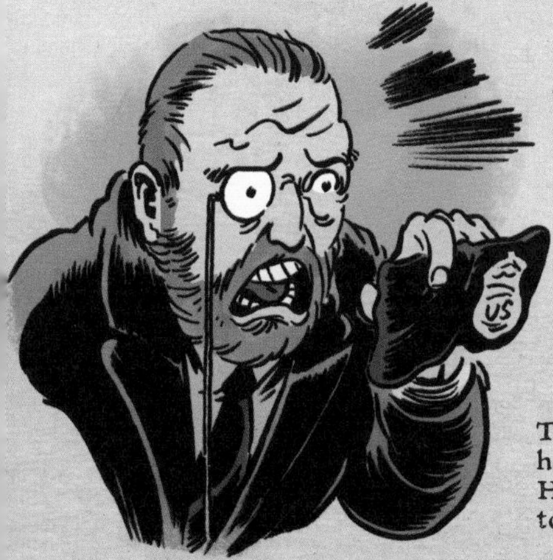
U.S.

The dead man is a federal marshal, his badge in a wallet, along with $400. The Ph.D. says everything is fucked and it's time to scatter. He names a dollar store in Cleveland and says to look for him there in a month or two.

He gives Lew a hug goodbye and hands you your share of what the marshal had in his wallet before he goes. Two minutes after he's out the door, you realize that in his hurry to get away, the Ph.D. forgot his hat. Five minutes after he disappears, you discover he's handed you a fat wad of one-dollar bills with a $20 wrapped around the outside.

The Ph.D. leaves you with a corpse, a nice hat, and $27. Couldn't resist one last rip-off. He got the wedding ring off the dead man, too, when no one was looking.

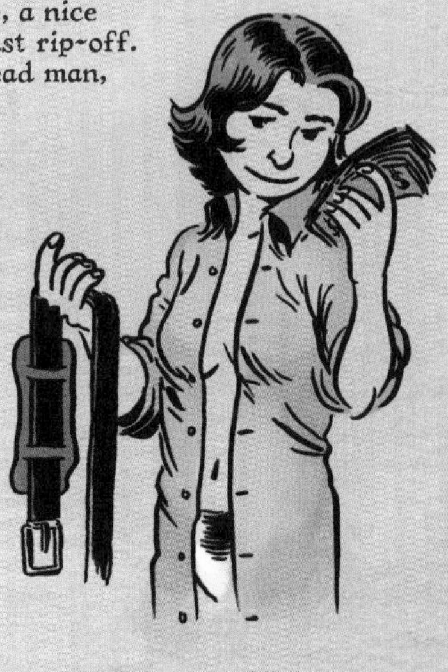

When you tell Lew you've been skinned for your share, she says that's the Ph.D. for you: snatching the little money, when the big money is right under his nose.

That's when she tells you she realized the dead man was wearing a money belt when she was on her knees, unbuckling it. She says she counted the cash in the bathroom, before she shot him. She says there's thirty grand.

Then she says he isn't a cop, either. She nicked that badge off a U.S. marshal months ago, back when she was still a pickpocket. She's been carrying it ever since, looking for a chance to use it. The man she shot is a gambler, on his way to a big poker game... only he just drew a losing hand.

"What are you telling me here? You killed him for the money? I thought you said you couldn't breathe."

She says, "I *couldn't* breathe, not when he touched me. Not when *any* of them touched me. Not unless I pretended I was with you.

"You promise me, Tom," she says, after the first kiss, the kiss you have been waiting for almost since the day you caught up to her at the bus station in Urbana. "You promise me I don't have to tell no more lies. I've always been a thief and now I'm a killer, but I ain't no grifter and I ain't no whore. You know that's what the Ph.D. wanted to make me, Tommy, the dirty sonofabitch."

You promise her. It might be the first promise you've ever made that you planned to keep.

You ask her what will happen when the Ph.D. finds out the two of you snared thirty gees and didn't share out with him. She asks you what you think will happen to the Ph.D. when the cops grab him trying to flee town with a dead man's wedding ring in his pocket. He didn't steal it: she planted it on him, during their last hug.

It isn't too late to warn him. You know the Ph.D. will go back to the motel cabin you've all been sharing, to grab his duds and take the car. You could call.

Then you remember McCarthy, Illinois, and how he ran without sparing a look back for you and Flynn. You remember his line about dropping the grift and turning pimp, letting the marks fuck Lew for a few bucks. You don't call.

The Ph.D. talks his way out of the murder rap~ of course he does~but they give him seven years for looting the corpse of a probable suicide. Flynn was seven years old when he drowned. You call it square and sleep fine at night.

You never hear why the cops picked him up in the first place and you don't dare ask Lew if she tipped them off about where to find him. All you know is that when you tell her the Ph.D. had been arrested, she won't look at you.

"Poor old guy," she says. "I hope he looks after himself. Prison can be rough for a fella his age. I hope no one tries to make him a whore."

The last of the twenties is nothing but sugar.

Thirty grand buys a faltering candy company and 5,000 acres of swamp in Cuba, which you publicize as being the most fertile sugar cane tract in the world. You offer investors a cloud of cotton candy and stocks in a company that you promise will rival Hershey's.

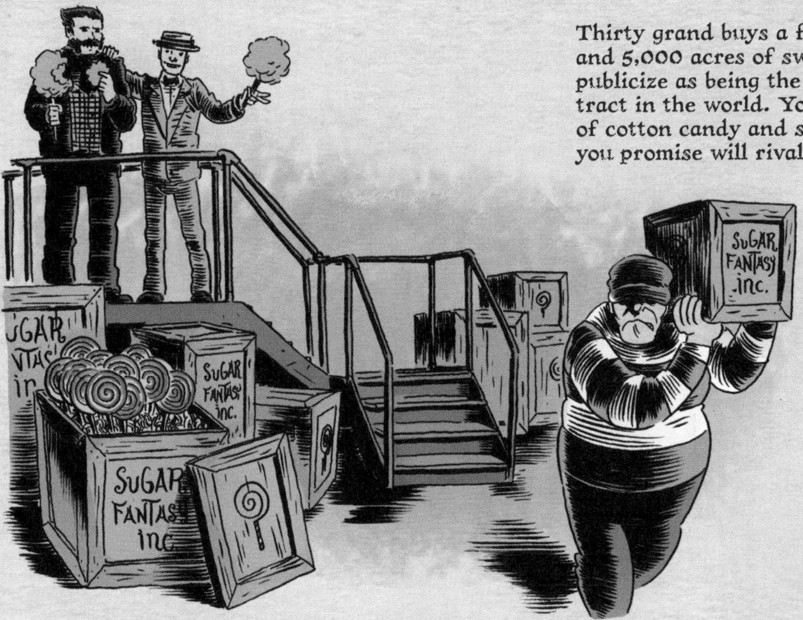
SUGAR FANTASY inc.
SUGAR FANTASY inc.
SUGAR FANTASY inc.

You sell them a dream of fat, greedy children, who will never have enough, who will always want more. The Huckleberries have no idea the children you are talking about is them.

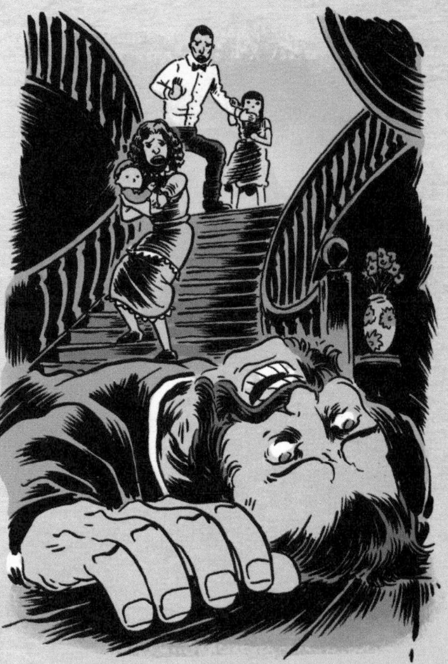

SUGAR FANTASY INCORPORATED collapses in the fall of 1929, along with everything else.

They say if you die in a dream, you die in real life. For some of your investors, waking from the collapse of Sugar Fantasy to find out they own worthless stocks in a Cuban mudhole is fatal.

If you wake from that same dream feeling like a million bucks, maybe that's because that's your rough net worth.

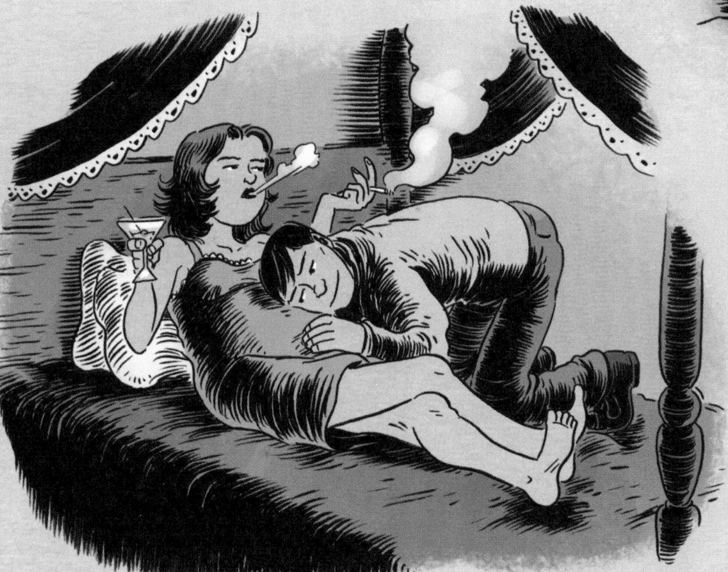

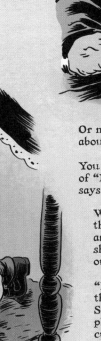

Or maybe it's because you're about to be a father.

You ask her what she thinks of "Flynn" if it's a boy. She says she likes it.

When you start talking about the next grift, she gets quiet, and then says if you go to jail, she won't be there when you get out. And neither will the child.

"I guess I better not go to jail, then," you tell her with a wink. She says if you ever give her a phony grifter wink again, she'll cut your eyelids off. "If I wanted to be with the Ph.D., I would've told *him* about the money belt."

The business of a con is to steal a man's most secret desires out of his own head and then sell them back to him for a pretty penny.

You aren't selling them stakes in a company that cans whitefish. You are selling them the fantasy that they are marked out for special things.

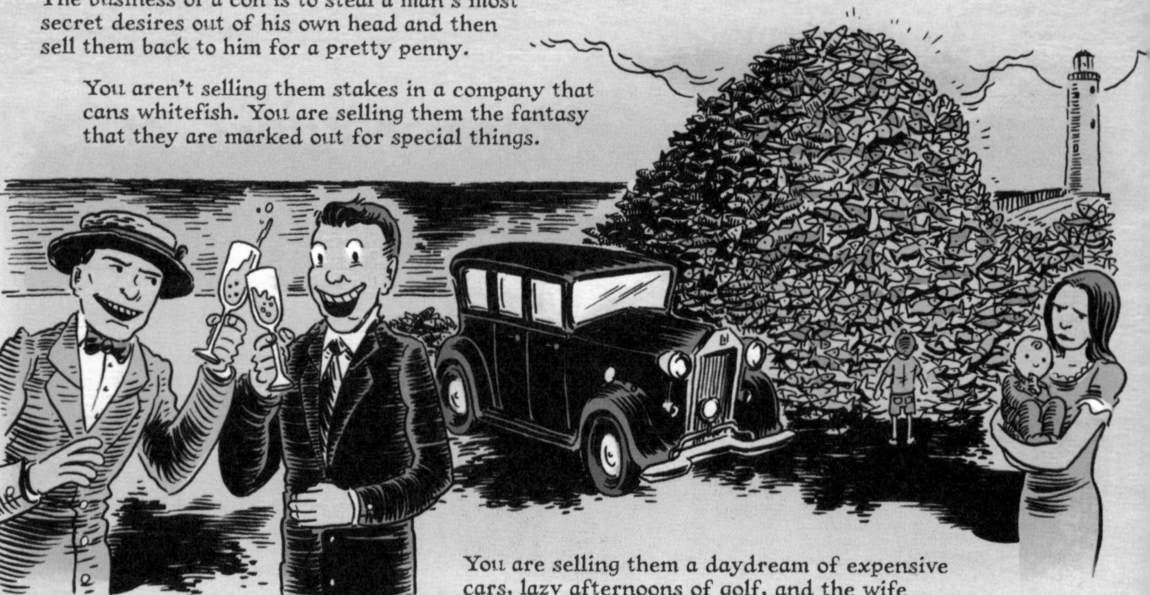

You are selling them a daydream of expensive cars, lazy afternoons of golf, and the wife waiting at home, naked under French silks.

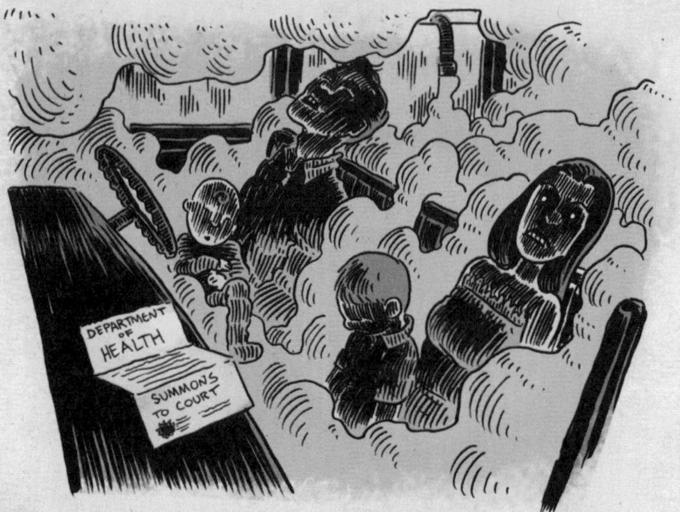
DEPARTMENT OF HEALTH
SUMMONS TO COURT

Is it your fault if they smell fish rotting in the sun and mistake it for the scent of money?

Are you to blame if they drown in the black rush of their own dream, once they discover the waters are too deep?

But you swim in the dreams of others like a fish.

AMERICAN WHITEFISH CATCH-AS-CATCH-CAN collapses after a botulism scare wipes out the unlucky investors. You walk away from the wreck unscratched...

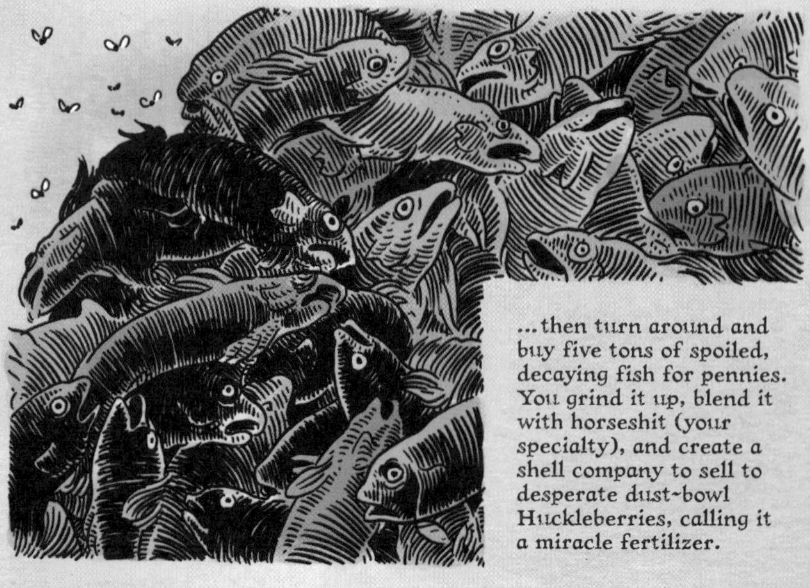

...then turn around and buy five tons of spoiled, decaying fish for pennies. You grind it up, blend it with horseshit (your specialty), and create a shell company to sell to desperate dust-bowl Huckleberries, calling it a miracle fertilizer.

The yokels farm the dried-out soil for small change.

You farm the yokels for another fortune.

"We've done fertilizer and fish, sugar and sex," Lew says. "What's next? Flynn wants a new sled for Christmas, Tommy. He talks about Christmas every day. If he had his way, we'd put the tree up tomorrow."

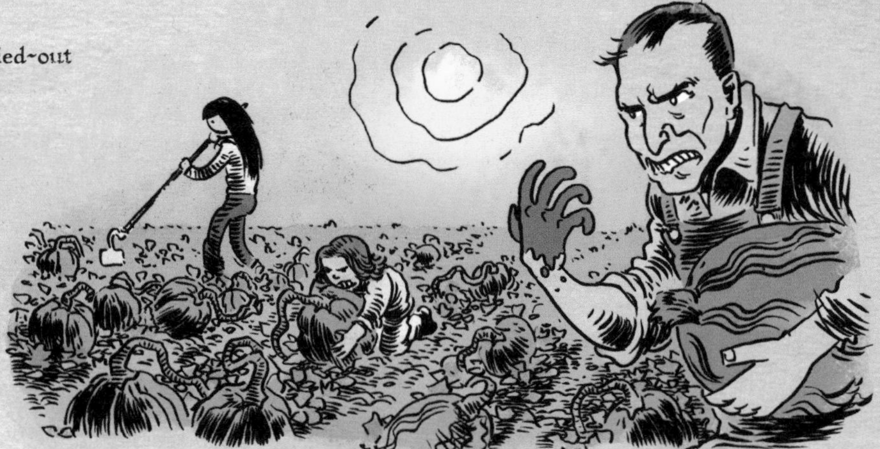

"Why settle for just one Christmas tree?" you say. "We're rich. How about a whole forest?"

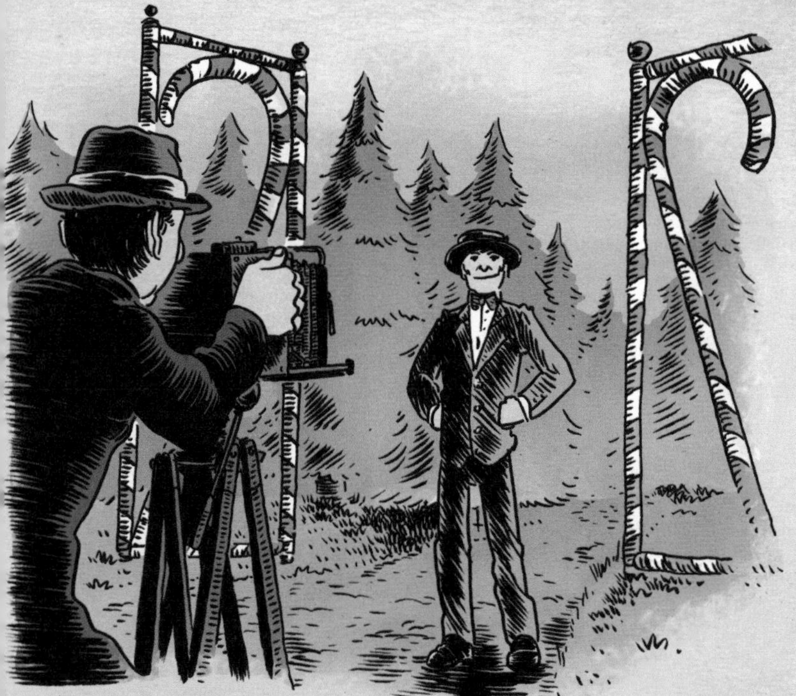

You drop twelve G-Notes on virgin forest in Colorado, and eighty dollars on big plastic candy canes.

You have the timber chopped down and sold for enough cash to make a sliver of profit, after you pay off the logging crew.

"How's it feel to make some honest money for once?" Lew asks you.

"Not good enough to make a habit of it," you tell her. "It's easier selling daydreams. Less overhead."

You hire another crew-not lumberjacks, but operators-and fan out across the Midwest.

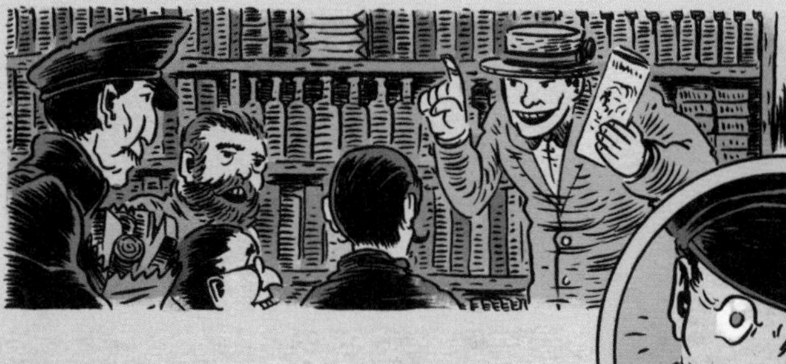

This time you're selling Christmas... the fantasy of a Christmas that never ends, a Christmas-land where being unhappy is against the law.

The Midwest is hot, dusty, and pitiful-everything dried up and blown away except for hope. You show them Christmas on the far side of a dark river.

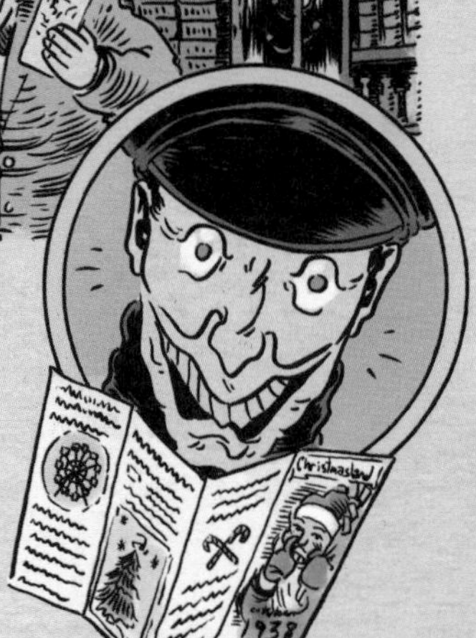
Christmasland
1938

They wade right in and are sucked away like Flynn. But they *aren't* like Flynn, not really. They're the ones who chased you and Flynn into the water. Drowning is fine for the likes of them.

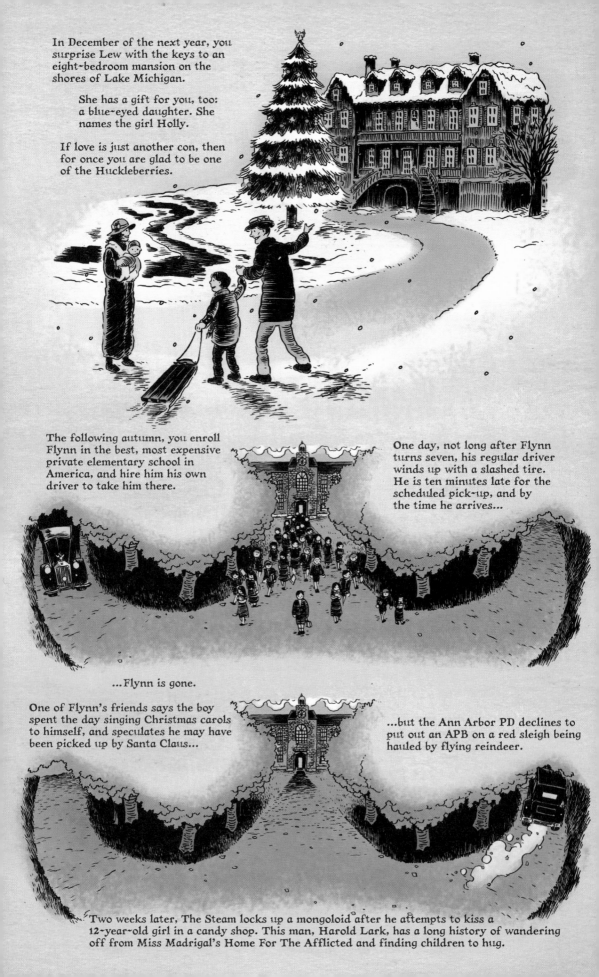

In December of the next year, you surprise Lew with the keys to an eight-bedroom mansion on the shores of Lake Michigan.

She has a gift for you, too: a blue-eyed daughter. She names the girl Holly.

If love is just another con, then for once you are glad to be one of the Huckleberries.

The following autumn, you enroll Flynn in the best, most expensive private elementary school in America, and hire him his own driver to take him there.

One day, not long after Flynn turns seven, his regular driver winds up with a slashed tire. He is ten minutes late for the scheduled pick-up, and by the time he arrives...

...Flynn is gone.

One of Flynn's friends says the boy spent the day singing Christmas carols to himself, and speculates he may have been picked up by Santa Claus...

...but the Ann Arbor PD declines to put out an APB on a red sleigh being hauled by flying reindeer.

Two weeks later, The Steam locks up a mongoloid after he attempts to kiss a 12-year-old girl in a candy shop. This man, Harold Lark, has a long history of wandering off from Miss Madrigal's Home For The Afflicted and finding children to hug.

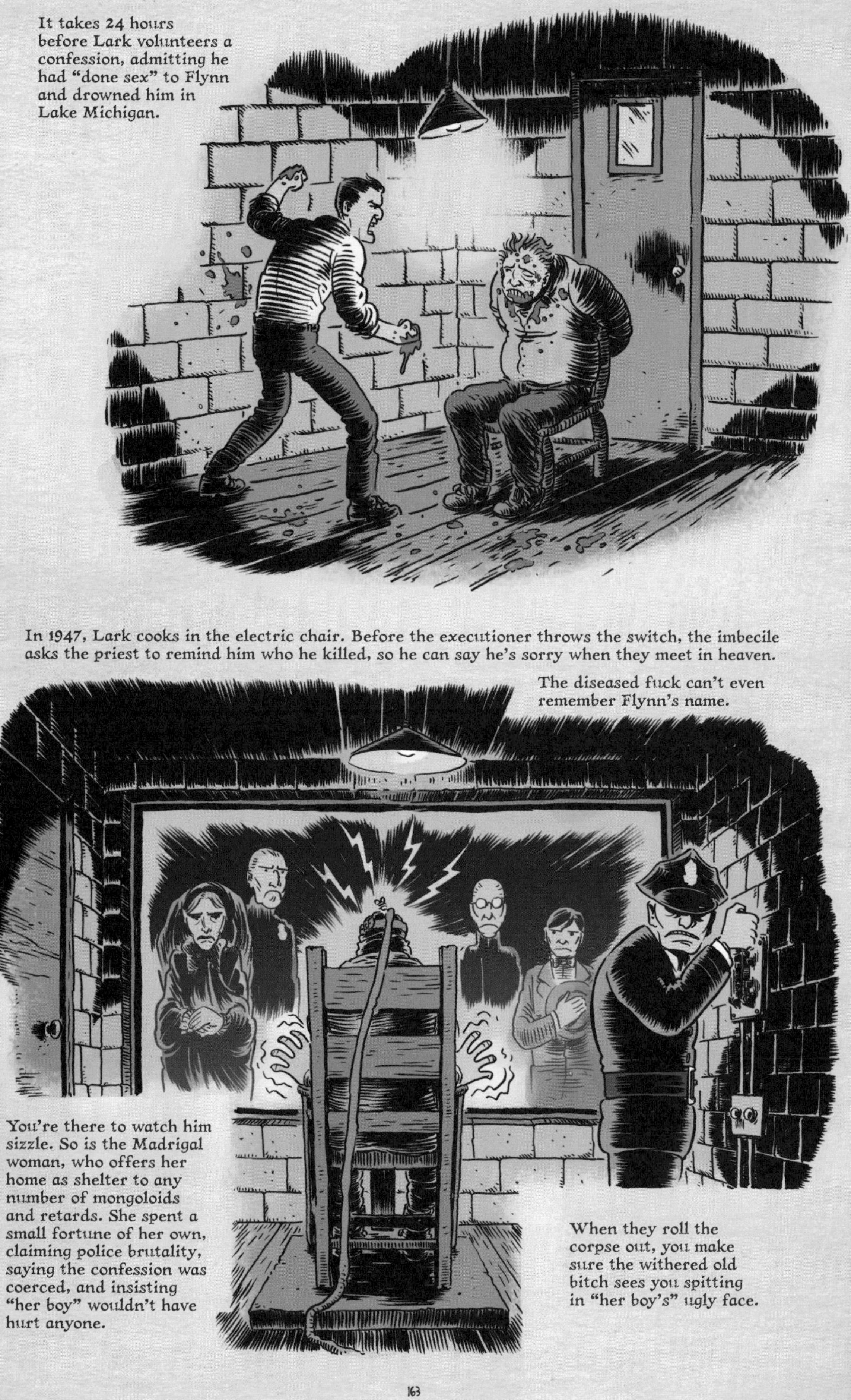
It takes 24 hours before Lark volunteers a confession, admitting he had "done sex" to Flynn and drowned him in Lake Michigan.
In 1947, Lark cooks in the electric chair. Before the executioner throws the switch, the imbecile asks the priest to remind him who he killed, so he can say he's sorry when they meet in heaven.
The diseased fuck can't even remember Flynn's name.
You're there to watch him sizzle. So is the Madrigal woman, who offers her home as shelter to any number of mongoloids and retards. She spent a small fortune of her own, claiming police brutality, saying the confession was coerced, and insisting "her boy" wouldn't have hurt anyone.
When they roll the corpse out, you make sure the withered old bitch sees you spitting in "her boy's" ugly face.

In the aftermath of Flynn's death, Lew is sentenced to die in the chair as well... the one with wheels. At least little Holly never hears her mother screaming or crying. Or singing Christmas carols. Somehow that's the worst: the way Lew will sit in the cold bathwater for hours on end, crooning the words to "Silent Night."

Holly never hears any of it because it turns out Holly was born deaf, wouldn't hear the gun going off if Lew tried to shoot herself.

But Lew doesn't try to shoot herself. She tries pills instead... the first time. The second time she takes a razor to the wrists, and after that, you have her placed in a private mental institution, very tony, very peaceful, with all the facilities of a modern Mediterranean spa. Only the best for your Lew.

Without Flynn, she becomes a kind of child again, unable to tell the difference between dream and reality.

Sometimes she pretends to be talking on the phone to her dead son, who she says will be sending a car soon to pick her up.

Six weeks after you check her into Deepwater, Lew checks herself out.

She drowns herself in the same river that took your little brother almost forty years before.

They drag the mud for three days without coming up with the body. You didn't expect them to find her. There was nothing of your brother or your son to bury, either.

They all slip away from you, like a handful of balloons escaping a child's grasp.

164

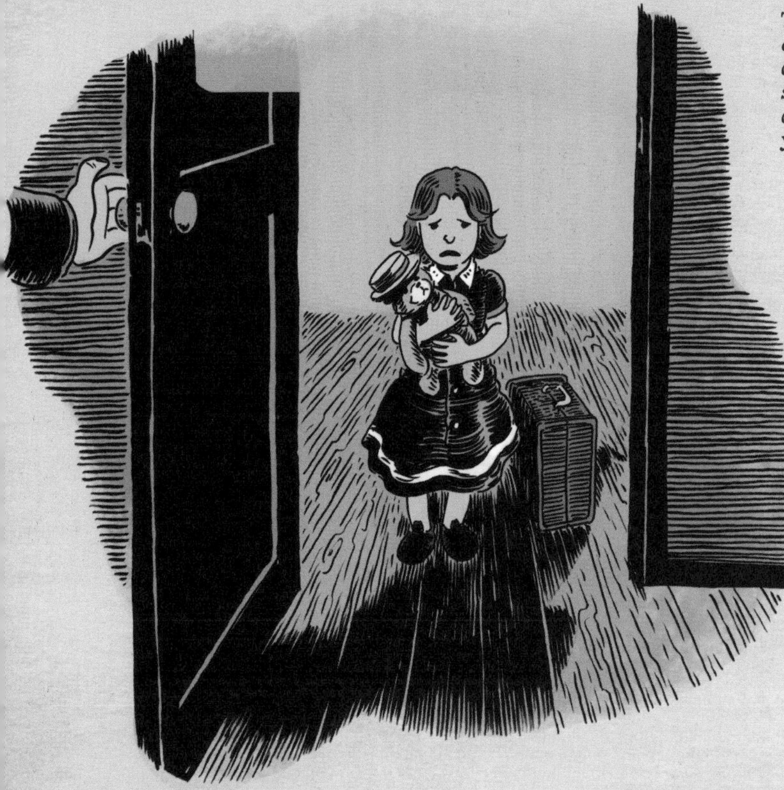

The world played you like a dim-witted mark, showing you all the good things, and then snatching them away from you, after you made an investment you can't ever have back.

You bet it all on the wife and children and respectability~ you bet a decade of your life, which is worse than betting money. Time you can't earn back. You would rather lose a hand or your tongue then have lost ten years of your life this way.

When you decide to let go of Holly, you view it as an act of fatherly love.

Holly is sleeping by the time you arrive at the orphanage. You're glad. You don't want to say goodbye. Not that she could hear you.

You can't be expected to look after a handicapped kid. Without the ability to absorb language, she'll wind up as empty-headed as Harold Lark.

You could've made a go at raising her with Lew, but no man could do it alone.

Besides. The world owes you and you're going to see that it pays. Holly doesn't need to be anywhere near that man.

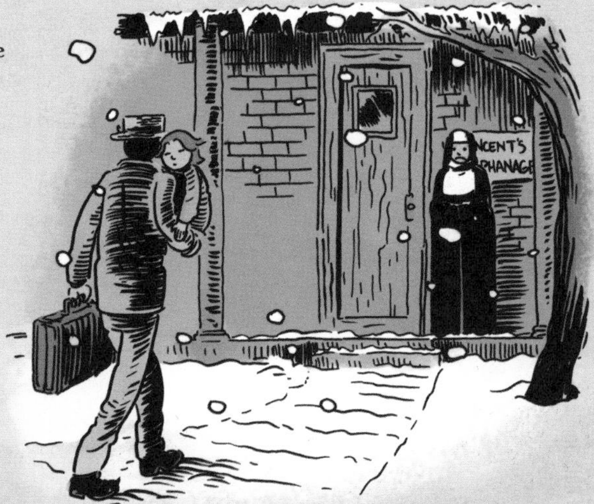

You send money for her care... until early April, when you get word that Holly has been adopted by a large, well-off family in Colorado. You are told she will have lots of brothers and sisters.

The Orphanage is legally barred from telling you much more, but one of the nuns whispers that the man who adopted her was named Christmas.

"She'll be Holly Christmas now! Isn't that delightful?"

But it isn't, somehow.

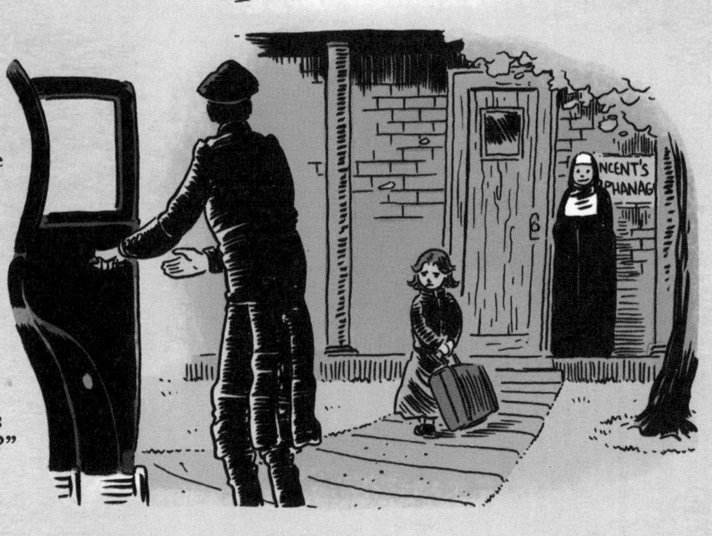

Your dreams are full of rushing water.

And drowned children.

Sometimes it feels like you have spent your whole life trying to cross the Fox River, your loved ones faithfully wading in after you to be swept away by the current. Both Flynns. Holly. Lew. Sweet Lew.

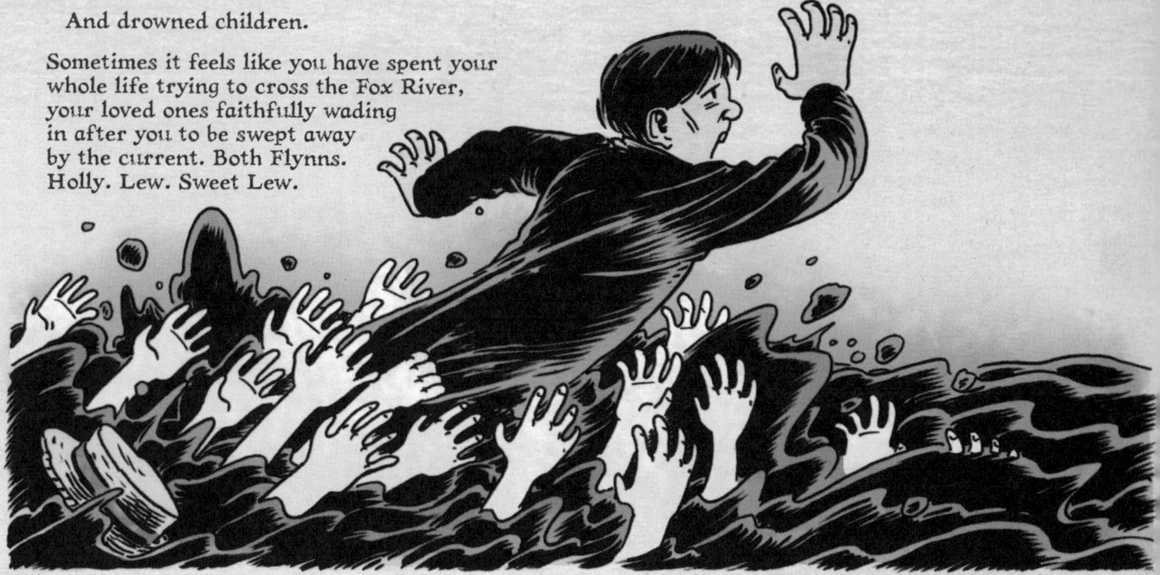

Just like the last time everything you love was swept away, the Ph.D. is waiting for you when you wade onto the far bank.

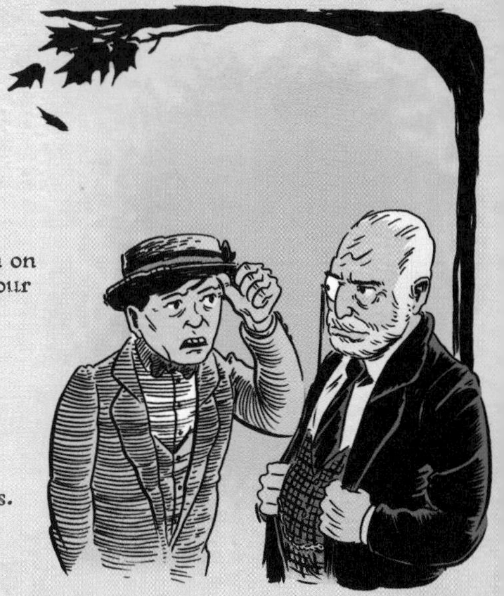

The last you heard of the Ph.D., he had been reformed by the love of a good woman, had married not long after getting out of jail, was raising a kid of his own. You took that to mean the old gigolo found some ugly rich broad to care for him in style.

But here he is, to see if you want in on a fat score, just when you are at your hungriest to dish out some hurt.

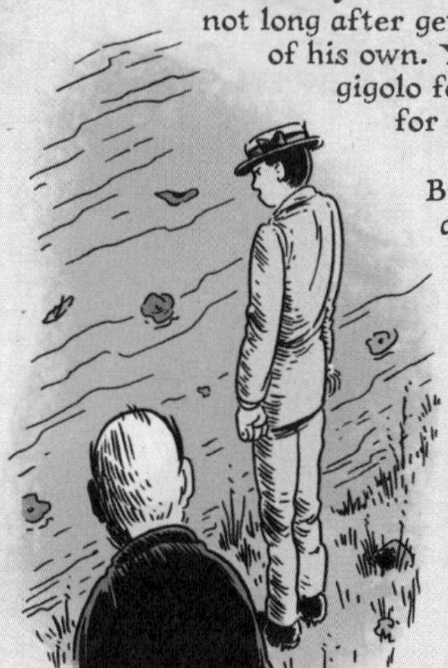

"What happened to true love?" you ask him.

"I had better sex in stir," he says. You laugh but cut it short when he only offers a thin smile.

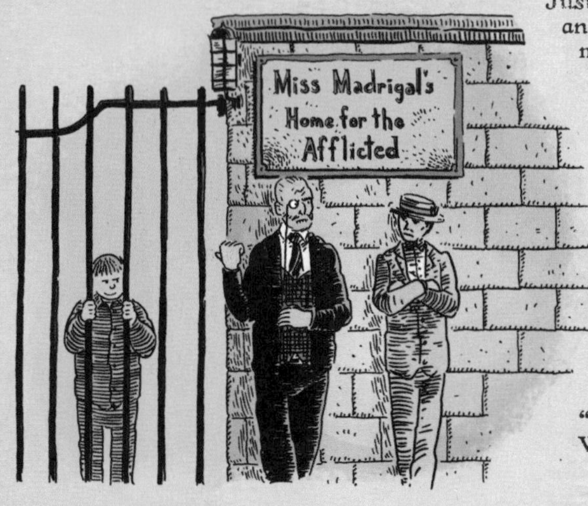
Miss Madrigal's Home for the Afflicted

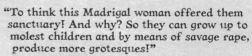

"I read about your little Flynn in the papers. Horrible! Just horrible. The mongoloid is an accident of nature and ought to be drowned at birth! That would be the merciful thing!

"To think this Madrigal woman offered them sanctuary! And why? So they can grow up to molest children and by means of savage rape, produce more grotesques!"

The Ph.D. continues, "I have it from a knowledgable source that the Madrigal woman is a lesbian with Communist sympathies. One cannot be surprised that a person like that would expect society to carry the weight of the feeble-minded... people who are born takers in this country of makers!

"Well... Madrigal and her ilk have taken enough. What's good for the goose, don't you think?"

You talk it over at Wrigley Field.
The Ph.D. has the play all worked out.

"The money she sank into the defense of Mr. Lark took a toll on her private fortune, but she's still got a million, and is thinking of opening another home for the deficients, now that things have quieted down.

"But if she's got a couple hundred thousand dollars to fling around, I imagine we can find a better use for her money, don't you?

"I'll pretend to be your butler, driver, and manservant," the Ph.D. tells you. "And you... you play yourself. Nobody but yourself.

"With my help, Madrigal is going to learn the truth about you. The true truth. Every last con and every last hustle. We're going to show her the evidence that would put you away for life."

"Are you crazy?" you ask him.

"Like a fox," he says. "Like a fox, m'boy." He lays it all out for you. And you know what? It's good. It's so good. It's not so different from his Stonewall Jackson scam, played out on a very large scale.

You are so caught up in the game the Ph.D. is describing, you hardly notice the game happening right in front of you.

The pitcher, Sam Jones, throws a no-hitter and everyone goes wild. A black guy, they're going nuts for. You still aren't used to the idea The Blacks are in the majors now.

What's next? Retards like Howard Lark being taught in schools alongside normal kids?

"Deal me in," you tell the Ph.D.

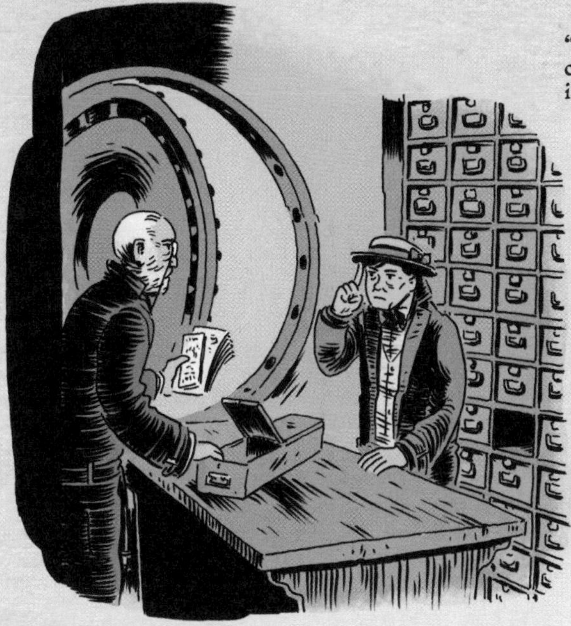

"Here's our play: all the paperwork on every scam you've ever pulled goes into the safety deposit box.

"She'll believe I am your long-suffering employee," the Ph.D. tells you. "I'll bring Madrigal here and give her a look at all of this—the facts and figures that could bury you. But I don't let her walk out with anything. I need compensation and protection, before I hand the evidence over to her.

"Why not show her faked-up documents?" you ask, although you already know the answer.

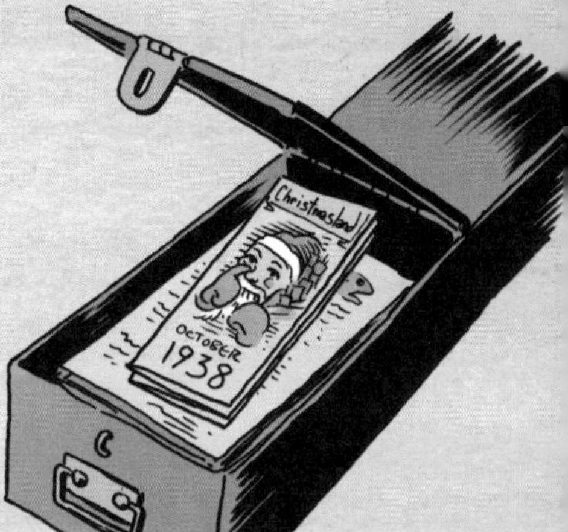
Christmasland
OCTOBER
1938

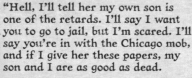

"Because I want her to take a good long look, and then go home and do the research. She'll find out the paperwork I showed her unmistakably ties you to real crimes, real scams.

"I'll persuade Madrigal I'm your trusted driver... that you place so much faith in me, you even put my name on the safety deposit box. Then I'll tell her that I'm haunted by the way you pushed for poor Harold Lark to get the death penalty.

"Hell, I'll tell her my own son is one of the retards. I'll say I want you to go to jail, but I'm scared. I'll say you're in with the Chicago mob, and if I give her these papers, my son and I are as good as dead.

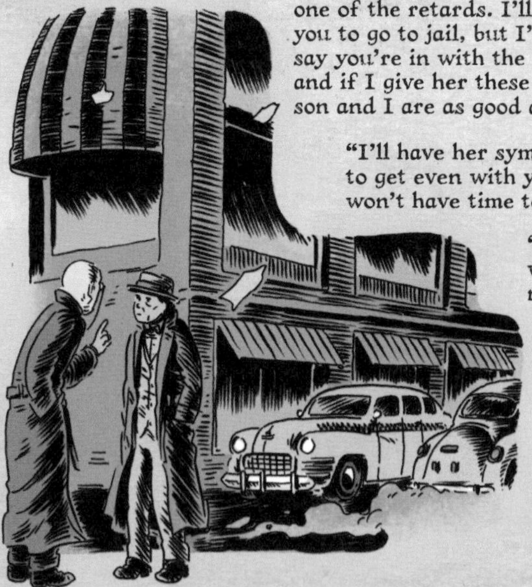

"I'll have her sympathy in one hand and her desire to get even with you in the other. But Madrigal won't have time to ask me many questions.

"I only have a few minutes to show her the papers, while you're around the corner visiting a dame. I need to be out at the car, ready to drive you home.

"We'll rent a limo and have it parked in front of the bank. I'll rush away, just in time to meet you. We'll let her spy on us from inside the bank, so she can see me bowing and scraping while you abuse me. That'll cinch it.

"Give her a couple weeks to stew, and then I touch her for 200 large—tell her I need that much to escape your wrath. She coughs up the cash, and I hand over the key to an empty safety deposit box. What do you think?"

You tell him, "I like the bit about you having a little retard of your own. I think with a detail like that you can touch her for 250."

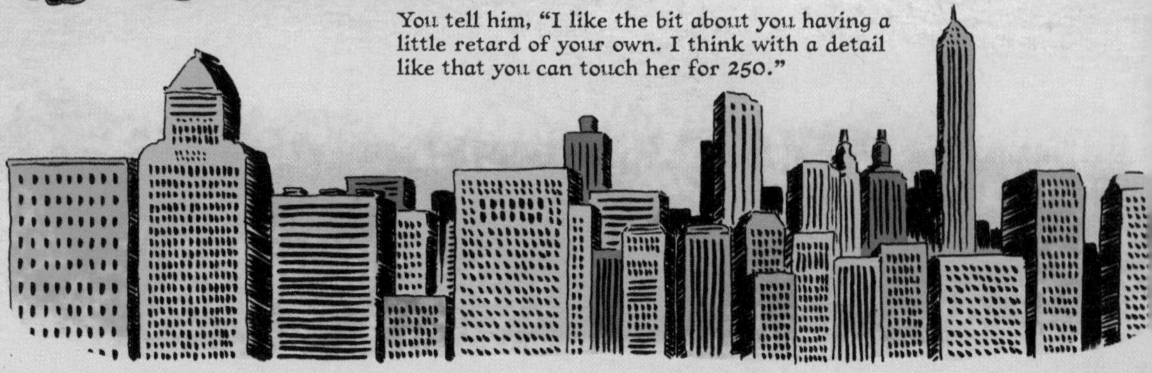

It takes just two weeks to set it all in motion.

This is the hardest part~giving Madrigal a look at the paperwork that could destroy the proper reputation you've cultivated in Chicago, and put you away for life.

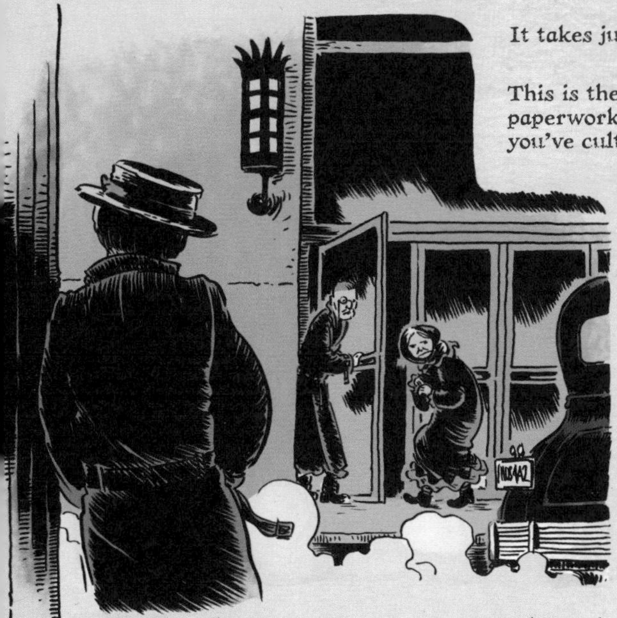

NOS4A2

You start your watch. In five minutes, you'll cross the street to the rented car. The Ph.D. will hustle Madrigal away from the safety deposit box with a promise to call her soon and arrange a deal. Then your trusted "chauffeur" will run outside to drive you home.

The tension is almost unbearable~less than a minute has passed before you're covered in a sick sweat~but you hold on. The Ph.D. is the oldest of old hands. He's always known just how to get a grip on someone, what to tell them to make them careless. How to walk the mark right over the trap door.

Unless... just maybe... he's *too* old. Something's wrong. Something feels off.

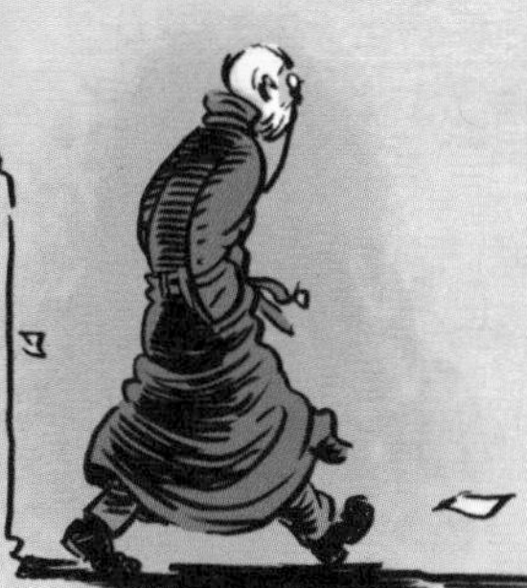

You're waiting by the rented car for too long before he comes out of the bank. He's supposed to put on a show of toadying and kissing ass, but instead he looks as carefree as a man who just had a whiskey and a blowjob. He opens the door to the rented Rolls and tells you to get in without even looking at you, seems to have forgotten all about following the script, bowing and scraping, letting you cuss him out.

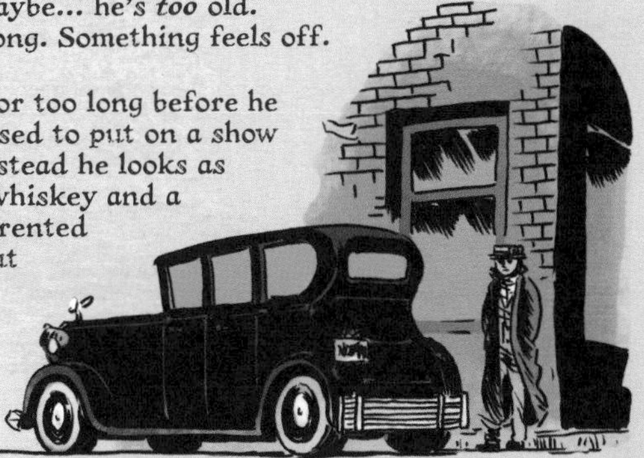

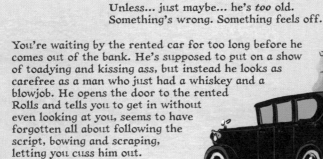

It gets worse.

As you climb into the car, you see Madrigal exiting the bank.

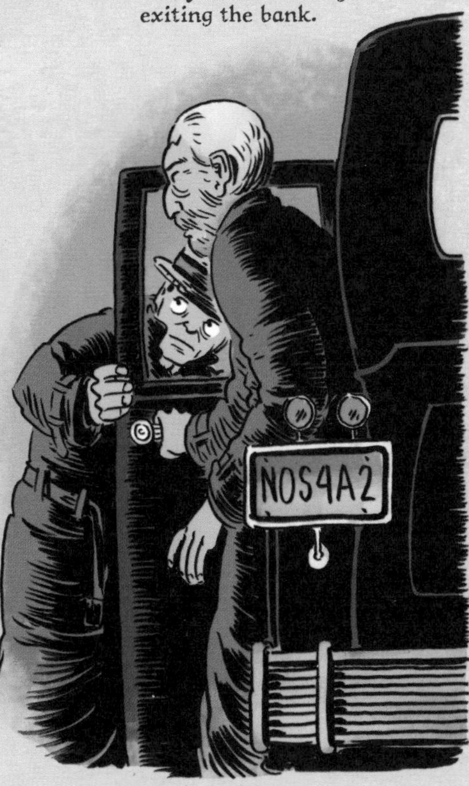

NOS4A2

And somehow she's holding all the papers the Ph.D. was only supposed to let her look at.

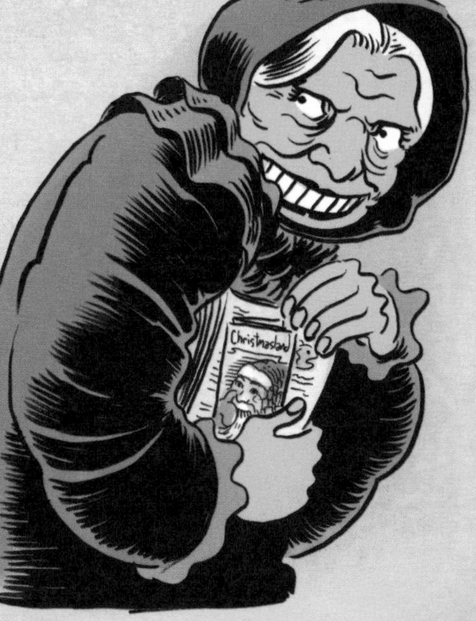

Christmasland

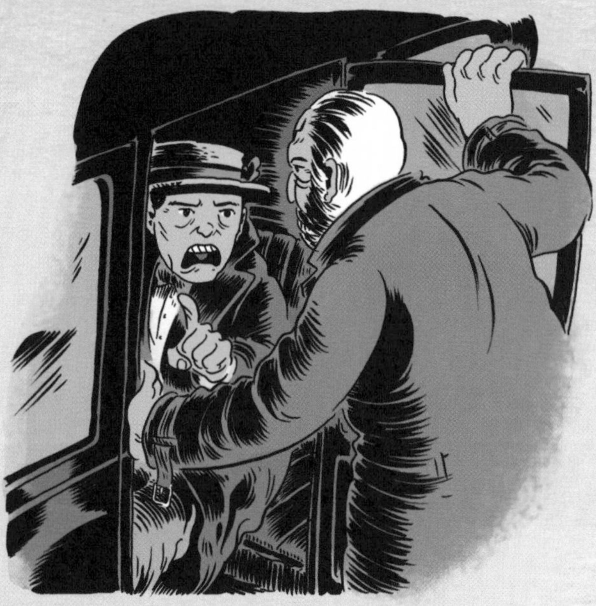

"What the fuck is this? She's walking out of there with the papers, man. What's wrong with you?" you cry.

"Nothing's wrong with me," the Ph.D. says. "But my son really is mentally handicapped. That lie was true.

"By the way, I think that's my old hat you're wearing. You can keep it, though. It looks better on you."

Then he slams the door.

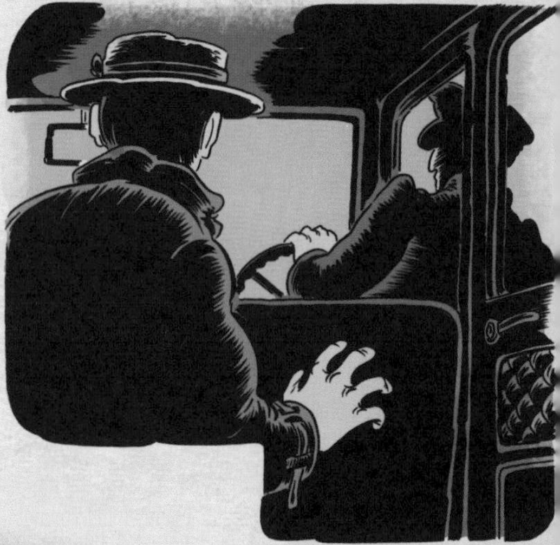

As the Ph.D. climbs into the front seat, you're thinking two things.

The first is that the old man hasn't lost the touch. He still knows how to walk a Huckleberry out over the trap door and drop them. It's just you've never been played for a Huckleberry before.

The second thing you're thinking is that if you were him, you wouldn't climb into the car.

But it isn't him.

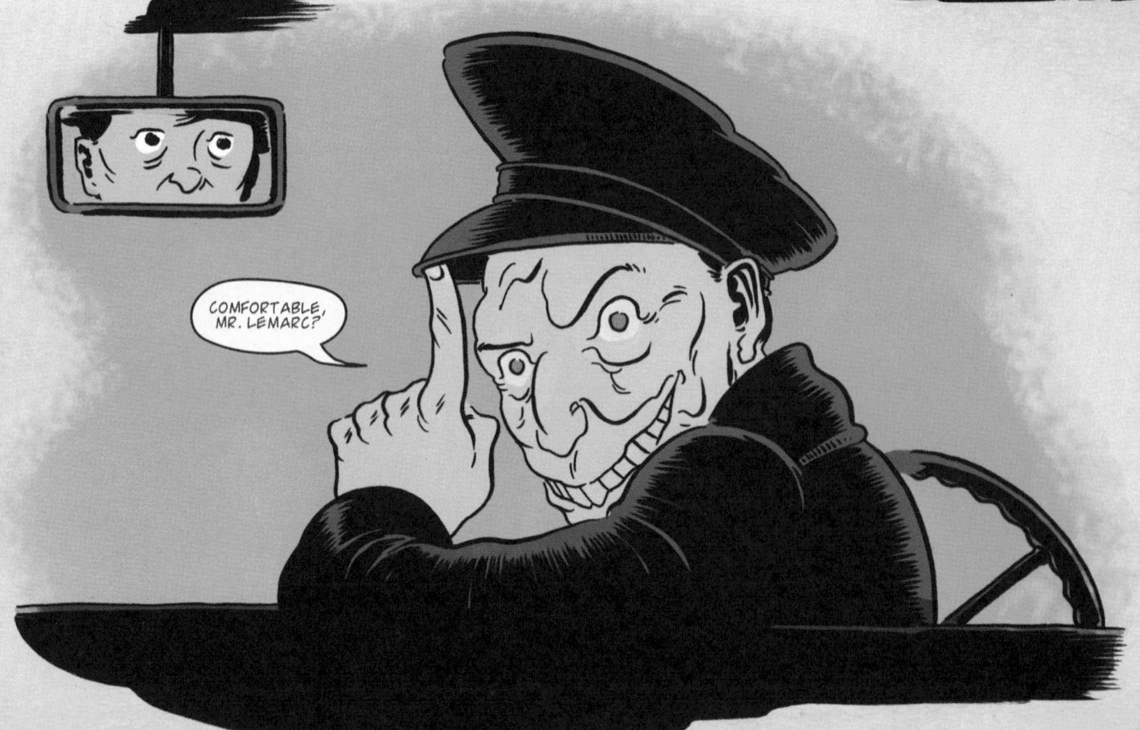
COMFORTABLE, MR. LEMARC?

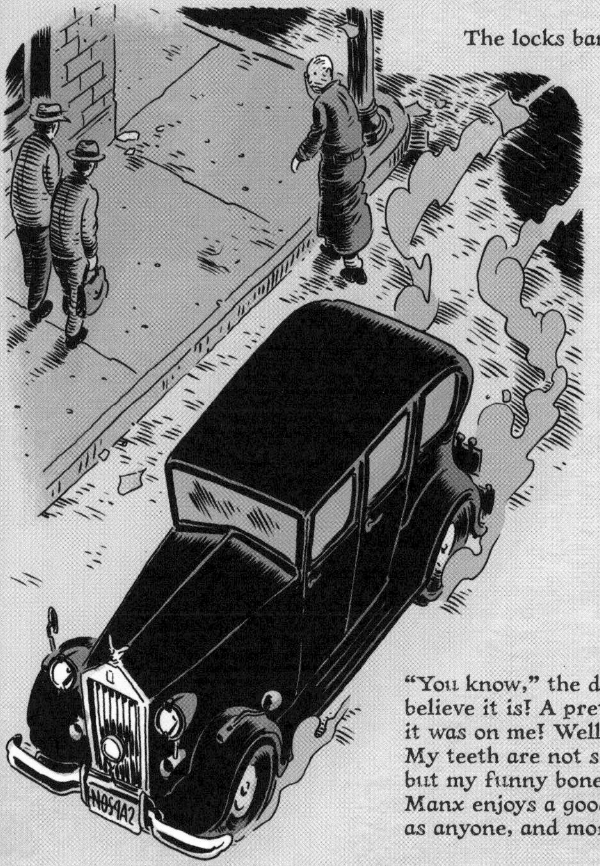

The locks bang down.

The old Rolls pulls away from the curb.

The Ph.D. watches you recede into traffic, his features somber and still, like a man watching a hearse roll by, containing the remains of a stranger.

"LeMarc?" you say. "What is that? A joke?"

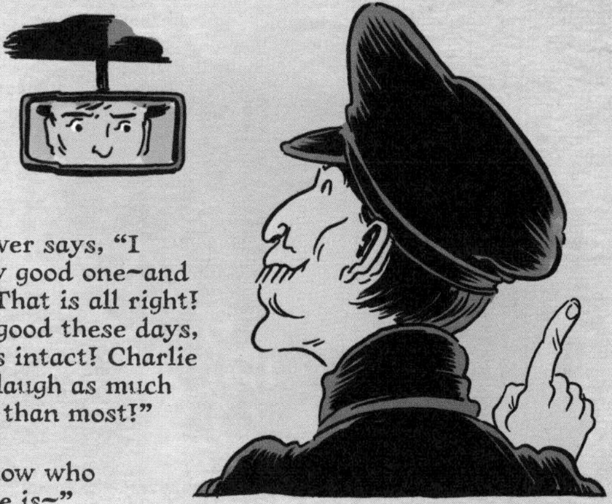

"You know," the driver says, "I believe it is! A pretty good one~and it was on me! Well. That is all right! My teeth are not so good these days, but my funny bone is intact! Charlie Manx enjoys a good laugh as much as anyone, and more than most!"

"Listen, Mister~I~I don't know who you think I am... but my name is~"

"It was Nicholas LeMarc the last time we met, and that will do for me! I can see you have forgotten who I am, but once upon a time you sold me a dream. And let me tell you... it was worth every penny! Yes, you don't remember me, but I could never forget you!"

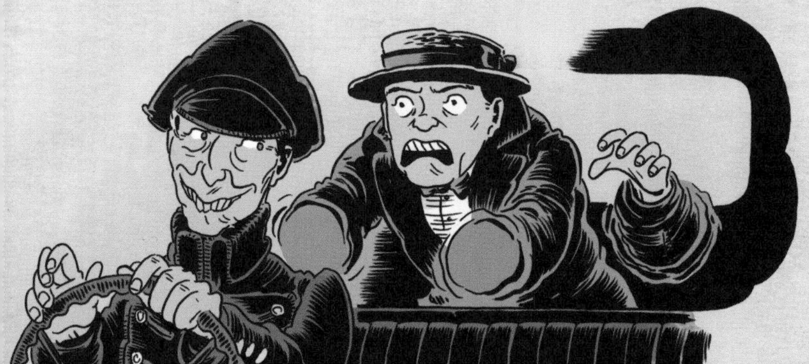

"What did you do to me?" you scream, when you try to reach up front and your hands melt away. "This can't be happening! You~you drugged me! This can't be real!"

"No, none of it was real... to *you*," says Charlie Manx. "You thought you had the best of your customers, selling them lies. But there really are no lies. There is only the world of being and the world of ideas, and neither has the greater claim to reality!

"Back in the world of being, you are about to be exposed as the fraudster you have always been. Which only serves you right! But don't worry about it. You won't have to answer for your crimes~there!

"I am taking you away from *that* world and into the *world of thought*, so you can see what you sold me all those years ago. Don't worry... you won't be lonely!"

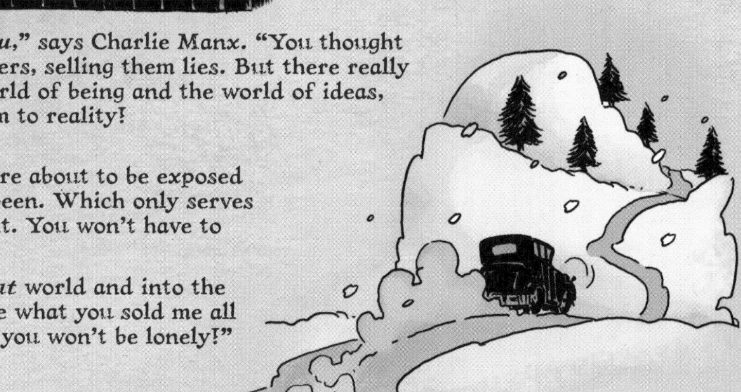

It is summer when you get in the car, but it is winter when you arrive at your destination. Maybe you were in the car one night or maybe for months. It feels like both.

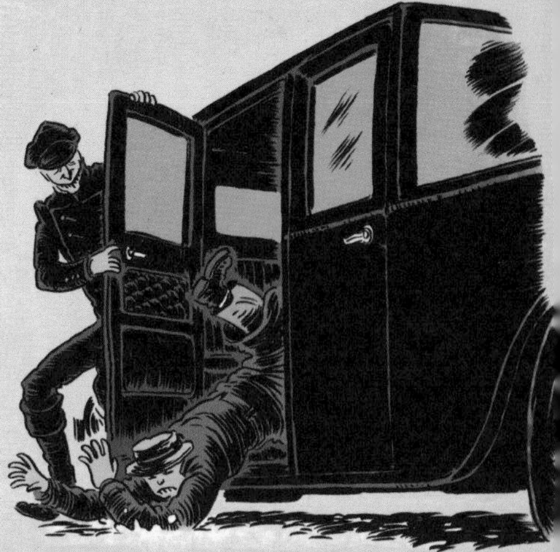

He talks the whole way: about inscapes and Christmasland and the children. His children.

A lot of it washes over you without registering. Although you listen close when he tells you about Lew.

"I've never been able to turn an adult before!" he says. "But she was a child inside and somehow that was enough! Good little Lew! If only you were more like her. But I doubt you were really a child even when you were a kid, Mr. LeMarc!"

He talks a lot of nonsense, but that part~that part is true enough.

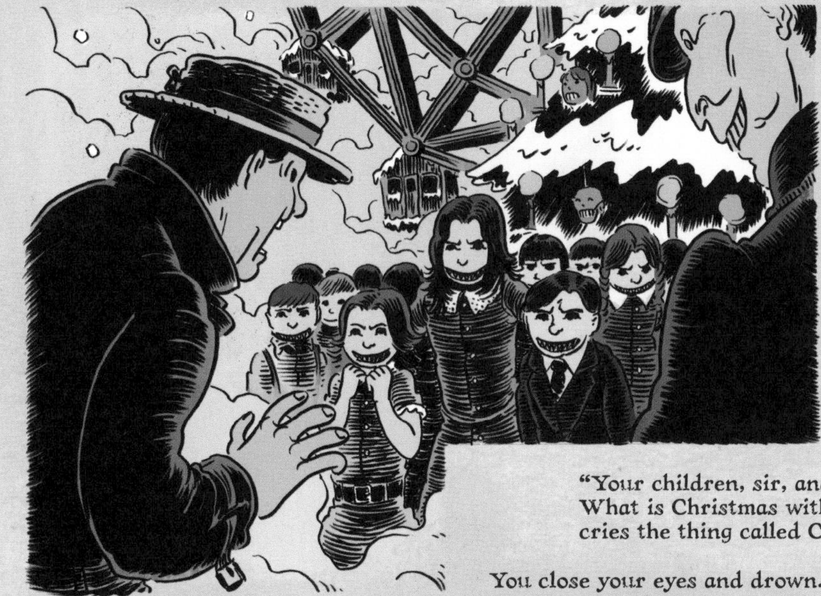

And there they are, just as he promised~your son and your daughter and Lew. Every good thing that was taken from you has been returned.

"Your children, sir, and your wife! What is Christmas without family?" cries the thing called Charlie Manx.

You close your eyes and drown.

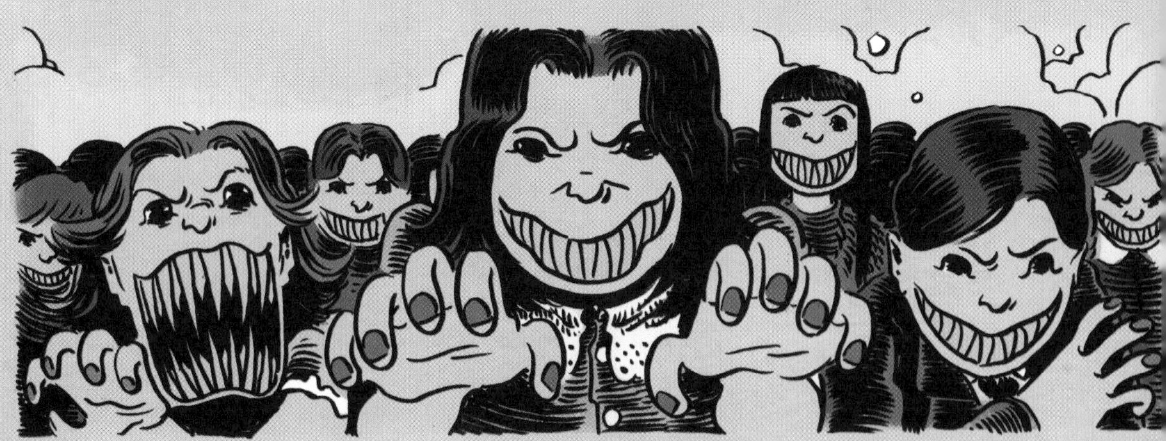

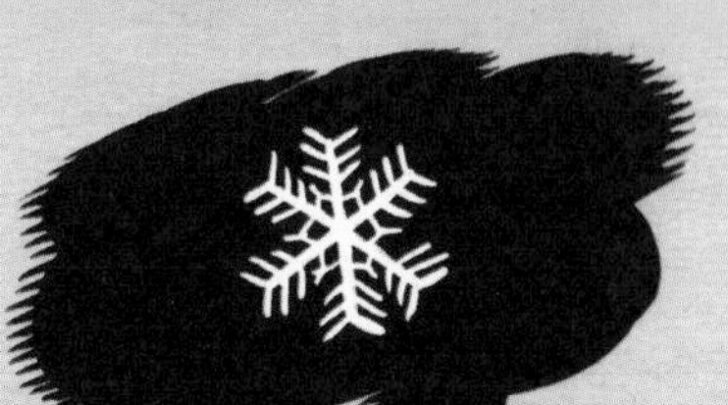

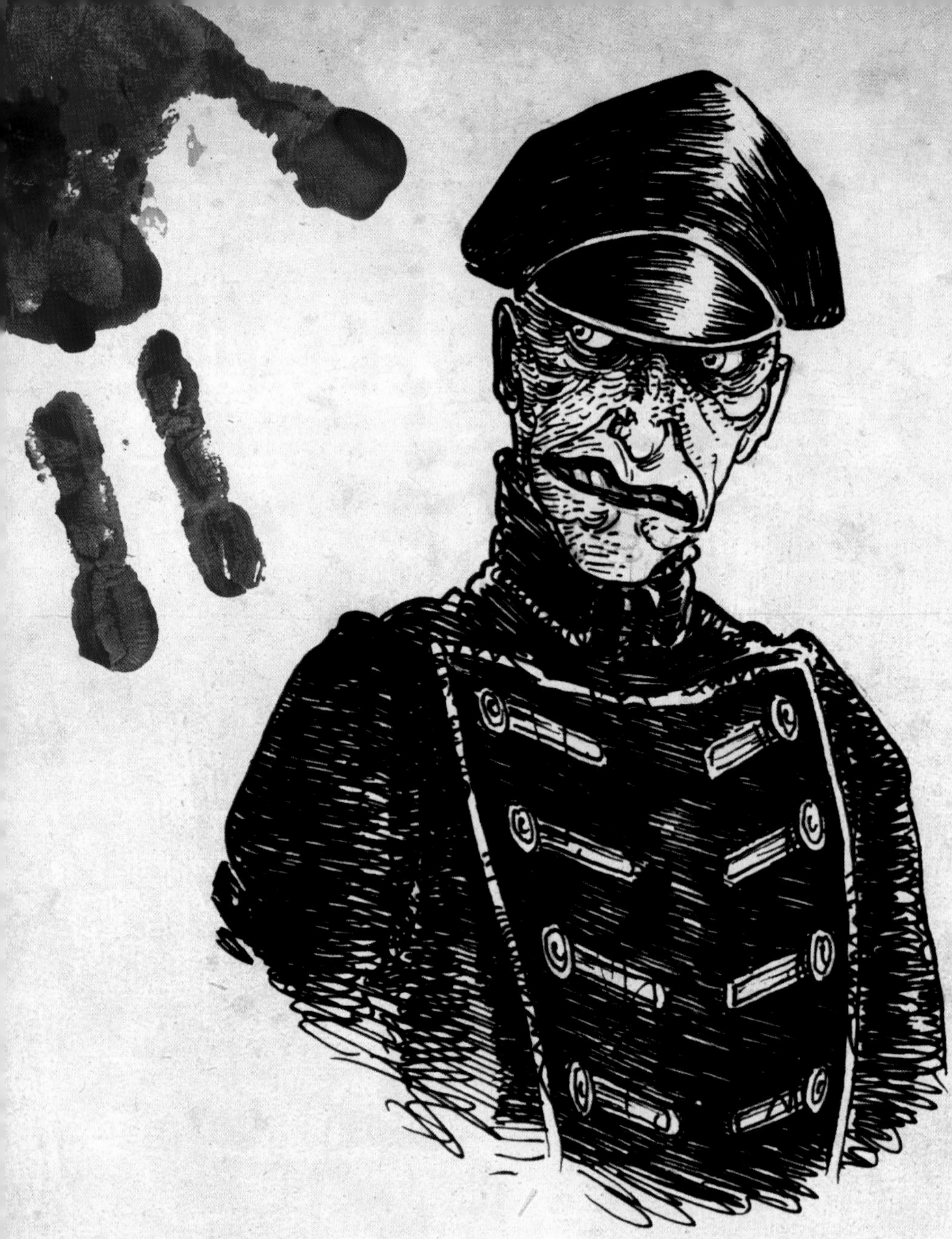

ART GALLERY

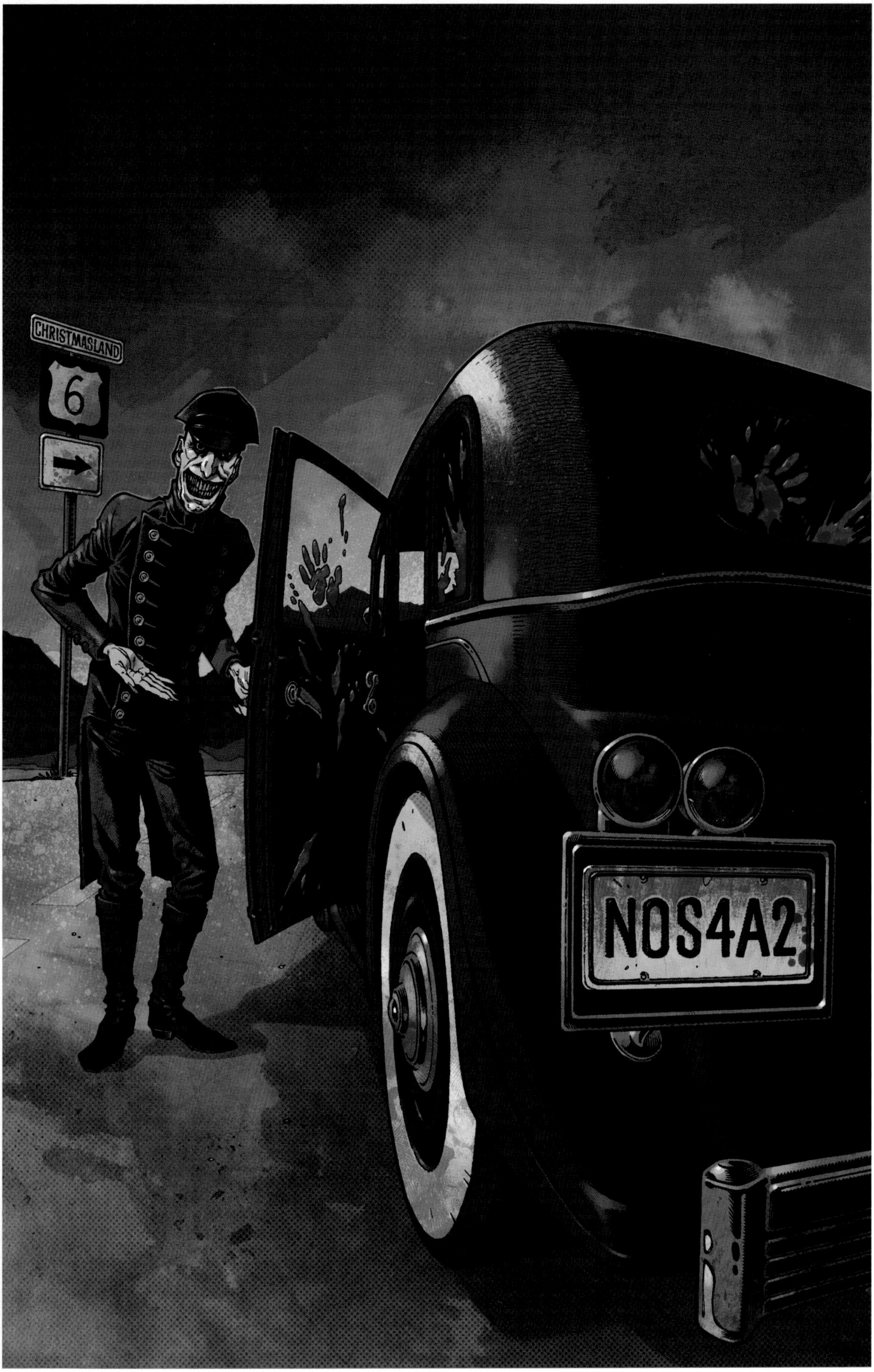
CHRISTMASLAND
6
NOS4A2

opposite page: art by Charles Paul Wilson III • *this page:* art by Gabriel Rodriguez, colors by Nelson Daniel

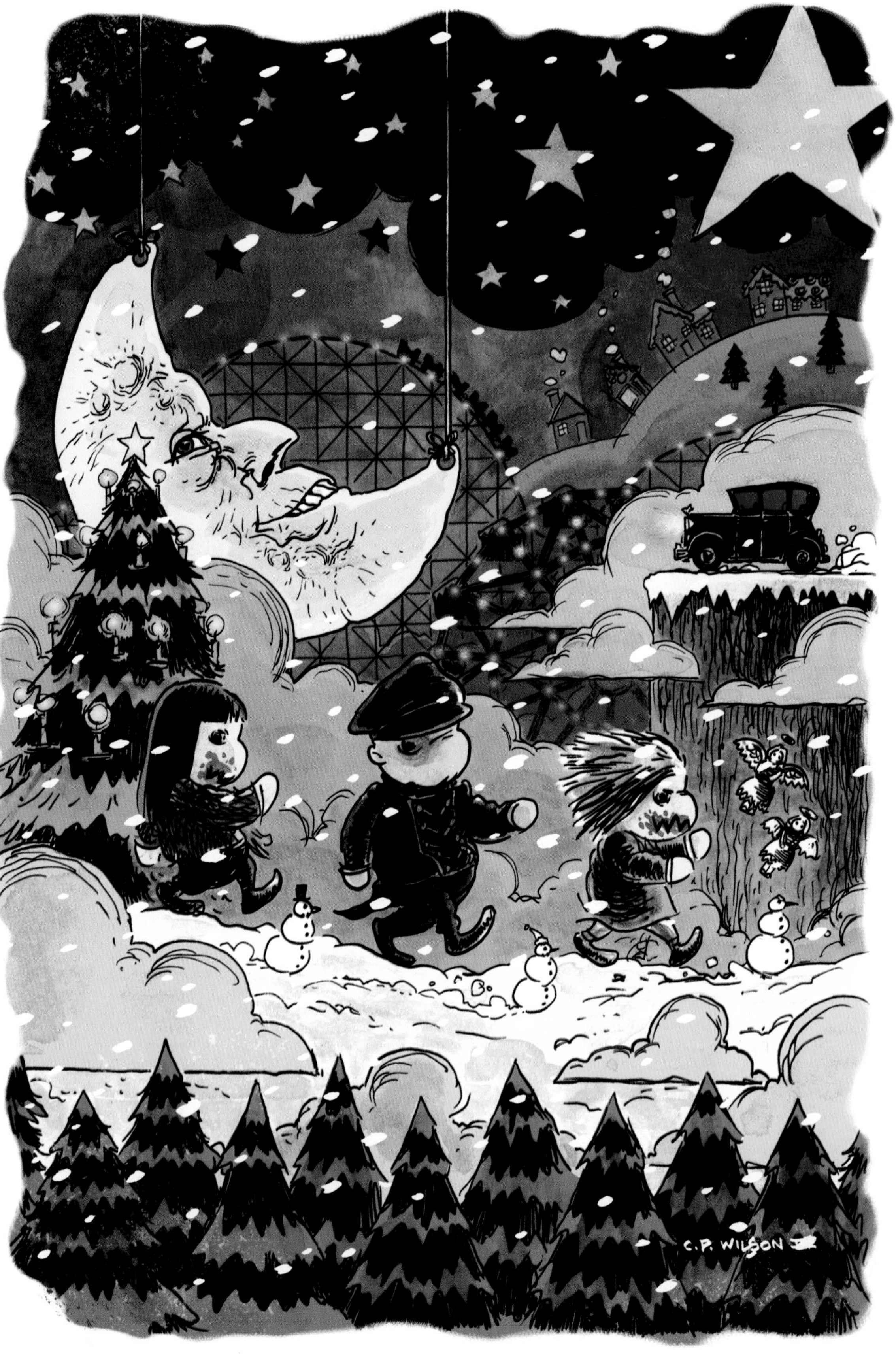
C.P. WILSON JR

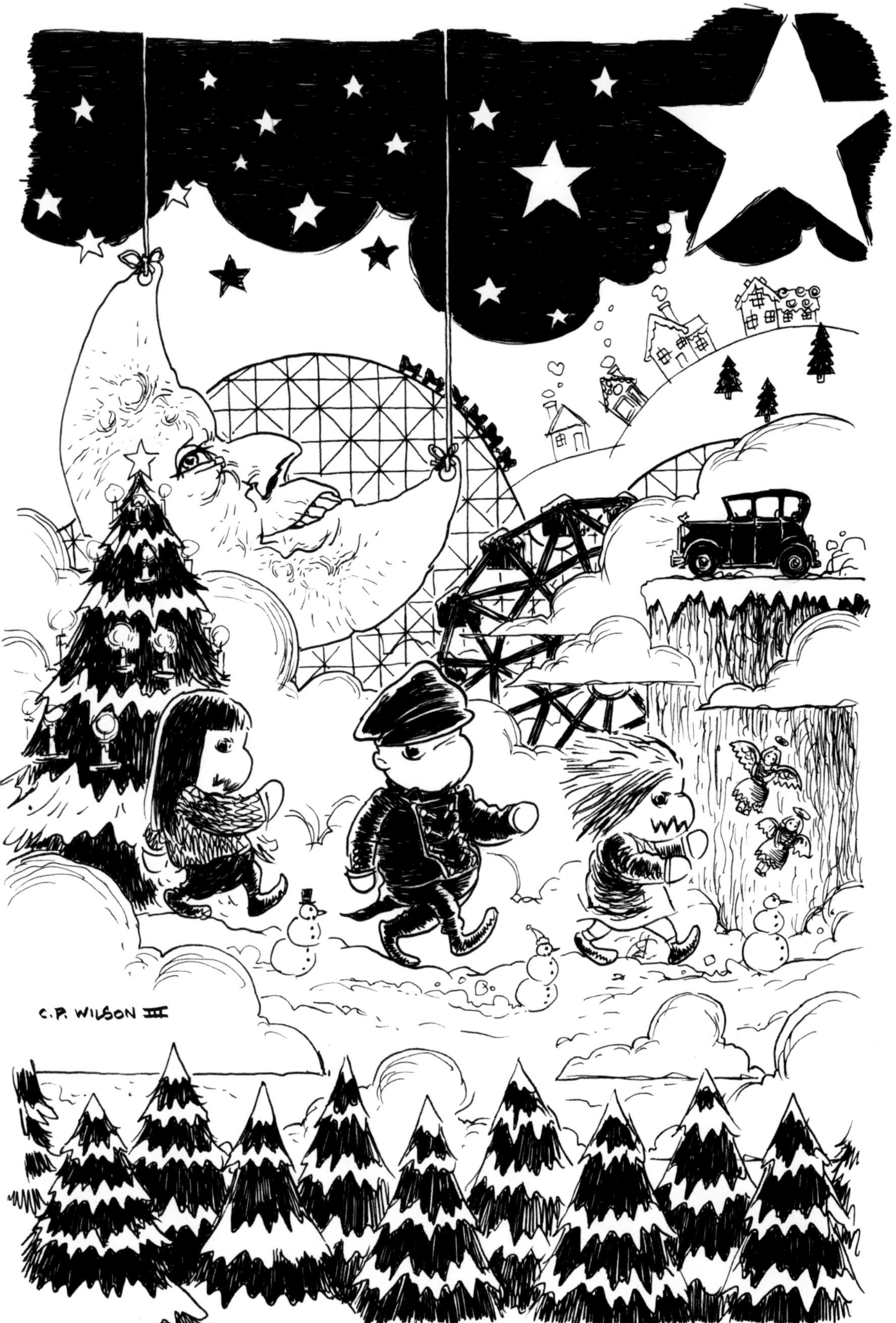
C.P. WILSON III

art and colors by Charles Paul Wilson III

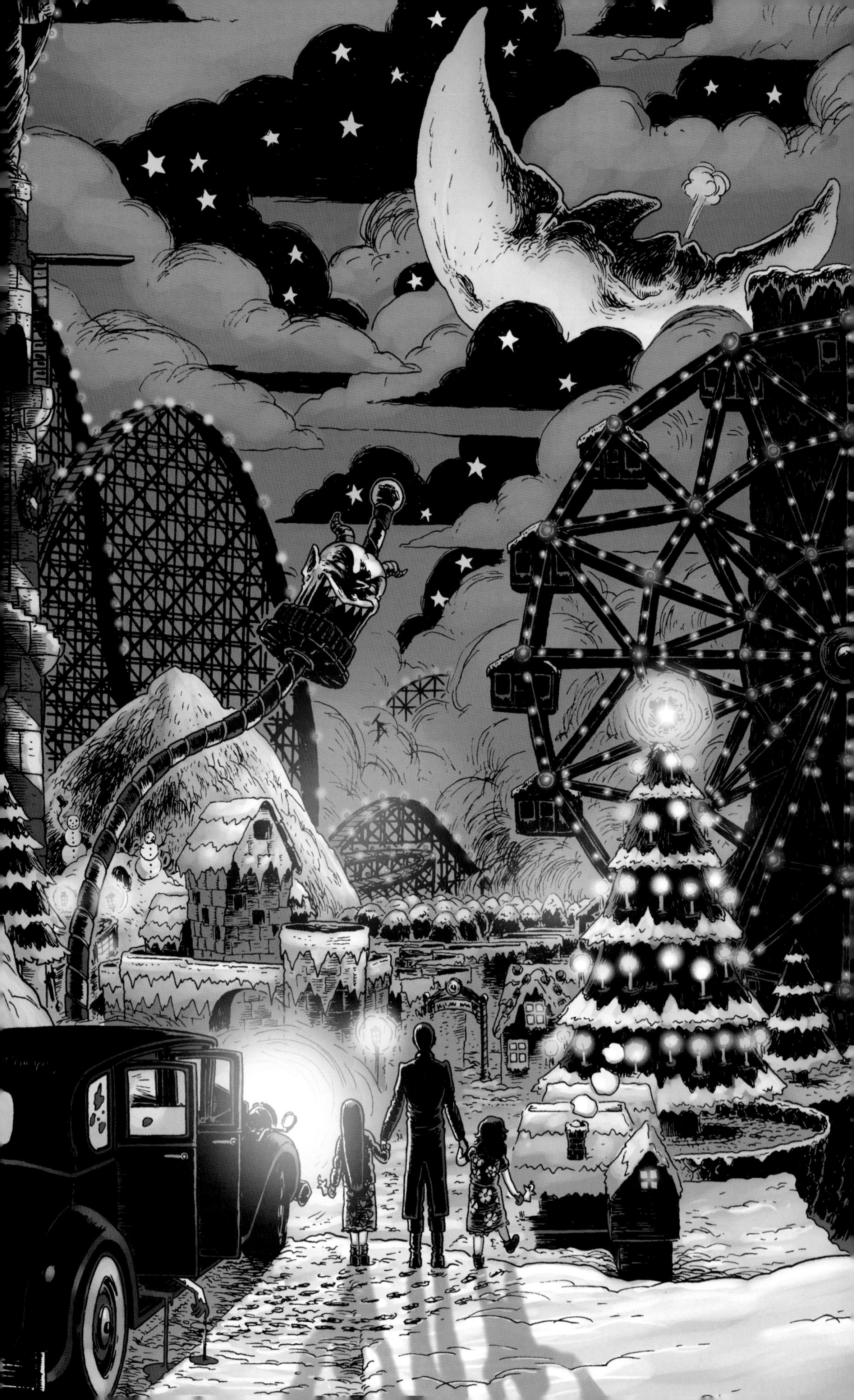

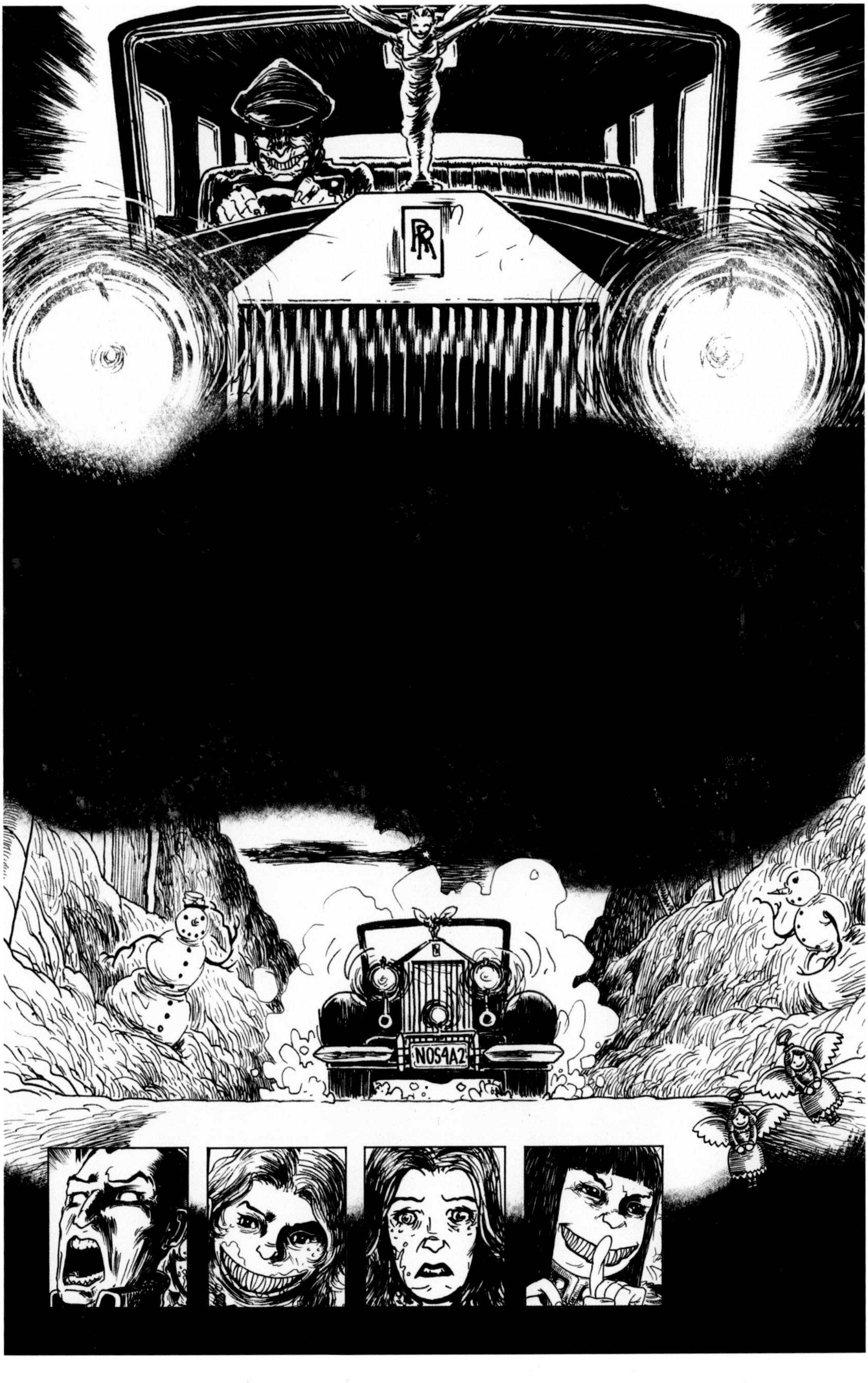
NOS4A2

opposite page: art by Charles Paul Wilson III, colors by Jay Fotos • *this page:* art by Charles Paul Wilson III

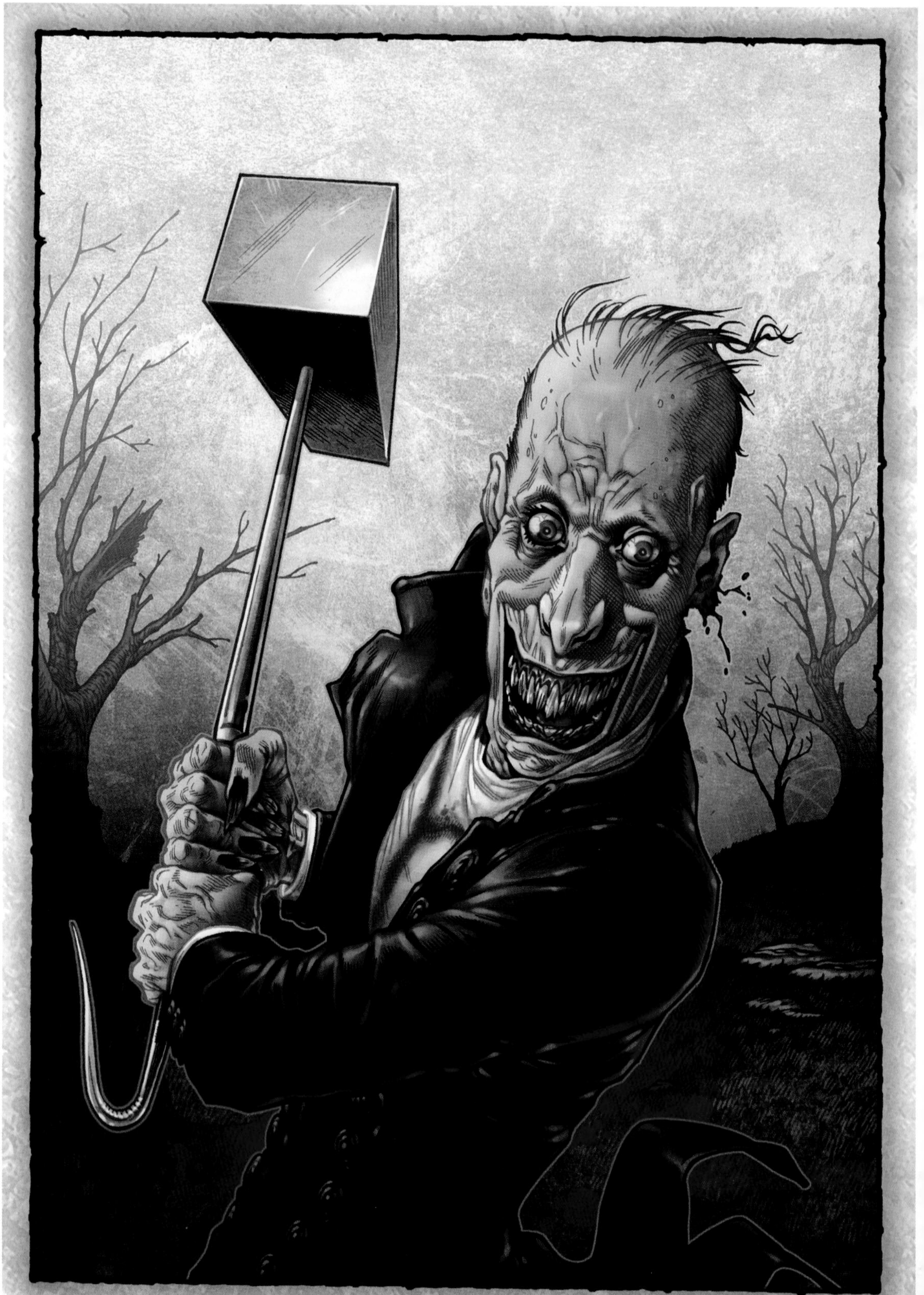

this page and opposite page: art and colors by Gabriel Rodriguez

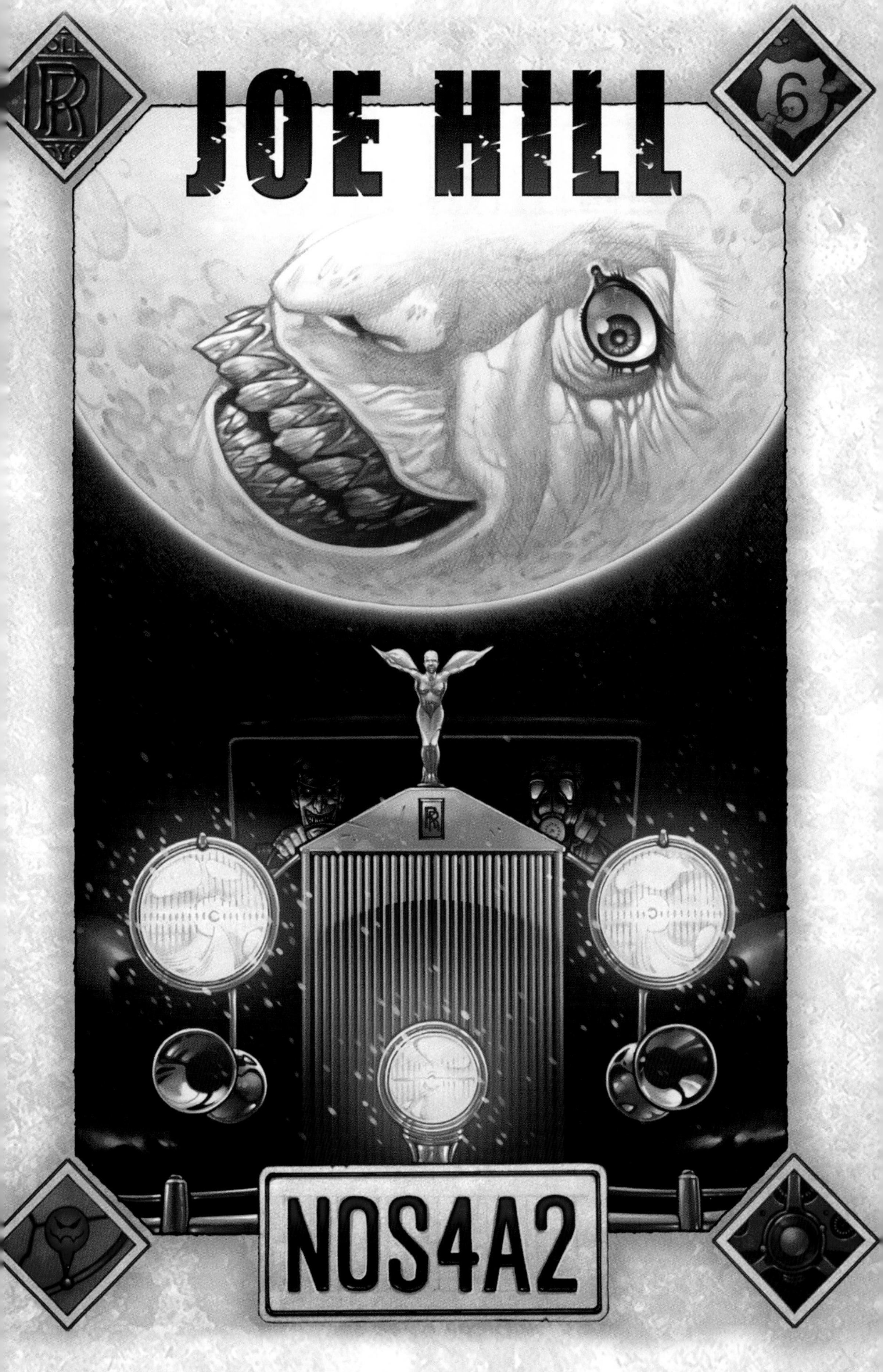
JOE HILL
6
NOS4A2

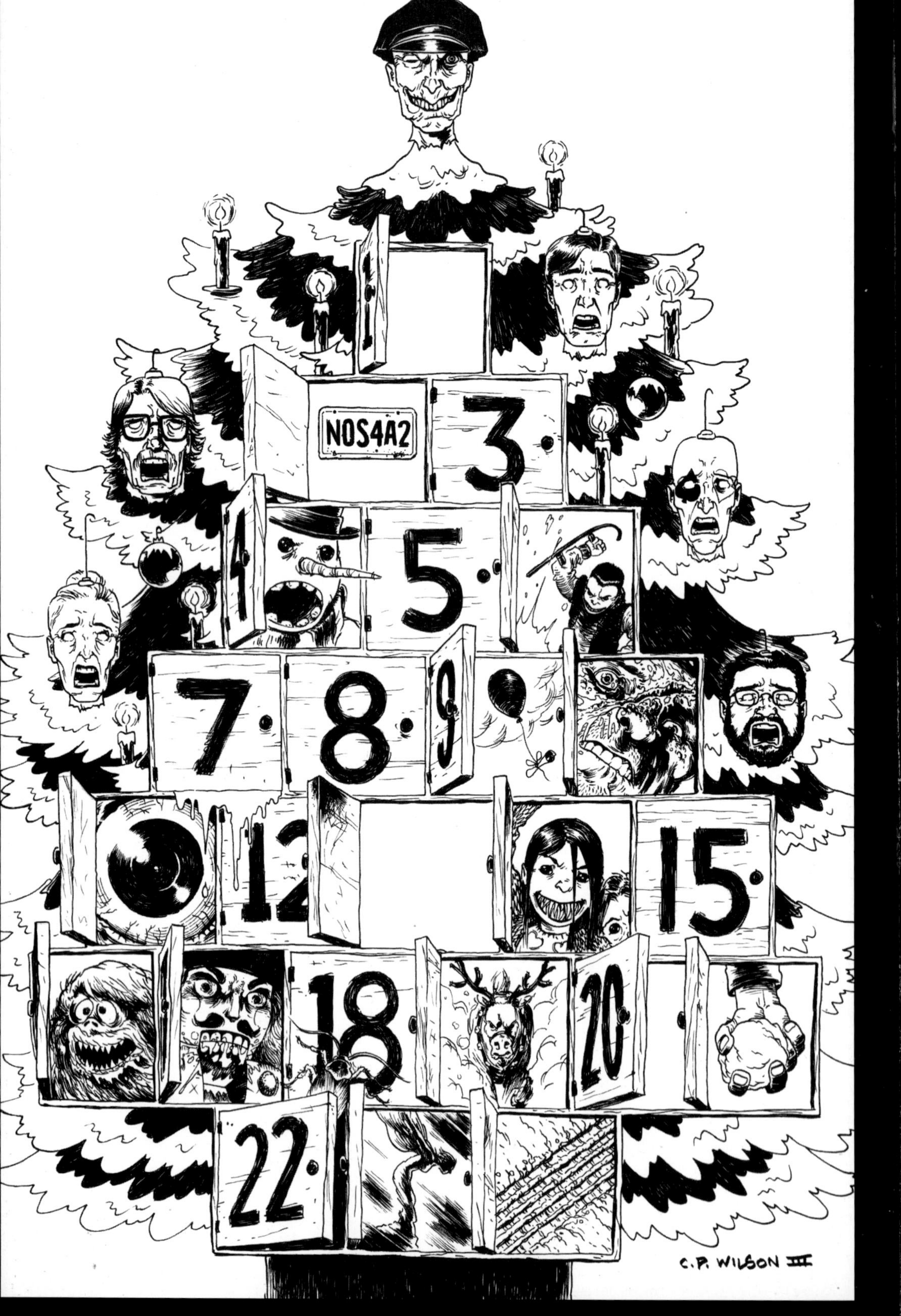
1
NOS4A2
3
4
5
7
8
9
12
15
18
20
22
C.P. WILSON III

art by Charles Paul Wilson III, colors by Jay Fotos

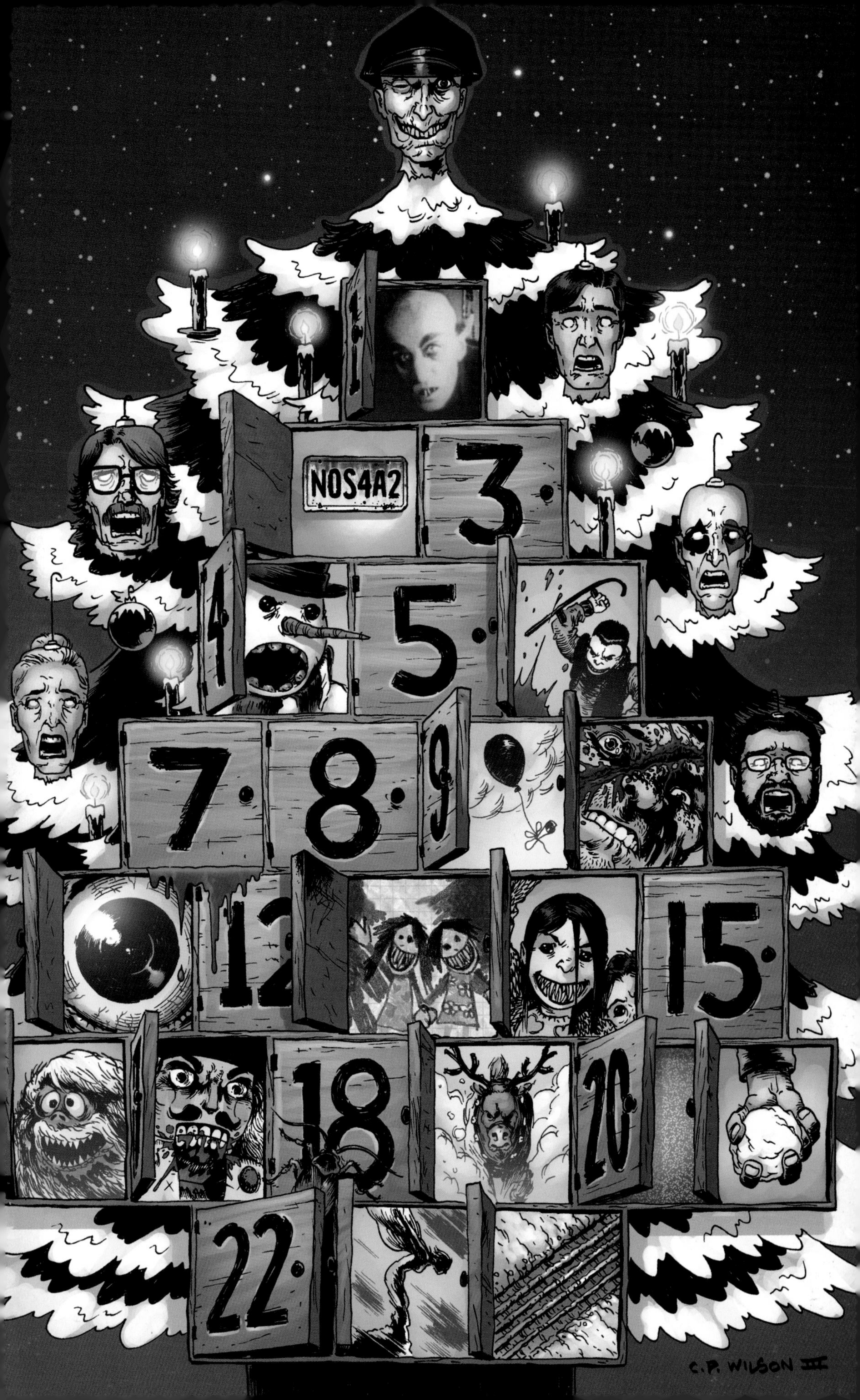

NOS4A2
3
4
5
7
8
9
12
15
18
20
22
C.P. WILSON III

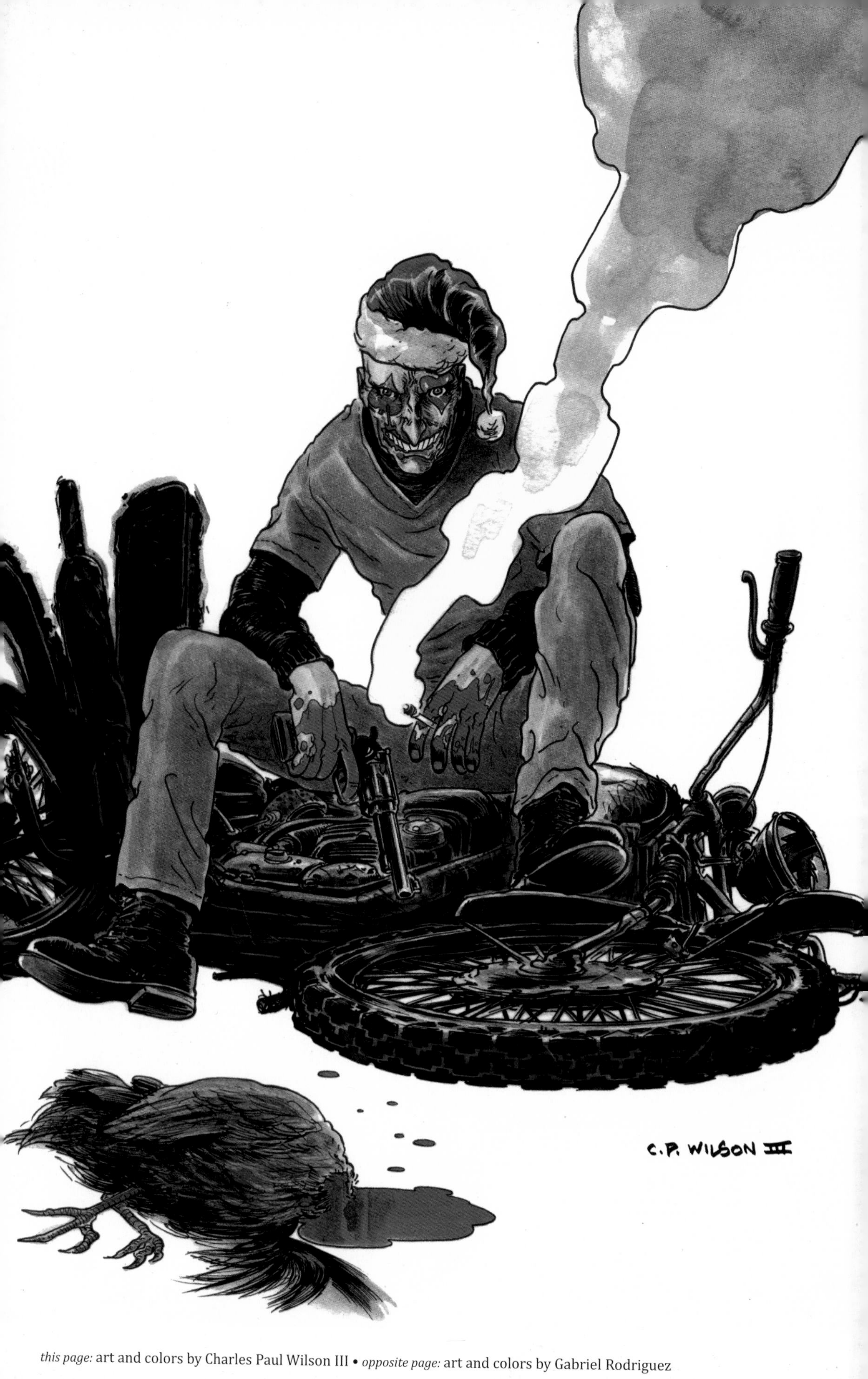
C.P. WILSON III

this page: art and colors by Charles Paul Wilson III • *opposite page:* art and colors by Gabriel Rodriguez

Millie Monx

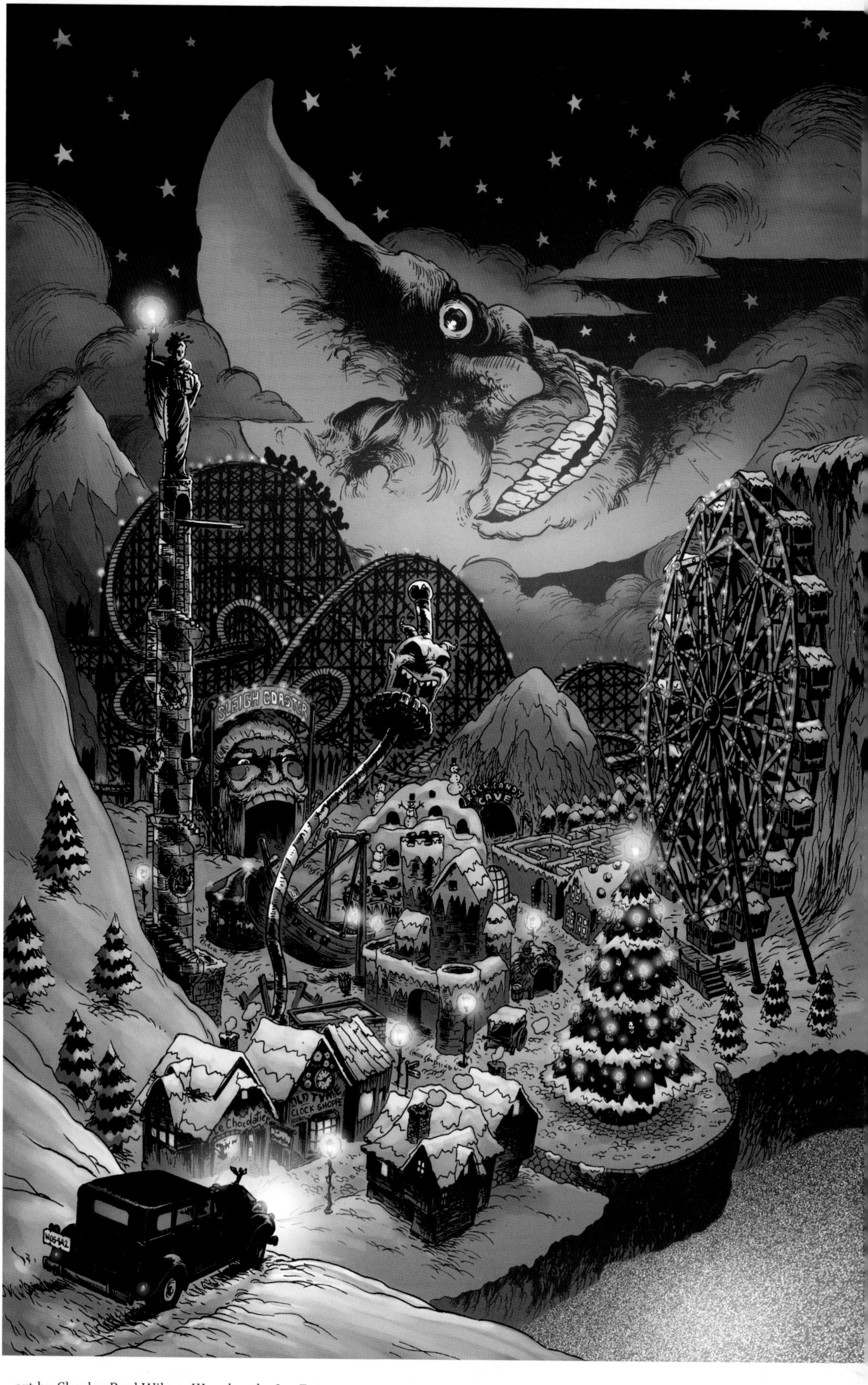
SLEIGH COASTER
ROCK CANDY CAVE
Le Chocolatier
CLOCK SHOPPE

art by Charles Paul Wilson III, colors by Jay Fotos

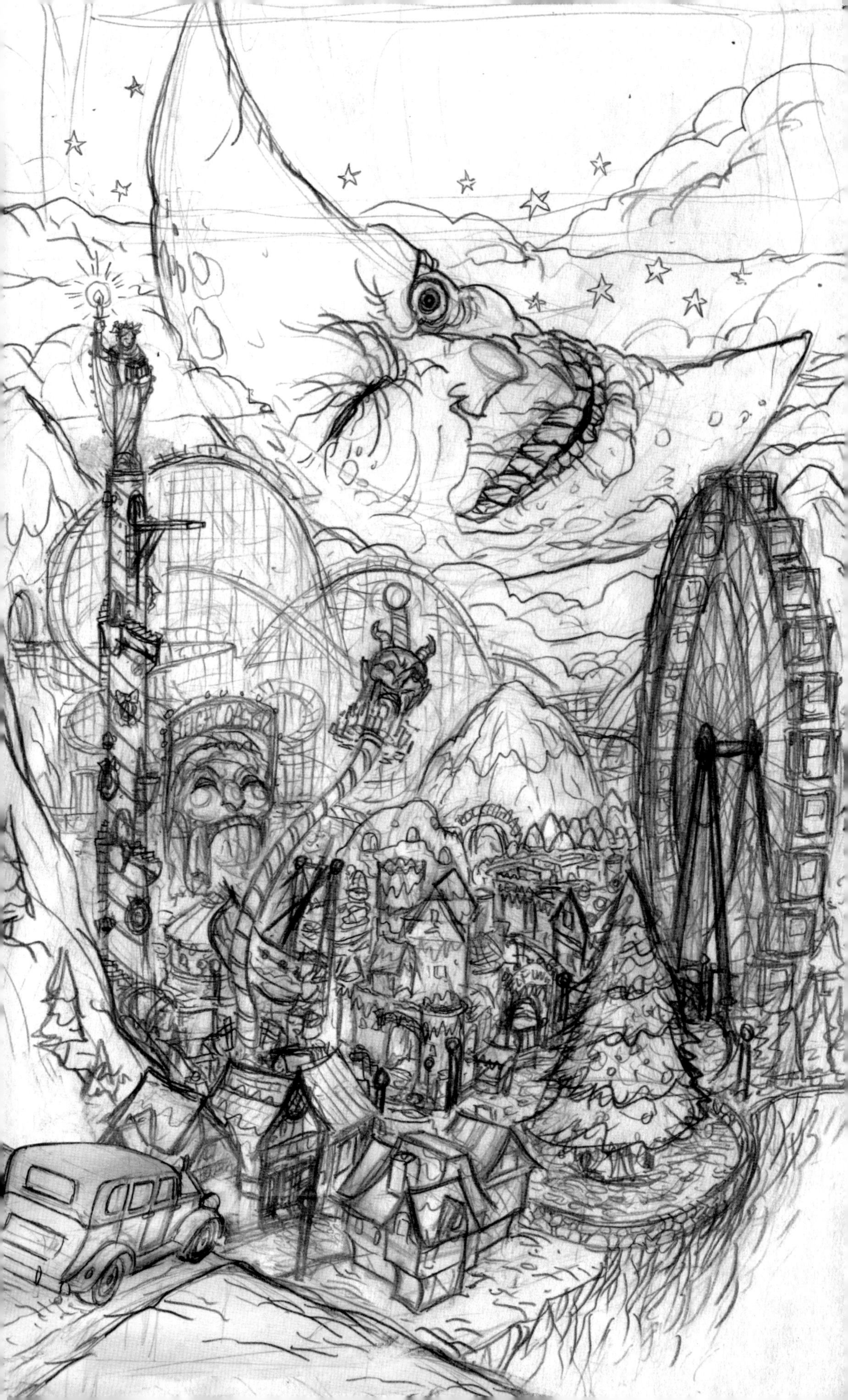

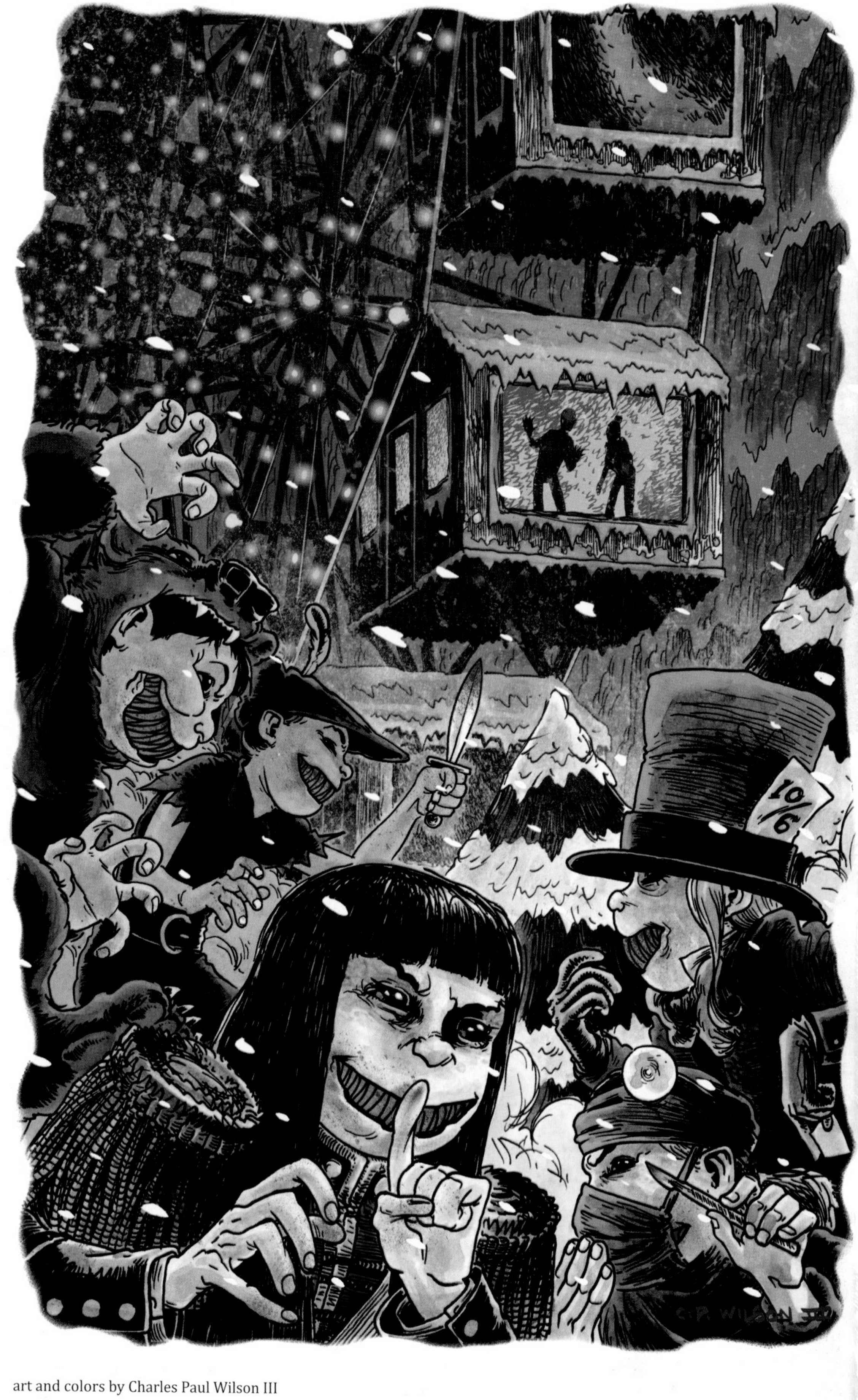
10/6

art and colors by Charles Paul Wilson III

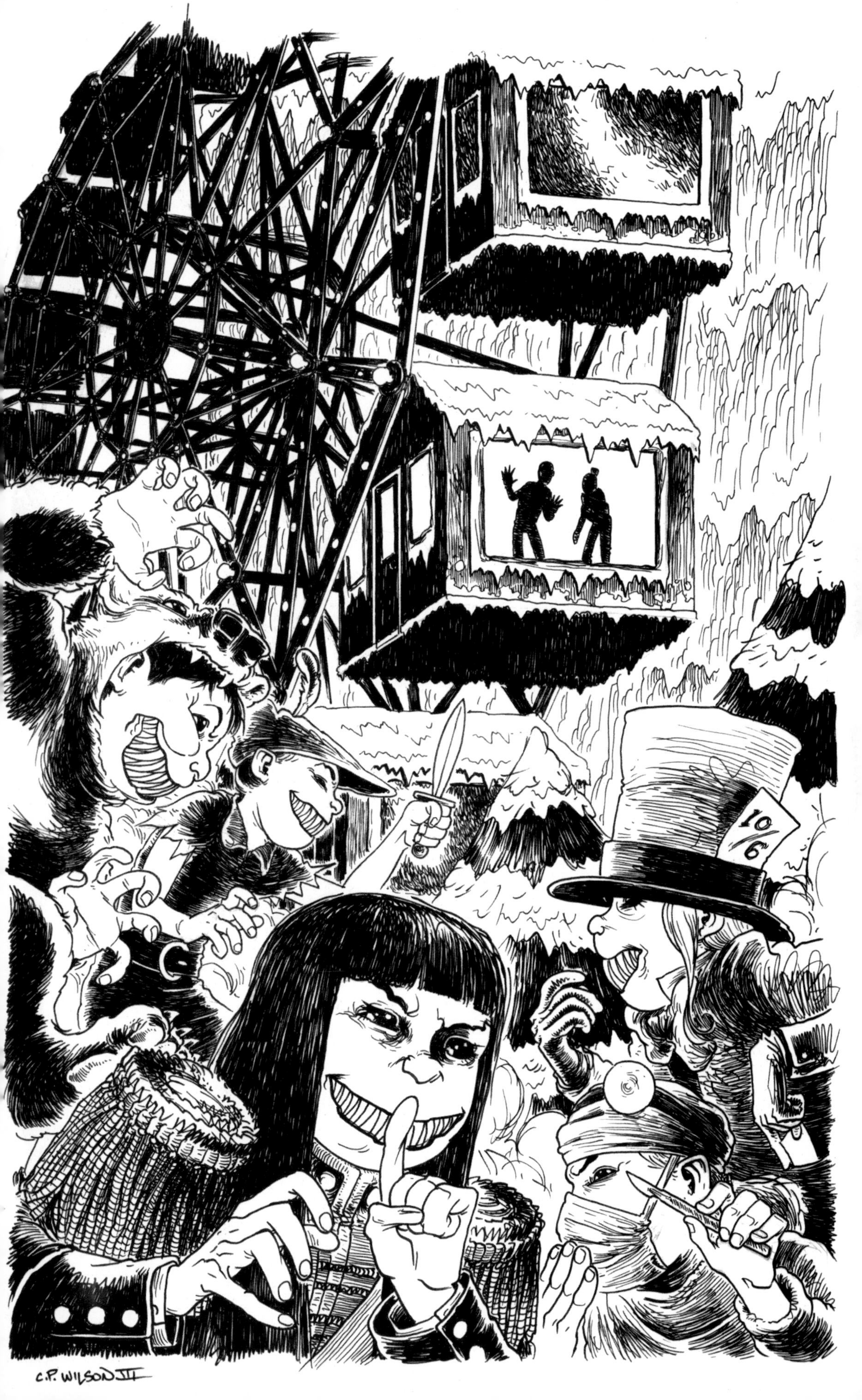
10/6
C.P. WILSON III

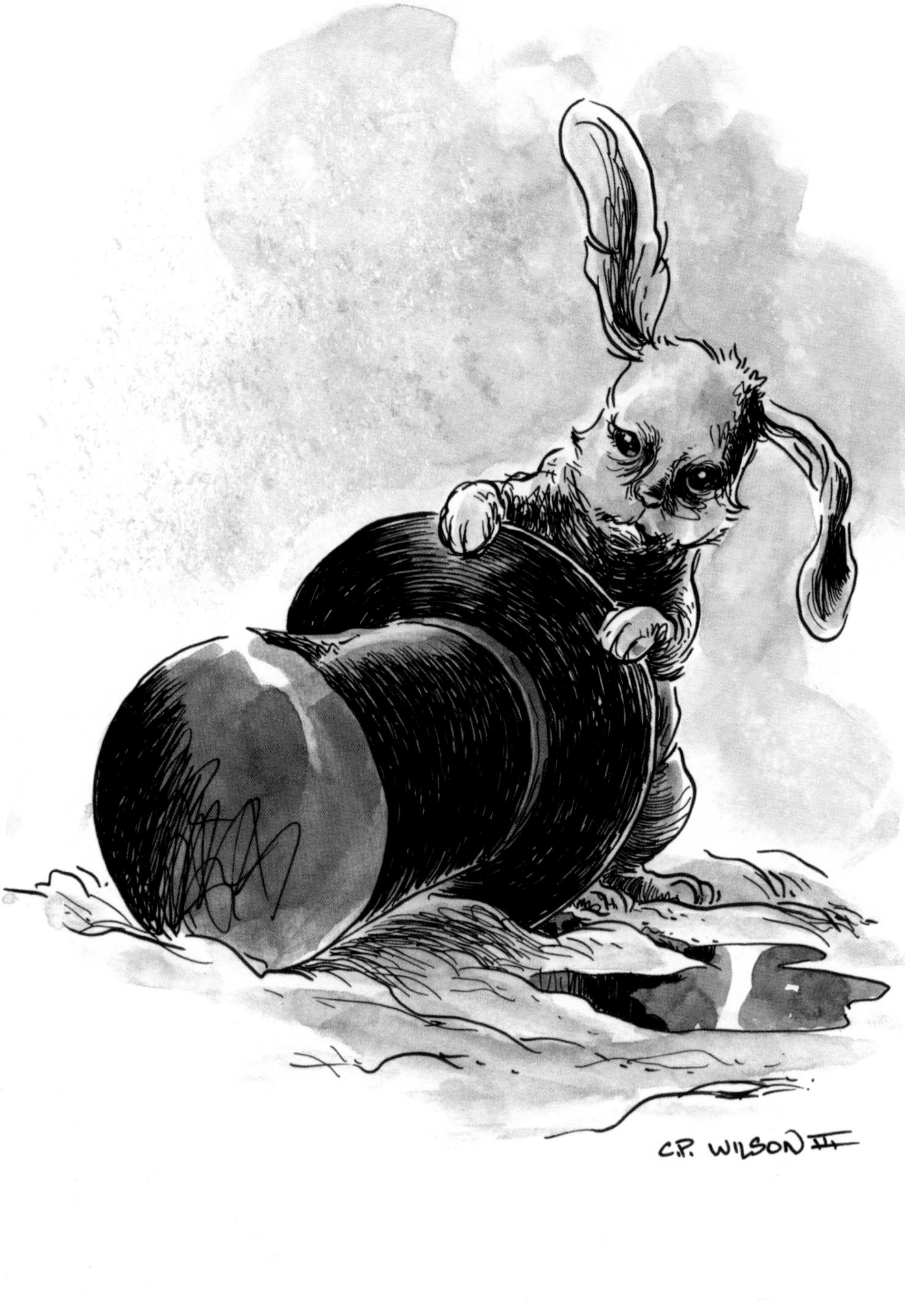
C.P. WILSON III

this page: art and colors by Charles Paul Wilson III • *opposite page:* art and colors by Francesco Francavilla

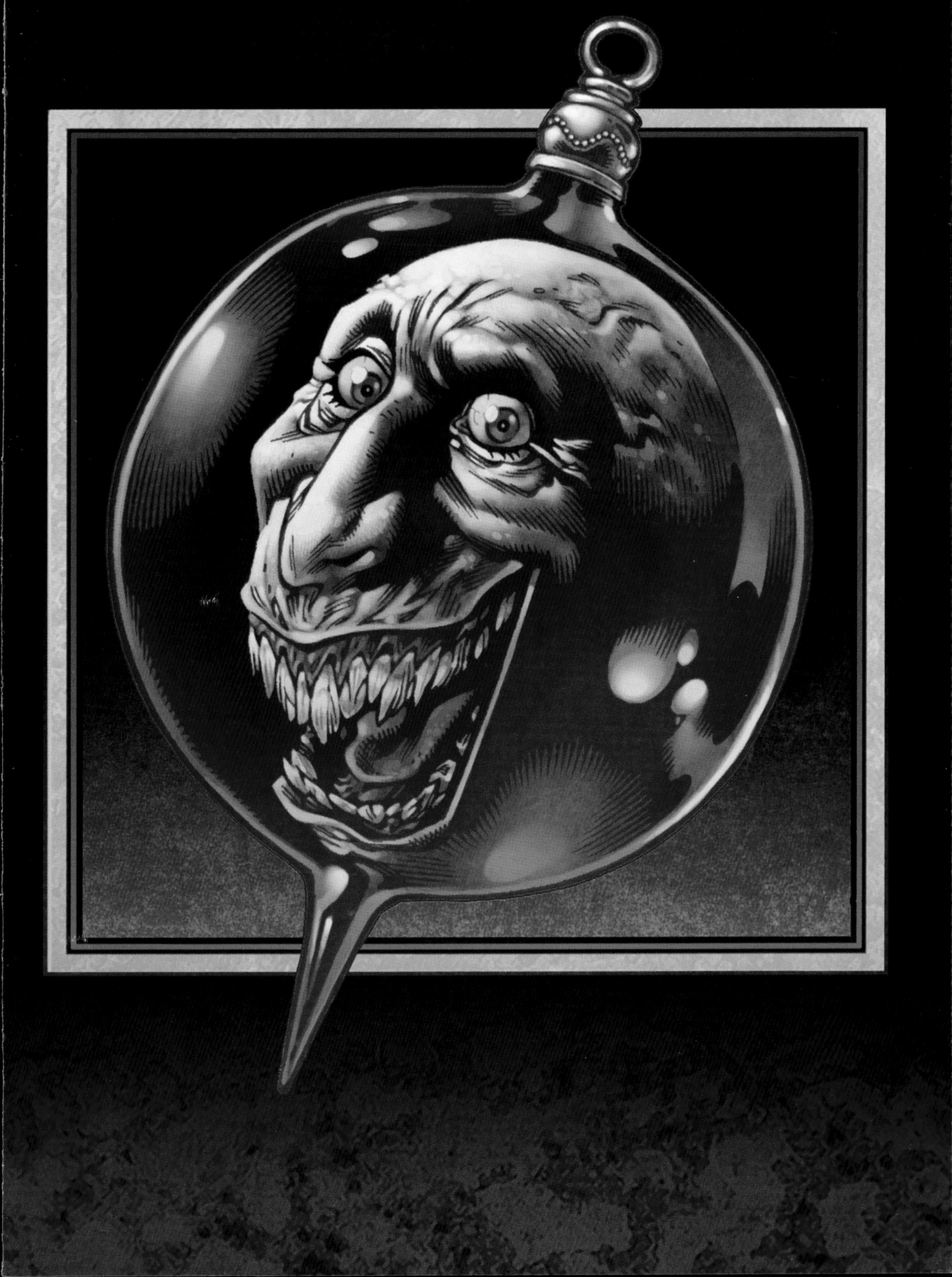

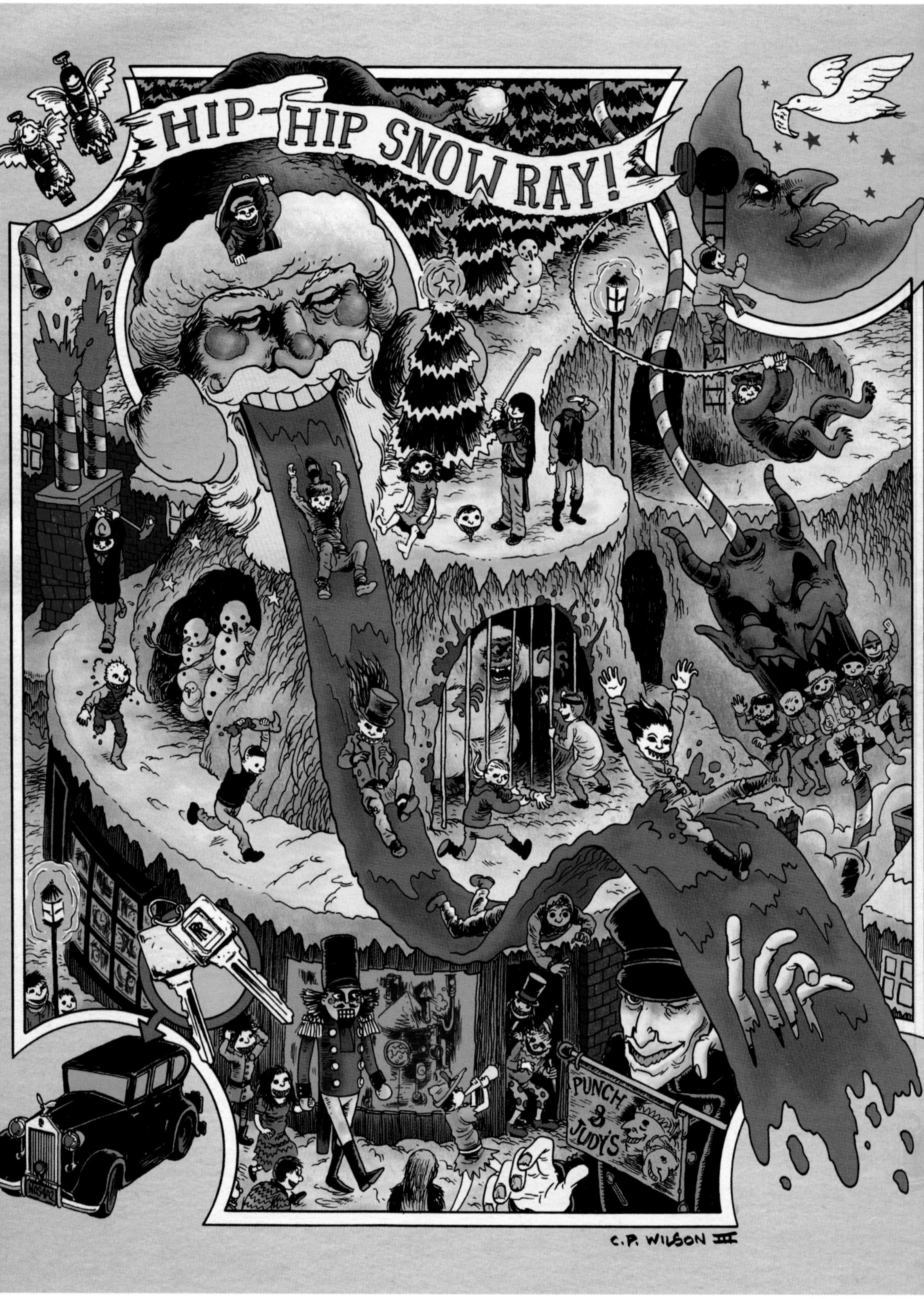
HIP-HIP SNOW RAY!
PUNCH & JUDY'S
NOS4A2
C.P. WILSON III

art and colors by Charles Paul Wilson III

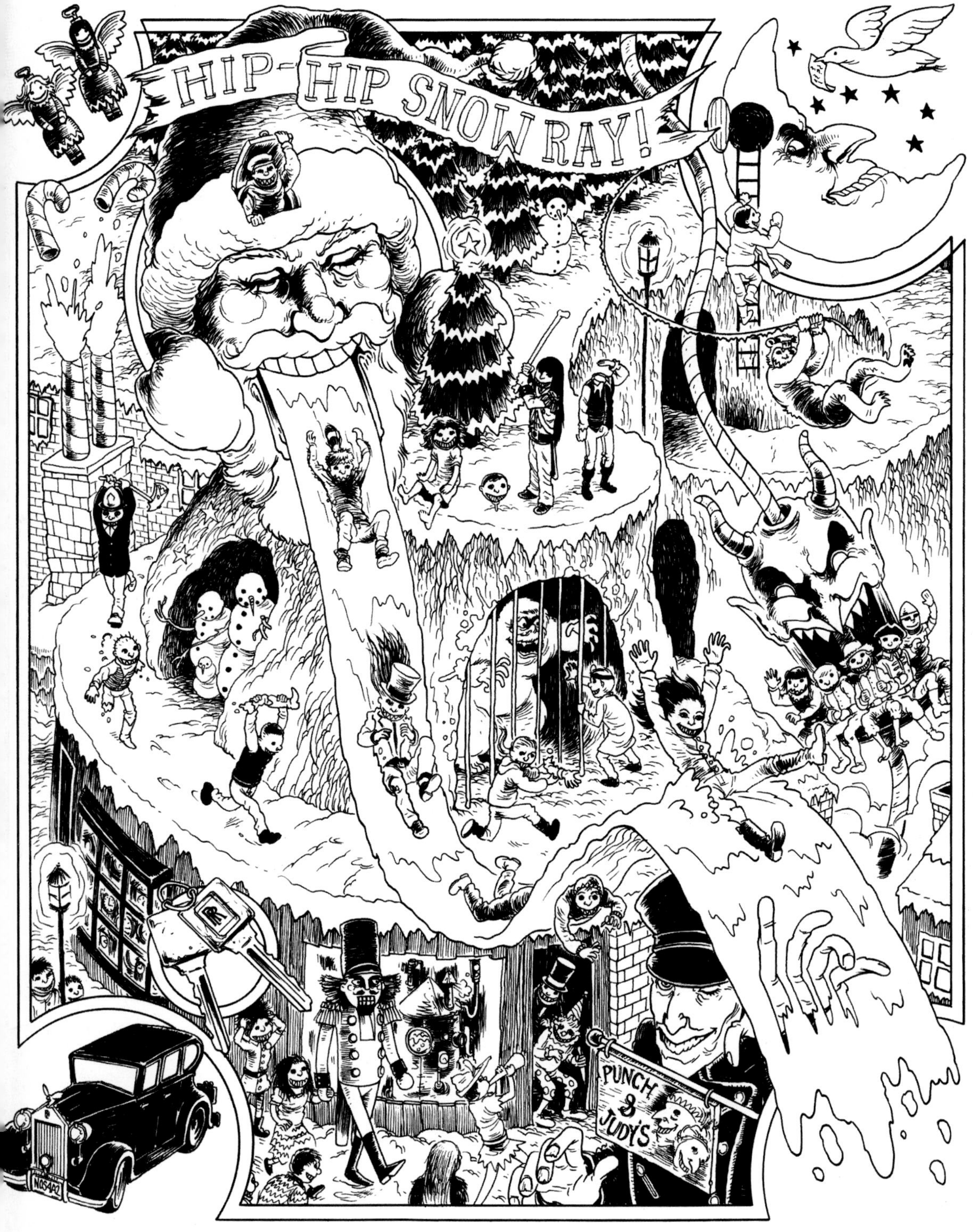
HIP-HIP SNOW RAY!
PUNCH & JUDY'S
NOS4A2

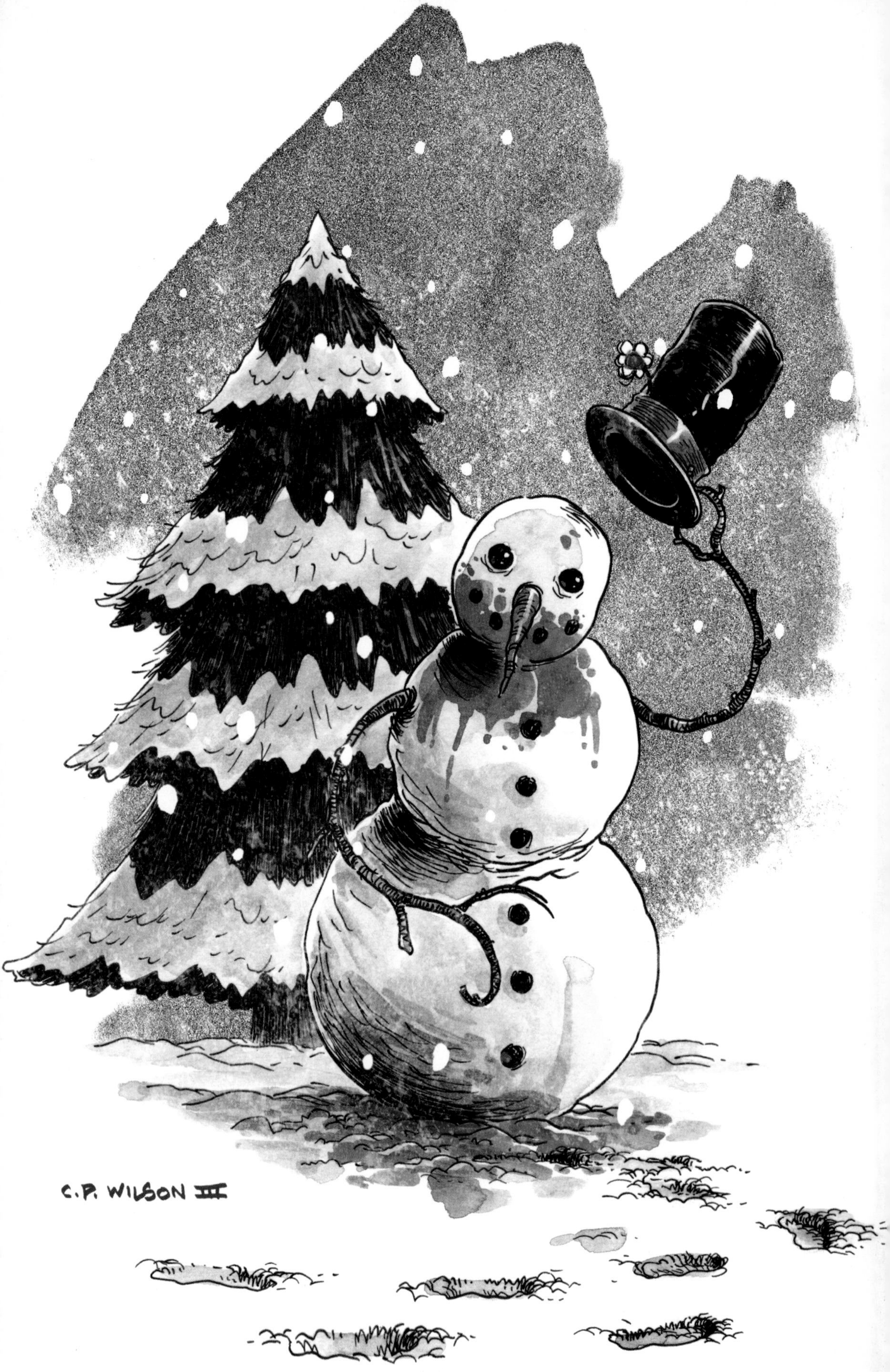
C.P. WILSON III

this page and opposite page: art and colors by Charles Paul Wilson III

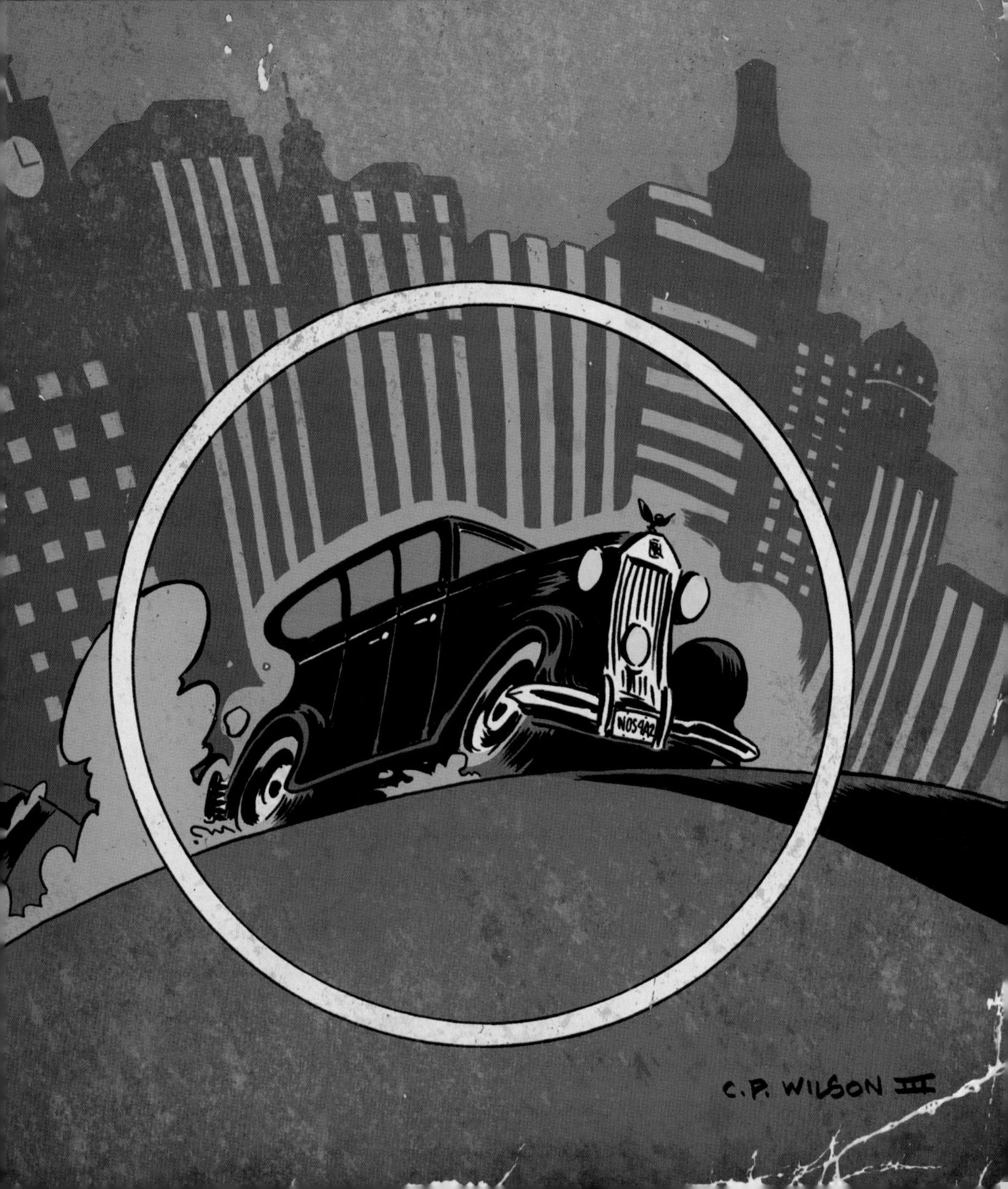
C.P. WILSON III

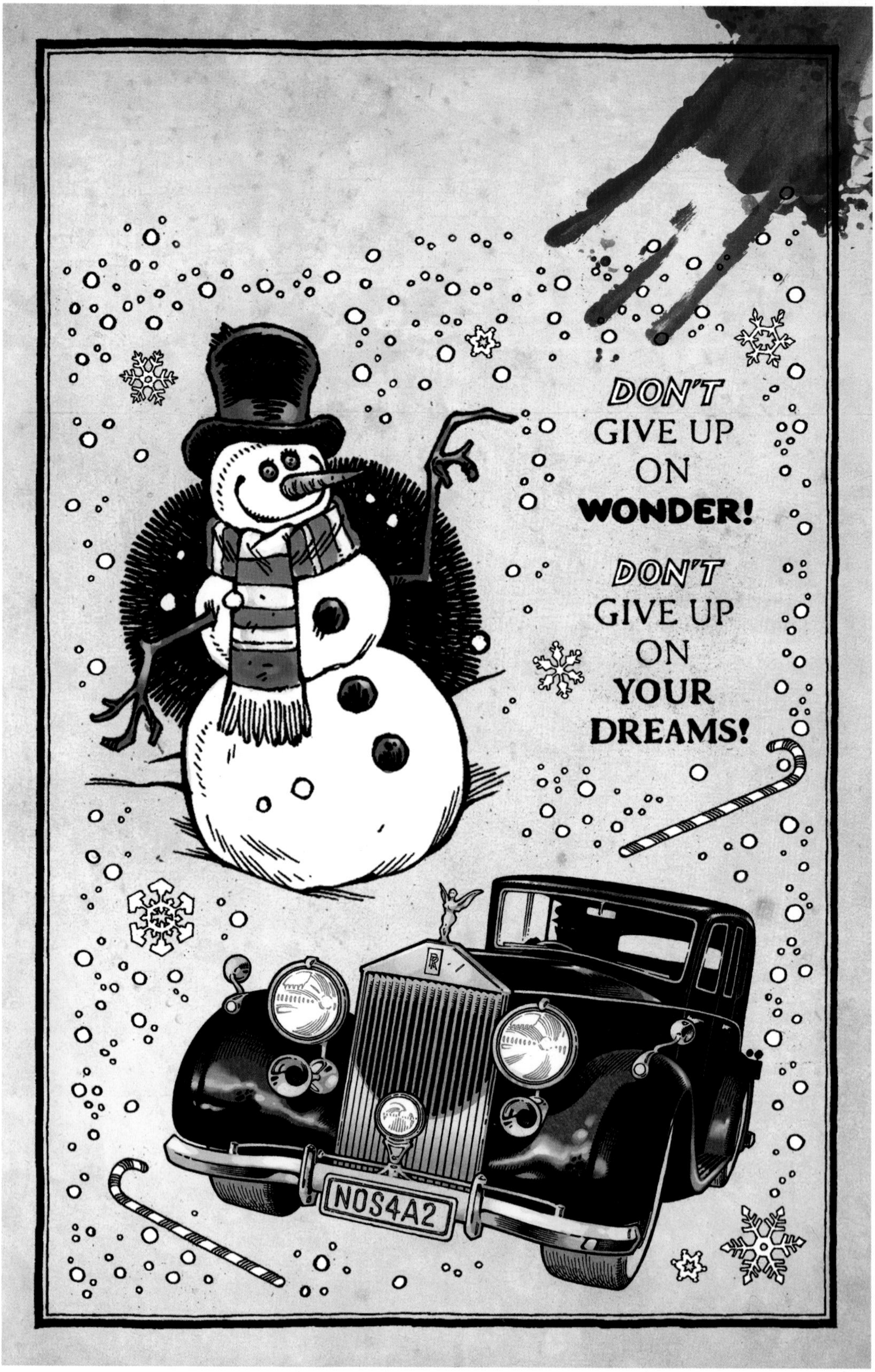
DON'T GIVE UP ON WONDER!
DON'T GIVE UP ON YOUR DREAMS!
NOS4A2

this page: art by Gabriel Rodriguez with Lucy Ryall, colors by Jay Fotos • *opposite page:* art and colors by David Stoupakis

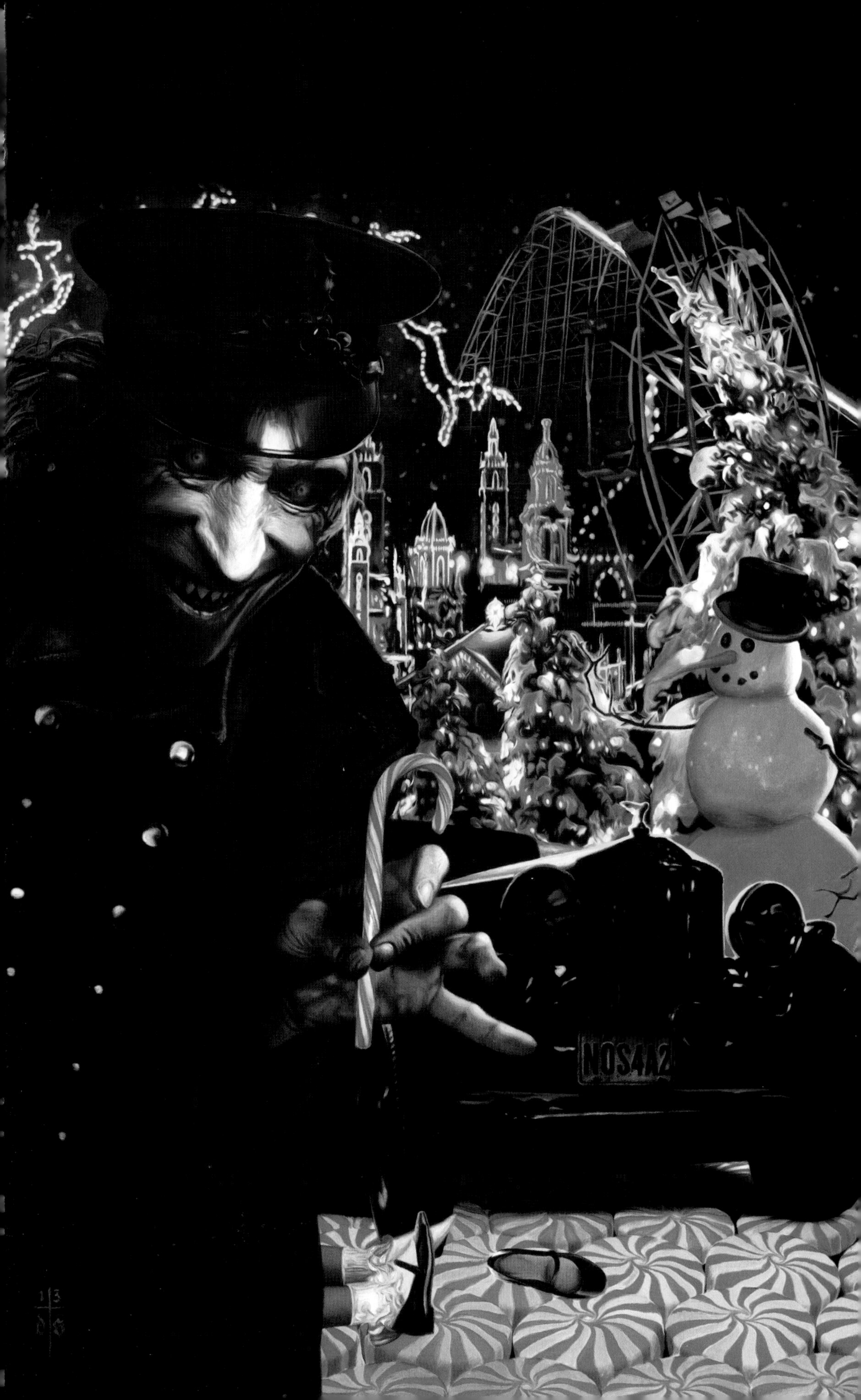
NOS4A2

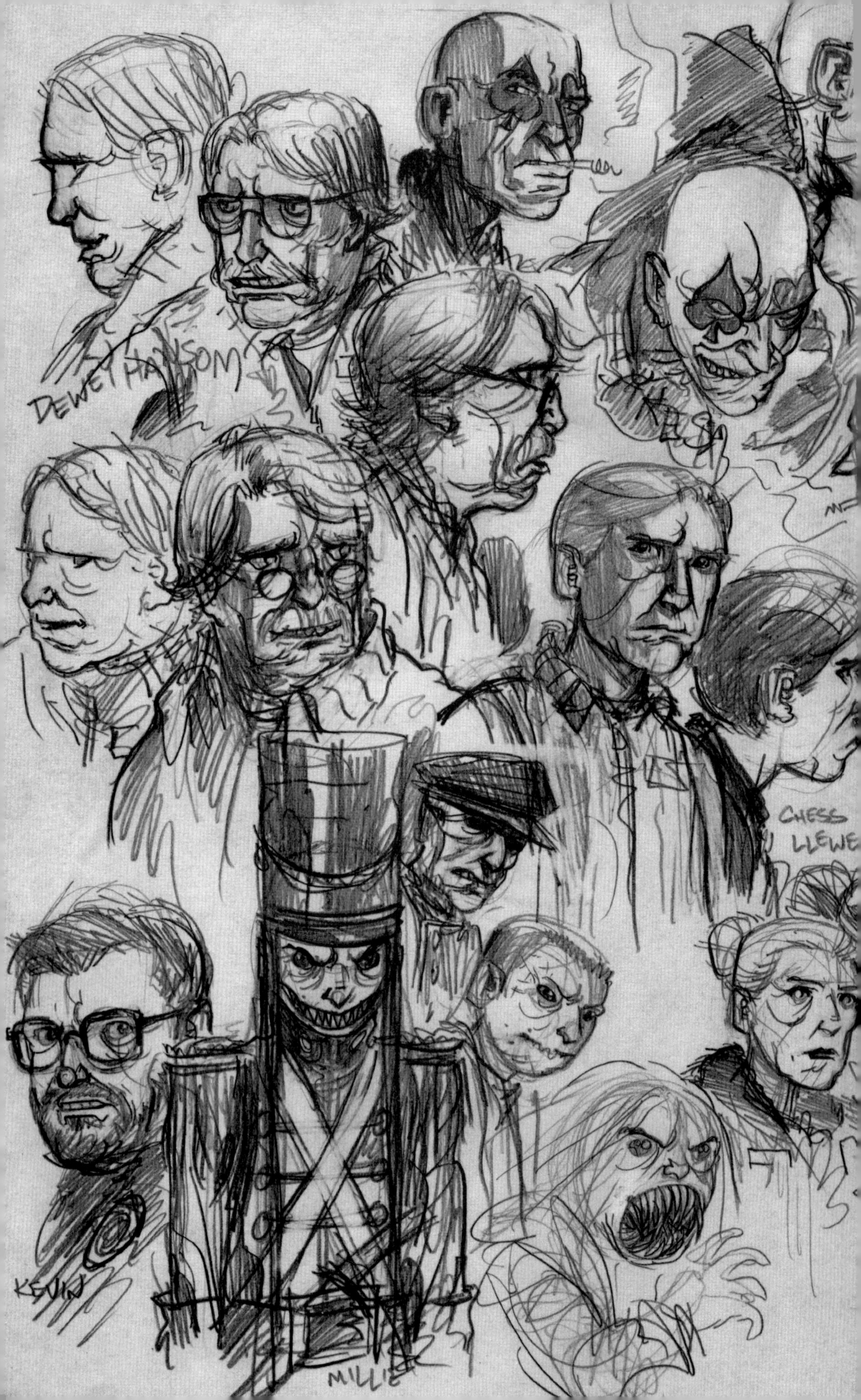
DEWEY HANSOM
CHESS
LLEWE
KEVIN
MILLIE

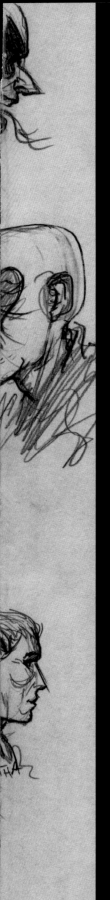
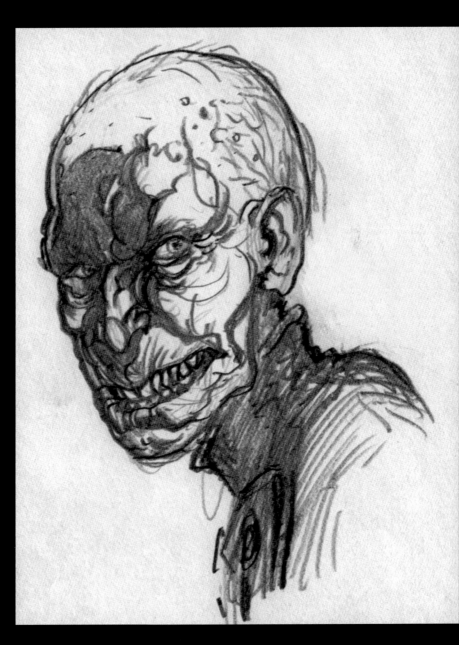

art by Charles Paul Wilson III

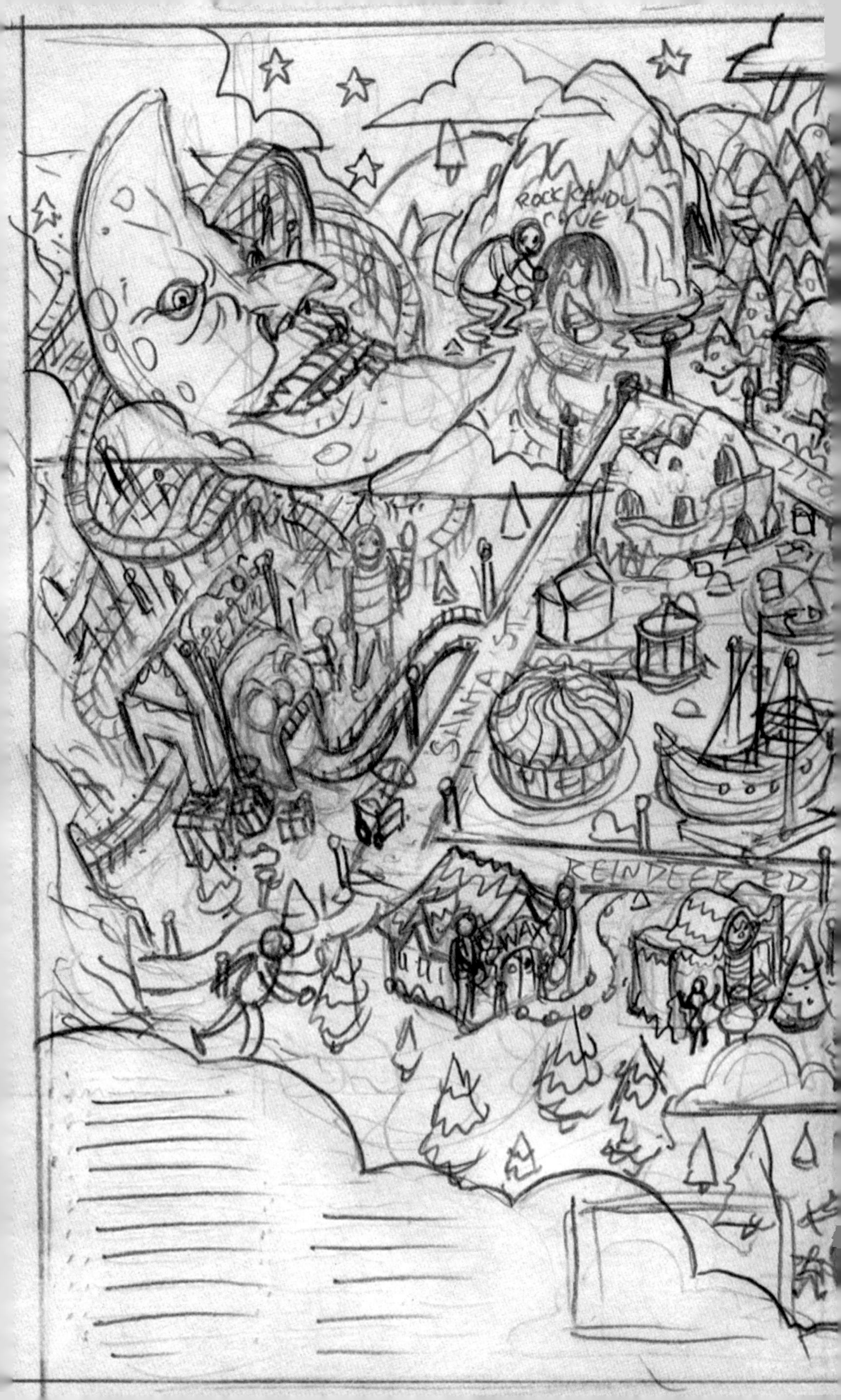

ROCK CANDY CAVE
SANTA ST.
REINDEER RD
WAX

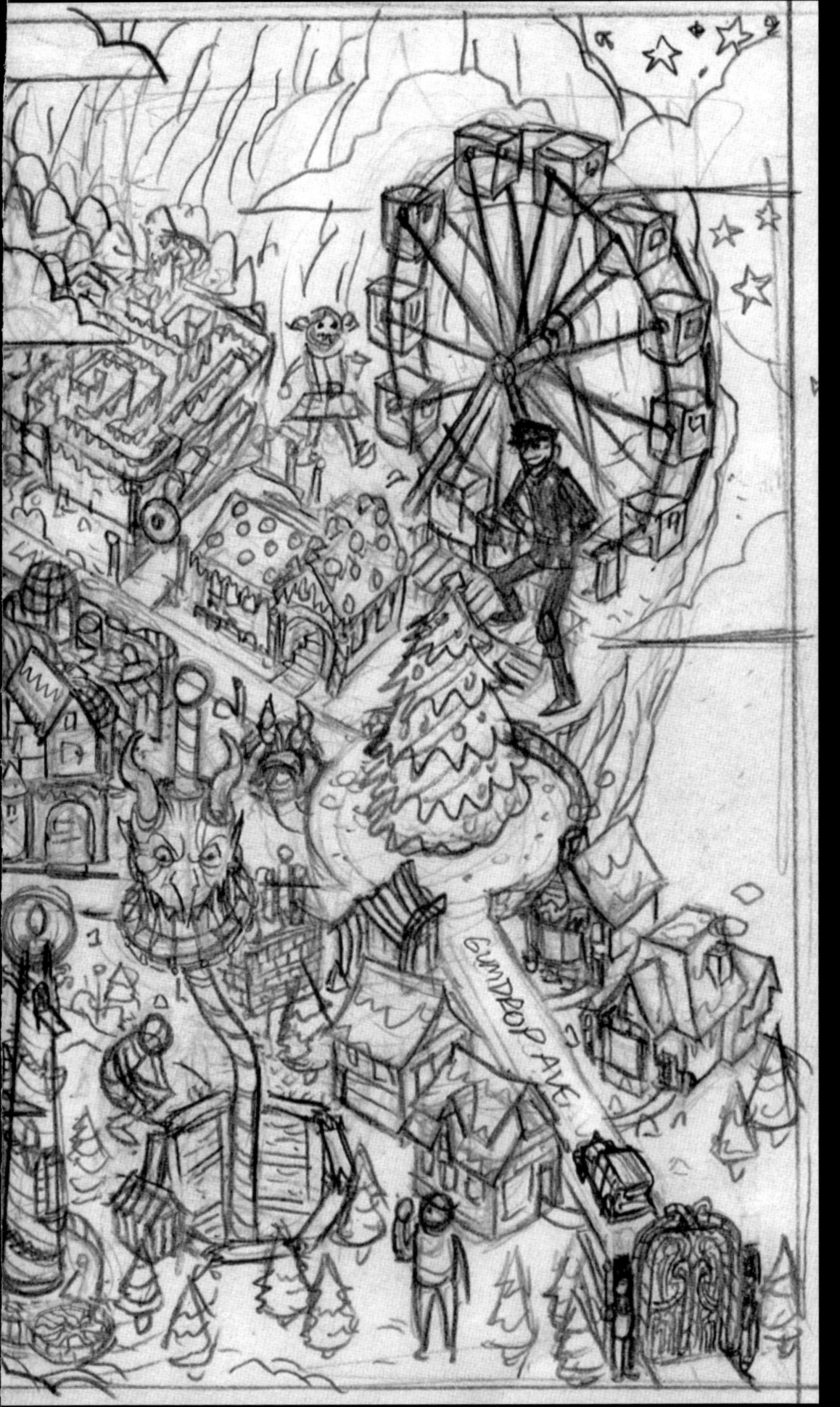
GUMDROP AVE.

art by Charles Paul Wilson

① chocolatier

② Punch & Judy's

③ Olde Tyme Clock shoppe

④ Manx's
  Mulled cider - shed

⑤ The March of the Toy Soldiers

⑥ Charlies costume Carnival

⑦ Gingerbread Inn

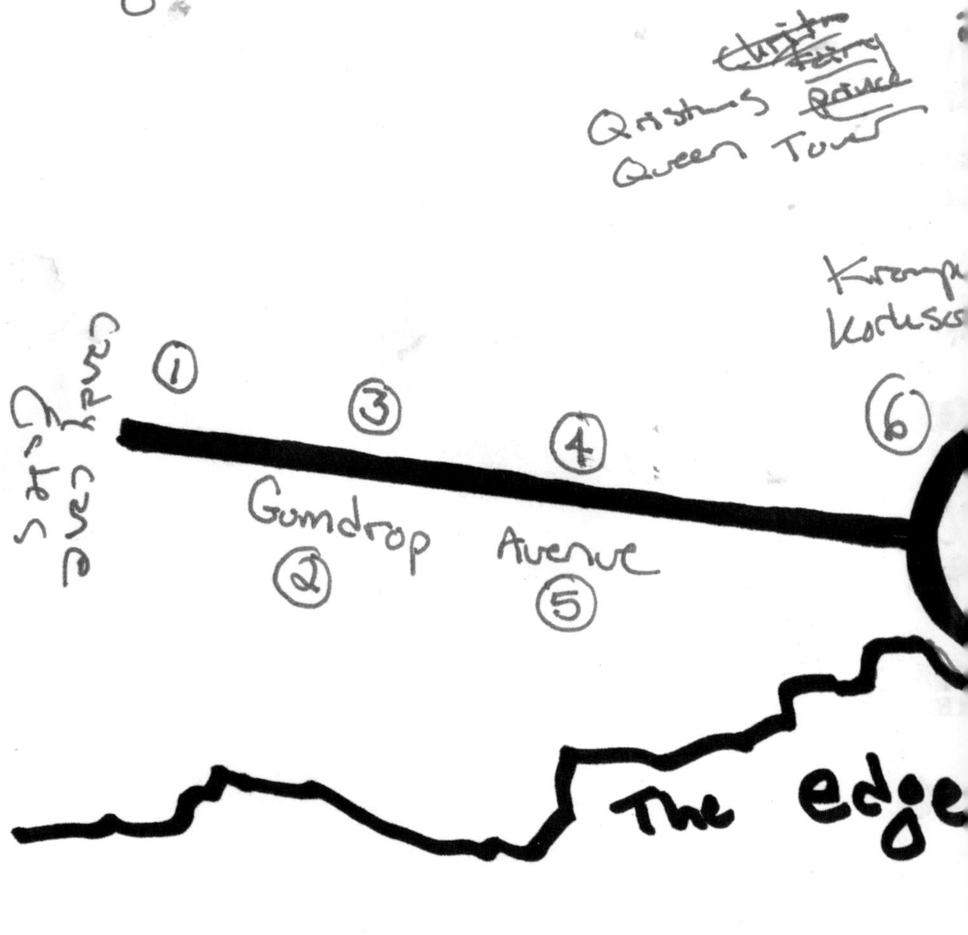

Rock Candy Cave

ARCTIC EXPRESS

Christmas
Queen Tour

Krampus
Kortusco

① ③ ④ ⑥

Candy Cane Stop

Gumdrop Avenue
② ⑤

The edge

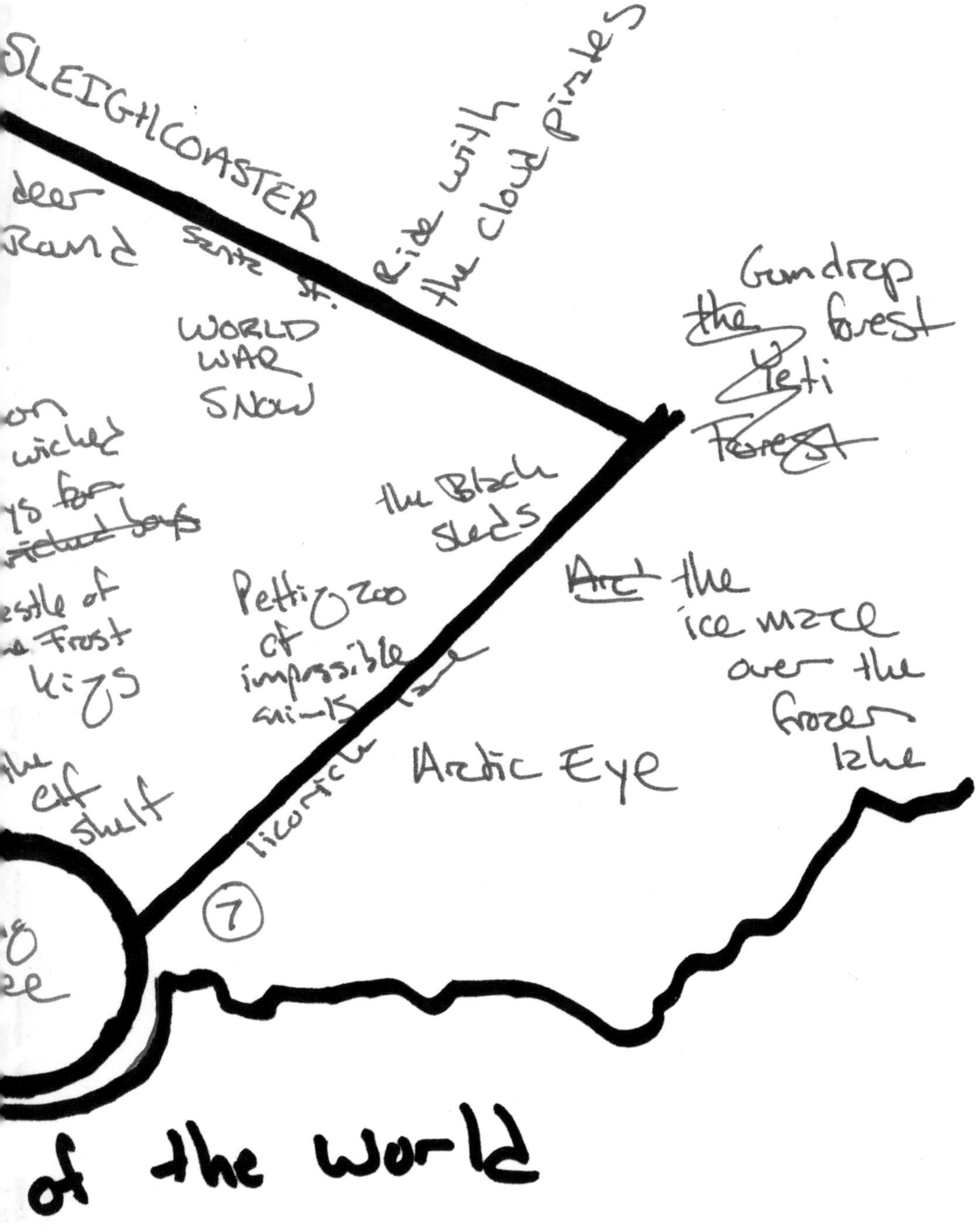
SLEIGHCOASTER
Ride with the cloud pirates
Gumdrop forest
WORLD WAR SNOW
the Black sleds
Petting zoo of impossible animals
the ice maze over the frozen lake
Arctic Eye
of the World

art by Joe Hill

WRAITH

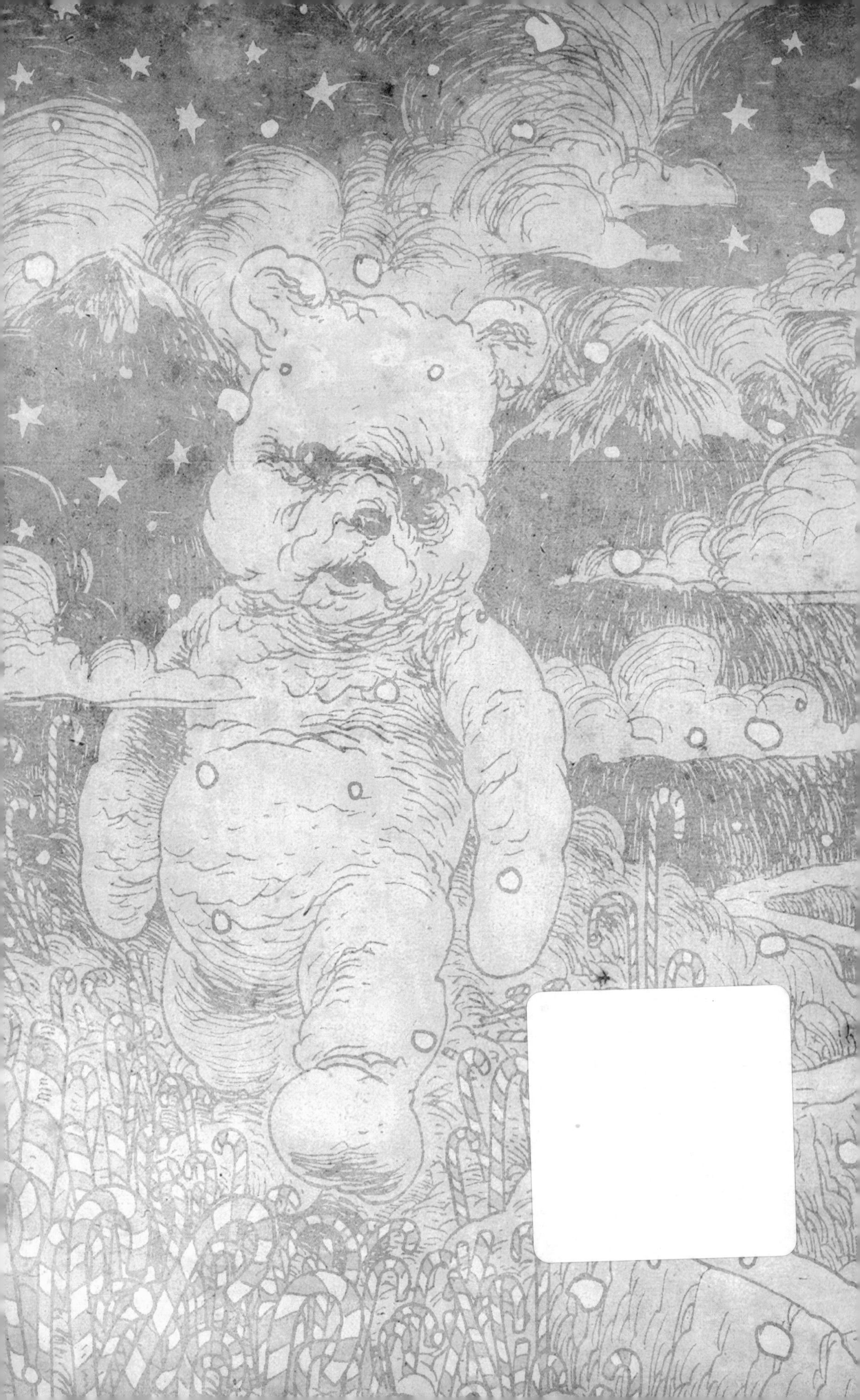